₳dvance ₱raise

"*A Girl Called Rumi* is a magical journey to a world of mystical delights, enchantment, and revelation. It's a page-turner that goes deep into the nature of reality beyond perception."

—Deepak Chopra, MD

"I was utterly captivated by this book. In *A Girl Called Rumi*, activist, artist, and writer Ari Honarvar manages to weave potent Sufi teaching stories, a gripping mystery set in the midst of the upheaval of the Iran-Iraq War, and beautiful writing into a magic carpet that transported me from the moment I opened the book to the moment I reluctantly turned the last page. Highly recommended."

—Mirabai Starr, author of *Wild Mercy*
and *Caravan of No Despair*

"Ari Honarvar's gorgeous debut novel, *A Girl Called Rumi*, shuttles between Iran and America as it grapples with the trauma of the Iran-Iraq War, the crackdown on female freedoms, and intergenerational conflict as well as the costs of resilience and forgiveness as children and parents are forced to make difficult decisions. This is a pulsating and culturally rich Iran seen through the eyes of its fables, its storytellers, its poetry, and its politics. In delicate and meditative prose, Honarvar takes her unforgettable characters— mystics, siblings, parents, best friends, enemies, fanatics—on a journey through the 'Seven Valleys of Love' eventually culminating in how healing happens, or doesn't, and how to move on. Iran's poets and poetry guide this heartfelt novel into a story as majestic as the thirty birds who make up the Simorgh, the fantastical being and mythical heartbeat of *A Girl Called Rumi*."

—Soniah Kamal, author of *Unmarriageable:*
Pride and Prejudice in Pakistan

"This is a lovely, illuminating and touching debut novel. I was moved to tears reading this manuscript. Ari Honarvar is a brilliant writer and readers hunger for stories like this—full of fascinating new worlds and redemptive outcomes."

—Rene Denfeld, author of *The Child Finder*

"From the horrors of the Iran-Iraq War to the complex reality of modern-day Iran, this is a novel that is as mesmerizing and dynamic as the Persian poetry it carries."

—Sahar Delijani, author of *Children of the Jacaranda Tree*

"Storytellers, mythical birds, and bombs collide in Honarvar's lyrical coming-of-age novel about Iran."

—Marivi Soliven, author of *The Mango Bride*

"*A Girl Called Rumi* is an amazing journey full of love, adventures, and dreams across different cultures, times, and perspectives. The real and the imaginary intertwine beautifully in this masterfully written novel by Ari Honarvar that reminds us of the best literature works of all time, from Rumi's mystical poetry to Gabriel Garcia Marquez's magical realism. Highly recommend!"

—Jesus Nebot, actor and producer

"My life is dedicated to social justice and migrant rights so I deal with a lot of vicarious trauma and often battle depression. This book has helped heal wounds I didn't know I had. I'm still reaping the benefits, and I know it'll have a similar effect on others. My life has literally been changed for the better as a result of reading *A Girl Called Rumi* as I entered a magical world called life and was lost and captivated with all its twists and turns. Suddenly I found I was not alone."

—Enrique Morones, human rights activist, Gente Unida

A Girl Called Rumi

A Girl Called

Rumi

Ari Honarvar

FOREST AVENUE PRESS
Portland, Oregon

Name: Honarvar, Ari, 1972- author.
Title: A girl called Rumi / Ari Honarvar.
Description: Portland, Oregon: Forest Avenue Press, [2021] | Summary: "A Girl Called Rumi, Ari Honarvar's debut novel, weaves a captivating tale of survival, redemption, and the power of storytelling. Kimia, a successful spiritual advisor whose Iranian childhood continues to haunt her, collides with a mysterious giant bird in her mother's California garage. She begins reliving her experience as a nine-year-old girl in war-torn Iran, including her friendship with a mystical storyteller who led her through the mythic Seven Valleys of Love. Grappling with her unresolved past, Kimia agrees to accompany her ailing mother back to Iran, only to arrive in the midst of the Green Uprising in the streets. Against the backdrop of the election protests, Kimia begins to unravel the secrets of the night that broke her mother and produced a dangerous enemy. As past and present collide, she must choose between running away again or completing her unfinished journey through the Valley of Death to save her brother"-- Provided by publisher.
Identifiers: LCCN 2021015175 (print) | LCCN 2021015176 (ebook) | ISBN 9781942436461 (paperback) | ISBN 9781942436478 (epub)
Subjects: LCSH: Iran--Fiction.
Classification: LCC PS3608.O4944364 G57 2021 (print) | LCC PS3608.O4944364 (ebook) | DDC 813/.6--dc23
LC record available at https://lccn.loc.gov/2021015175
LC ebook record available at https://lccn.loc.gov/2021015176

Distributed by Publishers Group West

Printed in the United States of America

Forest Avenue Press LLC
P.O. Box 80134
Portland, OR 97280
forestavenuepress.com

1 2 3 4 5 6 7 8 9

To Baba Joon, and to Shiraz

A Few Notes on the Text

THE POETIC VERSES IN this manuscript are author Ari Honarvar's own translations. Adhering to the original verses, they don't include punctuation.

IN LIEU OF A glossary for the Persian terms, the author has opted for footnotes for convenience.

THE COVER ART IS a calligram painting by the author, first published in *Rumi's Gift Oracle Cards*. The image depicted is the Simorgh. Her body and feathers are made of the words of this verse in Farsi:

> *Attar explored the Seven Valleys of Love*
> *We are still getting around one corner*

This verse is popularly attributed to Rumi, but no records suggest he was the author of these words.

THE DANCER CALLIGRAM USED in space breaks features this verse from *Rumi's Gift*:

> *Even if from the sky*
> *poison befalls all*
> *I'm still sweetness*
> *wrapped in sweetness*
> *wrapped in sweetness*
> *wrapped in sweetness . . .*

Family Tree

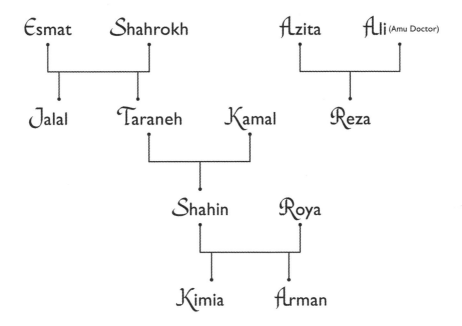

Part 1

Once there was.
Once there wasn't.
Once there was war.
Once there wasn't time for stories.
Once there were terrible laws.
Once there wasn't a way out.
Once there was a girl . . .

1. Kimia — SHIRAZ, IRAN, 1981

I WASN'T SUPPOSED TO be there. I'd been on my way to the bakery to buy naan for dinner. But then—the siren call. What nine-year-old can resist a story?

I squeezed the bread money in my sweaty hand and looked up as the cool breeze brought the first evening star above the mountains cradling Shiraz. The makeshift stage was directly in my path, right in the middle of Felekeh Ghasrodasht Square. On the stage, a middle-aged trio in worn suit jackets struck a bittersweet overture. The melody transitioned into a beguiling rendition of the centuries-old vatanam, a song that always reminded me of road-weary caravan travelers longing to go home. I closed my eyes and listened. I could sense the excitement of other children, barely holding still, eyes glued to the stage in anticipation. Their parents, busy with the usual banter about war and shortages of food and water, sat cross-legged on colorful blankets. Like all Shirazis, they were most comfortable when picnicking outdoors, eating from steaming bowls of vegetable aash and drinking fragrant rosewater tea.

I shifted from one foot to the other. I needed to head to the bakery, not stand near the stage, heart thumping with the music. "I'll just stay for a minute," I tried to convince my feet.

The music swelled in a flurry to an ecstatic crescendo, and by the time it settled into a steady tempo, I had all but forgotten about the naan. Behind a white screen, center stage, a light began to glow, hushing the crowd. Children pointed and bounced; adults paused in their conversations.

Out from the shadows, stage left, limped an old man wearing a tattered Bakhtiari tunic and a cap and shawl. Using a wooden cane, he shuffled across the stage and sat down just as the light came to its full brightness behind the white screen.

My feet stopped dancing.

A giant shadow puppet of the Simorgh appeared on the screen. The bird beat her magnificent wings in time with the music, the long silky plume on her head wind-tossed like a girl's hair. Unlike the Simorgh in my mother's poetry book, this one had the face of an eagle and a fierce beak. Flapping her elaborate feathers, the bird glided across an imaginary sky.

The other children jumped and shrieked with delight, but I stood still. The twilight spring air grew charged around me, and I leaned forward, feeling the magnetic pull of the bird. Then, from everywhere, a commanding tenor's voice filled the square with a single note: *"Huuu . . ."*

I searched for the source of the haunting sound and zeroed in on the old man. It was him, but he was barely pursing his lips or showing any sign of effort. Was I imagining it or was he also looking at me? Yes, his eyes pierced me with their intense gaze.

The old man brought his note to an end. He released me from his gaze and spoke, his voice calm and powerful. "Once there was. Once there wasn't. Besides God, no one was."

Even the smallest of the children in the audience became quiet.

He continued, "King Sahm was hoping for the perfect heir, but when his son was born, the child was as white as snow. King Sahm thought his wife had birthed a demon, so he ordered it to be taken to the foothills of the Alborz Mountains. The baby, Zaal, was alone and abandoned, cold and crying. But this calamity brought him the most wondrous gift. It changed his destiny and bonded him with the most majestic creature in heaven and on earth."

The musicians had disappeared into the background, but a bright sound of chimes reached us from a faraway land. The puppeteers, silent and almost invisible behind the screen, controlled the shadow puppets with precision and grace. In harmony with the melody, the stage grew dim.

"Suddenly the sky darkened, and a mighty wind lifted the infant up into the air. The birds gathered to hold his swaddle blanket with their beaks and claws, so he wouldn't fall. They flapped their wings and looked with awe to see a giant bird approaching. They had heard stories, but they hadn't known she was real. The Simorgh's wings spanned the whole mountain chain and some of the forest."

The puppeteers brought the Simorgh back to the screen. When the bird soared up in a fast, sudden movement, uncontrollable laughter rippled inside me and escaped from my mouth.

"When the Simorgh flapped her great wings, she shook loose the seeds of all the plants and trees and sent them flying throughout the world," the old man continued.

Sparkling confetti blew from the stage and landed on our heads. Children held out their hands to catch the drops of magical rain.

"The Simorgh heard the infant's cries and swooped down. Upon seeing him, she fell in love. The birds understood what they needed to do right away. They placed the bundle on the Simorgh's back and she headed up to the highest peak in Persia. The very top of Mount Damavand, to her nest . . ."

The bird lifted the bundle across the stage-sky to the edge of the screen. As the music picked up, she emerged from beyond the screen with iridescent wings and an emerald-green eye, sparkling brightly. The music grew even louder, masking the collective gasp of the audience. I marveled at the tiny embroidery on her wings. As the Simorgh took flight over the buildings surrounding the square, I squinted, watching her until her figure was a small bright dot, disappearing into the starry night.

Then I returned my focus to the stage. The old man was looking right at me. He winked.

Did his wink produce the deafening thump that shook the earth?

A fiery sun rose behind the stage, sending sparks over the rooftop. It took a moment for me to grasp that this wasn't part of the show. All around me people rushed about, their faces contorted in screams.

But a strange silence had enveloped me. I was motionless in the midst of the chaos, staring at the storyteller. He stood, smiling back at me. The backdrop that showed the Alborz Mountains collapsed in slow motion behind him as people hurried away. Children cried silently as parents swooped in to grab them.

I spotted my big brother, Arman, zigzagging through people, making his way to where I stood entranced.

I couldn't hear his screams, but Arman's breath, hot and urgent, grazed my face as he grabbed my shoulders and pulled me away from the stage. A nearby building burst into flames. I wanted to protest, but instead my lips stretched into a big smile. I felt Arman shaking me by the shoulders as he shouted words I could not hear.

Why does he keep shaking me? Wait, am I deaf?

No sooner had I completed the thought than a flood of sounds—explosions, screaming, ambulance sirens—came with a fury. The smoke burned my eyes, and I coughed, choking on its scorched bitterness.

"What's the matter with you?" Arman yelled, yanking my arm. "Let's go!"

"But the morshed," I protested, looking back at the stage as he dragged me away like a rag doll.

"What morshed?" Arman snapped.

There was no sign of the storyteller. The musicians had abandoned the stage. The puppeteers were jamming the delicate puppets into their suitcases. A few Simorgh feathers twirled a brief dance around the last remaining puppeteer, and then the square went dark. The power company, which was supposed to cut the electricity at the first sign of an air raid, must have been as surprised as we were and had only belatedly shut down its system.

Arman pulled me into a narrow side street.

"Let go of my arm!" I yelled.

"Not until we get home." He dragged me down the lane.

"Ow!" I cried, but I couldn't match his strength. I surrendered as my mind tried to piece together everything I had just witnessed.

We emerged from the lane onto a larger street. Men shouted and hauled equipment toward the fires.

My mother's familiar voice stopped us in our tracks. "Kimia!" she shouted, aiming her stout frame at us. Adding to my mother's bulk was the gray, raincoat-style Islamic uniform she wore. But this didn't seem to slow her as she sped over to us, her eyes radiating anger.

"Now you're gonna get it," Arman yelled in my ear.

I flinched, shielding my ear with my hand.

"Arman, Kimia!" My mother made her way across the street. Before I could protest, she grabbed my chin. "Where did you disappear to?"

I wanted to cry. "I went to—"

"She was just standing there," Arman interjected. "Right out in the open!"

"And what if another missile had hit?" my mother demanded. She slapped me hard. "Do you have any idea what I'm going through? Where is the naan?"

My face stung. "I . . . I . . ." Sobs were choking me.

Through a veil of tears, I saw Arman, whose righteousness had transformed to pity. His eyes were pinned to the ground, but his right hand twitched as if he wanted to put it on my mother's shoulder and shift her focus away from me.

My mother slapped me once again.

I heaved a startled breath, and my teeth became gritty with the soot in the air. Reeling in pain, I was about to yowl even harder when I felt the menacing glare of a bystander. The woman raced toward me, her stern face framed by the black chador flowing around her. I realized that my scarf had fallen from my head. The woman was coming over to chastise me for not wearing my hijab properly. Quickly I pulled my scarf back up, and like a modern-day talisman, my covered hair sent the woman in another direction.

My mother, oblivious to all this, crushed my hand in her grip. "I'll deal with you when we get home."

I closed my eyes, willing myself to disappear, something I tried every time I got into trouble.

My mother dragged my listless body through a tangle of streets and alleys and into the courtyard of our house. The garden was quiet. I opened my eyes.

It didn't work, I thought, disappointed that I lacked the magical skills to make myself vanish. An owl's *huuu* filled the silent air.

The arched door groaned and creaked as we entered. My mother yanked me into the entry hall as Arman followed in silence. There was nothing he could do now. My mother lit several candles, and we began removing our street shoes, slipping into our dampaee house slippers.

I caught my reflection in the taped-up mirror in the hallway. Dirty tear streaks marred my face, my scarf sagged around my neck, and my hair was matted and tangled. My bloodshot eyes looked like those of a trapped animal.

Arman rapped his knuckles on the stained glass of the hallway door, as he did after every missile or bomb attack. Fortunately, the explosions hadn't broken the mirror or the glass door. Like all our friends and neighbors, my mother had taped an X on each glass surface to save us some post-attack cleanup, since blast waves shattered glass as easily as they shattered the sound barrier. Once, when I asked my mother what would happen if a bomb or missile landed on the house itself, she said, "Well, housekeeping would have to take the back seat then, wouldn't it?"

I was beginning to forget my predicament when my mother's roar crashed over my head. "So, you just forget the naan and decide, without letting anyone know, to go bazigooshi? To make mischief? You want me to suffer!" She grabbed my chin. "Do you want your brother to suffer?"

I waited until she let go of me, then followed her into the kitchen. As she warmed a kettle for tea, her expression became serene, as if nothing in the world could disturb her, but I knew there was more to come. I joined Arman at the kitchen table and felt a rush of gratitude for him as he kept his head down in solidarity.

With the kettle heating and the loose-leaf tea in the pot, my mother turned and put her hands on her hips. I picked at the peeling veneer on the table, avoiding her glare.

"What am I going to do with you? If you keep this up, you'll end up like a street whore! Dirt of the world on your head!" She was getting more and more worked up. "Arman, go get your baba's belt," she barked without taking her eyes off of me.

Arman hesitated.

"Go!" my mother exploded.

THE NEXT DAY I woke up to the sound of someone wailing. Felfel, who was sleeping soundly on my pillow, stretched luxuriously as I stirred. She began to purr when I patted her calico coat. I faced the direction of the loud sobs. It was our elderly neighbor, Mrs. Kermani. Had someone close to her died in the war, or was she just bemoaning the blanket of sadness that had cloaked Shiraz lately? Even with my window closed, I could smell the foul smoke from the smoldering buildings. I wrinkled my nose and reached for the framed picture of my father on my bedside table. The motion brought a sharp pain to my shoulders, and I remembered last night's beating. Turning my wrist side to side revealed pink and purple marks covering older yellowing splotches.

I picked up my father's photo. Cheerful morning light shone on it, despite the bleak mood hovering over the house. My dad looked like a famous star in the spotlight.

A few days before my father left, I had asked him, "Why do they hate us?"

We were taking our usual walk, meandering through the garden around the willow tree and the rose bushes, holding hands.

"They don't even know us," my dad answered. "How could they hate us?" He took a long drag of his cigarette before passing it to me.

We had a secret tradition in which I finished off his cigarettes on the rare occasion when he smoked—never mind that I was a nine-year-old girl in post-revolution Iran. I took a couple of puffs and squashed the butt on the edge of the fountain.

"What is it like to lose your dad?" I asked.

He shook his head. "It's really hard."

Earlier that day, my entire third-grade class had gone silent as Roxana entered the room, her face showing long, angry scratches. *Would I claw my own face if I lost someone I loved?* Roxana and I were good friends, and I hated that I hadn't been there when she found out. Even worse, I didn't know what to say. So I had just sat there, staring at my hands, my ears still ringing from the explosions that had shaken the earth the night before.

Her dad had been visiting his sick mother in Tehran when a Scud missile got him. The missile also killed his mother, along with the hosts and all the guests attending a six-year-old's birthday party. They were all in the same apartment complex.

Even though we were used to going to funerals, it didn't get easier.

"Baba, if they don't hate us, then why do they bomb us?"

My dad was about to say something, but instead he changed course so as not to disturb a caravan of ants that spread across the walkway. I followed suit.

Once, when I was four, we had come across a similar caravan

on our walk. I had homed in on the biggest ant and crushed it with a rock.

"Why did you do that, Ooji?" my dad had asked, calling me by my nickname.

"I killed the big scary dragon," I said, as if it were the most obvious thing in the world.

"Do you want to know what I see?" he asked. He sat next to me and pointed at the ants. "That one there is Sara. She is the oldest daughter. She likes to tell jokes. Everyone always laughs at Sara's jokes. This one right here is Naneh Sheida. She makes the best baklava. And that little one over there, that's Sina. He is the youngest of all, just like you. He loves drawing with crayons. Do you know what Sina does with his crayons after he's done drawing a picture?"

I shook my head.

"He eats them! Who else does that?" he said, tickling me.

I laughed at first, but then, with a frown, I pointed at the rock covering the crushed ant.

"That was Baba Jafar," my dad whispered. "He was leaving for the store to buy Sina some more crayons."

Remembering that day from ages before, I looked up at my dad. He looked tired, and gray hairs that hadn't been there a few months earlier had sprouted like spring grass shoots all over his head. I didn't ask him any more questions about Iraqi pilots and bombs. I just squeezed his hand, and we continued our walk around the rose bushes and the willow tree.

The morning he left, my baba had told me to be a good listener. "I'm going to come back with more stories," he whispered in my ear. Then he slung his bag over his shoulder and left for the airport. He was a civil engineer on a secret government assignment that he couldn't tell us anything about. He didn't know when he would come back either.

In the first few days, I kept track of his movements in my mind: *Now he is fastening his seat belt . . . Now he is in his Ahvaz office, learning about his assignment . . . Now he is having dinner.* But as the weeks rolled by, it all became fuzzy, a tangle of pointless tidbits. When we talked on the phone, I didn't have much to say. I had promised to be a good listener, but this was much harder than I thought.

"Baba Joon, come back safe, okay?" I said to his framed picture.

"'The lost Youssef will come back to Canaan, do not despair. This forsaken land will become filled with flowers, do not despair.'" The verse from Hafez, Shiraz's very own poet, popped into my mind, consoling me. I kissed the cold glass covering my father's picture and set it back on my bedside table.

My mother, her eyes puffy and red, shuffled about the kitchen as she prepared breakfast. Laugh lines made parentheses around her pursed lips, but behind them the beast of her anger lurked, ready to pounce at the slightest provocation.

This wasn't the time to say anything about her misbuttoned blouse. I slid into a chair at the kitchen table, attempting to be casual. "Salaam," I whispered.

"Salaam," she mumbled.

She shoved a plate in front of me. I picked at my food and glanced at the newspaper report on last night's attack. There was a photo of a man holding a crying toddler, running toward the camera. They were both covered in dust, and clouds of smoke hovered over the rubble behind them.

"Another night you've ruined my sleep." My mother clucked her tongue. "All the lines are busy too. I can't get ahold of your father. Don't you think I have enough to worry about?"

I took an inventory of the responses bouncing around inside my head before forcing out the words "I'm sorry, Maman." Hearing my own cracked voice, my eyes welled up with tears.

"Don't make me come searching for you," she said with no malice.

"'Oh, pilgrims on your way to Hajj, where are you going? Your beloved is right here. Come back, come back.'" I was reciting Rumi.

"I'll die for you, my little poet." My mother's face brightened, and she kissed my head.

Arman, a halo of sleep hugging him tightly, frowned as he

walked into the kitchen. "Can't you two at least quote the Koran once in a while, instead of all this Rumi nonsense?"

My mother and I looked at him.

"What? I'm the only one keeping this family out of trouble!" Arman sat and crossed his arms.

Normally I would have rolled my eyes and made a snide comment, but I remembered his hesitation the night before when my mother had ordered him to fetch Baba's belt.

"And we women are so lucky to have Rostam the Brave to protect us!" My mother smiled as she poured him some tea.

Arman shoved his chair back and stood up. "Stop mocking me!"

My mother kissed him on his head. "Sit down and eat, sweetheart. You need your strength."

Arman sat, still cross, but soon he was distracted with buttering his naan. His sleepy face scrunched up in the same way it did when he solved math riddles.

My mother watched him as he slathered quince jam uniformly over the butter.

"Your brother worries about you too, Kimia. Thank God he, at least, knows how to act like an adult."

She pulled Arman's head to her. "Let me see your hair."

"Why?" Arman asked, his mouth full of his meticulously wrapped bite of naan.

"Even children your age are going gray from this war." My mother picked through his thick black hair. I had heard that rumor. I imagined what Arman and I would look like with gray hair.

"I'm a teenager!" Arman protested, but he didn't move.

"Maybe in America. Here you're my gol pesar.[1] I'm so proud of you for being so responsible . . . Always getting a perfect twenty in geometry."

"Speaking of geometry, Reza told me he needs help studying for his math exam, but I told him I had to help you with shopping," I blurted out.

---

1   boy flower

Arman was about to interject, but at the sight of my bruised arms he swallowed his words.

My mother sat next to Arman and placed another piece of naan on his plate.

"Azita Khanom and Amu Doctor have to attend the funeral of Mrs. Zamani's son, so I don't think they'll be able to help him," I went on. "Poor Reza. I could just show him a few tricks and I bet he'd ace that exam . . ."

"Drink your milk," my mother interrupted, pushing a small glass in front of me.

I complied. She must have woken up at the crack of dawn to stand in the rationed milk line. "Did you have milk and poetry this morning?" I asked, wiping my mouth with the back of my hand.

My mother nodded distractedly and faced the sun shining above the Poshteh Moleh Mountain through the kitchen window. Strands of her unkempt hair turned golden in the light. She cupped her hands around her warm tea.

"How was it?" I ventured.

She looked at me and blinked as if batting another thought away. "Oh, there were more poets than usual in the milk line today. Mr. Tavallali was there with a new poem. A pretty good one too." She bent her head to her estekan, sipping from her half-finished tea. "You have until eleven. Then you must meet me at the chai khooneh. You will stay at Amu Doctor's house, do you understand?"

I was already out of my chair. "Chashm, by my eye, I will! See you at eleven."

WITH MY SCARF FLUNG loosely about my head, I ran down the narrow, deserted alley. When two shapeless figures approached, I switched to a fast walk. There was a chance they might be Hezbollahi, the slang term we used to describe the religious right.

These conservatives didn't approve of girls running, and even though there weren't actual laws stating such ridiculous things, when enough women had been harassed or arrested, we began realizing our limitations.

As soon as women were forced to wear hijab, I had insisted on cutting my hair and had pretended to be a boy. But people began to recognize me and I had to stop, as even little girls didn't escape punishment. When Sanaz's younger sister was whipped by a fearsome-looking paasdar[2] for being on a swing, wearing a skirt and no head cover, my mother forbade me from breaking any of the strange new moral laws. I wanted to argue that the demented paasdar was carrying a whip, looking for a target, that there hadn't been any other similar incidents, but we were already spending so much of our time fighting.

I passed the two strangers and broke into a run again. Soon I was standing breathlessly before the thick wooden door of the Pirooz home. I banged the Hand of Fatemeh door knocker. That familiar carved cherry barrier was the only thing standing between me and my best friend in the world. "Reza! Reza!" I yelled. A bearded man strolled by and shot me a look. I pulled my scarf over my exposed hair.

"Come on, Reza!" I murmured. I was about to knock again when the door cracked open. "You won't believe what happened last night—" I stopped short as the door opened more fully and revealed Reza's dad, Dr. Pirooz.

"Good morning, golam,"[3] he said.

"Oh, hi, Amu Doctor, I thought—I . . ."

"You're looking for Reza, I presume?" Amu Doctor smiled.

"Yes!" I yelped.

I bit my lower lip, regretting my clear lack of eloquence. Amu Doctor, with his smart suit, his perfectly combed hair and trimmed mustache, made me suddenly self-conscious. I loved Dr. Pirooz

---

2   member of the Revolutionary Guard
3   my flower

like he was family. Ever since I could remember, I referred to him as my uncle, calling him Amu[4] Doctor, but his presence made me want to be more dignified and refined than I often appeared.

As Amu Doctor opened the door wider, I saw Reza, and all my frustrations vanished. He was almost a year older than me, but a bit shorter and younger looking. Clad in his favorite army fatigue jacket, he, too, spotted me and ran to the door.

"Kimia!" Reza exclaimed, yanking his Walkman headphones off his head.

"Reza, do you want to, uh . . ." I faltered. I hadn't planned on Amu Doctor's presence.

But Amu Doctor simply pushed Reza out the door.

"You two be careful out there, okay?"

We nodded simultaneously.

"Hey, are you bringing that?" I pointed to his Walkman. Reza had acquired it the previous summer on a lucky afternoon while vacationing in Dubai. He and the device had been nearly inseparable ever since. He caressed the chunky buttons of the blue-and-silver cassette player. There were times when we needed to be empty-handed and quick, like two animals. My excited face made it clear today was one of those days. He took the Walkman off carefully and handed it to his father.

"Now get out of here before your mother comes!" Amu Doctor said with a wink.

One of the new Islamic laws forbade boys and girls from touching one another, but the alley looked empty and my heart was leaping with joy. I grabbed Reza's hand and we ran, giggles falling like scattered cherry blossoms behind us.

"Do you have water today?" I yelled.

"No. Do you have electricity?" Reza yelled back.

"No!" I said and we both erupted in laughter.

We rounded a corner, still laughing. Three men in dark clothes and too much facial hair paused their conversation when they

---

4   paternal uncle

heard our chuckles. We unclasped our hands in a flash, shut our mouths, and looked down, assuming the most somber looks we could muster.

With my eyes still on the ground, I whispered, "Let's go see what the missile did!"

"Are you crazy?" Reza said, without looking at me. "We'll get in trouble."

"Not if they don't catch us!"

Reza grumbled something, but let me lead the way.

As we got closer to the impact site, the stench of the smoldering buildings grew stronger. The smell brought with it flashes of the chaos, Arman's silent screams, and the beating. I covered my nose and mouth with my scarf. Reza brought his forearm to his face, breathing into his jacket sleeve. We stuck to the alleys to avoid crowds on the larger streets. When the odor no longer bothered me, I brought my head close to Reza's and whispered, "I was there."

"Where the missile hit?" he asked, his voice high with incredulity.

"No, divooneh,[5] at the square! There was a storyteller I've never seen before. He was . . . strange, but, well, I don't know . . ." I switched to a whisper. "I think he's a magician or, at the very least, a friend to the jinn folks."[6]

Reza whispered back, "That's nonsense, plus you shouldn't be talking about magic. The Imam . . ."

I hushed him as I heard some men shout from around the corner.

"What?" Reza mouthed.

I eased a glance around the corner and then tugged on Reza's shirt. "Look!"

We both stared at the rubble of an office building that had collapsed onto the adjacent kabob shop.

---

5   silly
6   supernatural beings held responsible for misfortune, possession, and mischief-making

Reza stood transfixed. "When we had out-of-town guests, my baba brought home kabob barg from there." He pointed to the hulking pile.

Volunteers were combing through the rubble. I realized we were too exposed.

"Come on." I pulled at Reza again.

We found a partially destroyed garden wall and ducked behind it.

"Do you think there are dead people under all that?" Reza asked.

"Probably," I replied with a shrug, but I already knew no missing people had been reported in the paper.

Somehow that fib made the moment more exciting and our adventure more important. Without warning, I jumped over the lowest part of the wall and scrambled up the rubble pile. Since girls were not allowed to climb, I had to be lightning quick.

"Kimia!" Reza hissed.

But I climbed on. About two-thirds of the way up the rubble pile, I pulled a bright red scarf from a crevice. Despite the dust, it was in good condition and its heavy silkiness felt sublime in my hands. I tied it around my neck as if it were a cape and stood like a hijabi superhero with my fists on my hips. Reza started laughing. A couple of workmen spotted me and yelled. Reza lost his smile and motioned frantically. I glanced back at the workmen: they were clambering over the rubble toward me. I took one more look around from my perch, spread my arms out wide, and ran down the mountain of destruction, my red cape flying behind me.

2. KIMIA — SAN DIEGO, 2009

WHEN I COME TO, I'm sitting at my mother's kitchen table, holding an ice bag to my head. The last thing I remember was being in the garage, wondering how my mother, old, frail, and unhinged, had packed up her house in a few days. Then out of nowhere a large bird came flying at me.

"Maman," I ask, "did you know there is a bird in your garage? It's big, like an emu or a peacock. Maybe it escaped from the zoo."

"You need to eat," she says, arranging seven dishes in front of me. This is my mother's idea of a little snack.

I inhale the scent of khoreshte fesenjoon, suddenly famished. My mother places a ladle of the steaming stew on top of a mount of saffron-painted rice. She spoons yogurt and cucumber mixed with nuts and berries into a small bowl and piles Shirazi salad with chopped fresh mint on a plate.

"Bokhor aziz," she says as a reflex—"Eat, darling"—even though I have already begun eating.

"The food's delicious, Roya Jon," I say in between bites. I'm about to bring up the bird again when she kisses me on the head.

"Don't talk. Bokhor aziz," she commands before turning around to rummage through her kitchen cabinet. She is singing an old Iranian tune, but I don't recognize the lyrics. Maybe I have a concussion.

"You're fine," says my mother, as if she can read my thoughts. She puts a glass of warm water in front of me. "Nothing is broken. Nothing is swollen." She grabs my chin and looks at my eyes. I smell tea and saffron on her breath. "Your eyes focus with no problem. Amu Doctor always gave khaksheer to his patients who had taken a fall. If they threw it up, he knew they needed to go to the hospital." She pours the brown khaksheer powder in the water and stirs it. "These days, before they even look at you, they take a CAT scan and give you poisonous medicine with side effects that make you addicted." She adds honey in the glass and then holds a spoonful of the liquid mixture in front of me. I open my mouth like a baby bird, swallowing the earthy, sweet khaksheer, as I did a million times when I was little. "Our traditional medicine has worked for centuries. Why change?" She pushes the glass in front of me. "Drink the rest."

I obey while she watches me with all her attention. I put the empty glass on the table.

"I'll die for you," she says.

"Thank you, I feel better," I say. This isn't the proper response to her pronouncement. *I'll die for you* is the exaggerated and often overused Iranian catchall phrase for "I love you," "thank you," "you're welcome," and depending on what gesture you use, "not right now." *May God never will it* is the appropriate answer, but she has already turned away, pouring tea into two estekan cups.

I glance at the clock. It has been three hours since I arrived at my mother's garage, weaving through haphazard columns made from stacked boxes. I kicked a half-inflated exercise ball out of the way. I stepped over a milk crate topped off with a dish drainer and a Russian nesting doll. I heard a rustling noise coming from a far corner.

"Maman? Roya Jon . . . We need to talk," I said to the garage. "Hello?"

Navigating through heaps of old books and photo albums, my

foot caught the corner of a box. The contents spilled all over. *Great.* I bent to right the carton.

A shiny rose, brilliant and red, peeked through a pile of dusty knickknacks. I pulled on one of the petals and watched a rivulet of scarlet flow out from under the mess. It was my old red scarf. How had it made it to San Diego? I buried my face in the lush, slippery heaviness, inhaling dust and rosewater perfume. The dust tickled my nose and I suppressed a sneeze.

A framed picture lay near the pile. Wrapping the scarf around me, I fetched the frame and wiped the dusty glass with my sleeve.

Two fell down
One didn't rise
Which one? Which one?
Tell me no lies

The childhood verses surged forth from a labyrinth of disused memories. They chanted to a faraway beat of a broken drum. I angled the photo toward the light—Reza and me standing arm in arm. We sported matching haircuts. Reza presented to the camera something shiny in the open palm of his hand.

The rustling noise emerged from the same corner of the garage. My fingers tightened around the frame as I made my way toward the sound.

A strange squawk pierced my ears. An explosion of feathers knocked me backward. The frame flew out of my hand. I heard it smash against the wall just before my head struck the hard floor.

My mother, a hummingbird, graceful and lithe, is darting about the kitchen, clearing the dishes and spooning leftovers into a line of containers. I'm confused that she doesn't respond about the bird.

"Don't go to the garage until I check it out," I say.

She glances over at me.

"Do you know how it might have gotten in there?" I search her impassive face. "I think I need a bat and a flashlight to confront the thing."

"I don't know what you're talking."

I correct her English automatically. "I don't know what you're talking about."

"You slipped and fell," Roya says, and blows on the steam rising from her full teacup. I mull over the possibility that I might have imagined the whole thing.

"Never mind . . . Listen . . ." Putting my elbows on the kitchen table, I rest my face in my hands. Whether the bird is imaginary or not, I still need to talk some sense into my mother. She can't just pack up and move to Iran. "Roya Jon, please hear me out," I say, enjoying the notion that my current state may be giving me the upper hand for making my case. She can't possibly argue, seeing me like this. "There are so many opportunities for renewal. Major change doesn't have to come from an external source." My voice is feeble and I'm glad I don't have to make eye contact.

I can feel her watching me as she sips her tea.

"If you don't want to teach poetry, fine, but it would be wise to talk about your options before you make a rash decision."

The sound of shattering glass forces my eyes open. My mother is collapsing next to the broken teacup and saucer.

"Maman Jon!" I leap out of my chair. She is curled up on the floor. I gather her light body in my arms as she convulses like a freshly broken bird in my soft embrace.

"Shhh. It's all right," I whisper, holding her tighter, but I have no faith in my own words.

Two fell down
One didn't rise

My mother is a mouji—a street term for those who suffer from sporadic war-related tremors.

I caught sight of my first mouji one autumn morning right after the war began. My mother and I were heading to the ration line when he emerged from an alley. The man shook, his entire body caught in an uncontrollable hiccup. A couple of oranges fell out of the bag he carried, rolling onto the sidewalk. People gathered the oranges and put them back in his bag, but he shook again and they fell back out. He refused people's offer to carry his bag. We were transfixed. My mother had lost her job and my father was away on a dangerous war assignment, but this man had it far worse. Then, seven months later, my mother became a mouji herself.

Even after the worst of her spells, she refused to take any medication, telling us she would manage. Roya and I share an irrational distrust of medications, so I never insisted, but every time she had an episode, she implored me to kill her. She appeared to be in so much pain, and I felt the unforgiving hand of guilt tighten around my throat as I couldn't deliver the thing that would bring her solace. After she recovered, I would become angry and demand she see a doctor. "This is how you manage an attack? By begging me to kill you?" I would yell and regret it immediately.

"I'll get better. I promise," she said the last time it happened. And for years she did stop shaking. Until now.

I stroke her hair with my hand. The mouj[7] waves of the attack have subsided, but their echoes still reverberate around us. I watch tears flow down Roya's paper-thin cheeks. She sinks her head into the crook of my arm. "Baz havaye vatanam aarezoost.[8] Take me home," my mother says between sobs. "Please, take me home."

---

7   *Mouj* is the word for wave in Farsi. *Mouji* is the slang for those whose bodies are afflicted with uncontrollable and frequent waves—a manifestation of PTSD caused by explosions.

8   A common Persian refrain, originally composed by the seventeenth-century poet Feiz Kashani. It is translated as, "I wish to breathe the air of my homeland."

3. KIMIA — SHIRAZ, 1981

I WAS STILL WEARING my red cape as we arrived in the Ghasrodasht square, laughing. We had already committed several illegal acts, and the anticipation of setting a new record was making my feet itch. But all it took was one look at the mess left from the previous night and the laughter dried on our lips.

"Vay!" Reza cried. That sorry pile of concrete and debris couldn't be the magical square I had stood in a handful of hours ago. I squeezed Reza's hand, not caring if anyone saw us.

"Vay," Reza said again, echoing my shock.

We had attended performances and picnics in that square since we were babies. I remembered the smell of barbecued corn as Reza and I played ye ghol do ghol with pebbles on the picnic blanket and adults told jokes. I had even lost a tooth there. My father had wrapped it in a napkin, so we could bury it later in the garden. Each tooth was to become a surprise tree. The giant willow tree in our garden had sprouted out of my grandfather's buried tooth ages ago, or at least that's what my father told me.

Tears pooled in my eyes as my mother's recent poem came to mind. It was about the four-thousand-year-old cypress that longed for the forest of her youth—before the insatiable darkness of winter devoured pleasant memories of blue skies and sunshine and before gardeners became lumberjacks. My own pleasant prerevolution memories were fading like an old dream. I wanted to will back the days when everyone had the freedom to dress as they pleased and I could ride a bicycle and there was no war. But it was easy to doubt those days had ever existed.

I spat on the ground and shouted, "Come on!" and led Reza to the battered stage. We passed a couple of old women sweeping a corner of the square, but the cleanup had not begun in earnest, probably because there was worse destruction elsewhere.

When we arrived, Reza arranged a few broken props, the painted backdrops of the Alborz mountains and King Sahm's palace, so we were hidden from view. Without saying a word, we leaned against the stage, scanning our relatively unscathed surroundings. Nearby, a kid's dusty shoe poked out from underneath an abandoned picnic blanket. The breeze danced a plastic bag over a lone spoon, casting a certain dreaminess on our little corner. To the sound of traffic droning in the background, I rested my head against the stage and rubbed the edge of my new scarf between my thumb and forefinger.

"Look!" Reza's voice knocked me out of my reverie. He scurried toward a fallen prop and pulled out a trampled, broken drum.

"Keep it," I said. "Maybe we can fix it." I stood and tightened the red scarf beneath my chin. "Let's see what else we can find!" I kicked a small pile of confetti near my foot, scattering the colorful dots in the wind. "We're rich! We're rich!" I grabbed a fistful of the falling confetti, laughing.

"Kimia!"

Behind me, Reza held the half-burnt puppet of the Simorgh to the sun. I dropped the confetti and ran to him.

We looked in wonder at the intricate detail still evident in the damaged puppet, the sunlit dust falling on our faces. Tiny beads of every color decorated the bird's chest, and gleaming poolak sequins threatened to become undone around its busted tail feathers. We stashed the puppet and the drum by the backdrops and continued to search.

Something glinted on the far edge of the stage. I ran to the shiny thing, recognizing a gold button that must have fallen off King Sahm's vest. As I bent to inspect it, I realized I could easily fit under the stage. The breeze changed directions, and I smelled a strange perfume.

"Not again!" I heard Reza's annoyed voice as I crawled under. "What are you up to now?"

I showed him the button before sticking it in my pocket, and turned away, crawling on all fours, searching for more treasures. My fingers brushed against the cool metal of a handle sticking out of the ground. "Look!" I yelled. "I think it's a trapdoor!"

"I think we should leave it alone," Reza pleaded.

"Help me with this!" I barked at Reza, tugging on the handle.

Reza obeyed, and after a few moments of struggle, we managed to pull the door open. The heavy cast iron landed with a low thud in the dirt.

We rushed to look inside and our heads collided. "Akh!" We both laughed as we tried once again. As our eyes adjusted to the darkness inside, we took in the perfume wafting up to welcome us.

"Smells like jasmine. We're going in," I said into the darkness.

"It's orange blossom. And you're insane!" Reza said.

"Reza! Look, there are stairs! Come on!" I grabbed his arm, begging.

"I don't care if there's an elevator—I'm not going in!" He pulled his arm away. In his face I saw there was no winning this one.

From the corner of my eye, I spotted dusty boots from the other side of the street, heading our way. "Uh-oh," I said, pointing.

Reza wiped his hands on his pants. "I'll, uh, I'll wait for you over by the street," he whispered before scrambling out from under the stage.

I heard his light, fast steps as he ran the opposite direction, undetected by the approaching men. The boots were getting closer, and before I thought it through, I was diving down the stairs, heaving the trapdoor shut above me.

The door thudded into place. I was in almost total darkness, except for a rectangular sliver of light framing the edges of the door above. As I waited for my eyes to adjust, I imagined the trapdoor was the mouth of a mighty whale that had swallowed the city noise and was drawing me into its mysterious belly. I stood at the top of the stairs. *I should go back up and meet Reza.*

My left hand ran along the stone wall as I eased myself down the first few steps. With the light from above illuminating my path, I became more confident halfway down. I began taking two steps at a time. *Reza will be so jealous he didn't come with me.*

Near the bottom, the smooth texture of the wall changed to a rugged surface with dramatic peaks and valleys. I paused and examined a stone carving of the giant Simorgh stretched out before me. When my hand reached the eye of the bird, the emerald stone fell to the ground. I bent down and tucked it into my palm.

"You can keep it. It will bring you good luck!"

Startled by a voice coming from nowhere, I gasped and righted myself, ready to run. There stood the old storyteller, a few steps below, smiling as he had the night before. I turned toward the exit and bolted.

I must have run fast, because soon I was out of breath, clambering out of the trapdoor and speeding across the square. It took one glare from a stranger for me to realize I was running out in the open. With my head down, I switched to a quick walk. Reza stepped out from behind a mass of honeysuckle blooms draped over one wall of the alley.

"What happened?" Reza spat out a flower bereft of nectar.

"Keep walking. I'll tell you later," I said, glancing at my watch. "I'm supposed to meet my mother at the chai khooneh. She'll kill me if I'm late." I turned to him and huffed. "Are you coming?"

Reza hurried to catch up. I ignored my legs' plea for a fast gallop, and in turn they trembled in protest. Finally we arrived at the entrance of the old teahouse and paused at the threshold, taking in the majesty of the scene.

Soothing setar music calmed my nerves. I fiddled with the eye of the Simorgh in my pocket as Reza studied the tile mural of a battle scene from the myths of *Shahnameh*. The scent of fresh-brewed tea flirted with the tobacco smoke and hovered over the old men and their hookahs. The smoke rose up to the giant mural, giving it a hazy feel, as if the battle depicted had just ended. The scene showed a man on a horse, carrying a bloody saber. On the ground lay the body of a woman, her head severed near the horse's hooves. I hated that mural. I scrunched my nose, turning toward the crowd to search for my mother.

Across the way, a young couple sipped steaming estekan cups of tea while their two children played. Ice cream was smeared all over the little girl's face. Her older brother kept hiding under the table and jumping out to surprise her. She was surprised every time, and her repeated delighted yelps made everyone around them laugh, too.

As sunbeams entered from high windows and cut through the smoke and din, our eyes followed the servers, carrying large trays of tea and an assortment of desserts. We grabbed our cups of paloodeh from our server's tray and weaved through tables. I couldn't wait to share my adventure with Reza, but for now, I was safe, I was with my best friend, and sweets and poetry surrounded us.

"There she is," said Reza. He had spotted my mother first. She was holding forth at a crowded table. As she began, my mother's hands made graceful movements in accordance with her words as if the poem had made her into both the conductor and the symphony. The crowd grew quiet when she whispered a line like it was a precious secret and collectively leaned to receive the next verse.

We had settled on a bench when I noticed I was still wearing my cape. At least no one had caught me in it. *Has anyone been arrested for wearing a cape?* I shrugged and put my paloodeh on the table. My mouth watered at the thought of taking the first bite of the sweet frozen vermicelli drenched in fresh lime juice and sour cherry sauce.

As I raised my hand to take off my cape, I caught Reza looking at my bruised wrist. We locked eyes for a moment and in unison diverted our gaze to the fancy tile floor. We ate our paloodeh in silence.

"'Forgive the wars among seventy-two nations. Unwilling to see the truth, they were led by fantasies.'" My mother quoted Hafez with her booming voice.

Everyone, including the children, clapped. As more people gathered around her, we had to jockey for a better position in the crowd.

"No one brings life into poems like you, Mrs. Shams," said someone in the audience. Others nodded and clapped.

"Now! How about one of your own?" an admirer demanded.

"Well, chashm." My mother proudly complied.

I watched her face, a blossoming lotus, as the poem unfolded.

"'Your bird is our guide. How else could we survive the Seven Valleys of Love? Soon all valleys will dissolve in your presence. And we shall bask in the light of your sun.'"

I closed my eyes, savoring the last verse as applause erupted, the sweet, cold taste of paloodeh still on my tongue.

We emerged proud as a lioness and two cubs from the teahouse. The splendor of the chai khooneh extended itself to the outdoors. The sun played hide-and-seek with the cypresses lining both sides of the street, inviting us to stay in the world of myth and poetry.

"Well, it's time to go to the ration lines," my mother said.

A few people turned around and glanced our direction, as she still had her deklameh[9] voice on. Unfazed, she grabbed my hand, and we headed to the line. Many stood expressionless, still shaken by the previous night's attack. Cars whizzed by the long line, and the shouts of the bus-driver-helper boys, half-hanging out of the

---

9   spoken poetry

buses, calling out upcoming street names, rose and fell away. Two women, holding their chador veils tight under their chins, were having a spirited discussion about the lack of electricity and water.

"My neighbor has a water tank to save water," the older woman said. "But I can't afford one. Everything is so expensive these days. May God curse Saddam. Did you have electricity today?"

"Nah, how about you?" the tall, slightly stooped woman replied in her relaxed Shirazi drawl.

Reza and I exchanged furtive looks and smiled.

"Kimia Joon, after you get the eggs from this line, you need to go to these other lines. Basheh?[10] Oh, and here are the ration coupons." She handed me a wrinkled and ink-smudged list and several coupons printed on cheap, flimsy paper.

"Reza Joon, you don't have to wait in line," she added.

"It's okay, Roya Khanom, we have a lot to talk about. I mean, Kimia is still helping me with my homework."

I shot him an angry glance. *Don't mess this up, Reza. Not now!*

"Okay, then, I'll meet you back here in a couple of hours," my mother said, distracted.

"Bye," Reza and I said in unison.

My mother sped away, but to us, she moved in slow motion as seconds took centuries. When she turned the corner and disappeared from view, Reza said, "Tell me!"

"I can do better than that! Close your eyes and hold out your hands," I said.

Reza complied, his face pinched in excitement around his closed eyes. I placed the warm stone eye in Reza's hands.

"Wow, what is this?" he asked suspiciously after he opened his eyes.

"The eye of the Simorgh, divooneh!" I said.

"What do you mean?" Reza asked.

"I plucked it from the Simorgh in the world below the stage!" I said impatiently.

---

10 Okay?

"There's a Simorgh down there?" Reza's eyes widened.

"Of course! And it's probably guarding some great treasure! But I couldn't really find out because—"

Before I could finish, Reza's expression changed, and someone smacked me on the back of the head. I spun around to see my big brother standing behind me.

"What are you two bacheh nokhodchi[11] doing here?" Arman said, with an air of bravado.

"You're a nokhodchi!" I shot back ineptly, holding the back of my head.

I was mad that after we had finally secured the space to have our private conversation, we were so jarringly interrupted. I was embarrassed that I was exposed and made into a spectacle for the bored people standing in line. I was furious at Arman's freakish ability to find me mid-adventure and trample my fun. But mostly, I was livid that I didn't have a proper retort for my obnoxious brother. My hands formed into fists, but the balloon of my rage deflated as I recognized Arman's small gang of Mobarezin, the morality police wannabes, a few steps behind him. My fingernails dug into my hands as I stole a glance, wanting to meet Reza's eyes. He was busy stuffing the stone in his pocket, looking as worried as I felt. The boys, in various stages of puberty, flanked their leader. People's attention shifted from us to them. The leader, taller than the rest, and with a face that claimed the most mature beard in the group, frowned at an anxious Reza. The hot noon sun added more intensity to the situation, making me want to ditch the line and run. Reza took a step back, sweating.

"Well, Reza, what are you doing here?" Following his leader's cue, Arman stepped up to Reza.

"Uh, uh . . . ," Reza stammered.

"Leave him alone!" I cried out.

Now we were all in the spotlight. People near us, glad to have

---

11   baby garbanzos

the distraction from the tedium of perpetual waiting, stopped their conversations.

"Brother Shams, who's this boy with your sister?" the leader asked, glad for the audience to showcase his authority.

Arman, who hadn't planned for this scenario, grimaced. "Morteza, I mean Brother Hashemi, Reza's, uh, our cousin. Little pest, that's all," he answered, smacking Reza on the head.

Reza mouthed *ow* and rubbed where Arman had hit him.

"And why are they unaccompanied?" asked the leader, towering over Arman.

"My mom is just around the corner. She'll be back in one minute," I said, looking the leader in the eyes. He averted his own. Pious men do not make eye contact with women.

"You know you're not supposed to hang out with boys unaccompanied. We'll let it go this time, but I don't want to catch you two together again," said Arman.

"Got it?" added the leader.

We nodded, and for the thousandth time that day we looked down. The leader motioned to the gang that it was time to leave. They disappeared into the crowd, Arman glancing back at us.

4. KIMIA — SAN DIEGO, 2009

I AWAKEN TO THE comforting smell of sautéed onions in cumin and turmeric. I rub my eyes and survey my surroundings. There used to be two long Miniature-style paintings hanging from the wall across from this sofa. Men on horses hunted deer with impossibly thin legs, and women tended a giant cauldron. My father had brought the paintings, along with my black box, from Isfahan.

He had arrived with the winter air on his jacket and in his hair. He swept me up into his arms as soon as he walked into the kitchen, kissing me with his bristly face. "Ooji, where have you been?" he bellowed, laughing from his depths.

Arman, now attached to Baba's leg, tugged at my foot, and so my father set me down and hoisted him up. "Look how big you are," he said to Arman.

After he and Maman had exchanged pecks on the cheek, she returned to dinner preparations. "Look at these treasures!" he exclaimed, opening his suitcase. Arman and I stared at his crumpled clothes, disappointment registering on our faces. My dad smiled and grabbed a bundle of shirts, and with a few quick motions, unraveled the clothes to reveal the paintings and the box.

Maman looked up from the simmering aash anaar, gave the

presents a brief glance, then wagged her ladle in the air, dripping pomegranate sauce on the floor. "Why did you waste your money on *that*?" she chided my father, zeroing in on the box. My father only chuckled. "Kimia"—she nodded at the floor—"get a rag."

The box was intended as a gift for my mother, but her rejection meant it would come to me or Arman. Luckily, Arman was much more enamored of the Rubik's Cube that had also tumbled out of Baba's clothing.

My black box is hidden in a nook in my closet. The nail hooks poking out of lighter colored rectangles on Roya's wall tell me the paintings are somewhere in the garage with the rest of her belongings. They tell me this is not a dream. They tell me my mother still wants me to take her to Iran. I pull myself up, my heart sinking.

After her mouji attack last night, I took Roya to bed. I sat on a chair near her, trying to meditate the unsettling hours away. "Coming back to the breath is the quickest path to the present moment," I tell my clients. "When your breath doesn't flow freely, take charge. Free the breath and the breath sets you free."

So I belly-breathed, mindful of the chill, stubborn knot in my stomach. Only, with each inhale, I grew more agitated. A faint headache began to pulse between my temples. I reached for a glass of water.

"Salaam," she said in her sleep, her eyes moving behind her closed lids. "How have you been?"

My mother is a restless sleeper, waking up several times at night. When I first began my mindfulness practice, I had encouraged her to join our weekly meditation sangha to help her sleep more soundly.

"I'll disturb everyone's peace," she said with a serious look in her eyes. "When I sit quiet, the ghosts come to visit and it'll be rude not to greet them." I wondered if she was hosting one of her ghosts now.

"Make like a turtle," she said, distress wrinkling her forehead.

I recalled the air raids of my youth. The instructions were

drilled into every elementary school kid's head: crouch on the floor, with your head touching your knees, like a turtle.

"No, no," Roya whimpered, her hands grabbing at darkness.

"Shhh." I massaged her shoulders. Her hands fell limp by her sides. "You're safe." I stroked her forehead. "You're in America."

When my mother's breathing became rhythmic, I abandoned my attempt to meditate and headed for the garage, holding a broom to defend myself.

Roya was right. The garage was empty except for the clutter of soon-to-be discarded memories. I stared at the tipped box, its contents spilled out on the cold floor. No strange bird here. It must have been my imagination. But instead of being reassured, I felt the cold spread from my center, like frost on a windowsill. I stayed long enough to see that Roya had swept the broken glass pieces and had placed the photo on top of the exercise ball. I rushed out of the garage, still clutching the broom.

Now, in the kitchen, Roya is singing to herself, assembling a proper Persian lunch, which will take all morning to prepare. I flatten my hair against my head and ask how she is feeling.

"I'm doing great," she says without turning around. An apron cinches the tasteful dress around her thin frame. She adds a splash of olive oil to the pan, and onions sizzle louder. "Arman is coming over for lunch. Eat your breakfast and then join us."

I eye the spread on the table—soaked walnuts, boiled eggs, warm lavash bread, butter and jam, and a pot of tea. "I actually have a lot to do, but are you sure you're okay?"

She whips around to point her spatula at me. "Bebin!"[12] Throughout the years, she has pointed enough kitchen utensils at me that the thought of her conjures this very image. "It's been ages since we all have had a meal together," she says. "I feel good. And I want my children to eat with me." Her hair is gathered in a neat bun, and a bright lipstick makes her smile more pronounced.

---

12   Look!

"Good," I say, lowering myself into a chair. "I'll just switch some things around."

I'll have to ask Vikas to lead the Introduction to Mindfulness class. If lunch goes smoothly, I can still make my volunteer shift at Willow Grove Elder Care.

"You don't look so good, darling." Roya points to the blanket I have wrapped around me.

"I'm all right. I'm just a bit chilly," I say, hugging the blanket tighter. My mind races, churning out random images: A red scarf. Roya shaking on the floor. A large hand slapping my small face. A burst of iridescent feathers.

I am not all right. I can hear my unsettledness louder than the sizzling onions in the pan.

5. Arman — SAN DIEGO, 2009

I CALL MYSELF TONY, a name that, like an undersized wool sweater, neither fits me nor feels comfortable. But it suits me far better than my birth name.

I wake up right in the middle of a dream for no apparent reason, and then notice my phone is flashing. It doesn't surprise me that it's Kimia—even when I silence my phone, I still sense she wants to reach me. We have a bond of sorts.

When my mom became pregnant, I asked for a brother. But Kimia came along and I treated her like a boy. I taught her to play football and took her and Reza on neighborhood adventures. We were inseparable. Then, in a matter of months, women lost the right to run in public and girls couldn't play with boys. Our father left for a war assignment. Kimia changed. I got busy with my Mobarezin training. But even decades later, I still can't free myself of this inexplicable and inconvenient cord that ties me to my sister.

"Weren't you supposed to be at Roya's for lunch?" Kimia says, her reproach crackling over the phone line.

It looks like I've overslept. My living room reeks of old booze and stale loneliness. Sweat circles stain the underarms of my new Gucci shirt. I'm sprawled on my couch.

"Listen, Arman." She says my birth name like a curse. "Roya told me not to tell you over the phone, but since you couldn't bother to show up today, here we go. She had an attack."

Guilt wrenches my insides. It's been years since our mother has had one of her episodes. And it had to be today of all days. Maman takes pride in her self-reliance and would never ask for help, so it's up to us to keep an eye on her—something I often fail to do.

Before I can digest any of this, Kimia plows on. "When she came to, she said she wants to go to Iran. She needs someone to take her. I think you should go with her."

My mouth falls open like the broken glove box of my Mercedes. This is turning out to be the worst phone call ever. I hem and haw a little and then try to explain to Kimia that I can't just leave work.

Her response hurts more than a slap in the face. "Have it your way," she says in her cool, detached voice.

I plead, "Don't be like that, man." My sister has no idea. She's all successful, living in posh digs in La Jolla while I've been struggling. I finally have a good thing going. Can't she understand that?

"I understand," she says. "You're the only man left in our family and you choose some nightclub gig over your own mother."

Then the click. She knows how to twist that knife.

I throw the phone next to my box on the cluttered coffee table. I curse Kimia under my breath for stomping on my dream and disrupting my life. I curse the cosmic lottery that made Iran my place of birth. Why couldn't I be from Tahiti or the Cayman Islands—somewhere I wouldn't dread visiting?

The cell-phone clock shows I still have time to go back to sleep before my shift begins. I reach for my box.

This stash box wasn't special when I first found it at a garage sale a few years ago. But in a fit of inspiration, I sanded and stained the damaged exterior and relined the inside with aromatic cedar wood. I carefully carved out spaces for my favorite glass pipe, my Bic lighter, and a Ziploc bag filled with pot.

"Besmellah,"[13] I say. The words are shards of glass in my mouth. Sometimes there is an insurmountable distance from Persian-ness to American-ness. In my weaker moments, I slide backward into my old self, becoming awkward and jittery. I cluck my tongue to clear my palate from the ancient words and pull the bag of weed free from its elastic loop. I load the pipe and take a greedy toke. And another. And another.

I collapse back on the couch and close my eyes, waiting for ordinary dreams, the kind that don't remind me of that awful country. But of course, instead of dreaming about California beaches and women in bikinis, I dream of Iran.

In my dream, I'm not the scrawny thirteen-year-old I used to be, but tall and muscular, like Morteza Hashemi, our squad leader. I run my hand over my head. I've got a full head of hair. Sweet.

The Mobarezin commander says my name, asking me to join the queue. I stand at attention next to the others.

"You are all heroes," the commander shouts. "As our Imam Khomeini has said, 'Our leader is the twelve-year-old child who strapped explosives to his chest and threw himself under a tank.' And if you are fortunate enough to be a martyr, your place will be in paradise among Hazrat e Mohammad and his descendants."

I don't want to throw myself under a tank. I don't want to become a martyr. I hate that kid for being the gold standard for a true revolutionary.

The commander puts his hands on my shoulders. His scraggly hair is matted on his forehead, and he smells of old sweat. Like Morteza, the commander has a great, thick beard. "You are ready, Brother Shams. You are ready to serve God."

What am I supposed to say to that? Dehydrated and dizzy, I try to swallow the lump in my throat. Luckily everyone chants, "I

---

13   In the name of God

testify there is only one God and Mohammad is His prophet!" I shout, too, but no words escape my mouth.

The commander fastens a headband decorated with Arabic writings on my forehead.

My eyes wander to the chosen boys, a hormonal potpourri of teenage growth, standing at attention. Several boys are lanky, their faces dotted with zits. Javad is built like a linebacker. Three have a handful of whiskers, but Morteza's stern face has more facial hair than all of us combined. What I wouldn't give for that! I'm not sure of much: Am I going to live a heroic life like the Marvel comics men I've secretly stashed under the mattress? Or will I be a martyr like Imam Hossain? I don't want to die but if I have to, can I at least wait till I have a killer beard?

I wake up, smelling like the commander. My neck is stiff from sleeping on the couch. I run my hand over my three-day stubble and head to the shower.

THE PARKING LOT OF the Pink Poodle is littered with orange splatters. I pull up next to a beat-up pickup truck, crushing more palm fruit under my tires. The sideview mirror flashes back my shaved head and my perfected tough-guy look. It reminds me of a Phoenician death mask I once saw at the Museum of Man. And all of a sudden, I want to cry.

Something enormous, like a silent plane, flies above, its shadow sucking the heat from the hot asphalt around my car. I lift my head toward the sky, but the pain in my neck stops my eyes on the flashy new Pink Poodle sign. I had imagined the sign would make the place seem more updated, but instead it draws attention to the shabbiness of the run-down building. I'm always polishing a turd.

The bar is already packed with the happy-hour crowd, but this doesn't make a dent in my unassailable fucked-upness. For months, the club has been all I could think about. Now, I'm not so sure. I bump into a waitress carrying a tray filled with drinks. Glasses shatter on the floor, the way the antique blue jug did. The way the storyteller's hookah did.

Without saying a word, I bend to gather pieces of broken glass.

The waitress shoots me an annoyed look and squats down with her tray. "It's all right," she lies.

"That's cool. Pedro can take care of it." Jason, my business partner, is standing above us. He motions to a busboy. "What's going on, Arman?" he asks.

"Shhh!" I whisper and nod toward the bar.

"I mean, Tony," Jason says in a conspiratorial whisper as we head to the bar. "You seem kind of distracted. Is everything all right?"

"Right. I'm sorry, man." I stop. I look at the kitschy disco ball. It just spins, mocking me with its gaudiness. Behind us, Pedro is cleaning my mess. *My mess.* I taste bitterness in my throat. I see Reza's face, lit with the ferociousness of a thousand suns. I see the deep crimson of Shirazi wine splatter against the morshed's wall.

Jason slips behind the bar and mixes two rum and Cokes. He slides one toward me.

"I might have to go to Iran," I blurt out. "My mother wants to go back. I mean, my sister could go with her. I can't just leave you with all the work."

"Oh." Jason lets this sink in.

I watch him, hoping he'll say he needs me here.

"Hey, you know what? I'll see to the grand opening. Why don't you take some time off and be with her?"

"That's really nice, but . . ."

"No buts! See, that's what I appreciate about the Old World: Family always comes first." Jason raises his glass and clicks it to mine.

"To family," Jason says.

6. Kimia — SHIRAZ, 1981

THE WIND CARRIED THE boys' intermittent shouts across the street and over our school's courtyard wall. The boys' school was holding one of their pro-war rallies. If my mother had been with me, she would have said they sounded like castrated cats. I imagined Reza and Arman standing in different lines, shouting as they raised their fists with the others. I couldn't wait till I saw Reza. But first there was school.

The bell rang, and the frowning vice principals got busy herding us, a mass of girls in black head coverings and gray uniforms. I watched Zahra as she whispered in Golsa's ear. Both girls giggled quietly. Zahra's cheeks were flushed and she looked . . . different.

"She's getting married tomorrow," said Jamileh in my ear.

"What?" I said louder than I wanted, startled both by Jamileh and this news.

"Quiet!" said Mrs. Bayaat as she walked past us to the front of the line.

"What are you talking about?" I asked Jamileh more quietly.

"Yeah, her parents are hitching her to some hotshot mullah, Imam Jannati or something."

I flicked a glance in Zahra's direction, her small figure hunched over her backpack, digging out a notebook. I had lost people to war and to the regime's crackdowns on political dissidents. We all had. But the last thing I expected was to lose a friend to marriage. I had heard rumors that in remote villages, girls my age were getting married to big, hairy men. I shuddered at the thought and felt deeply sad for Zahra, even though she didn't seem to be too upset.

Zahra disappeared in the midst of girls in morose uniforms, and Jamileh and I skirted the unfinished bomb shelter dug in the middle of the outdoor basketball court. I could still make out the white lines defining the court's perimeter. I peered into the bomb-shelter hole with longing. As frightening as the bombs and missiles were, all my experiences with them, including the night in the square, had somehow invigorated me. I joined others in the line, secretly wishing for the red siren.

Ever since the war began on that brisk autumn day in 1980, the sirens warning of Iraqi air raids had been color coded. The siren colors were vibrant like autumn leaves, but their sound filled the air with a dark terror. Each siren included an announcement, indicating the level of danger. The yellow was the siren of caution, a possibility that an attack would ensue, while the siren warning of Situation Red wailed a piercing scream predicting death and mayhem. The white siren brought news of the passing of the attack, but by then we were too shaken to enjoy it.

Everyone had a battery-operated transistor radio. Shopkeepers, maids, doctors, and bus drivers all had a radio on low volume just so they could hear the siren. We slept with the radio on, and sometimes the red siren, like a shrill and undignified grim reaper, awakened us from deep sleep. Covered in cold sweat, our hearts racing, we would grab small valuables and run to the basement or a makeshift bomb shelter. We equipped our basements with axes and shovels, just in case we got buried under the rubble. We taped the windows and mirrors just in case and called our loved ones in other towns when the phone lines weren't too jammed. *Just in case* had taken over our lives. Even so, I much preferred the red siren to the suffocating tyranny of the daily compliance on the streets and at school.

Only once in that school year did I climb inside the bomb shelter that felt more like a tomb for a giant than a sanctuary protecting us from bombs. I reckon we climbed down into that potential mass grave for no other reason than it provided an illusion of safety for the adults.

When the red siren blared, the principal's and teachers' voices faltered with fear as they guided us into the shelter. Children cried for their mothers. We descended the ladder, sometimes stepping on each other's hands in the rush to get down. We scrambled to find places on the dirt floor. Sitting there cross-legged, looking at the dusty, tear-stained faces of my schoolmates, I saw for the first time the beauty of being so close to death. Time slowed and the shelter appeared in Technicolor as I marveled at the flimsy web of life sagging and shivering precariously. I wanted to throw my head back and laugh. I wanted to rip off my scarf. To the music of an untimely rooster crooning in the distance and cries of the girls, I wanted to dance a wicked dance.

Instead, I walked calmly to the principal and grabbed the bull-horn from her trembling hand. Mimicking the voices of the stars of the hit children's show *Madreseye Mooshha*,[14] I put on an impromptu performance, recounting the latest episode. A few kids could mimic the voice of Kopol, the walnut-obsessed mouse-star of the show. But no one in the entire school was able to match the voice of my favorite, Narenji, the waif mouse with delicate feelings. Upon hearing my precise imitation of her voice, the shelter became quiet.

Perhaps our principal, Mrs. Khatami, thought of objecting, but the girls had stopped crying, so she didn't interrupt. When nervous parents rushed in, they found their daughters laughing. The girls didn't want to leave the bomb shelter.

"Boro digeh!"[15] Jamileh's loud voice jarred me out of my reverie. "Shams! Go already!" I peeled my eyes away from the

---

14   *School of Mice*
15   Go then!

hole. While I was daydreaming, most girls had found their place in line. Jamileh nudged me. "Are you asleep?" she asked. "Nah," I answered and headed toward the queue.

The vice principals, wrapped head to chin in heavy maghnaeh hijab, worked their way down the line, measuring each girl's pant leg with their measuring tapes. Students wearing pants tighter than twenty centimeters in width received an automatic suspension. The two dedicated bureaucrats eyed the length of our uniforms and sniffed each girl for traces of perfume. Our uniforms were to fall below the knee, and perfumes were strictly forbidden. We all submitted ourselves to the inspection that promised to preserve the moral fiber of society—whatever that was. Our uniform color, a tragic gray, perfectly reflected the mood in the air.

The line began to move students into their classrooms. When my turn came, I picked up two stones from a bucket to throw at effigies of Uncle Sam and Saddam Hussein. I never learned whose idea it was to make puppets out of enemies, just so they'd be stoned by a bunch of schoolgirls. I only knew I felt absurd engaging in this bizarre, school-mandated ritual.

I held the stones in my hand and bit my lower lip. I wound up and aimed at a classroom window. But at the last second, I changed direction and threw the stones at the silly-looking handmade dolls. Like every kid before me I shouted, "Death to America! Death to Saddam!"

The wind brought the smoke and the harsh smell of scorched synthetic fabric from the burning American flag at the boys' school. My eyes began watering. Oh, how I longed to hear the blood-red wail of the siren.

I DIDN'T HAVE MUCH time. My mother wanted me home to help with dinner, but I made up a fib about a mandatory after-school rally. I wasn't sure whether it was the war, my baba's absence,

or that she had been laid off from her teaching job for taking a
photo with the deposed shah, but my mother's ever-present
temper flared with a new, raw severity. It was as if all the beauty
she had depended on for her poetry was getting stripped away
from her world. You see, poets are like flowers. Some bloom in
the cold shade of despair. Others can't get enough of the bountiful
gold of the sun, exposing both the wondrous and the wretched.
My mother needed grounding beauty and light to nurture her, to
give voice to her deepest, most guarded wounds. The regime had
pruned her of her poetry.

When she was in a fit of rage, I wondered if she somehow
blamed me for the world falling apart around us. If I'd been smart,
I would have been more careful, but my secret outings were as
precious to me as the air I breathed.

I was standing with my backpack against the crumbling wall,
squinting into the bright sunlight, when I felt someone touch my
arm. My sun-soaked eyes followed the touch, and although I
couldn't make out his face, I knew it was Reza. I broke into a smile.
Not even my hijab could restrain the elation beaming from me.

"Have you got electricity today?" said Reza with laughter in
his voice.

"No. Have you got water? Hey, where have you been? I've
been waiting forever!" I said, punching him in the arm.

"Akh! We had to join the prayers after school," he said, holding
his arm.

I made an ugly face. "C'mon, let's get back to the stage!"

"What? Kimia, they've probably closed off that stairway by
now. Besides . . ." He pulled free of my grip. "We have to be careful
about being seen in public together."

He was right. It seemed like there were eyes everywhere
watching our every move. I shooed the thought away quickly.
"When has that ever stopped us? Come on, tarsoo![16] We have to
find out what's in there!"

---

16   scaredy-cat

"I don't know," said Reza, taking a step back.

"Look, I'll give you the eye of the Simorgh," I said, trying to keep desperation out of my voice. After our encounter with Arman and those gholdor bullies, I had asked for the stone eye back. Reza reached in his pocket reluctantly and handed it back to me. That night, I stashed it under my pillow, convinced it was going to give me some magical power. But if we went to the underground world, who knew what other treasures we would find . . .

"What? Really? Let's see it!" Reza interrupted.

"I don't got it on me! I'll give it to you right after we go into the underground world."

"We?"

"You want the eye or not?"

"Okay, okay!" And off we ran.

When we got to the square, I threw my book bag under the stage before sliding after it. Reza, trailing behind, stooped and followed me. We began brushing the ground, looking for the trapdoor. I brushed furiously, while Reza swept his hand as if he were polishing a delicate piece of furniture.

"Here it is! Help me!" I said.

We tugged at the door, grunting. It opened with an ancient groan.

"It's still pitch-black down there," Reza whispered.

"Not for long!" I said as I opened my book bag and fished out a small flashlight.

I turned it on and started down the stairs.

"Great. You thought of everything." Reza sighed.

"Hurry up!" I hissed, looking up at the halo of light that framed his face.

Reza stood and dusted off his pants. I watched him take a careful step forward to let himself down.

"Kimia?"

"What?" I shone my flashlight in his face. I was way ahead.

"I only have to go down this one time to get the eye, right?" Reza asked as he shielded his eyes.

"Yeah, divooneh. But after you see this, you're going to beg me to come back here!"

"You're dreaming," Reza muttered as he tried to catch up. My skin prickled with anticipation as we reached the bottom. I wanted Reza to see the Simorgh in its full majesty. He joined me in front of the wall and I intentionally held the flashlight low until he was there beside me.

"Ready?" I asked. He nodded, and I aimed my light at the wall.

He gasped, which of course was the effect I was going for. My light followed the prismatic tail plumage, slowly tracing the carved smaller feathers of the body, all the way to the Simorgh's face. Reza examined the raised texture of the bird's face with his hand and outlined its eye socket with his index finger. We looked at each other with wide eyes.

"See?" I said, satisfied.

But Reza pointed behind me. "Kimia, look!"

Down the dark hallway, light bled from underneath what appeared to be a door. I pointed the flashlight that direction, a move Reza was ready for. In one smooth motion, he grabbed the flashlight and shook his head as he turned it off. Before I could protest, the door swung open with a loud creak, pouring light into the dark hallway. I shielded my eyes. Reza let out a tiny yelp and ran back up the stairs.

"Reza! Wait," I whisper-shouted.

For a moment I entertained the idea of running after Reza and away from this mysterious and quite possibly dangerous underworld, but my feet were rooted to the spot.

Holding my breath, I took tentative steps toward the doorway as I allowed my eyes to adjust to the light. There they were, a pair of giant green eyes staring right into mine. I gasped as my pounding heart told my brain to hustle and make sense of this.

This can't be real, I thought.

My eyes finally peeled away from the monster's, but I stood still, scanning for clues. I followed the burgundy shape of an embossed dragon curled on the wall of an oval room, back to its green eyes. He had spikes along his spine and tail and his open mouth was home to a fireplace. His eyes glinted as they reflected the small fire burning behind his sharp teeth. *It's not a monster. It's just a fireplace.* I took a hesitant step inside the room.

A large carved-in bookcase adorned the curve next to the tail of the dragon. The opposite side was a tile mural of Omar Khayyam and the maiden, pouring wine.

"Hello," said a familiar voice.

I looked around, searching. The chatter of birds came from branches of lush trees planted in giant ceramic pots in the center of the room. A few trees soared to the high ceiling. A black bird flew out of one of those trees and circled the ornate mahogany desk on the far side of the room before landing on top of the chair behind the desk.

"Hello?" I said, my voice sounding small.

"Hello," the black bird answered.

I blinked a few times, and instead of the chair, another shape came into focus. The storyteller from the square was sitting at his desk with the bird perched comfortably on his shoulder. The old man was so still that he blended perfectly with the inanimate objects surrounding him. His beard gray and long, his cheeks rosy and glowing, and his wrinkles a map of roads less traveled, the morshed was smiling at me.

"Some people argue we have free will," he said, apropos of nothing at all.

"What?" I said, still disoriented.

"Free will—the freedom to choose. For example, you could choose to follow your friend, or you could choose to come in. Do you think you have this choice?" the old man asked as he clasped his hands.

"Of course I do!"

"Very well," he said. He picked up a feather quill, dipped it in jet-black ink, and began writing in his book. I waited, but he continued to write as if he had forgotten about me.

"I think I'll go find my friend," I said.

"Suit yourself," the old man murmured without looking up.

I couldn't remember the last time an adult had left it up to me to do anything. I edged back. "See, I have a choice. Right now, I could stay or go, or I could do something else—maybe something you don't expect!"

His keen gaze locked mine. "It appears that way, doesn't it?"

"What do you mean?" I asked.

"Please have some tea," he said.

The morshed glided over to a little table set with two estekan cups of tea, a small plate of nuts, and a bowl of sugar cubes. This surprised me nearly as much as the tall trees and the birds in this strange underground dwelling. How had he been able to procure sugar cubes when no sugar ration coupons had been issued in months? The last time we had something sweet at home was when my baba had found a batch of stale koloucheh on the black market.

The old man motioned to me to have a seat and presented me with an estekan and saucer. I examined his hands: twisted cypress branches, gnarled yet dignified.

"No, thank you," I said, remembering to mind my manners. "Wait. You already poured two cups?" I frowned as I took the estekan. "It's hot . . . Is this a trap?" I said in sudden fear.

"Dear, it's just tea!" he bellowed, laughing.

His response eased my suspicion, but why did I feel like I was in the middle of a test?

"No, wait. If I don't drink the tea, then I've proven you wrong, haven't I? You thought I would drink it!"

"You got me there! Well, then, I am forced to admit defeat," he said playfully.

I gave him a defiant look and walked over to the bookcase. Besides Ferdowsi, Hafez, Saadi, and the rest of the great Persian classics, there were books by contemporary poets and poetesses. An impressive section was devoted to world literature—Dante, Gibran, Tolstoy, Voltaire, and many more names I couldn't pronounce. I craned my neck and saw even more books whose titles I couldn't read without the help of a ladder. The wall of books relaxed me in an unexpected way. It was as if they provided an insulation from the grimness that was waiting for me in the world above.

I stole a glance at the old man, who was sipping tea like he had all the time in the world, before weaving through the plants and potted trees. They encircled a raised octagonal hoze[17] with a running fountain. In our own downstairs living room, we had a small hoze with goldfish, originally decorated with Persian rugs and plush cushions and cots for afternoon naps. It was now a bomb shelter.

I left the goldfish shimmying under the trickling fountain of the hoze and found my way to a backgammon set in one of the alcoves of the round wall. "Backgammon is illegal, you know," I said.

"Is that so?" he asked.

Black and white game pieces sat on the indigo and gold mandalas that decorated the surface of the magnificent khatam box.

"The white pieces were carved from one grand tusk of a giant elephant; the black ones from a rare Indian gemstone. The chess set on the next table is made by the same artisan," he said.

I picked up a black queen and explored the changing textures of her gemstone shape with my fingers. Her outstretched hand held a shield, and she stared at me with dark, knowing eyes.

"You could get into big trouble with the morality police if I told them." I eyed the old man.

"Well then, I am at your mercy." He bowed slightly.

Unsure of what to do next, I put the chess piece down and wandered to the morshed's wine rack.

"Each bottle is made from a different lot of delicate, hand-picked Shirazi grapes, nectar of the gods! Too bad you're so young, or I'd offer you some," said the old man.

I first smiled with self-importance at the thought of being offered wine, but then my eyes widened: "Do you know what the penalty is for alcohol? You could be flogged . . . even executed!"

---

17   pool

"'My beloved Mansoor for whom the head of the gallows rose, what was his crime? Revealing the Secret.'" His deklameh recitation filled the room.

"That's Hafez." I had heard my mother recite that verse.

"Very good!" His eyebrows arched.

I bit the inside of my cheek, concealing a smile. But as warm pride flushed my face, I thought of my mother, who, even though she would never admit it, was superstitious. What if this old morshed had access to the jinn folks? Of course, I would never have dared explore that topic with her, as I had a pretty good idea of how she would react. My stomach sank at the thought of my mother finding out where I was right then. But could this sweet old man have the jinn folks and pari fairies on his side? *Maman will never find out. I'm the best at keeping secrets*, I thought.

Taking deliberate steps, I sat across from the old man. He picked a pistachio from the nut tray and gave it to the bird on his shoulder. The bird took it in her bright yellow beak, which matched her feet and the skin surrounding her eyes.

She effortlessly shelled and gobbled down the treat.

"Merci," she said.

Laughing, I covered my mouth with my hand. "What's her name?"

The old man made a loose fist and extended his index finger. The bird flew down to his hand and perched there. "Her name is Myna. She comes all the way from the lush jungles of Hindustan," he said, patting the bird's head.

Once, my dad and I came across a man on the street who had a small monkey on his shoulders. The monkey appeared to be searching for something in the man's hair. My dad explained monkeys were experts at grooming and this one was looking for lice. He said in Hindustan there were all sorts of exotic animals, including monkeys and talking parrots and mynas. The myna looked at me with curious eyes. "I have a friend named Myna," I said. I then realized I didn't know the morshed's name either. "What's your name?" I asked.

"They call me Baba Morshed," he answered. "How about you, my daughter? What is your name?"

Nice going, Kimia. I hadn't expected I would reveal anything about myself. Who was this man, anyway? What if he was some sort of bache baz,[18] like my aunt Malek warned me about? What if he was connected to the jinn folks and my name gave him some sort of power over me?

"Um . . . They call me . . ." I looked around the room. There was a book of Molavi's *Masnavi* sitting on the corner of the old man's desk. "Rumi," I said, finally.

"As in Molavi?[19] Molana Jalaluddin Mohammad Balkhi Rumi?"

I nodded. My mouth was as parched as a dry well.

"Interesting name for a girl," Baba Morshed said thoughtfully and reached for his estekan. Myna flew back to his shoulder. He sipped his tea as if no one was in the room.

I was relieved Baba Morshed didn't ask any more questions. In fact, he looked so content just sitting there, silent. I stared at Rumi's book, unsure of what to say next. I picked up the estekan in front of me and took a sip absentmindedly, thinking about how Reza would react to all this. As I swallowed, I froze. *Ahmagh idiot!* I thought. *If rather than trying to impress him, I had just avoided the tea* . . . He'd bested me so handily, and I'd helped him.

Watching me, Baba Morshed laughed, his shoulders shaking, making the bird flap its wings to regain balance.

I couldn't help but smile too. I was about to press him about how he knew when I remembered all that was waiting for me at home. I looked at my watch and panicked once again. Standing up, I slammed the estekan down on the tea table. "I gotta go! Goodbye!" I said as I ran toward the door.

"Khoda negahdar."[20] I heard his amused voice bidding me goodbye.

---

18   pedophile
19   Rumi's other name
20   Take care.

7. ARMAN — SAN DIEGO, 2009

I LIGHT MY ONE-HITTER and inhale the smoke deep into my lungs. As I tossed and turned in bed last night, my mind kept wandering back to my conversation with Kimia. I'd called Maman as soon as I woke up this morning and apologized for missing lunch.

"Come over today," she'd said. "I'm making baghali polo."

I roll down the window now and blow the smoke into Maman's driveway. I still don't have a plan, but it's time to leave my stuffy car and go inside. All I know is that going to Iran is as batshit an idea for Maman as it is for me.

I knock and enter through the unlocked door. The smell of lamb stew and fava bean rice meets me at the door. I haven't had breakfast, and the weed is giving me cotton mouth. "Maman," I shout. Nothing. I find her in the kitchen, doing her dishes. She slowly runs the sponge over a plate, watching the soapy water wash away the lingering food and grease.

"What's this? Are you starting to be all mindful and meditative, like Kimia?" I joke.

"No," she says. "I just wish I could do the same to my mistakes . . . wash them away."

I help myself to a glass of water and wait. A few stacked boxes and a suitcase sit by the garage door. The house has an eerie feeling, being so empty. Maman dries her hands on a dish towel and goes to the worn leather-bound book on her kitchen table. She recites, "'I am madness and the silence that engulfs it. I am the target and the arrow that pierces it.'"

I ease myself onto the chair next to her, smelling the distinct must of old books even with the scent of lunch in the air. "Is that Rumi?" I ask.

"No, it's my new poem." Maman beams. She turns to a page, her eyes wandering over to a picture of the Simorgh. She traces its long peacock-like plumage to a crooked hand-drawn mustache on the Simorgh's foxlike face. She starts laughing. And doesn't stop— like she's high . . . or crazy. Surely, she's seen the mustache before. Still laughing, she wipes a tear with the pad of her thumb.

"Did you do this?" She heaves, pointing to the mustache.

"No, Khanom. That's Kimia's handiwork," I say. My foot taps the ground nervously. I want to eat and then deal with the whole Iran question, but this clearly isn't the right time.

"I knew it!" Maman claps her hands, sending a jolt through my spine. "The poor Simorgh has had this mustache for more than thirty years, but this is the first time it's made me laugh. This *Masnavi* was my great-grandfather's. Limited edition. I must have been so mad."

"It's a very nice book." I swirl the water in my glass. My stomach is grumbling.

"Let's have some tea," Maman says, uncharacteristically oblivious to my hunger. She closes the book and walks to her samovar on the kitchen counter. "This samovar, like the *Masnavi*, has survived regime changes, bombings, and trips across how many continents to end up here?" she asks without wanting an answer. "The day my grandfather brought it back from one of his trips to Russian Azerbaijan, I begged to hold it." Maman caresses one of the samovar's double-scroll handles.

"'It's not a toy, dear. Let's boil water in its belly and make tea!'"

my maman bozorg[21] said. But seeing my pout, my grandfather went to his suitcase and took out a matryoshka doll. Have I ever told you that?"

I shake my head no. Maman isn't the type of mother who waxes nostalgic about her childhood.

She opens a container of loose-leaf tea. She adds the tea leaves and a pinch of orange blossom to the teapot. "This samovar and I are both dented and bruised. But time leaves pockmarks on all of us."

I'm about to tell her she looks great, but she recites another poem:

"'The cauldron that stirred my childish notions has finished simmering. All you see inside is eternal love. I am ready now.' Now, that's Rumi."

Boiling water gurgles in the samovar's bronze belly. She turns the pierced spigot key. The water rushes into the teapot beneath it.

"Come, smell this." Maman holds the teapot under my nose. "Freshly brewed tea with orange blossom. I wish for this to be the last thing I smell before I die."

"May God never will it," I say. "You have many long, happy years ahead of you."

"My cousin Zaleh sent me this tea from Lahijan," Maman says, ignoring me. "Contraband-style, in a bunch of interwrapped plastic bags, like it was hashish. Aren't you hungry?"

My mother places lamb stew on top of rice on my plate. She looks so small and childlike, I can't help but see her as a five-year-old. I've come over to take her samovar away without offering her a Russian nesting doll.

"Bokhor aziz. Eat, darling," she says.

"Chashm." I dig into the tahdeeg, the special crusted rice, from the bottom of the pot.

She brings the bowl of Shirazi salad to the table and sits, holding her tea. She plucks a sugar cube from its bowl and tucks it inside the corner of her mouth. She takes long sips, staring inside her cup.

---

21 grandmother

I search the cannabis-encrusted recesses of my mind for a way to stop her move. I used to talk her off the ledge every time she was about to kill Kimia in Iran, but I'm pretty rusty now. I can't appeal to the danger of going to Iran. We both know Iranian American families who vacation there every summer and have a great time.

"It always begins with a tickle at the base of my spine," Maman says.

"What?" I ask, my mouth full of Shirazi salad.

"My episodes. It's like a butterfly flapping its wings inside my lower back. When it happened last, I was watching your sister ramble on. She was trying to sound logical and calm, helping me make the right choice. I ignored her and drank my tea, like I am now." She takes another sip. "What does she know about choices, anyway?"

My mother's eyes are on her cup, but she seems far away. "The ripples first appeared in my tea, then the estekan began to rattle in the saucer. I knew it was happening again. I'm always completely helpless. Each wave takes me back to the day the bombs fell. But this time, I knew I had made the right decision." She puts her tea on the table. "I want to taste the breath of Shiraz on my tongue. I want to see Amu Doctor one last time."

"Oh," I say. Maybe the solution has arrived after all. I had hoped I wouldn't have to face Amu Doctor ever again, but if I have to, I'd much rather see him here than travel to that godforsaken place. "Well, why don't I apply for a visa and buy Amu Doctor a ticket to come visit? That way you don't have to leave your pretty garden and this sweet house," I say, my voice echoing in the empty dining room.

She stares at me with incandescent eyes. Then her roar fills the house:

"'Those ripped away from their beloved know my wail. Having been cut from the source, they long to return.'"[22]

---

22   from Rumi's *Divan e Shams*

8. KIMIA — SHIRAZ, 1981

I WANTED TO TELL Reza everything about Baba Morshed's underground world. I wanted to tell him about the talking myna and the dragon fireplace and my baffling conversation with the old man. But this wasn't the right place for it.

The ration line was predictably long and full of patter about the shortage of essentials. Reza and I craned our necks to measure our distance to the entrance of the shop.

I recognized Reza's cousins, Hassan and Shahnaz. The brother and sister stood silently in the queue near the front of the line. While, like us, they endured the monotony of the ration line with rhythmic foot-shifting, I imagined that somewhere in Khuzestan, their father was on the front line trying to keep his exhausted and traumatized troops alive so they could fight another day. I pictured him somewhere near my baba, protecting his office building and hotel. It didn't matter that my father was neither in the army nor geographically close to Major Saeedi's troops. I was happy making as many logical leaps as needed to keep my baba safe from harm.

I signaled Reza with my head that we should go talk with Hassan and Shahnaz. He looked back to the end of the line, not wanting to lose our hard-won place. I wasn't thrilled about the prospect of waiting out my youth in line either, but I wanted to talk to them, and I wanted Reza with me. I gave him a look and he followed.

"Salaam, Shahnaz. Salaam, Hassan. How are things going?" I said with a big smile.

"Salaam. It's going all right, I guess," said the heavily veiled Shahnaz. "I can't wait till I'm done here. I have a ton of homework I need to get to."

I envied her ease in handling her chador. While I often struggled with my hijab and hated how it made my head itch, she was wearing it as if it were a second skin, comfortable and natural.

"Any news from your father?" I asked, and held my breath.

"He phoned last week." Hassan answered this time, his unpredictable pubescent voice squeaking. "He is doing all right. He didn't say anything else."

I didn't know what news I expected from them, but that wasn't it. I took a step toward the back of the line but stopped abruptly. Reza, who followed me without missing a beat, nearly crashed into me.

"I'll do your math homework for three days if you get these few things for me," I whispered to Shahnaz. "I have the coupons and the money right here." Cutting in line was taboo. I opened my palm, revealing the contents to Shahnaz. She gave me a guarded look.

"A week," she said.

"Okay, a week." I was very aware of the going rate. I handed them the coupons and money and looked at Reza and then the corn vendor down the street. He nodded slightly and walked away. I followed him.

WE WATCHED THE CORN vendor pull a hot corncob from the flames of a manghal grill, dip it in a bucket of salt water, plunge it in a container of melted butter, and then hand it to a customer. We stood behind several other people and suppressed our laughter about how we had moved from one line to the other. But I had a more important topic to discuss.

"Reza, you have to see his place!" I struggled to keep my voice to a whisper. "He's got a backgammon set and all kinds of books I've never seen before . . ."

"Shhh!" Reza's look was severe. No one was paying attention to us, and he wanted it kept that way.

I glanced around and leaned in closer. "And a huge fireplace in the shape of a dragon's mouth."

"What?" Reza frowned.

We shuffled forward in line. Reza reached into his pocket to retrieve his coins.

"It's not scary, I swear. He's, um, he's got some mysterious power. I mean he has trees and birds living there," I said.

"Is he a sorcerer?" Reza asked with wide eyes. His hand froze in his pocket.

"No, no," I said, pointing him to the impatient corn vendor. "He is just well-educated and interesting. I was able to challenge him right back. We had a debate, you know." I lowered my chin to hide my pride.

Reza paid, and the vendor handed him two hot ears of corn. We stepped into the shade to blow on the steam. I took my first tentative bites of the warm, sweet saltiness of charred corn topped with butter. Reza, too, became busy chomping on his corncob.

Torn between needing to convince Reza and savoring the taste, I juggled the kernels on my tongue. "Look, all we have to do is drop the groceries at home and go over there. Nothing bad's going to happen. Nobody's going to find out, I promise," I said. "Come on, tarsoo!"

A couple turned around, curious. We looked at the ground, and when the coast was clear, Reza smiled, and I knew I had convinced him.

"Oh, and call me Rumi when we're over there," I added.

REZA AND I MADE our way through the empty streets toward the square. The early-afternoon rain had painted Shiraz the indigo color of dusk, providing a perfect excuse for shopkeepers to close their doors for a long siesta. The smell of kerosene heaters beckoned us to take a break from the damp, cool streets, but I was anything but sleepy. A fleeting worry fluttered inside my chest that we would be interrupted—or worse, found out—but the square appeared deserted.

As we yanked open the trapdoor, Reza insisted I introduce him as Kaveh Ahangar,[23] the hero who took on the evil serpent emperor Zahhak in one of the *Shahnameh*'s epic tales. He and I had reenacted the battle scenes, taking turns killing Zahhak at the end. We climbed down the stairs, the scent of orange blossom unwinding the tightness within me.

As much as I had tried to assuage his worries, Reza still held on to some of his reservations. I was prone to exaggeration, and he had been taught not to interact with strangers. But when we arrived, the old man and his birds put Reza at ease immediately.

Now, he stood motionless in front of the fire. The flames inside the dragon's mouth danced a snake-like rhythm before him, and he seemed impressed and not at all worried. I sipped my tea, thinking I was so lucky to have Reza to share this treasure with.

My raincoat-style uniform and scarf sat on top of my book bag in the corner. With my short hair and Daffy Duck T-shirt, I didn't look that different from Reza. Months before, I had tried pretending to be a boy, so we could be together, as we were before the Revolution. My parents had gone along with this, and my mother had even cut my hair. But a couple of well-meaning, nosy neighbors recognized me and told my parents. After that, my mother became unyielding, demanding I only take off my hijab at

---

23   blacksmith

home or places I trusted. When I saw Baba Morshed's wine collection in my first visit, I was confident he wasn't some Hezbollahi who would take issue with my appearance. After all, he was more vulnerable to the authorities than I was.

I had so many questions. What was Baba Morshed's real name? Was I clever enough to ask him without getting into a mess like I had last time? How did he get the trees to grow underground?

"Baba Morshed, tell us more about the Simorgh!" I said.

"And why are you interested in the Simorgh? She is ancient and mostly forgotten. You modern children have busy lives. You have TV and the Walkman," Baba Morshed said, adding a log to the fire.

"Pretty much all good music is illegal, and the TV only has three channels—all boring news about the war," said Reza. He circled his fingers on the dragon's jade-green eye.

"Ah, so it is escape you seek," said Baba Morshed, his eyes drifting up to Myna, who was perched on the tallest branch.

"Yes, when you tell your stories, Baba Morshed, I forget all about the war," I said, following the morshed's gaze to the top of the branch. "Plus, school is just full of rules, and so many horrible things happen every day . . ." My voice trailed off as my arms folded in a self-hug, my fingers touching the fresh purple bruises.

I could sense Reza struggling to say something comforting when Baba Morshed walked briskly to his desk and opened a massive book. We turned and watched. Like a timeworn gate that hadn't been unlocked in nine hundred years, the book opened with a loud yawn. It was a strange, commanding sound, as if all of life's secrets were coiled inside it. Even the birds, who had been busy chirping, silenced to an occasional tweet. Myna flew to the storyteller's shoulder as he settled in his chair. The only noise in the room was the soothing crackling of the sprightly fire.

"You are not wrong to seek stories," said Baba Morshed as we made our way to the ancient desk. "As my most revered teacher said, 'Whoever doesn't love stories doesn't love God, as God is the best storyteller of all.'" Baba Morshed paused and ran his hand over his long beard. He looked at us with the eyes of a cunning child. "Do you want to know a secret?"

Reza and I nodded and leaned forward against the desk.

"A well-told story reveals more precious truths than a thousand lessons," he said, whispering. "But I must warn you," he continued, "the Simorgh will teach you that if you want to truly live, you won't seek escape from life. To truly live, you must enter the Seven Valleys of Love!" There was a shift in the old man's voice. It became deep and resonant, like that night in the square. He motioned to us and we joined him, each on either side of his chair. He leafed through the open book, revealing two luminous pages.

"Vay!" mouthed Reza.

Baba Morshed turned the book to face us. Hundreds of birds in shimmery colors spread through the pages. Some sat on the grass, and many more perched on the branches of luxuriant trees. Light and shadows danced on the leaves as if a breeze moved through the picture. The scalloped leaves flickered between lighter and darker shades of green. The birds themselves looked as vivid and full of life as their real counterparts. I could almost hear the torrent of the waterfall that tumbled below the birds. I looked at Reza in disbelief, but he was bug-eyed, glued to the book.

Baba Morshed's voice came from everywhere:

"All the birds of the great, wide world were gathered together. This had never happened before—imagine the scene! Peacock's tail, bright and iridescent, trails behind him like a finely designed Persian rug. Rosy Red Finch darts around, showing off his agility. Majestic Eagle, with her elegant wings utterly still, soars above all. Meanwhile, Nightingale sings and sings, and Owl hoots out of tune.

"The birds had traveled from all different corners of the world. There must have been over ninety-five thousand of them. The vast meadow was filled with different plumage colors and heavenly sounds. Why were they all there, you ask? Well, because Great Hoopoe, who many considered a brave leader, had sent them an invitation to join him on a journey to find the mysterious Simorgh."

Baba Morshed paused and took a sip of his tea. I could feel

the excitement of the birds in my own belly. Taking his time, Baba Morshed turned the page. "Then Great Hoopoe arrives. Seeing his tired eyes and his majestic golden crown, the birds fall silent. His powerful voice fills the arena: 'Friends. I admire your courage. This will be the most difficult challenge of your lives, and before you reach your destination, many of you will give up or perish.' Some birds flapped their wings nervously and a few squawked before they fell silent again. 'But those who succeed will reach the Simorgh and will be free of bondage forever,' he continued."

The old man looked right at us. "You see, Hoopoe knew the birds better than they knew themselves. He knew even though they could fly as freely as they chose, they were still afflicted with various degrees of suffering. Suffering kept them in bondage, and that was why they were there. They wanted to be truly free. But as it turned out, for many, the desire to be free of bondage was overcome by the fear of a difficult and dangerous journey. Bird after bird came up with excuses not to take part in this perilous venture.

"Nightingale was the first to plead his case: 'I am in love and I cannot part with my beloved. My beloved is the rose, and I bow to her. If she should disappear, I would lose all reason to live. If I leave her, my song will fail. Worshipping her is enough for me. Being with her is my world. You see, it is for me she flowers. Besides, nightingales are not robust or strong, and the path to find the Simorgh is too long and arduous.'

"Falcon thought it would be mad to leave his important position in the king's court. Owl loved searching the ancient ruins where she nested, and hoped one day she would find a treasure that would make her the richest being in the world. Parrot wanted to find his true friend. Duck didn't want to leave her precious water, and so on . . . But Great Hoopoe was ready. He dismantled each excuse with bull's-eye precision. What he offered was beyond all that each bird valued most. Something was missing in these birds' lives. Something that couldn't be replaced with a good career, a decent place to live, or even a passionate love affair. You couldn't befriend anyone to ask for it and you couldn't go to war to possess it. The Simorgh was their only chance to see what was missing. And those who listened knew he was right."

At that point, the old man paused and folded his hands in his lap. The sound of the bell from the mahogany-carved grandfather clock broke the silence and lingered in the air. I looked at Baba Morshed with eager expectation. *Just a bit longer*, I pleaded with my eyes.

"We better get going before you get into trouble," Reza said, gently touching my arm.

9. Kimia — SAN DIEGO, 2009

THE SHATTERED BRICKS, THE dust, the sirens: that was Iran. The voice: that is his. But my bed is here, in America, and I am awake again. In the blackest darkness, I can sense his hand extending from underneath the rubble. "Kimia! Kimia!" he calls.

The great heaving shoulder of the Pacific, hiding itself in chilly gloom, shoves into the shore below my perch. The bottle filled with sleeping pills sits on my nightstand next to a pouch filled with lavender. None of these things let me sleep, so I kick my blankets off and pull on my robe, staring out the window of my pretentious house, into the gray.

The sun will burn off the gloom, in time, and reveal blue water that looks so innocent and sparkling. Expensive SUVs will nose out of driveways and carry my clients to their morning yoga, Pilates, and coffee. So much, so much abundance and so little . . . flavor.

I make my way downstairs to the kitchen, my feet padding on the cool Saltillo tile, and start the kettle boiling. I wash off dirty limes I picked yesterday.

After we arrived in America, and I went to my first supermarket, I could not believe the divine-looking fruit piled in mountains of perfection. I grabbed apples bigger and more beautiful than the largest pomegranates in Iran. How could strawberries grow so humongous? I grabbed them, too, and oranges and out-of-season grapes that must have been pulled from a painting.

We paid the money to the smiling lady at the checkout and rolled the shopping cart into the parking lot, where I could contain myself no longer. I yanked a shiny red apple from a bag and sank my teeth into it, closing my eyes to better appreciate the explosion of flavor in my mouth. But all I tasted was crunchy water with a hint of something that resembled apple. I stood, chewing, in disbelief. Surely the strawberries must have some flavor! I fumbled with the plastic package, chose the ripest-looking berry in the pack, and took a bite . . .

I accept this about my new home, never sharing my petty gripe with another soul. This is the land of infinite choices. America has afforded me a suitable path. It has allowed me to leave red sirens, ration lines, and daily funerals behind.

I squeeze a lime in the hot water and stir in honey. I hold the cup, sitting at the kitchen island, my mind wandering. Is the flavor of Shiraz enticing enough for my mother to throw away her life here? Why am I so hard on Arman? I wonder if the river of my familial love flows only when my mother and brother do nothing to inconvenience me.

I bend my head to my cup. The lime water has turned lukewarm. For the first time I can recall, I'm not looking forward to meeting a new client. Erin said on the phone she needed spiritual counseling to help her cope with a contentious divorce.

I have grown my practice by word of mouth. Since I don't have a title or business cards, my clients call me their spiritual counselor, life coach, mindfulness instructor, or even healer. I cringe equally at each title but never correct them. I don't know what to call myself either. My methods include research-based practices and another ingredient I can't exactly define. My former colleagues and acquaintances balked at first, but in times of desperation, they end up seeking my help. When I prove to be helpful, they refer others to me. The macro-enabled spreadsheet on my laptop aggregates results of different categories—repeat clients, referral rates, the percentage of sold-out retreats, and single sessions followed with a thank-you note or a phone call. My success rate hovers around 85 percent, and dealing with divorces is my specialty, so I'm reasonably confident I can help Erin. But I'm as excited about my session with her as I would be about biting into another wax-covered supermarket apple.

I peel myself from the stool, wash my face with a warm washcloth, put on my long white skirt, and spray my home office with a calming essential-oil mixture. The doorbell rings, and I pause as I do before every session, setting my intention to help my client to the best of my ability.

I swing the door open, welcoming Erin with the warmest smile I can muster. Attractive and middle-aged, she hides behind expensive sunglasses but returns my smile. I lead her with slow steps to the white sofa, inhaling a lungful of air enlivened with notes of fir and bergamot. Erin's breath falls in line and she lets out a deep sigh. I take time, making myself comfortable in my seat while I study her. Erin removes her sunglasses, stuffs them in her purse, and follows my lead, settling into the sofa. Her red hair frames her tired face, and she appears resigned and furious at the same time, but her body has relaxed into her seat.

When she is ready, I ask, "What brings you here?"

"My husband and I are divorcing, and I can't seem to forgive that prick," Erin says, spitting the word *prick* like it's a bitter tablet. Blinking to adjust to the light, her pale blue eyes fix on the bay window behind me. I don't ask her to tell me more about her husband but follow her gaze, turning to the window. A hummingbird pecks at the feeder, its lustrous fuchsia throat sparkling in the sun. I watch him until he's had his fill. He flies away, beating his impossibly fast wings.

"So beautiful," I say, facing Erin.

"Yeah. When I was growing up in Ojai, we had a birdfeeder," she says, her voice calmer than a moment ago. "I loved watching my father fill the thing and waiting for different kinds of birds to come visit." She plays with the lotus part of her necklace.

"Let's take a moment and be with the love you felt watching the birds. Close your eyes and notice what comes forth," I say.

Erin closes her eyes, a faint smile relaxing her face. "I feel my neck loosening," she says and turns her head from side to side. Her hand goes to her solar plexus. "The love I felt watching my dad fill the birdfeeder is right here." I scan her body, paying close attention to the muscles around her closed eyes, her shoulders and her hips. Soon a different wave of emotion will wash over her, and I must be prepared. As expected, her smile disappears, a gradual shadow masking her features. She opens her eyes with a start. "But my dad left me," she says in a younger voice.

I can redirect Erin's attention to our surroundings or a sensation in her body, or let her finish this train of thought. I choose the latter and nod for her to continue.

"My mother physically abused me. But she was mentally ill, and I've forgiven her. My dad . . . instead of protecting me, he abandoned us. He didn't give a shit about me," Erin says. I watch her without interruption as, like all my clients, her face transforms to a younger version of herself. Through experience, I have learned this is the turning point. For some, it takes several sessions, but Erin is ready. She reaches for a tissue out of the Kleenex box, her eyes swimming in tears. "I'm sorry."

"No need to apologize. This is what you're here for," I say. "And I'm right here."

As Erin sobs, she becomes the little girl who has never stopped grieving her father.

"How do you know your dad didn't give a shit about you?" I ask when she has quieted.

"If he cared, he wouldn't have left." She searches my face to see if this is the correct answer, but doubt has already tinged the edges of her words.

"We spend so much of our time allowing thoughts to lead us, to pigeonhole us and our loved ones in unfortunate patterns. But we can choose which thoughts to follow and which thoughts to ignore. 'If he cared, he wouldn't have left.' Does this thought bring you freedom or constriction?" I ask.

Erin's doubts multiply as her hand goes to her necklace again. This used to be my favorite part of the session, witnessing the client become their own solution. But as the lawn mower buzzes in the distance and the indoor fountain bubbles, I can also hear echoes of dark thoughts clanking against the door of my mind.

"I don't feel free right now, so I'd say the thought is constricting," says Erin, and I'm grateful for her interruption. "But why would he leave me if he cared?"

"What if it caused him great pain to leave you? Is this at all possible?"

"I suppose it's possible."

"Good," I say encouragingly. "Is this thought constricting or expanding?"

"Expanding. Definitely."

"Good. Now, let's close our eyes and imagine how your life would be without the burden of these thoughts about your father. What would it feel like if you dropped them altogether?"

I stifle a yawn and set my meditation timer to twenty minutes. Erin closes her eyes. Instead of closing my own eyes, I focus on the digits of the timer, but after a minute my eyelids grow heavy. What if I dropped my thoughts of 1981 altogether? I try to maintain my gaze, but the luxurious warmth of fatigue wins and I close my eyes.

> *Sara and Dara*
> *Looking at a map*
> *Lightning thunder*
> *clap, clap, clap*
> *Two fell down*
> *One didn't rise*
> *Which one? Which one?*
> *Tell me no lies*

We had become blood brothers on a cool summer night, Reza and I.

On the balcony, the adults listened to the songs playing on Voice of America while they ate sweet Persian melon. My mother boisterously taunted Amu Doctor over a game of backgammon. Arman hovered around, as he was to play the victor. My dad, who was nowhere near as competitive as my mother, helped Azita Khanom solve a word puzzle in the paper. While everyone was engaged, Reza and I seized the opportunity. We tiptoed our way to the kitchen, turned off the lights, and lit candles.

Earlier, while we sat on the swing set, balancing our dinner plates on our thighs, I had explained the ritual to Reza. "And then we're going to cut the palms of our hands and mix the blood together," I said through a mouth full of rice and khoreshte karafs.

Reza held his spoon suspended in midair as he contemplated this. "We're going to cut ourselves? I don't know about that. It's going to hurt. A lot. And what am I going to tell my parents about my bloody hand?"

"Don't worry, khareh khoda, you donkey brain! We're just gonna prick our palms. And I've got Band-Aids hidden in the kitchen already."

Ever since I'd read my first Mark Twain book the previous year, I had fancied myself a Persian Tom Sawyer. Once, I spent a whole afternoon sweeping our entire yard with the front gate wide open. Every time a kid walked by, I shouted, "This is so much fun! This is better than any game I've ever played!" But unlike Tom Sawyer, no one gave me more than a glance, much less volunteered to help.

Eventually, "It's time for dinner, Kimia koochooloo. What are you doing out there anyway?" my mother had yelled. She didn't wait for a response. "Put the broom away and wash up."

I didn't try that trick again, but when I read the second chapter of *The Adventures of Huckleberry Finn*, my brain went to work immediately. The next day, I revised Tom Sawyer's blood oath to my own liking. I didn't have Tom Sawyer's gang of robbers, but I had Reza. We had to officially become blood brothers.

That night, under the flickering of the candlelight, I stabbed my palm with the kitchen knife. Even though I had expected it, the pain radiating from my open gash sent a flash of surprise to my eyes.

"See! It didn't hurt at all," I lied, forcing my voice to be as steady as the open palm I held to Reza. "We will never betray each other. We will always have each other's back. We'll tell each other everything. Promise?" I whispered, still holding the knife.

Reza, staring at my bloody hand, offered me his own. I grabbed it and pressed the blade on his palm, drawing blood.

"Akh!" yelped Reza.

I smashed my palm against Reza's and pressed my lips to his for a fraction of a second. The kiss was not a planned part of the ritual. I fell back into my chair. I had kissed Reza to shut him up, but now for a rare moment, I was the one who was tongue-tied. We looked at our palms, our blood mingled and our thoughts mangled.

"I promise," said Reza, his face flushed.

"It's a real beautiful oath," I whispered, stealing the line from the Huck Finn book. I then took the Band-Aid and carefully placed it on Reza's palm. He returned the favor.

Sara and Dara

Looking at a map—

The gong of the meditation timer snaps my eyes open. Erin sits, straight-backed, her demeanor suggesting she is ready to speak.

I pull myself together, a smile wobbling to my lips. "Do you have any insights to share?" I ask in a serene voice.

"I thought about my dad and how close I felt to him when he was around. Yes, he left me, but just now I could feel the sense of security of those times so palpably," Erin says with a disbelieving look on her face. "The more I tapped into the feeling of security, the less I was bothered by other thoughts. I thought about Brett and how he drives me crazy and I realized I'm punishing myself by holding onto spiteful thoughts about him. I would feel a lot freer if I just let go of these negative thoughts."

"Why don't you take a moment and be with this sense of freedom."

"Okay," Erin says and closes her eyes. After a minute, she whispers, "It's that easy, isn't it?" She opens her eyes, touching her arm and her face as if to orient herself in the room.

I nod, biting my lower lip. "What has your attention now?"

"The fresh smell in the air. The Buddha statue between the potted plants. My own breathing."

"How are you now?"

"I feel wonderful," she says, her eyes wide and clear.

I summon the authority of the respected expert, who only a week ago had sworn by the soundness of her own techniques. "Dwelling in the past brings suffering. Worrying about the future brings suffering. Freedom is right here." I deliver the trifecta mantra as I do with every client. "But be sure to have compassion with yourself. Your old thoughts will most likely return, especially when you're ill or in any way stressed. What you just experienced will always be with you, and with enough meditation and practice, you can conjure it at will."

When I reach to take Erin's check, I pull my sleeve down, even though my tasteful cuff bracelets are dutifully hiding my scars.

I HOLD MY BLACK box on my lap, sitting at my vanity. The reflection in the mirror is mine, except for my eyes. They are the eyes of the trapped animal staring back at me through the taped-over mirror of our old house in Shiraz.

I had hoped it wouldn't come to this, but all other options have been exhausted. *Violence is the last refuge of the incompetent.*[24] I'm sure Asimov wasn't considering this scenario, but nevertheless, he was right. I open the box and hold the knife in both hands.

When I took the knife to the sharpener a few days ago, the man said it was really a dagger. Perhaps. Its silver-plated copper

---

24   a quote by Isaac Asimov

blade was designed during the Qajar dynasty, and engraved Persian texts embellish its golden handle and scabbard. I bought the dagger one sleepless night, finding it on eBay under the title *Aladdin Arabic Persian Dagger with Sheath*. The sharpener said, "An antique beauty like this should be decorational only. Why do you need it sharpened, anyway?"

I can no longer bear to look at myself in the mirror. Unlike what I sold Erin, my life is no longer a series of separate moments but a loud, chaotic parade of stubborn stories, each eluding deconstruction. Darkness has sprung leaks in the fortified wall of my serenity, and inside my upright and confident torso beats the heart of an impostor.

I slip the knife out of its golden sheath and press the blade over the first of my three thin wrist scars. The sting sends a warning to my senses, making my heart beat faster. At the sight of the red droplet forming on my wrist, my mind pops into focus.

I lean over the sink. In the emptiness of my mind, like the night-blooming jasmine, old secrets come to life. From the safeguard of their black prison, they tease me, they beckon me with their dance of seven veils, but I am their prison guard and they are my faceless prisoners. For now, the past is back where it belongs.

I examine my wrist. Over the years I have developed the Goldilocks precision of a surgeon—not so deep as to cause a mess and not so shallow as to be inadequate. Inhaling my first full breath of the day, I take the first aid kit out of the box and remove the bandages, scissors, and sterile alcohol pads. With one hand, I bandage my wrist. I clean the beads of blood from the vanity with a wet wipe. Pink water swirls down the drain as I wash the knife. I pat the knife dry and place it back in the box, my distorted reflection on the blade staring back at me.

I perch for the next hour on my bedroom balcony, listening to the empty echoing quiet in my mind. Down below, the marine layer lifts away slowly, rolling from the blue-gray sea toward the horizon. I am no longer cold. A new thought, like a tumbleweed, blows into the vast desert of my consciousness—I'm going to Iran.

PART II

Attar explored the Seven Valleys of Love
We are still getting around one corner
— Anonymous (attributed to Rumi)

10. Kimia — THE VALLEY OF QUEST

I KEPT WATCH FROM the rooftop balcony with my father's small binoculars. A balmy spring morning brought with it the buzzing of bees and the fluttering of monarchs zigzagging among them. A few clouds cast shade on the verdant garden below; the willow tree's lackadaisical branches swayed above violet pansies and yellow roses. To my right stretched Poshteh Moleh Mountain. Ages ago, on Fridays before sunrise, Arman and I had each held one of our father's large hands, crossed a creek, and climbed Poshteh Moleh to watch the sun make its glorious appearance over Shiraz. We sat on top as the golden light bathed our town, pointing out different buildings and landmarks to one another. We used the small binoculars to find our own house. Even though we had repeated this ritual dozens of times, more often than not, we found a new building, or a tree we hadn't spotted before.

Across from where I now kept watch lay Sleeping Man Mountain, its belly adorned with a blanket of the late spring snow, glistening against the blue sky. My father had told me the sad legend of unrequited love that took place on that mountain range. Like my father, I couldn't recall most of the details. The legend was of the simple shepherd who had fallen head over heels for a rich man's daughter. When he was denied her hand, the shepherd went to the mountain, let his sheep roam free and went to sleep. He never woke up. The mountain, the only true witness of his plight, took pity on him and, in his honor, stretched itself out to look like the sleeping shepherd.

I dropped the binoculars. Hanging by their straps, they dangled lightly, tapping my chest. The last time my family had been together on this balcony was the previous autumn. My father had just bought a case of fresh pomegranates. Sitting on a picnic blanket, we ate and laughed, our faces and hands gleaming with ruby juice.

A few weeks later, he was called on a secret project near the Iraqi border. What we'd thought would be a short assignment had stretched into five months.

I missed his hands most of all. I used to grab a pinky of those magnificent hands in my own as we walked in the garden. He would tell me the story of "the bespectacled snake teacher" who managed a classroom of jungle animals. The mouse and the elephant were best friends, and the tiger, the class clown, would get herself into a different trouble each time. When the story was over, I would tug on his pant leg and squeal, "Again!" He repeated a different version of that story a hundred times for me. He had put his hand on my forehead and prayed when I was sick with the flu. His touch and the mumbling of the Arabic words were more healing than any prescription written by Amu Doctor.

I wiped my tears with my sleeve and brought the binoculars back to my eyes. A young man strolled the street below, laughing to himself. A woman shielded her child as they passed him. Only a madman could laugh out loud in these times.

Reza's small body, carrying his heavy book bag, his headphones on, appeared behind them. I focused on his face with my binoculars. The bubble gum Reza was blowing had grown to the size of a small balloon. When he reached my door, the bubble gum burst, giving him first a look of shock and then a quiet laughter as he gathered the sticky goo from his face with his fingers. My own face broke into a grin. I grabbed my book bag and ran down to the door.

Matching our steps, we walked the empty Enayat Abad Street, like we had every day as far back as we could remember. Even blindfolded, we knew the place of every tree, every building, and every crack on the sidewalk.

We loved making up games and new traditions on our koocheh.[25] When the Revolutionary Guards started painting Imam Khomeini quotations on people's walls, we made a game of reading these supposed nuggets of wisdom. We stood in front of the quotation as if we were in a gallery, examining a fascinating piece of modern art. We played with the words of the quote or inserted nonsensical additions. The game presented unexpected challenges: Sometimes in the middle of the night, antirevolutionaries painted obscenities over those quotations. This was a dangerous game. If caught, the offenders could be imprisoned, publicly lashed, or worse. Regardless, the next day, the dutiful Revolutionary Guards painted over the defaced canvas. This cat-and-mouse game was better than most programs on TV. I sometimes took out my Magic Marker, but Reza wrestled it away before I could reach the wall.

"Nakon,[26] divooneh! Do you want to get killed like Nushin?" he asked.

"She didn't get arrested for this," I said, even though I didn't know her charges.

Nushin was barely a teenager when she was executed. Sometime later, my dad ran into the slain girl's father and asked about the charges. The man shook his head. "They never told us."

Once, I threatened Reza that either I would write an obscenity about the regime or he would have to deface the wall. He relented

---

25   street
26   Don't do it.

and yanked the Magic Marker out of my hand. He wrote in tiny letters, *K+R=BB*. Kimia and Reza are blood brothers.

That day, we barely noticed the new quotation painted on Zamani's wall:

> *In the world there is no democracy better than our*
> *democracy. Such a thing has never before been seen.*
> —*Ayatollah Khomeini*

Ah, such an easy statement to mangle—any other time, we would have had a field day with this, replacing *democracy* with *bullshit* or *insanity* and so on.

"Do you have water?"

"No, do you have electricity?"

"No."

Some rituals, however, were nonnegotiable.

"Hey, what were you just listening to?" I pointed to the Walkman headphones around his neck.

"Bruce Spingstin. My uncle sent it from America. It's no Duran Duran, but it's new."

"You mean Sprinstine?"

"No, Spingstin," he corrected. And then he sang, terribly, "I got a rush on you."

"Knock it off! I bet you're singing it wrong. Anyway, you better watch out. Gashteh Baghiatallah[27] are cracking down on Walkmans now," I warned him.

"I know. I have a tape of Koran verses that I've started keeping in here, just in case." He pointed at his beat-up backpack.

"And what are you going to do with this Spanksteen tape when they catch you, Reza Khan?" I quizzed him.

"I'll take out the illegal tape and stick it in your pocket, Kimia Khanom." He nudged my rib.

"Stop it!" I pinched him on the arm.

The street was starting to get busy. Without a word, we parted ways.

---

27   the morality police of Shiraz

THE HOZE FOUNTAIN SPLASHED around the birds as Reza and I entered the old man's den. The finches, now used to the presence of their small human guests, bobbed up and down under the waterfall. Unselfconscious, they fluttered their wings to repel the water, seeming uninterested in the story that was to unfold. Reza and I huddled silently over the great book. Neither the alluring fire burning inside the dragon's mouth nor the oval silver tray filled with pastries could pull our attention away. We took turns staring first at the book and then at the storyteller. But neither of us had any intention of appearing rude, or worse, childishly impatient.

Baba Morshed puffed on a hookah pipe. I loved that familiar sound of bubbling water. My grandmother had an old hookah she brought to our house when she visited. Hers, like many ornate hookahs, showcased the picture of Nasiruddin Shah on its vase. The vase on Baba Morshed's hookah, however, was made of transparent turquoise glass. When he puffed on the hose, I could watch the water bubbling, and the tobacco and charcoal burning red in the bowl at the same time. He turned to the ficus tree, exhaling a long slow breath, blowing the smoke toward it. "She likes the smoke," Baba Morshed said as his eyes followed the hazy spirals reaching the tree's green leaves. The finches, finished with their bath, flew back into the branches. At last, the old man took the hookah off his massive desk and placed it on the floor. He opened the book, and his voice filled the room:

"'The first valley is the Valley of Quest,' said Hoopoe gravely. 'In the Valley of Quest, you must pass a hundred tests, knowing that with each breath a new difficulty arises,'" the old man read aloud. We watched the illustrations of the hoopoe bird, his crown shimmering against the page, amid the thousands of birds, each with a different expression, looking up at him.

"'The birds shivered with terror at the thought of what lay

before them. The wrens flapped their wings in panic, and the parakeets squawked with fear. Many birds took off without a word; the
sheer number of them made the sky dark as they flew home. Those
who stayed also wanted to flee, but they knew they couldn't return
to their old lives even if they wanted to. They had no choice but to
continue the journey.'"

Why didn't the birds have a choice? I thought. But I held the question. Baba Morshed turned the page and continued.

"'You will spend years in this valley, and you will struggle.
But that is not all,' said Hoopoe, looking directly at Nightingale.
'You must let go of all that you hold precious.' Nightingale's heart
was crushed knowing he had to leave his beloved rose behind. But
standing in front of Hoopoe, he knew the rose deserved a lover
who wasn't riddled with fear and anxiety. So Nightingale took
the most important step of his life as a true seeker: He aligned his
mind with his heart and chose to go through the Valley of Quest."

I released myself from Nightingale's eyes. So much was
contained in those eyes, I couldn't bear to look again. If I hadn't
been so engrossed in the story, I might have wondered how such
thick papyrus-like paper could be nearly transparent. How could
the delicate paintings of the bird feathers have the iridescence of
an orchid in sunlight? How could Nightingale's face be so full
of sorrow? I stole a glance at Reza, who wrapped his headphone
wire around his finger. He loosened the wire from his finger and
rewrapped once again.

"Hoopoe went on, 'Having nothing in your possession, you
still will have to detach yourself from all that exists. Then you
will no longer fear the dragons, the guardians of the valley, which
seek to devour you. Your courage will transform the dragons into
your guides.'"

Baba Morshed gave a faint lopsided smile and leaned back in
his chair. Reza took a rosewater noghl[28] candy from the silver bowl
and chewed it slowly. All I could do was raise my hand high as if

---

28   sugar-coated almond slivers

I were in a classroom having a bathroom emergency. The old man nodded slightly, giving me permission to speak.

"Give up everything? I can't even get Reza to give me his Walkman for a day!" I said, grateful I could get that off my chest.

"Hey, first of all, it's a Sony TPS-L2, the latest version. Secondly, me giving up my Walkman has nothing to do with the story," Reza said, his grip tightening around his Walkman. "You know, Imam Jomeh kind of says the same thing as the hoopoe."

Well played, Reza, changing the subject, I thought.

"He says any sacrifice made in the name of Allah will be rewarded greatly. He talks about how becoming a martyr while killing the infidels can earn you the highest status in paradise." Reza sat upright with a satisfied smile.

"Do they indeed say the same thing?" asked Baba Morshed before I could protest.

"No! Hoopoe doesn't ask them to kill," I jumped in.

"Ha! You're not paying attention," Reza said in the tone he used when he wanted to assert that he was older and obviously wiser. "Both leaders are talking about sacrifice for something more important."

"Vay! Sacrifice? Says the person who won't even give up their Walkman," I said, turning to him, ready for battle. Suddenly I felt the storyteller's eyes on me and stopped. Embarrassed that we couldn't keep it together, even for a few minutes, without bickering, I slowly turned back to face Baba Morshed.

"Story is the shell protecting the hidden pearl of truth. The shell becomes nicked and damaged as the ocean water, creatures, and time have their way with it, but the pearl remains the untouched gem."

I thought about this. My baba once told me we have so many wars because people confuse truth with myth. "But how do you know which is the pearl and which is the shell?"

"It all depends on who is listening to the story, doesn't it? The pearl might appear as a shell to you," Baba Morshed said, gesturing toward me. "And the shell might look like the pearl to you," he said to Reza. "Until you can see with the eyes of the Simorgh. Then certainty will lose its hold, and at the same time, all questions will fall away."

I didn't understand what the old man was saying, yet I was riveted. His words were like a song in the language of sirens, incomprehensible yet irresistible. Moments before, I had wanted to know which one of us was right. I had been ready to debate my point. But now, I couldn't think of anything to say.

"Perhaps the more relevant question is, who are you?" He slapped the desk with his hand. Both Reza and I jumped.

Baba Morshed laughed and continued. "You're never too young for this question, although most people don't begin self-inquiry until the autumn or winter of their lives. What makes you, Rumi, and what makes you, Kaveh?" he said, gesturing to me and then to Reza.

Out of habit, I opened my mouth to answer, but the words and the thoughts behind them kept falling away.

"You don't have to answer now, Rumi Jon. Be patient. Let the question simmer inside," he said.

We sat quiet for a while. Then Baba Morshed looked up at the grandfather clock a moment before it signaled the end of our time together.

Reza, pensive, began to gather his belongings while I sat, hunched over and frowning, my mind hard at work. I still wasn't used to the odd feeling of leaving with more questions than I had arrived with. But what competed for my attention was the new sensation that had stirred inside my belly. Like all children of war, I was well-versed in anxiety; I knew by heart all its subtle tweaks and jabs. But this was brand new.

11. ARMAN — SHIRAZ, 1981

WE WEREN'T GIVEN WEAPONS, so we seemed more like newborn giraffes, clunky and uncoordinated and not the tough soldiers we tried so hard to emulate. Saddam and his buddies would have had a good laugh at the sight of us jogging and shouting slogans. But I wore fatigues and a black headband like a real soldier, and that made me feel more in control of my life.

Ever since my father had left for his assignment, Maman and Kimia had become two different people. It started so gradually that none of us noticed at first. But the more demanding Maman became, the more Kimia responded with defiance. Her behavior made Maman livid. It wasn't easy for me to be the only disciplined, pious person in that madhouse while they acted like two reckless jinns bent on destroying each other. I blamed Kimia for being the source of the lunacy that made my home life unbearable. But then I would remember her face every time Maman struck her with the belt. That image always drained me of anger.

The commander, pleased with his new crop, sent us out on our first assignment. Morteza led us in setting up the barricaded checkpoints leading to Charah Moshir Street. People hurried to work, and minibuses, taxis, and motorbikes circled the round-about. We took our time, thankful we had been given a task within our grasp. Morteza methodically inspected our work. Of course, the inspection was completely unnecessary, but so was the task itself. He ordered us to stand guard. We quickly created forma-tions we had been taught and watched with eagerness as Morteza held his hand up to an approaching car. We suppressed our smiles when the car actually came to a stop.

This is for real, I thought.

Morteza walked to the driver and bent to window level. "Hello, brother. Driver's license and birth certificate, please," he said with a stern, deep voice.

The middle-aged man, who had lost the color in his cheeks, fumbled for his papers. Other boys, injected with a jolt of power, took Morteza's lead and began checking other approaching vehi-cles. Never mind that this exercise was a mild form of harassment at best. Unlike the official morality police, Gashteh Baghiatallah, we were just a bunch of rattled teens led by a volunteer-commander who had as much authority as a football coach. We had no cars. We had no weapons. We had no way of arresting people. Even if we did, how would looking at people's papers provide us with grounds to arrest them?

I quietly dismissed these concerns. Instead, as my comrades took command of the street, I found myself thinking about Marvel comics and Imam Hossain. If I was honest, I didn't want to be there at all. Deep down, I longed for glory, for a chance to be a hero, not another pissant waiting for further instructions. I mean, living a life with supernatural powers, fighting crime and corruption was so appealing, and at the same time martyrdom seemed so . . . so glamorous . . .

It wasn't until Morteza gave me a quick glance between searches that I was sent into full panic mode. I looked around for something to do. My eyes darted to find an available target. All the cars were taken by my squad mates. In desperation, I homed in on an old lady hobbling along with a bag of groceries.

"Driver's license and birth certificate, please," I said, my voice cracking.

"What?" said the old lady, squinting at me.

"Driver's license and birth certificate, please," I said. Taken aback by my own voice, I noticed others were looking in my direction.

"I don't drive—never have!" said the agitated old lady. She resumed walking.

Even though I knew I would regret my next move, I stepped in front of her. I had no choice. I had to prove myself as the authority in front of my squad mates, especially Morteza.

"I'm sorry, but I need to see some identification, please." I began the sentence whispering, but my voice got louder toward the end.

"I can't even read or write. I never carry papers with me." She waved me off as she began walking a bit faster this time.

There was no going back now. I felt Morteza's cool gaze watching me, weighing me, wondering if I was worthy to be his equal. I caught up and stood in front of the woman, blocking her way.

"Ah, ah," she barked. "Why are you attacking an old lady? Let me go!" She swung her grocery bag and hit me repeatedly with it.

What would Spider-Man or Imam Hossain do? I bet this wouldn't happen if I had a beard, I thought as I hunched over, protecting my face. When I was composed enough to stand, the old lady was far away. I turned to see the entire squad, along with the drivers they had stopped, staring at me.

12. Morteza — SHIRAZ, 2009

I PERCH MY GLASSES on top of my head and walk to the window. Watching the boys as they perform their drills in the parking lot fills me with a fatherly pride. Some of my brightest memories were shaped in that very parking lot when I was a teen volunteer myself. My own two boys will join their ranks in a few years, Inshallah. I close the window latch and the boys' chants become muffled.

I drain the last of my lukewarm tea and return to the ledger on my desk. Without my glasses, the numbers appear rounded and blurry, but there is nothing soft about these numbers. They represent expenses for the Basiji supplies and accommodation. These volunteers of the Revolutionary Guard Corps have been doing God's work for years, ridding the Islamic Republic of unsavory and corrupt elements. I take care of my Basiji brothers so they can take care of the people.

I press the intercom button. "Mr. Dashti, could you bring me another glass of tea?"

There is nothing unusual about this request. My assistant is a good, pious man, but he makes weak tea, and I'm forced to keep drinking it all day. I never criticize Mr. Dashti's tea-making. He is many years my senior. Besides, his son became a shahid, a martyr, in the war. His eyes are always so full of sadness, I can't bear to add to his sorrow. But when expecting guests, I make the tea myself.

"Befarma,[29] sir," whispers Mr. Dashti. He has quietly entered the room and gently places the estekan in front of me.

"Thanks," I say, but Mr. Dashti has left as quickly as he entered, taking the full ashtray with him.

I unlock my desk drawer and take out the chess piece. The black queen resembles the carvings of Persepolis. I drink my tea and, as every evening, I roll the piece between my fingers, feeling the bumpy curves. On good days, the black queen reminds me of my accomplishments—major ones like rising to the rank of commander at such a young age, shaping young minds at the head-quarters and at home, and small ones, like finishing my reports on time. Other days, the chess piece makes me remember what I have lost, and that which I'm still looking for. One day yes. One day no.

A large shadow glides over my desk, darkening the ledger. I gaze up just as a light knock raps on my door. The queen tumbles out of my hand.

"One minute," I say, my heart racing. I grab the queen off the floor and throw it in the drawer. I close the ledger and place it on top of the queen, and turn the key in the lock. "Baleh?[30] Come in."

Taghi pokes his head in, his hair disheveled. "Salaam," the boy squeaks. Apprehension wrinkles his brow, and post-workout sweat dots his forehead.

I forgot that I had asked him to stop by after the drills. I slide the key in my uniform pocket and wave the boy in. "Salaam. Come in, son."

The boy shuffles forward, his plaid shirt a size too small, its sleeves failing to cover his skinny brown wrists. He stands hunched, panting.

"Brother Nasri tells me that your math grades are falling. Is that right?"

---

29   Welcome
30   Yes?

"Baleh, agha,"[31] says Taghi through chapped lips.

"Why is that?" I demand.

"I'm just no good at math, agha."

"Is this what you've been telling yourself?" I stand, walk around my desk, and pause in front of the boy. Taghi smells of sweat, teenage hormones, and angst. "Do you think I had everything handed to me without trying?"

The boy shakes his head.

"My father, may God have mercy upon his soul, was a cement factory worker, and we both thought I would follow in his footsteps. But God's grace has been with me. I finished high school and overcame more adversity than I can count in a ledger." I slowly pull up my uniform sleeve to expose my forearm. The damaged skin, gnarled like a half-coiled snake, makes Taghi suck in his teeth.

"Akh," he says, wincing.

I try to focus on Taghi's satisfying reaction and not the beast's eyes, the unbearable heat, fire leaping toward me, and the pain—searing, breathtaking pain. I set my jaw, ridding my mind of traces of the pain, the commander's tiny glaring eyes, and the phantom howls of curdled loyalty. "There were times when I thought I'd lost everything," I continue. "My friends, my commander, my place in the world . . ."

"I wish I could've fought alongside you in the war," Taghi says with a determined expression.

I am not talking about the Iran-Iraq War as Taghi assumes, but I don't correct the boy. "Pesar Jon, I didn't give up," I say, my voice taking on the cadence of the motivational speech I have delivered a hundred times. "I didn't say things like, 'I'm just no good at this.' I persevered. From you, action; from God, benediction. You see?"

"Baleh, agha," the boy shouts, his shoulders pulled back.

"Now go home and work on your math homework. I'll have Donyaee tutor you a few times a week."

"Thank you, agha! May God give you a long life," says the

31   Yes, sir

resolute young man. Zeal shines in his eyes with a pulsing, glimmering brilliance. It was zeal that propelled a preteen suicide bomber under the enemy tank. And it is zeal that has sustained our mighty republic for three decades.

The boy leaves, and I spray a pump of deodorizer into the air, the cool orange scent masking the residue of cigarette smoke. I take a pinch of dry rice from a small bowl in the corner of my neatly organized desk and toss it into the birdcage by the window. "See?" I grin at the bird. "That's how you lead, Lalu."

The bird turns away in her cage. I laugh but glance toward the ceiling. An uneasiness slithers within me. "I have to go. Sakineh is making aab ghoosht for dinner," I tell Lalu, my voice sinking in my chest.

I bid Mr. Dashti goodbye and lock the office door. As I make my way outside, across the uneven sidewalk to the noonvai,[32] I recite a protective prayer under my breath. I haven't had a hallucination in years. I have been poring over documents for hours and this perhaps is taking a toll on my eyesight.

Along the way, every shopkeeper letting in the cool evening air greets me. I buy a pack of bubble gum from a street peddler who has set up his merchandise under the bright green leaves of a walnut tree. My boys had oral exams today, and if they report they performed well, each will get a piece.

In the breadline, people step aside, giving up their place. I refuse, of course. "I insist!" says a fat man with an impressive mustache. Before I can respond, he says, "I won't take no for an answer."

When I first took my position as the commander of the Shiraz Basiji troops, this deference surprised me. But now it has become as routine as the sun rising over Poshteh Moleh every morning. I stand at the front of the line, feeling more like myself, counting the bricks around the arched opening of the sangak[33]oven. As a child, I loved peering into the orange fire lighting the inside of the arch. The naan, also in the shape of a cutout arch, lies on top

---

32   bakery
33   a type of bread made on hot pebbles

of a sea of glowing pebbles, exuding a scent that would make me hungry even if I had just eaten. But for years, I haven't looked inside the oven.

"Salaam Jenab, your excellency! Your usual, sir?" says the baker. I'm about to answer when at the edge of my vision, I see *him*. I gasp. *It can't be*. "Sir?" asks the baker. But I wave him off and push through the breadline. I break into a jog through the crowded sidewalks, never taking my eyes from my target.

People try to get out of my way, but now I'm running full tilt, clipping shoulders and knocking groceries to the ground. I can't let the man duck into an alley and disappear. I gain on the figure, a long-overdue satisfaction beginning to fill my body. I catch him as he is about to cross a busy intersection. From behind, I put my hand on the man's shoulder.

"I've found you!" I say, out of breath. An old man twists around. It's not him.

The old man trembles like the leaves of a willow tree. "Bebakhshid, agha!"[34] he says. "Have I done something wrong?"

"Jenab! Jenab!" I hear Agha Davood yell behind me. He is holding the bread in his outstretched arms like a sacrificial offering. "Your bread, sir," the baker says. He, too, is breathing hard.

Annoyed, I dig into my pocket to fish out change. "Thank you, Agha Davood."

"Sir. Am I free to go?" asks the old man.

"You can go," I say without looking at him and hand the money to the baker. The old man runs across the street. A car honks and its driver yells an obscenity. He is about to follow that with something worse when he catches my glare. The driver closes his mouth and pulls away.

"It's not worthy of you!" The baker hands me the bread and refuses his money.

At home, I eat my aab goosht in silence and go to bed early, only to stare at the ceiling.

---

34   I'm sorry, sir!

I leave for work before dawn, the packet of bubble gum still untouched in my pocket. I forgot to ask my boys about their exams last night.

I am grateful when Mr. Dashti arrives in the office, but then I remember what day it is. Every year on June 7, Mr. Dashti comes to the office, dressed in black from head to toe. Every year on June 6, I ask him to take the next day off, but Mr. Dashti never accepts the offer. He says working helps keep his mind off Mehdi. But every conversation eventually turns to Mr. Dashti's martyred son anyway.

"Today would be his thirty-seventh birthday," Mr. Dashti says with a sigh. He places a new potted peace lily on my desk.

"Mehdi's place is in behesht,"[35] I say, conjuring the enthusiasm of a true revolutionary who thirsts for martyrdom, but Mr. Dashti still looks forlorn.

"I know . . . I know," he says. "They didn't find a key on him, but I can't think of any other place than behesht for him. Mehdi was a sweet boy." He gazes out the window onto the parking lot where kids are lining up to march.

There was a rumor during the war that young soldiers were issued golden plastic "paradise keys," each one symbolizing guaranteed entry into heaven. But I wasn't given a key and hadn't seen one myself. I was older of course, nineteen, when I enlisted. Mehdi had been fourteen at the time of his martyrdom.

"How are your granddaughters?" I change the subject to a more pleasant topic for Mr. Dashti.

"They're growing like cedar trees." Mr. Dashti says, his face brightening. "Sharareh, my eldest, has placed high on the konkoor entrance exam. The light of my eyes . . . she is going for medicine . . . Mashallah,[36] she is in the top three hundred."

"Great. Great," I say, relieved we have moved on.

He lifts the peace lily and dusts underneath as he continues talking about his family. I enjoy watching Mr. Dashti's thoroughness,

---

35   heaven
36   What God has willed.

appreciating that he keeps the reception area and my office in such immaculate condition.

"You know, Sharareh is so excited she can vote for the very first time tomorrow," says Mr. Dashti.

My loyalty lies with Mr. Ahmadinejad. The current administration, with Imam Khamenei's blessing and Mr. Ahmadinejad's leadership, has been funneling some revenue from oil to the hardworking poor and rural populations. Most of my Basiji volunteers come from these areas, as they are some of our strongest supporters. Plus, some trickles of this big, sloshing sea of oil money come to me, making my operations possible. Unfortunately, Mousavi, Ahmadinejad's opponent, appears to enjoy more popularity.

"Your granddaughter will be voting for Mr. Ahmadinejad, right?" I say.

"She is actually very excited about Mousavi. She thinks Mousavi will help with individual freedom. You know how young people are these days . . ."

I throw my head back and laugh, startling Mr. Dashti. "Ha! Doesn't she know that individual liberty is a false capitalist concept created to destabilize us?"

Mr. Dashti's hands stop moving about the desk. He stands still, watching me.

"I see this every day," I can't help but continue. "These intelligent, well-educated people lured by a Western imperialist mirage."

"I think what she wants—" Mr. Dashti says quietly.

"No!" I cut him off. "If one person drills a hole in the boat, everyone sinks. Period."

I stomp into my office and slam the door. The bird flaps her wings in her cage. I unlock my drawer and retrieve the chess piece. The black queen, her outstretched hand holding a shield, peers at me with cold, hard eyes. I have to catch the storyteller.

13. KIMIA — SHIRAZ, 1981

AT EXACTLY 7:15 A.M. on every school day, like a punctual bureaucrat, a piercing pain began to burrow a hole in my belly. This day was no exception. I grabbed my schoolbag and winced. The pain brought with it the usual entourage of anxiety, tension, and dread. Stepping out of the house, I took a whiff of the massive honeysuckle vine blooming on the fence and snatched a flower for my journey to school. Continuing the morning ritual, I put it under my nose, inhaling the fragrance to untangle my nerves and soothe my pain. I thought about Baba Morshed's place and my breathing slowed. Then I remembered his odd question and kicked a pebble. I had never questioned who I was before that day. This was even harder than the riddles Arman used to ask me. I had talked to Reza, but he, too, was at a loss.

"Who are you?" I had asked him on our way home from the storyteller's.

"I'm Reza," he said.

"And what makes you different from a million other idiots named Reza?" I asked, annoyed.

"Well, this body," he said, pointing to himself. "And my soul, I guess."

That seemed like a pretty good answer. "Our name, our body, and our soul," I said, counting with my fingers.

But when we went back to Baba Morshed's, he wasn't satisfied.

"Soul, you say?" The old man stared us down. "What is your soul made of? Where does it come from? Does your soul grow like your body, or is it unchanging? Where does it go when you die?"

I opened my mouth, but the storyteller held out a finger. "Sabr,[37] Rumi! Some questions you must answer right away without letting your mind grab ahold. Other questions need to cook inside your fire!"

"Baba Morshed, I'm still confused. Don't Hoopoe and Imam Jomeh say the same thing? Was I not right?" Reza asked.

"The real question is, what makes Imam Jomeh who he is? Did he make every choice for himself, including all his thoughts and beliefs, or is it his ghesmat,[38] written in a secret book of life?" He looked at Reza, who stayed silent. "I will tell you that while Imam Jomeh encourages external destruction, Hoopoe is concerned with the annihilation of internal obstacles," Baba Morshed continued.

"Wait . . . I don't understand. What is 'annihilation of internal obstacles'?" I asked.

"Sometimes we wear our habits like clothes that no longer fit us. We forget they're just undersized garments to be shed." Baba Morshed paused and fed Myna, who was now by his side. "Do you know the story of the peacock and the hunter's net?" he asked.

We shook our heads.

"I love that story," said Myna in a squawky voice. Reza and I looked at each other in astonishment.

"She can talk *and* understand what we're saying?" Reza asked Baba Morshed.

"Baleh," answered Myna.

Reza and I laughed, delighted.

The old man fed her another pistachio and began. "Once there was. Once there wasn't. Besides God, no one was."

---

37 patience
38 destiny

I closed my eyes and relaxed into my seat.

"Peacock was the most beautiful and celebrated of all the animals in the forest. He knew this, but he wasn't arrogant or rude. He simply saw his beauty as a means to serve his friends. Every evening, when the animals gathered, he spread his plumage and danced for them. All animals were grateful for Peacock's graceful movements, the rainbow colors of his feathers, and the majesty of the umbrella they made.

"One day, as he was foraging for food, Peacock came across a long line of seeds. He ate them one by one until he was far away from his home and his friends. But the seeds were the most delicious he had ever tasted, so he continued eating them, moving farther and farther away. Suddenly, a hunter's net fell on Peacock. He gasped and squawked. He struggled to get free. He yelled for help, but his friends were too far away to hear him. After much struggle and screaming, he gave up. It was getting dark. He slept, waking the next day in the net. He began toiling and yelling for help again. But nobody came.

"After some time, he realized he could squeeze his head and neck through the net. There was a mound of seeds nearby. So he ate until he was full. He yelped a few times. Again, no one came. So, he fell asleep. This went on for a number of days.

"In the meantime, Peacock's friends were worried about him. When he didn't put on his show the first evening, they thought he needed to take a break. By the second night, they started searching for him. But Peacock was so far away they couldn't find him. Owl, who was the eldest and the wisest of all the animals, decided it was time to organize a search party. Groups of animals set out to look for their beloved friend. And they searched and searched. It was Fox, with his keen sense of smell, who found Peacock sleeping inside the net.

"'Oh, beloved Peacock! How glad we are to see you!' Fox exclaimed.

"Peacock, upon hearing Fox's voice, stirred awake. But he looked blankly at the animals standing before him. Other friends came forth and told Peacock how much they had missed him. But Peacock just stared at them suspiciously. The animals were surprised, as their friend usually had so much to say.

"Finally, Fox came forward and said, 'Let me set you free with my sharp teeth.' And he began chewing on the netting that had imprisoned his friend. But Peacock began squawking, 'What are you doing, you old fool? You're tearing my flesh with your razor-sharp teeth.'"

At that moment, Myna whistled and said, "Bah bah, bravo! Great story!"

"No longer an external obstacle, the net for Peacock became an internal one," Baba Morshed said, stroking Myna's head gently.

THE SOUND OF FOOTSTEPS brought me back to the street. I was heading to school, staring at the honeysuckle flower in my hand. Our neighbor's teenage daughter, Neda, was on the other side of the street. But she didn't notice me.

She was pulling her bangs out of her head cover. Neda, like many girls her age, defied the strict Islamic dress code by rebelling the best she could. Some girls were proficient at making Molotov cocktails. Others wrote anti-regime rhetoric on walls. But fashion, it turned out, was these young women's greatest secret weapon. They rolled up their pants to show their colorful socks or pulled up their sleeves to bare their wrists, but most commonly they pulled back their scarves to reveal their hair. If they had bangs, they tucked a finger beneath their head cover and coaxed them out. Following her lead, I pulled my scarf back as I crossed the street to join her.

"Salaam," I mumbled.

"Salaam," she said.

A couple of boys whistled at Neda as they passed us. She lowered her eyes, smiling as she looked at the ground. Turning

back, I frowned, ready to hurl an insult at them for their rudeness toward Neda. But really, I was offended they hadn't paid me
any attention. Before I could say anything, a vehicle resembling a
morality police SUV made a slow approach.

"Gashteh Baghiatallah," I whispered as I fixed my scarf over
my hair.

Swift and seamless as a seasoned pickpocket, Neda placed her
bangs neatly under her scarf. We both stuffed our hands in our
baggy raincoat-style uniform pockets and fixed our gaze on the
ground as the SUV passed by. My heartbeat thrashed in my ear as
the vehicle slowed down. I felt the men's scrutinizing stares on our
downturned heads, and a trickle of sweat ran down my back. But
they didn't stop.

When the SUV became smaller, Neda and I looked at each
other and gave a slight, almost imperceptible nod as if to say,
Disaster averted.

You see, we were sisters of sorts. Tragedy is the best adhesive:
A few months earlier, Neda's mother, Elaheh Khanom, who was
terminally ill with a brain tumor, had pushed past the chemo drugs
and gathered all her strength to throw her daughter a birthday party.

My mother and I had attended the party while Arman was
busy with his Mobarezin training. The air was filled with music
and perfume. The guests who had momentarily forgotten their
woes had made a circle around the birthday girl. They laughed
and danced around Neda, who beamed with delight. But I couldn't
enjoy myself. Like a sick kid who knows much too much about
procedures, tests, and white blood cell counts, I knew much too
much about the new laws. Unlike Reza and me during our adventures, we were sitting ducks here. The burn in my stomach pinned
me to the chair, and I held my belly with my hands as my ulcer
dutifully warned me of all the things that could go wrong. And
at that party, there were plenty: Unrelated men and women in the
same room. A vodka bottle. Dancing. Music.

Soon a whirling wave of panic spread through the house as
someone screamed the dreaded words: "The morality police!" Now,

everyone's belly was filled with gut-wrenching angst. Somewhere between ousting the shah and post-revolution's soured jubilance, attending a birthday party had become a crime.

Like trained athletes, the guests, including old women, jumped the wall into our yard. My mother quickly gathered all her chador veils and handed one to each woman descending our wall. Their feet bare, some limping from a bad landing, the guests ran to the street. Some caught cabs, others walked home, trying their best to look inconspicuous. One guest managed to pull her car around to our house and stuff her husband into the trunk before speeding away. He was an army officer and could have faced serious charges.

Elaheh Khanom's cancer was not her ally during the raid. She was the last one to come over the wall, and by that time the two bearded men in fatigues were following her into our house. They pointed their AK-47s at her. Elaheh Khanom fell to her knees.

"Please, agha, she is sick," my mother pleaded.

"So?" said the shorter Revolutionary Guard as the other turned his rifle toward us. I froze. My mother stepped in front of me.

"We need to search your house," said the short one.

"Suit yourself," my mother said calmly, but even I could hear her heartbeat.

"You two, come with me," he said, pointing his weapon at us. My mother twisted toward Elaheh Khanom. She had sprawled on the ground, shaking with a seizure caused by the stress.

"Please brother, let me help her. She's going to die," my mother begged.

"Let her die." The tall silent one spoke his first words as he blocked my mother with his rifle.

The summer before, I had witnessed a wild dog sink his teeth into the back of a kitten, shaking the little guy furiously. I wanted to free the poor thing, but every time I stepped forward, the dog growled and shook the kitten even harder until its body went limp. I felt the same bitter bile of helplessness in my throat.

"Come on!" said the short one. "And if you have any playing cards, bottles of alcohol, backgammon sets, or contraband literature, you're coming with us. Deviant behavior is punished to the fullest extent of the law to protect the moral fabric of our Islamic Republic." His agitated words, like bullets of a machine gun, sprayed over the yard. It was as if he had grown embittered giving the same speech for the thousandth time to unruly children who were intent on defying him. He motioned with his gun for us to move.

My mother grabbed my hand and held it tightly in her own. Although we were dying to do so, neither of us looked back to see Elaheh. Instead, holding each other's sweaty hands, we watched the men in fatigues tear up our house.

We had some playing cards hidden in the basement, but Felfel, who had just given birth to kittens, stared at them with her wild green eyes and they turned away, distracted. I buried my head in my mother's chest, muffling my sobs of relief. I could feel my mom's warm breath on my ear as she whispered, "The cat saved us."

The short one, disappointed he hadn't found anything juicy, asked why we were harboring fugitives.

"We did no such thing," said my mother, in her most indignant voice. "Out of nowhere people jumped over the wall into my house and onto the street. What was I supposed to do?" She then pointed to our neighbor who was now lying motionless under the willow tree.

"She is innocent. They probably jumped the wall into her home too!"

The guards whispered to each other as I wiped my tears with my sleeves. My mother squeezed my hand and subtly turned toward Elaheh Khanom.

"Okay. We're gonna go now. But we'll be watching this neighborhood closely," said the short one.

As soon as the door was closed, we rushed to Elaheh Khanom. My mother cradled her head in her lap and told me to fetch some water. After that night, Elaheh Khanom became bedridden and died a short while later. Neda told me later she would have given anything to have been there with her mother instead of hiding at her aunt's house that night. She told me that she would never be able to celebrate her own birthday again.

I PULLED THE REMAINS of the honeysuckle out of my pocket. I had squeezed it dead. Sighing, I threw the crushed flower in the bushes.

14. KIMIA — SAN DIEGO, 2009

I AM NEVER SO aware of impermanence as I am after I cut myself. The black box I hold in my hands, like the dagger it contains, will one day be no more. I will one day be no more.

This thought neither frightens me nor brings me solace. Like all other thoughts, it comes and goes without much fanfare. Life doesn't look like the set of an old movie. Time doesn't slow. I'm not giddy with awe, but I can sense the tenuous web of life just as I did as a nine-year-old in the bomb shelter.

I study the box—the meticulous inlay border, the walnut wood, stained to an obsidian blackness of tremendous depth. This is not a typical Persian box. The entire visible surface of a standard khatam craft, like the trinkets packed in Roya's garage, is inlaid with complex mosaic designs. I caress the simple pattern wrapped around the lid—bone slivers, gold, and betel. I can almost hear my dad's voice. *Ooji, where have you been?*

I put my box in its hiding place in the closet and fetch my planner. I have already canceled my future appointments, citing a family emergency, but my to-do list still runs several pages long. When I phone Bernice to let her know this will be my last volunteer shift before heading to Iran, she says, "Lunch is on me."

Bernice, half-Lebanese herself, loves Persian food. Roya, who loves Persian-food lovers, often prepares Tupperware containers filled with rice, stew, and salad, which Bernice and I eat during our breaks.

Bernice is a veteran. She returned a few years ago from Afghanistan with a back injury. Neither of us is eager to share our war stories. What we share is a love of food, and that is enough. She makes satisfied noises after her first bites and I polish off the last morsels on my plate, like I did as a child.

On my way to Willow Grove, I drive past the line of oleander trees casting shade on the ground cover. Right there in the middle of ice plants sits a crooked cross with threadbare fake flowers. *Who died there?*

I go through the lobby and head to Tom's room. He usually asks me to read him Joyce, but today he points to the Bible by his bedside. He is a former judge. He has stage-four pancreatic cancer. Elena, in the next room, has leukemia. Once, after her pain medication kicked in, I held her hand as she sang in Bulgarian and laughed. Gladys has suffered a stroke and can't speak, but her face blooms like a flower when I take her to the courtyard garden. Volunteering at an elder care and hospice facility means eventually walking in on an empty bed or finding a new patient where an old friend used to be. With each patient's passing, Bernice performs a small ceremony and places flowers on their vacant bed.

Ruth was the first to go. She was a genetics professor who had opted out of a life-prolonging but painful heart surgery. We worked on Sudoku puzzles together.

"Ruth is gone," Bernice had said when I entered the lobby that day.

"Oh," was all I could manage. I worried a sleeve thread between my fingers.

"Everyone has a different way of handling it," Bernice said. "'This life is our playground and death our nighttime. We must play, returning at night empty-handed and tired.'"

This sounded like something my mother would say.

"It's Rumi," Bernice said, her honey-colored eyes searching my face. "You're a fan?"

The truth is, Rumi belongs in my past, and I change the subject when my clients want to talk poetry. Roya, on the other hand, goes into battle mode as soon as an American brings up the thirteenth-century poet. She'll say bitterly, "*This* isn't Rumi but a hack translation by white men who don't speak Farsi."

"I came across the quote the other day and thought you might like it," Bernice said.

"My mother . . . she loves Rumi."

Bernice gave me her splendid smile. It was that smile and the gap in between her front teeth that had put me at ease immediately the first time I met her. That day, she stayed with me until I was comfortable enough to meet Ruth's replacement.

In Tom's room, I read the King James Bible to him. His hooded eyes are fixed ahead on the painting of a blue guitar leaning against a dilapidated wall. Bony shoulders jut through his hospital gown, and his wheezing breaths are uneven. The grayish pallor of his skin tells me he doesn't have many more days. I turn the page and continue.

Like Tom, this state of being is also impermanent. My equanimity will eventually wear off and the storm of thoughts will return. I will oscillate between being mortified about what I have done and dismissing cutting as a benign eccentricity. *I'm not suicidal*, I'll rationalize. Some cutters cause themselves harm so they can stop feeling numb. I cut myself so I can witness my feelings without drowning in them. It's not a habit per se, since if I repeat the deed before the wounds have healed, it only hurts without producing desirable results. But then the literature on the subject suggests one grows out of self-harm over time. Apparently, I'm an exception.

Bernice is waiting for me by the courtyard entrance, holding an old-fashioned picnic basket. We make our way past a row of yellow-flowering succulents to an unoccupied table. She takes the food out of the basket—fresh baked bread, an assortment of olives, hummus, tabouli, feta cheese, and dolma. I tell her about my plan to accompany Roya to Iran.

"I'd like to go back to Afghanistan someday," she says. "I'm sponsoring my interpreter so she can immigrate to the US. But I love her whole family and I want to visit them again." She stops, a spoon full of tabouli hovering over her plate. She must've noticed the stunned look on my face. She tilts her head, waiting for me to say something.

"How did you do it?" I whisper. "Get over what happened to you there?" It's an unskillful question and I suddenly feel embarrassed, even though I still can't understand wanting to go back to a place that hurt her. "I'm sorry," I say.

"It's cool." Her rotund face breaks into that disarming smile. She smooths a flyaway hair from my face. "My parents were pretty shocked when I enlisted. They're hippies, you know."

I wouldn't describe them as such. Bernice's mother is a professor specializing in postcolonial Africa. Her father, an anthropologist at UC San Diego, focuses on the Middle East.

"Try the date hummus," Bernice says, offering me the container. "Everything else is Lebanese, but the hummus is made by this Syrian family I know. It's amazing."

I spread the hummus on my bread. Bernice bites into the sandwich she's made, her face glowing with pleasure. "Mmmm," she says.

We eat in silence for a few minutes. Gladys—"the sitting Buddha," as Bernice calls her—is wheeled out by an attendant. He turns to her favorite spot near the geraniums.

"Anyway, my parents tried to stop me, but I didn't budge," Bernice continues. "When I came back from war, I was sure they'd be angry and tell me I should've listened to them. But they weren't mad. They just supported me the way they knew how."

Bernice tells me her mother held her hand every night like when she was a girl, waking up from a nightmare. Her father had a different approach. As a teenager, he had worked at a Lebanese restaurant. He had spent closing time drumming and dancing with the rest of the staff.

"Things would get wild," Bernice says. "People would laugh uncontrollably, someone would be shaking on the floor, someone would cry." She leans forward. "My dad said it was really healing for him. When I came back, I was in a bad way. My dad asked our extended family, my former classmates, my friends, neighbors, everyone, to come with instruments and hold a drum circle for me. People sang and danced. Those who came empty-handed were given pots and pans. It was a scene . . . pretty chaotic at first." She laughs. "But following the beat was something I could focus on. Seeing everyone gathered around, just for me, was really touching. They did this every week for the first six months."

She opens a container of baklava and puts one on my plate. "One day, my dad breaks into a Lebanese song he used to sing to me when I was little. Everyone is drumming along and I'm loving it. But right then, someone begins crying super loudly. It was kind of distracting, and I couldn't hear the song. I wanted to tell them to shut up." Bernice gazes at the row of palm trees in the distance. "Then, I realized it was me . . . sobbing." When she looks back at me, I can see her tears.

I'm right here. I hold her eyes in mine. I can see the child in her and the old woman she will become. Her face shines with time-less innocence—the same innocence I lost ages ago. She shrugs, smiling. "I still go to therapy, you know. So, while I wouldn't say I'm over it, I can sleep at night. I'm still a work in progress, but I'm super thankful to my family and friends."

Bernice is the only person I socialize with outside Roya and Arman. It's hard to imagine having so many supportive people in one's life. To me, more people means more unpredictable variables to wrangle.

"Hey," she says, rousing me from my thoughts. "I reckon it must've been so hard for you to be in a new country with no one you know."

"Oh, I managed," I say, pulling down my sleeve.

IT HAS BEEN YEARS since I have set foot inside a bar, and I'm not sure what to expect. I am curious to see Arman's latest venture and what kind of people frequent a place named the Pink Poodle. Since Arman quit college in his senior year, he has been an actor, a carpenter's apprentice, off and on a fast-food worker, a birthday party magician, and a Latin dance instructor. But none of his other gigs lasted this long.

I push the door open. The place is buzzing with a happy-hour crowd of stylish people, belying the low-rent exterior. Different cliques congregate around hexagonal tables. The place itself feels like a beehive. Worker bees gather around the queen, drinking flavored drinks. A couple of drones play pool. A cluster of bees dance.

Arman waves from the other side of the bar. He called this afternoon, saying he was heading to work but wanted to talk about Maman. "I want to talk in person," he whispered into the phone.

In his club clothes, he looks more like an extra in a cheaply produced Iranian music video than someone who studied at MIT. We place awkward kisses on each other's cheeks. I inhale his familiar smell beneath the expensive cologne. A forgotten sadness gnaws at me. I follow him along a bizarre pink fur wall to the back of the building.

In Arman's office, a well-dressed Asian man is reading a magazine on the sofa.

"I'm Jason," says the man, jumping up to shake my hand.

I had imagined Arman's partner as a hairy-knuckled-thug type. But Jason's face has an air of royalty, as if he is a prince from the Ming dynasty. There is something charming about the boyish fluster coloring his otherwise elegant demeanor. Before I can ask any questions about how the two met, Jason leaves.

"Thank you for coming. Have a seat," Arman says in a formal tone. He moves a batch of Pink Poodle calendars from the chair to his messy office desk.

His trip to Roya's turned out to be pretty much disastrous. Rather than convincing her to stay, he left our mother's house with his Iranian passport and a Tupperware container so filled with baghali polo that the lid had to be secured with a rubber band. Roya likes to keep me informed of the whereabouts of her leftovers.

"Healthiest man alive, huh?" I gesture to the burger wrapper and half-eaten onion rings sitting on top of a pile of bills and paperwork. Arman is always vowing to start going the gym or begin a vegetarian diet. Every time we visit, he promises the next time we meet, he will be the healthiest man alive.

"You mark my words!" he says, raising one finger. And with the other hand he sweeps the food into the garbage bin. He looks at me as if to say, *What else have you got?*

I switch to Farsi to throw him off balance. "So, 'Tony,' what have you told your partner—that you're from Tehran, Italy?"

"Dude, just lay off, okay? Let's talk about Mom," he says, sticking with English.

I look at my brother, and for the first time in years, I see the fiery frustration of his youth. Is it true that family members' eyes trap one another in the amber of childhood? Or have I not really looked at him in all these years?

"Roya tells me you have your Iranian passport now," I say, setting my purse on his desk. "I'm booking our tickets tomorrow."

"Her name is Maman. Besides, we can still change her mind," Arman says reassuringly, but his eyes show me he can't even convince himself.

"You know there is no changing anything, right? You weren't there. Her episode was really bad this time. She doesn't think she's going to make it much longer . . . and I don't either. This is what she wants." I stop talking. Different emotions flash on my brother's face.

"Do you need help with airfare?" Arman asks.

I stare at him, stone cold.

Arman puts his hands out and tries to push back from the desk. The wall behind him prevents this. "This plan sounds insane.

What's in Iran anyway? Everyone has left—or they're dead!"

"Not true," I say. "Lots of people are still there. Amu Doctor is still there."

"So what?" Arman's eyes flit about the room. "Hey, what about that place you volunteer at—Pussy Willow or whatever?"

I sigh.

"Now that—that's what she needs!" Arman turns in his cramped space and gestures with his arms. "She needs professionals, you know, psychiatrists and nurses and all that. Amu Doctor couldn't take care of her in this state."

"Listen to yourself, Arman. She would fight so hard, they'd have to strap her down, restrain her, drug her. Is that how you want to see your mother?"

"No, goddamn it, no!" Arman rubs his hands over his face. "I know this place doesn't look like much to you. I know you think I should be some kind of engineer, but I've finally done something that matters to me. I've started something good, and I don't want to lose it."

"It would only be for a week . . . ten days tops. We'll just get her settled and come back. She is convinced she's going to die soon," I say, my voice dipping.

"She doesn't know that. How could she know that?" Arman shoots back. "She could outlive both of us."

I sit, silent.

Arman yanks on a lower desk drawer and pulls out a wad of cash. "Here," he says, counting out bills. "Here's Mom's airfare and yours. Take her back and I'll water your plants."

I stand, grab my purse, and walk out.

"Aw, come on! Kimia!" Arman yells after me. "Kimia!"

15. KIMIA — THE VALLEY OF THE BELOVED

"OF ALL THE BIRDS who traveled through the Valley of Quest, only a fraction survived. Many of those bore scars, some were injured, and all were tired. But the birds felt lighter and more alive than they ever had before. Awaiting the arrival of Hoopoe, they quietly recounted their adventures to one another. They nodded with kindness and listened attentively. Owl and Parrot, with a handful of other birds, took it upon themselves to look after the injured. The spirit of camaraderie gave them strength. Their courage lifted their hearts and prepared them for continuing to the second valley. They were ready.

"'This valley is the Valley of the Beloved,' Hoopoe bellowed. 'To enter it, one must be a glowing flame. The heart of the lover must burn with the passion of fire as with love; there is no second guessing. Love is so complete, right and wrong cease to exist.' Hoopoe's voice echoed inside Nightingale's head. The air was electric. Every bird could feel passion ignite inside their heart. Falcon was ready to soar into the sky. Hummingbird couldn't stop flapping his tiny wings.

"'Love is fire. Mind is smoke. The eyes of the mind are blind to Love because when Love arrives, the mind disappears. That's when every bit of the manifest universe is compelled to reveal itself to the eyes of Love. She who undertakes this journey must have a hundred thousand hearts so that she can sacrifice one with each breath. You must allow the fire of your heart to burn away all that is not Love.'"

The old man threw a fistful of powder from a pouch into the dragon's mouth. The fire roared even higher. A bright reflection danced on Reza's dazzled face as his hand went to his mouth.

"Brave Nightingale, who had left his beloved rose behind, let the flame of Love consume him. He perched inside the fire as the flames rose but did not back away. He cried with pain and sorrow but did not move. Wherever his teardrops fell, the fire died and a rose sprang from the ashes. Soon, he was surrounded by a field of roses."

I SLID INTO THE bench at the back of the classroom and took out my notebook. Everyone was deeply engaged in discussion. I usually was one of the loudest, but this time I put my head down and began scribbling furiously.

I pretended to be working, but I wanted a few moments to recount every detail of our time with Baba Morshed. When I closed my eyes, his place appeared, and I was back inside the story. Yet I was so afraid I would forget something. I had a sharp memory, but just as with dreams, I didn't trust myself to remember all the particulars of the strange recent events. If anyone came across the notes, I would say it was a story or a dream.

For a moment, I stopped writing and again imagined how my mother would react if she found out the truth of my secret outings. She would horsewhip me, I knew it.

Two summers before, when my parents had refused to buy a

horse for Arman, he decided to buy one himself, and in exchange for my silence, he'd grant me riding privileges.

"Where are we going to keep it?" I asked.

"In the basement. We'll ride it during the day, and when it gets dark, I'll make an excuse to go out. I'll bring the horse in then, while you keep Maman and Baba occupied."

The next day, he broke his piggy bank and counted the money he was saving for a new bike. Arman then rode his old bike with squeaky breaks to the Poshteh Moleh village, and traded it along with his savings for a horse. The plan had worked miraculously, but being twelve years old, with no experience in big purchases or equine upkeep, Arman had ended up with a sick horse. That may have had something to do with its surprisingly cheap price. Unaware of this, we fed him, washed him, and brought him in every night in secret.

Rather than stairs, the pathway to our basement was a sloped driveway, convenient for parking one car, or sneaking one horse.

We were careful and didn't put the horse in the living-room part of the basement that stayed cool all summer. This vast room had grand paintings hung on the soothing mint-colored walls, a small hoze, and old Persian rugs that would most certainly be ruined by horse hooves and droppings. Instead, at night, we took the boxes out of the smaller adjacent storage room. We left the horse there with a bowl of water and some hay.

When our parents left for work, we scrubbed the storage area of horse droppings and then the two of us, along with the rest of the neighborhood kids, took turns riding the poor horse in a nearby plain, just out of the adults' sight. The horse, naturally, exhibited signs of decline. When he began to writhe on the ground, we knew he was dying. We dug a shallow hole behind our house and waited. When the horse took its last breath, with great difficulty and the help of other kids, we dragged the beast into the hole. We covered the body with some dirt, and like in American movies, stuck a cross made of two sticks on top of the dirt. A few days later, when the whole neighborhood stank with the smell of the rotting carcass, our secret was uncovered, and we were lashed with the same horsewhip that had come with the recently deceased horse. Fariba, the neighbor girl who had discovered us digging a hole, had happily told my mother all about it.

REMEMBERING THE LASHING, MY grip tightened around my pencil and the tip broke on the paper. I took another one out of my backpack, cursing the brittle Chinese pencils that wouldn't sharpen. Oh, how I loathed being at school.

I was about to begin writing again when shushing sounds replaced conversations. My head jerked up to see our teacher, Ms. Hemmati, arrive. She was dressed in black with bloodshot eyes. My inner world disappeared.

Last week, the principal had told us Ms. Hemmati's brother had become a martyr of the war.

"How old was he?" Rama asked.

"Sixteen," said the principal. We cast furtive glances at each other, sad but also relieved he wasn't our age. At least he'd lived a long life, we thought.

Ms. Hemmati winced as she took her seat. She didn't look like herself.

"Let's begin," she said with a hoarse voice.

Seeing our beloved teacher in such anguish, we opened our textbooks immediately. The lump in my throat made the noose of my school hijab feel tighter. I tugged at it and stared at my textbook.

"DO YOU WANT TO learn to play canasta?" said Dayi[39] Payam as soon as I came home from school.

"Baleh!" I said, grateful to have a distraction from the weight in my chest. Ms. Hemmati had burst into tears in the middle of the lesson, and several kids had also started sobbing. Soon tears had trickled down my own cheeks. After some time, she had resumed the lesson as if we had just been interrupted by the sound of thunder and no pause or explanation was needed.

"Eight times nine is . . . ," she said.

"Seventy-two," we responded.

Dayi Payam, my mother's younger brother, had shown up unannounced at our house, but this wasn't unusual. His ten-year marriage had been a rocky one and he would leave Isfahan for long stretches, returning when he and his wife both had cooled down and forgotten what the latest scuffle was about.

The last time I saw him was the previous autumn during an intense crackdown period. Even so, he disappeared late at night, playing cards with his friends, and didn't return until morning. My father always had freshly brewed tea ready for him when he walked into the kitchen. Baba would put his newspaper down and immediately launch into a discussion about the favorites for the next World Cup. Dayi Payam would sip his tea, his eyes full of sleep, and rub Arman's head.

"Who is the best footballer in the world?" my uncle would ask Arman, having little interest in the answer.

Late one night, when I woke to use the bathroom, I overheard my mother and father discussing Dayi Payam.

"Shahin, I'm really afraid," my mother whispered. I tiptoed close to their bedroom door and pressed my ear against it.

"They're not just playing cards. I know it! Payam is gambling and smoking shireh,"[40] she said.

I swallowed hard. Playing cards carried a stiff penalty, but gambling and drug use were punishable by death.

---

39   maternal uncle
40   opium

"And with all this bombing . . . Payam never gives me the phone number of his friends, no matter how much I ask. He always has an excuse—Masood's phone lines are down. He's going to Saeed's house first, but then Jafar is going to pick him up later and he doesn't know where he will end up." She sighed. "What if something happens to him?"

My dad said something I couldn't hear. I pressed my ear harder to the door.

"I know he doesn't want to get us into trouble, so he lies to me," my mother said, anguish ringing in her voice. "But it doesn't help. I don't feel protected. I feel shut out and scared to death for him . . . and for us." She began to cry.

The last time Dayi Payam was around, he taught me gin rummy and spades, which we played every day as soon as I arrived home from school, not stopping until dinner time. After dinner, I hastily finished my homework, and then we played again until it was long past my bedtime. My uncle then would look at his watch and say, "I've got to get ready."

When Dayi Payam stayed at our house, my parents left me alone for the most part. My grades began slipping, but I became a formidable opponent in cards.

This time, when I arrived from school, Dayi Payam was watering the rose bushes, a cigarette dangling from his lips. I laughed and leaped into his arms, especially happy to see him. My mother was always gentler and less punitive around her younger brother. Plus, thanks to the storyteller, like Dayi Payam, I now had a clandestine place I could disappear to and never speak of during the card game.

That afternoon, right after he taught me canasta, I watched him in his black shirt and slacks, looking at his own somber reflection in the mirror. Under his breath he said goodbye and left the house. Thankfully I was invited to Reza's house for dinner, so I left shortly after my dayi.

I headed to Ghasrodasht Avenue. The sun was setting behind the Sleeping Man, giving a soft glow that diminished the harshness of the street covered with black flags and revolutionary slogans.

Once a year, during the two lunar months of Moharram and Safar, we were to mourn the massacre of Hassan and Hossain, the grandsons of the Prophet Mohammad, and their families. Religious folks had always observed those months, and now the entire country followed suit. Never mind it was 1,400 years since the death of the martyrs; the Shiites injected the occasion with such feverish importance that an outsider would be convinced the murders had happened yesterday. Perhaps it was their way of telling the world they alone were the rightful successors of the Prophet. Or maybe it was just habit.

Unlike the Persian solar calendar that corresponds accurately with the beginning of each season, the Islamic lunar calendar had received a revival after the Revolution. This was all well and good for the religious or those for whom this provided a benefit, but the practical implications for children, their secular adult counterparts, those affiliated with any other religion, or anyone who did not care to be sad for something that happened a millennium ago were monumental. For one thing, the morality police were extra vigilant, flooding the streets with more paasdar guards on patrol. For another, people were expected to carry an even more sullen expression than usual. If one had the misfortune of having a birthday during those months (and everyone had a turn since it was a lunar calendar), they had to forgo celebrating. No weddings were scheduled, either, and people wore black outfits. Any other color was frowned upon.

Although public display of affection was permanently banned, public display of self-flagellation—anything from beating your chest to cutting your scalp with a sharp instrument—was permitted and condoned for the duration of the mourning. Mullahs made more public appearances during these months than Santa Claus during Christmas season. They repeated their sorrowful tales of the martyrdom, and people wept.

My school girlfriends and I found this surreal carnival of

sadness to be comical. On one occasion, when we had to put on our obligatory sad faces, we feigned crying until we were all laughing uncontrollably. My face buried in my friend's shoulder, I mockingly pretended to blow my nose in her hijab. That led to an eruption of laughter that was thankfully masked by the wailing of the crowd.

I made my way to Reza's house, focusing on the soft pink clouds. I was thankful I could go on foot rather than asking my mother for a ride. Even after years of driving, Roya was still a nervous wreck behind the wheel of a car and inevitably unloaded her frustration on her passengers, making the journey more unpleasant than crossing a turbulent sea on a ship filled with typhoid-infested convicts. And that was on good days, when we didn't end up getting lost.

I stopped in front of Zamani's house. The entire wall was filled with small print:

> Dear students, you must watch the behavior and the activities of your teachers and professors so that if, God forbid, they say something wrong, you see them deviating in any way, you must report them to the responsible officials. Teachers and professors, you must be alert to watch your own colleagues to see if some of them are trying to teach deviating thoughts during their lessons to the children of our Islamic nation so that they can be stopped. If this does not work, directly communicate with officials. My dear children, if you observe that some enemies in the appearance of friends or schoolmates are trying to attract your friends, introduce them to the responsible officials, and try to do all these things very secretly. Committed mothers and fathers, watch the comings and goings of your children and observe their activities!
>
> —Ayatollah Khomeini

I took a snapshot of the quotation with my mind. I couldn't wait to share it with Reza.

My steps quickened as I approached his house. I loved that Amu Doctor called me golam—my flower—and Azita Khanom always had a small present for me. But the best part was Azita Khanom's unbelievable albaloo polo with pitted sour cherries. The marvelous scent of a slow-cooked stew and saffron rice with fresh butter met me by the door. Yes. Life could have been better all around, but in that moment, anticipating the warmth of Reza's house, his sweet laughter, and by God, the amazing food made specially for me, it was enough honor just to be alive.

16. Arman — SAN DIEGO, 2009

AFTER KIMIA LEFT, I called and apologized. Something I've been doing a lot of lately. Then I bought my ticket to Iran.

Jason keeps insisting I go home and get some rest before my flight. But I stall, telling him I've got some paperwork I want to finish.

I pick up my Rubik's Cube, mess it up, and solve it again. Some of the small cubes have lost their color altogether, others are chipped or peeling, but I know each cube's place by heart. When we left Iran, my mother packed her tea set, a couple of small paintings, and one or two knickknacks. But besides a duffel bag full of clothes, this Rubik's Cube was the only thing I brought—the only thing that connects me to my dad. I mess it up again and figure out the puzzle.

On the sofa across from me, Jason sips his chamomile tea and reads a tattered copy of *The Portable Nietzsche*. He lost his dad too. His father doesn't sound anything like Baba, though. When his dad was alive, he smoked like a chimney and was too busy with his factories in China to spend any time with Jason. "So he could make a bunch of crap," Jason told me one day. "We're talking number-two pencils that fall apart, imitation Legos, and unsticky adhesives. When he was on his deathbed, all I could think was, 'I don't even know this man.'" My own dad would have given anything to spend more time with us.

"We're in the black, J," I say, pointing to the mess of paperwork on my desk.

"Oh yeah?" Jason says. He looks up from his book, his designer reading glasses perched on his nose.

"Went through it twice." I indicate the paperwork with a sweep of my arm.

Jason nods and returns to his book. "Nice."

I can't help but be grateful for him right now. Jason's so low-key and collected. In contrast, I seem to always be full of turmoil— even when I first met him for the second time. It was right after my speed-dating fiasco—the one that had me at the downtown hotel bar. I was knocking back a few, feeling exceptionally lost. Maybe once upon a time I was crystal clear about my purpose for existing, but in that moment, for the life of me I couldn't remember.

Just then, "Remember me?" said a handsome Chinese man I also didn't remember. He was sitting next to me, doodling on a napkin.

"Pardon?" I mumbled, searching through the index of faces in my memory, not entirely sure he was talking to me.

He put his pen on top of the napkin, obscuring his drawing. "We were in a couple of classes together at MIT. You tutored me in linear algebra. Tony, right?" Disarmingly friendly, Jason extended his hand.

"Oh, hi. Great memory!" I shook his hand, smiled, and had no idea what to do next.

Now, Jason closes his book and arches a bemused eyebrow. I've been staring at him.

"I don't want to go," I blurt out.

"Why? It's just for a few days. You said you still have family there, and the food is great." He sits up and drops the book on the coffee table. "Listen, I'll take care of things, I promise."

"I don't know, man," I say. My eyes become hot with tears.

"This somehow makes me feel more officially American—you know, 'successful entrepreneurs' contributing to the economy and all that shit."

"This is why you don't want to take a few days off?" Jason asks.

"No. I don't wanna lose what I've built," I say.

He is about to reply, but I keep going. "You know what? That's not it." Jason often accuses me of oversharing. *TMI, man. TMI*, he says. But I haven't shared the most important detail of my life with him. I had hoped to keep it that way. For the first time in ages, I'm living my life instead of my life living me. But it's all slipping out of control. I twist the Rubik's Cube again. "You're always reading these books on philosophy and ethics and all, right?"

"Yeah," Jason says. "Is this about your trip or contributing to the American dream—"

"Let me ask you a question," I interrupt. "When you do something, how many parts is you doing the thing and how many parts are other factors conspiring for you to do it? I mean, how much responsibility does a person have, given near infinite variables influencing a single act?"

"What in the world are you talking about?" He takes off his glasses and sets them on his book.

The cube's edge digs into the palm of my hand as I grip it tighter. "Man. I'm really scared," I admit.

Jason leans forward. "Hey, you said it was safe to travel there. If you think you'll be in danger . . ."

"That's not it either." I sigh. I'm dying to tell him, but imagining the disappointment—no, revulsion on Jason's face, I bite my tongue. I force a smile. "Maybe I'm going through some kind of existential crisis." I throw the cube on the desk and stand. "Say, theoretically, you did something awful when you were a kid, but nobody knows about it."

"Theoretically?" Jason bends his head to his cup, watching me.

"Theoretically." I begin to pace the room. "Now, say you have a chance to come clean, but that might make things worse, not only for you but for those who were affected in the first place. Would you come clean or would you keep it to yourself?"

"I see," Jason says. "Since you know me, you also know I'm kind of analytical . . . so mind if I ask you a couple of questions about this theoretical scenario?"

"Shoot," I say, still pacing.

"All right. Now, how awful was this act I committed? Did someone get hurt?"

"Yup."

"Was it permanent damage?"

"Yes to that too," I say.

"Was there intent? In other words, did I mean to cause harm?" Jason says.

"No, no. No way."

"All right. You said I was a kid when I did this thing, right?"

I stop pacing and nod.

"And how do I feel about this awful thing now?"

"I don't know. Like shit." I drop my head in my hands.

"Hey, are you all right?" Jason asks.

"Oh yeah." I straighten up and resume pacing the room. "I'm being hypothetically upset." I wave my hand. "Please go on."

He says, "In general, I favor moral particularism. Instead of leaning on any moral principles, I'd weigh the circumstances to determine a specific response."

"Okay. So, what would you do?"

"I guess I'd learn about the other people involved and what their response might be. I'd educate myself on ramifications. I'd make a list of the pros and cons of spilling the beans versus keeping silent." He puts down his cup and crosses his arms. "Then my chances of making the right decision should be pretty decent."

My frown relaxes, and I'm beginning to walk back to my desk when he says, "This, of course, presupposes that one: I know myself well enough to predict how I'll digest this information. And two: there is such a thing as free will."

I throw my hands up in the air. "Will you just give me an answer?"

Jason laughs. "I'm sorry, man. I don't mean to be difficult. I guess if I were pressed, I would trust I'd make the right decision and try not to worry about it." He taps his lips with his index finger. "What might be a more pertinent question, though, is not how I'll proceed, but how I'll respond to the consequences of my decision. Will I accept my fate, or will I stew in the torture soup of 'What if I had made the other choice?'"

"Shit." I sit in my chair and run my hand over my head. "Let's change the subject. We'll pick this up after I come back, okay?"

"Yeah. Sure," says Jason, but he looks like he's suppressing the urge to push the conversation further. He wraps his hands around the empty teacup and glances around the room, searching. "All right. Tell me about your sister."

"What? Right. Kimia. What do you wanna know?" I suddenly remember how nervous Jason had become when he met Kimia. I've never seen him blush around women.

"You never talk about her," he says. "What's she like? Are you two close?"

"We were close a million years ago, but then we realized we had nothing in common. Then I quit school, as you know. She got married. We drifted apart even more."

"She's married?"

"Nah. Divorced. Her husband was a piece of work. He cheated on her."

"I'm sorry to hear that."

"Yeah. She's always had guys clamoring to date her, but then she got into her meditation and counseling. Now she just scares them off. I think she's happier that way."

Even though we've moved on, the residue of my dilemma still hangs in the air between us.

17. Kimia — FLIGHT 5276, BRITISH AIRWAYS, 2009

FROM OUR DEPARTURE GATE, I turn, looking for Arman. He called right after I met him at his bar. "I'm buying my ticket as we speak," he said. But where is he?

I picture him running toward us. I imagine him biting his lower lip like when he was a boy, but now, the fluorescent light reflects off the top of his head and his gold chain bounces against his chest.

"Boarding pass, please," the gate agent says again.

I resist the compulsion to look at my phone or back at the terminal. I hand over my boarding pass and follow Roya to the plane.

"All that matters is this moment," I say to myself as we board the plane. Following the mindfulness tip I teach my clients, I relax my shoulders and focus on putting one foot in front of the other.

Roya and I are assigned the middle and the aisle seats. The window seat belongs to a punk rocker sporting a purple mohawk and different-size safety pins attached to his eyebrows and ears.

"I'll go in the middle, Roya Joon," I say to my mother.

"Oh, no. You take the aisle seat. I'll be fine. You will use the restroom more."

She is right. I hated how, on road trips, my ex-husband, Lance, used to joke that he was an American driving a German car with an Iranian woman who had a Japanese bladder. I still remember the humiliation of my soaked pants when my first-grade teacher refused to give me permission to go to the bathroom. With my eyes pinned to the clock that wouldn't budge, I had waited for my father while the kids gathered around my wet shoes and held their noses chanting, "Shashoo, shashoo."

When my dad finally arrived, I broke down into tears in the back seat and begged him not to tell Maman. I don't know to this day whether he did. What I do know is that Roya was much gentler in the days after that incident. As was Mrs. Kayhan, my first-grade teacher, who became more yielding and attentive.

My mother herself had suffered from urinary-related traumas in her childhood. She told me and Arman of the time when, while she was still asleep, her stepfather had thrown her with the mattress, blanket and all, into the pool. This was to cure the four-year-old Roya from bed-wetting. Later in life, she was rushed to the emergency room with an infected kidney that had to be removed. She also never learned to swim.

From my aisle seat, I eye Roya. She seems undaunted by the hours of travel still ahead. When she faces me, I busy myself with fastening my seat belt. My hard-won equanimity waxes and wanes, and a conversation with my mother will only disturb my peace. I close my eyes and relax into my seat.

Within a few minutes of takeoff, my mother has a spread of feta cheese, naan, pistachios, dried figs, and kookoo sabzi on her food tray.

"Please, help yourself," she says to the punk rocker. Of course, she hasn't touched any of the food yet herself.

The guy pulls off his earphones. "Oh, no thank you," he mumbles.

"Absolutely not. You must have some. You are my guest and it's a long flight."

I want to intervene, but I know my mother. I remember our frequent picnic outings back in Shiraz, where she sent a plate full of goodies to the neighboring picnickers. Taarof is one cultural habit that remains nearly untouched by the changes in political climate or even war. Taarof allows complete strangers to quickly establish a sense of camaraderie and find an outlet for their generosity. Roya would look for pregnant women while picnicking and send Arman with an overflowing bowl of hot aash sabzi. But taarof goes beyond food. If someone likes your shirt, the typical response would be *Ghabel nadareh,*[41] *it's yours.*

This conditioning is so ingrained in each Iranian that upon arriving in the US, I was shocked when an acquaintance ate an entire orange in my presence without offering me even a single wedge. But now my mouth purses in discomfort as I watch this awkward exchange between Roya and the punk rocker. He has set his earphones aside. He places a pistachio inside a dried fig as my mother has demonstrated for him. She watches him with anticipation as he swallows.

"It's delicious, no?" Roya asks.

"Hmmm," he nods, but reaches for his earphones and almost succeeds in jamming them in his ears, but my mother is too quick. She grabs his tattooed arm. "Now try this!"

I reach for my own earbuds. The humming of the plane at cruising altitude has eased the angst in my belly, and my eyelids are comfortably heavy. *Sorry punk rocker, you're on your own.*

---

41   It's not worthy of you.

18. ROYA — FLIGHT 5276, BRITISH AIRWAYS, 2009

I GAZE AT MY daughter's profile. She has Shahin's nose and my brother Payam's jaw. Having lost both men, I look for pieces of them wherever I can. I see Payam's hunched shoulders, standing in the supermarket line. I hear Shahin's deep-throated laughter in Arman. I don't talk about Shahin to anyone, but oh, how I miss him.

I pretend to cough to cover my sob. I needn't worry—Kimia has already retreated to her own secret world.

Shahin and I had no secrets between us. What we couldn't say in person, we wrote in letters to each other.

I met him at his mother's funeral, of all places. Tahereh Khanom, a seasoned Persian literature teacher, was also my mentor. I spent summer afternoons with her and her brother Jalal Jon as they helped me with my poetry over tea and noon khamei pastries. He was a philosophy buff, and she was a fierce back-gammon player.

As I was leaving the funeral, I caught the sight of an ornate backgammon set sitting on a table in the corner of the living room. This was before we had to hide our playing cards and backgammon sets. Tahereh Khanom used to throw the dice on the board like she was some pro backgammon player mashti.[42] She wasn't a braggart, but when she got a double six, the edges of her eyes crinkled, and I knew she was going to decimate me. The wave of memories brought a gush of tears. As I reached for my napkin, I glanced across the room and the world stopped.

Shahin later wrote me a letter about the moment: "My belly was a tangled knot of sorrow, but my eyes caught those of a Persian Audrey Hepburn. Her tousled long brown hair danced in the breeze. When our eyes touched, her damp long eyelashes fluttered the tears away and she looked down. I never forgot that moment. I never went back to America."

He was on the other side of the living room, but his green eyes snared my heart. I could see his smile lines when he greeted the guests. He had a poet's lips.

I hadn't met Shahin before that moment because he was working on the Wells Dam project in Washington. Of course, in those days no one dreamed that one day Iran and America would become enemies.

Dams, he used to say, were the most exquisite multidimensional riddles ever created. He told our kids about DaVinci's dam, the one that kept the Florentine empire prosperous and defeated their longtime rival, Pisa. He told us that long before that, our ancestors in the Sasanian dynasty of the Persian Empire built Band-e Kaisar Dam, providing hydropower through water wheels that furnished an ample water supply for an entire city. "History aside, the construction of a dam required a certain ingenuity that's more inherent than learned," he explained in a matter-of-fact tone.

My Shahin was gifted with that ingenuity. He was in the midst of solving a "dam riddle," as he called it, when he received the phone call from his father. He told Shahin his mother "had a cold." Even though Shahin had spent many years away from Iran, he was well aware of the cultural imperative that prevented his father

---

42   a tough dude (originally meant to describe a pilgrim of the holy city Mashhad)

from telling him what was really going on. He grabbed the next flight to Tehran.

Seeing his father's red, swollen eyes at the airport crushed Shahin. He collapsed onto his luggage, sobbing.

"But then you met me," I would remind him when we told the story. He would pause and kiss me, and Arman would say, "Yuck," while Kimia made kissy noises.

After the funeral, Jalal Jon arranged for a gathering where we could meet. Shahin later told me he had arrived with sweat on his forehead and butterflies in his belly. Magic crackled in the air around us when I opened the door. I spoke to him of passion and poetry, and he asked me to *Cool Hand Luke*. My skin tingled with anticipation of our future unfurling into the most glorious possibilities.

For months after his mother died, Shahin stayed in Shiraz, helping with his father and uncle's law firm. Shahin filed layeheh[43] papers, greeted clients, and answered phone calls.

We were in love. My heart beat a little faster when I heard his footsteps outside my door. "'I have come! I have come, bearing a gift from the Beloved. I have come to relieve your sorrow!'" He would whisper this Rumi verse through the door.

If I wasn't the person I am now, I would have said it's difficult to pick which was our happiest moment—when we wed, when our children were born, or when we all, hand-in-hand, walked into our new house with gleaming stained-glass windows. But for me it's simple. The happiest moments are all lumped together in the bland, reliable clay of contentment yet to be hardened and cracked by boredom—me washing dishes, the kids playing, and Shahin sweeping in the background.

How I wish it was boredom that had spoiled my contentment. But this wasn't our ghesmat. The stress of the regime crackdowns and the war began chipping away at our happiness. I became irritable and lashed out. Shahin moved in the opposite direction,

---

43   legal bill

turning contemplative and spending much of his free time quietly telling stories to the children. Then one of our own was arrested.

Jalal Jon was set up by his enemies in his law office. How did a man like Jalal Jon produce such powerful enemies who destroyed him with such ease? Was it as trivial as accidentally cutting someone off in traffic? Had he slighted someone with one of the cases he won? Was someone envious of him? No one will ever know. But it was that simple. Jaasoos[44] agents were everywhere, watching, waiting for a slip.

How did it come to be like this—neighbor betraying neighbor? One young man's mother, on national television, shamed him for being antirevolutionary and sent him to his execution. *Tof!* I spit on the curse that turns people into such demons.

On one awful noon hour in the month of Ramadan, Jalal Jon had laid out a modest spread of noon o panir o sabzi on his desk. He had taken his first bite when the paasdar guards stormed the office. They arrested him for breaking the holy fast. They flogged him publicly.

After the lashing, he was a broken man. He lost hearing in one ear and the spark in his eyes. The flame in his heart died. We couldn't get him to talk either of poetry or philosophy. Jalal Jon always had an excuse to be alone. Shahin's father, Kamal, unable to manage on his own without the help of his brother-in-law, closed their law office. Jalal Jon died not long after. I didn't know this then, but he was only the first in our large family to become a sacrificial offering to the insatiable snakes of hatred and fanaticism.

---

44   spy

19. KIMIA — SHIRAZ, 1981

"DO YOU HAVE WATER?"

"No. Do you have electricity?"

"No." I wanted to launch into recounting my good dream, the one filled with roses and laughter. Our families, including my baba, sat cross-legged on a picnic blanket made of rose petals. We were in the center of the empty square, a slow rain of red and white petals falling from the sky, landing on our heads and clothes. I put a fragrant petal to my nostrils. I breathed in, and the petal stuck to my nose. Laughing, we lay down, letting a blanket of rose petals cover us. This was the first pleasant dream I'd had in a long while, and I was eager to share it with Reza, but I stopped myself.

"Something is different," I said, looking Reza up and down. "Where is your Walkman?"

"I left it at Jamshid's last time I was there," he said, putting his schoolbooks away.

"Wow. What is brought by the wind will be carried away by the wind. I didn't know you could live a day without that thing."

"It's no big deal. Are you ready to go?" Reza asked, putting on his faded Converse shoes.

"I'm always ready, Reza Khan," I said, not quite convinced I had heard the whole story.

Reza appeared older and calmer as we meandered through the streets. It wasn't like him to keep secrets from me, but he seemed content to walk in silence. I, however, couldn't contain myself.

"Hey, you have to tell me everything. We're blood brothers!" I stopped, held up my palm, and pointed to the thin scar. "Now spill!"

"I gave the Walkman to Khalil, the gardener's son," Reza said in one breath and started walking again.

"Wait! What?" I ran to catch up to him.

"You think I'm crazy," he said, his eyes fixed ahead. "But coming home from Baba Morshed's, all I could hear was his voice, you know: 'Nightingale knew the rose deserved a lover who wasn't riddled with fear and anxiety, a lover who was true to himself.' It was right then when Nightingale decided to go through the Valley of the Beloved." Reza took a deep breath and veered around a pothole in the alley. "When I closed my eyes at night, all I could see was Nightingale's eyes . . . how they had changed once the little bird made his decision. You think I'm nuts, right?" He looked at me as if it pained him to tear away the secret that fit so snugly against his heart. He didn't seem sure I would treat his confession with the tenderness it deserved.

"No! You're not nuts. I couldn't stop thinking about Nightingale either," I said, wanting to hug him, but it wasn't safe. "Why did you give your Walkman to Khalil?"

"It's hard to say why I did it. But you know how it is for me to be around people . . . I was thinking more about that than the Walkman. You know how . . ." His voice trailed off. Across the street, three official-looking women in black chadors stopped a young woman in a short manteau. They towered over her as she hunched, wiping off lipstick with the back of her hand. She shouldn't have left the house wearing lipstick.

We turned the corner and Reza whispered, "You know how afraid I am."

I did know. Reza's home was a sanctuary where everything was manageable. Even the hardest math problems were soft as powdered sugar on halva for him. And when he was with me, he had no problem with the babble of the chai khooneh or the crowds at Vakil Bazaar. The trouble was school. The trouble was the loud streets and bombastic strangers. The air sucked out of the room and whirled around him during tests. When I quizzed him at home, he got every answer right. Something changed when he was at school.

One evening, when we were making a stone tower in his courtyard, he broke down in frustration. He described his day, how he had to stand in front of the entire class with his heart in his throat, stammering out incoherent answers. Answers that in the sanctuary of his home would roll out like his favorite Hafez verses. Of course, except for a few showoffs, oral exams were terrifying for all of us. The worst moment was right before the teacher pulled the trigger and called someone to the front of the room. If one was blessed with exceptional hearing, they would hear the quiet shallow breaths, or legs twitching, or fingers sliding over textbook pages for frantic last-minute reviews. If one could read minds, they would see nazr promises made to God and desperate pleas to the Twelve Imams for granting one simple request: *Please, please don't let the teacher call my name.* We all suffered, but oral quizzes perpetually tormented Reza in new, excruciating ways.

"Everyone thinks I'm lazy and stupid. What's wrong with me?" he said through his tears that day.

I hated seeing him like that, but I was at a loss myself. So I fished a textbook out of his backpack and quizzed him over and over again.

As we continued on the path to Poshteh Moleh, Reza told me what had really happened to his Walkman. "I woke up today like every other day. Every morning, I reach for my Walkman on the nightstand as soon as I open my eyes, but this morning, instead of popping the headphones on my head and pressing play, I decided to get up and find its box."

He had placed the Walkman in the box and headed for the door, not knowing what he was going to do with it. But he knew he had to make a choice.

We passed a woman dragging a young girl behind her. The girl's limp feet scraped the ground as she whined, "I don't want to go to Aunt Feri's house." The woman gathered the girl in her arms and hurried past us, carrying her, the girl wailing in her ear.

When we arrived at a quiet street, Reza continued. "Khalil was picking weeds from the herb garden. When he saw me, he stood. There was a patch of dirt on his forehead, right here," he said, pointing below his hairline.

"He said hi—you know the way he always calls me Agha Reza. I said I was off to school and would see him later. I reached for the gate handle, but stopped and called Khalil. I held out my Walkman to him and said, 'I hope you enjoy this. I know I did.' Masht Fatolah was nearby, watering the violets and whistling. He dropped the hose and hurried over. He insisted that I take the Walkman back, that it was too much, but I handed it back to Khalil, who hugged it.

"You should have seen the look on their faces, Kimia. They were so happy even though they had no idea what a Walkman was. I mean, Khalil took the box and shook it against his ear before opening it. I gave him a couple of tapes and showed him how to use it. Masht Fatolah said, 'Khoda omret bedeh, pesaram.'"[45] Reza smiled and looked down.

I took his hand.

The Poshteh Moleh Creek filled our nostrils with a whiff of algae and new grass. In the distance, a man pumped his flat bicycle tire. We found a bush that obscured our bodies from the world, but still we could hear the rhythmic sound of air breathing life into the

---

45   May God grant you a long life, my son.

tire. I watched Reza gather smooth stones. I wondered why I had never noticed the dimple in his chin.

"The moment I gave away the Walkman, I felt a strange hole inside me," Reza said, sitting back next to me. "It didn't hurt, but it was sure empty. I scratched my ear where the headphones would have normally sat and crossed the street. I crossed the street, Kimia!" His eyes glimmered with astonishment.

Crossing the street had always been an ordeal for Reza. While I would readily stand in the middle of two lanes before I ran to the other side, he waited until both lanes were empty. Sometimes for an eternity. When he was alone, standing at the edge of Afif Abad Street, he'd crank the volume of his Walkman to maximum, and wait for a rare reprieve from the madness. He watched angry cars barreling down on him and blue minibuses honking at the tiny motorbikes weaving through traffic. But that morning, he hadn't reached to turn up the music, nor had he realized he had crossed the street until it was over. He walked away from Afif Abad, the same street that had always made his palms sweaty and made him nearly late for the morning assembly.

He gave me a few stones, and we began skipping them one by one on the creek bank.

"I would usually be running at full speed to make it to school on time, but not today. I was calm and I had time. So I bought a quarter kilo of fresh greengage gojeh sabz[46] and threw one in my mouth. I was about to eat another one when I saw a woman sitting on the ground in a frayed chador. She held her sleeping toddler with dried boogers and tears on his face. I gave the woman the bag. 'No, thank you sir,' she said, but I was insistent. 'Please take it. It'll be a good snack for your child.' Then she wished me a long life, just like Masht Fatollah. That's good luck, right?" He brushed back his hair from his eye and laughed.

There couldn't still be a hole in Reza's heart where the Walkman

---

46   green plums

used to be. If his eyes were an indication, his heart was as big and clear as the Caspian Sea. I, too, laughed.

"In class, I was the first one picked for the pop quiz," Reza continued, skipping a stone on the water. I imagined him taking soft purposeful steps toward the front of the class. I could almost hear audible sighs of relief replacing the tense quiet. Whatever promise had been made to Imam Zaman and Hazrat Abbas had worked for the rest of the class.

"I stood in front of my classmates. They looked like a crowd gathering to witness an execution. But rather than panicking when I saw their faces, rather than a hundred thoughts cramming my head, my mind was clear. I wiped my hands on my pants. They were dry!" Reza paused and looked at me.

His face looked so bright and sweet just then, it broke my heart. I brushed a leaf off his knee and motioned for him to continue.

"'What is the primary export of Peru?' Mr. Mehraban barked. He was looking at me over his reading glasses. He was thirsty for blood, I tell you. 'Copper, gold, zinc, textiles, and chemicals,' I answered. 'What is the capital of Ethiopia?' 'Addis Ababa'—I said it that fast. The class was stunned. They expected a massacre, and instead they saw a tennis match between two pros. I was John McEnroe . . . minus the cussing. Everyone's eyes were on me as I walked back to take my seat. A perfect twenty grade." He rubbed a stone, checking it absentmindedly for smoothness. A family of ducks landed in the creek.

"Vay! That's amazing." I bumped my shoulder to his. "What happened next?"

"Well, some boys looked like they were jealous . . . Afshin and Pouya later told me they were proud of me. But everyone is looking at me differently now, you know? It's all really great, but . . ."

"What?" I asked.

He spoke to the ground between his knees. "What if this all ends? What if I go back to being a pathetic loser?"

"Hey! Don't get ahead of yourself," I said, putting my arm around him. "You'll be fine. I promise."

"I THINK THIS TIME it's for real," I overheard Dayi Payam whisper to my mother one night after dinner.

I tiptoed to the living room and watched them through the cracked door. Earlier, hoping we would play canasta, I had knocked lightly on Dayi Payam's door. When there was no answer, I peeked in to see him asleep, covers pulled over his head.

"Bita is leaving me," Dayi Payam said with slumped shoulders, his elbows on his knees.

"I've never liked her, and you know that. But you're the one who is always on the run. Mard baash[47] and confront her." My mother spat. "*Tof!* Bita is a bully and needs someone to shut her down."

"I'll never hit her, Roya. Or anyone. I swear to my ancestors' graves! I will never be Agha. Even now when I rem-em-em-member his b-b-b-belt . . . ," he stuttered, pointing to a scar above his left eyebrow. "Plus, it's no use to stand up to her after all these years. Maybe it's best to let things take their course," he said, staring out the window into the darkness of the garden.

"What does that mean? What are you going to do?" my mother asked.

"I don't know. Maybe stay here for a while and get my bearings and then go back to Isfahan and see what she wants to do."

"What do you want to do?"

There was a long pause, and then I saw Dayi Payam stand. I tiptoed away to my room, recalling Bita, her hazel eyes and her Isfahani accent. I was too young to have any ideas about the specifics of their quarrels, but when Dayi Payam told one of his hilarious stories at gatherings, others held their bellies and laughed as Bita ironed out the creases of her skirt with her hands.

I didn't know this when I tiptoed away, but his unraveling

---

47   Be a man

began shortly after that night. Dayi Payam and Bita were childless, and without the glue of parenting guilt, reconciliation didn't stand a chance. He became more reckless, risking high stakes both in card games and in real life. Eventually his depression stripped him of his loud laughter and his rosary beads. He stopped being careful as he continued his illicit activities and disappeared sometime after we left Iran. Later, Amu Doctor wrote that he couldn't find Dayi Payam's name in the prisoner list or hospitals. We mourned him just the same. There was little chance he was still alive and free.

20. $\mathcal{K}$IMIA — FLIGHT 5276
BRITISH AIRWAYS, 2009

ROYA'S CRY STARTLES ME awake. I yank out my earbuds. She has grasped the punk rocker's arm with both hands, her eyes squeezed shut, her lips moving in prayer. *She's having another attack,* I think. I scramble to unbuckle my seatbelt. But upon a closer look at her face and the suppressed smile on the punk rocker's lips, I remember why my mother hasn't traveled in all her years in America—the slightest turbulence sends her tumbling down a dark panic spiral.

"Ya Hazrat e Imam Reza," she shrieks.

I lean close and try to pry her off the punk rocker. "Maman. It's okay. We're just hitting some air pockets."

"Ahhh. Ya Imam Ali!" She yells her prayer to the saint as the plane shakes again. She buries her face in the punk rocker's arm.

"Shhhhhh. Maman. People are looking," I whisper in her ear. A few passengers are turned to look at the woman screaming Arabic words. I redouble my efforts.

"Please keep your voice down . . . Pray in English," I plead, even though it's an absurd request. "Sorry about this," I say to the punk rocker. I smile at the other passengers.

Eventually the turbulence passes, my mother relaxes in her seat, and the punk rocker goes back to his movie. Roya turns to me as soon as the shaking stops. "Eat something. You're so skinny." She makes a bite of naan and kookoo and holds it in front of me.

By now, I am accustomed to my mother's outbursts, the most notable one being at my wedding. Roya never had any qualms about sharing her opinions on Lance's family, but I didn't think she would go that far. At my wedding, right before we cut the cake, she yelled Rumi in Farsi, saying: "'The old man searched and searched . . . He said, "I am sick and tired of these monsters and demons. I am looking for a true human being."'" Then she collapsed onto the floor, crying. She hadn't planned the last bit, but I don't think she had planned to scream in Farsi either. When Arman, with the help of a few caterers, carried her outside, you could hear a fly flap its wings. The most memorable part of my wedding day turned out to be Roya's tantrum.

I'm not quite sure which came first, Lance's family's opposition to our relationship or Roya's distaste toward them, but the vitriol swung back and forth like the pendulum of a reliable clock. I endured more than a few brunches where Lance's mom, tipsy from her Bloody Mary, shared with the table that, "Yes, Lance's father had a chance to be stationed in Iran, but I wouldn't hear of it. Those Arabs are too backward."

Once, as I walked Roya to her car, she whispered, "Why do you let them treat you this way?"

I pretended I didn't hear her. "What else do you have planned for today?" I asked, hoping she would drop the subject.

"You were a lion when you were a girl!" She stepped in front of me, grabbing my arm.

I looked away.

"What happened to you?" she pleaded.

"Things change." I shrugged.

Something in her must have known that I married Lance to

get away from her. He was simply a part of that plan. Regardless, it must have hurt her to no end.

The plan itself was simple: To get from point A to point B. But like a prisoner plotting a careful and foolproof escape, the strategy through which it was executed consisted of a multidimensional kludge of objectives, ideas, variables, and contingencies.

Fairy-tale romance, this was not. Selecting Lance was a culmination of well-calculated analytics resulting in a favorable union. My methodology and findings were impeccable. The criteria included affluence, even temper, and stability. I had a chart with the name of each eligible bachelor, his grade point average, sports he played, the quality of his friends and family, and any other obscure yet applicable data.

Lance had the highest scores in all pertinent categories. A native Texan in his third year of law school, he was from a well-to-do family. His father, a navy admiral, and his doting mother had been in a strong happy marriage for twenty-nine years. Lance didn't indulge in drugs or alcohol and had a couple of steady relationships under his belt. Finding a way to date him was easy. I befriended his best friend's girlfriend, who set us up. A year later, we were married. He became a corporate attorney. And after receiving my degree in actuarial science, I became, well, an actuary.

I didn't love him anyway, I said to myself when Lance left me for our real estate agent. But the realization that I had sacrificed love for security and in the end was left with neither broke my heart in an unexpected way.

21. KIMIA — SHIRAZ, 1981

ON WARM DAYS, I hated my hijab more than school. That lunch hour, rather than enduring it, I set out to persuade Jamileh and three other girls to retreat back to our classroom. Life had been good, and I had become more daring. Ways of appeasing Roya and other grown-ups came to me in effortless inspirations. Reza was blossoming, and I was happy for him. We visited Baba Morshed when we had time, and even my dad's absence was more manageable. I found myself smiling the cat-that-ate-the-canary smile.

"We're not going to get into trouble, are we?" Jamileh asked.

"Never. We are just going to have a bit of fun," I said, watching rows of schoolgirls jockeying for shade against the wall.

My friends deliberated for some time as I turned away from them and the sun.

"Okay," I heard Jamileh say. A smile trembled on my lips as I led my coconspirators inside. I took off my hijab and folded it on the teacher's desk as the girls, with their crossed arms and pursed lips, watched me. I had promised and they had expected me to entertain them.

Tough audience, I thought, and began singing a Googoosh

song. The girls, not fully convinced, took their seats. I watched their expressionless faces as I tapped my feet on the linoleum tile, singing a number from the musical *Shahre Ghesseh*. As different voices emerged from my lips, their fingers began to drum on the desks, their mouths moving to the words. I continued with more fervor, louder, dancing over to each girl, making a face, watching each smile build into laughter. I didn't stop until the air became heavy with our collective singing. Soon we were stomping around in a primal frenzy, our voices raised, our maghnaeh hijabs strewn around the desks, and sweat trickling down our uncovered scalps onto our necks and backs. When Vice Principal Safavi entered the room, we were standing on desks, singing and clapping, so engrossed that we didn't know she had been watching us for some time.

"Daste Abbase Ali az tan joda shod,"[48] I sang from the top of my lungs and banged on the teacher's desk like it was a tonbak drum.

"Daste Abbase Ali az tan joda shod," the laughing girls shrieked to my call. It was an old joke about a mullah whose religious tale of sorrow had taken a hilarious turn to become a danceable song.

Jamileh's blank stare toward the door made me swallow the next verse.

Like fallen angels, one by one we descended from the desks. I secured my maghnaeh over my bowed head. My legs quivering, I sank into my seat.

"So many brothers and sisters are sacrificing their lives every day, and you're singing and celebrating?" said Mrs. Safavi in a low voice. She walked straight to me, her nostrils flaring with disgust. She was close enough that I could see the thick powdered makeup sinking into the grooves of her pockmarked face.

"Is this how you're using your recess time? You should be ashamed of yourselves. Whose wretched idea was this?"

The fallen angels' reluctant gaze fell on me. I smelled sweat and my own fear.

---

48   The hand of Abbas of Ali was severed.

"That does it, Shams." Mrs. Safavi's voice curdled with disgust. "You'll stay after school for a week and help the janitors. You'll have double homework for the rest of the year."

Then, like Ezraeel, the angel of death, she pointed her long finger toward the open door, the light behind casting a shadow on her face. "Now get out and prepare for the next class. Everyone! Out!"

REZA, CONFIDENT AND NIMBLE, glided around the playground. He didn't seem to mind the cacophony of boys yelling or the unpredictable chaos of the ball darting in and out of the middle of the game. It was as if his body knew when to duck and when to jump. He was the only player left to defend his dodgeball team. His teammates were now screaming his name. He saw me and his mother outside the playground and waved. Before he could turn to face the rival team, a tall and angry boy wound up and threw the ball at Reza with a guttural roar. The ball was hurtling toward Reza's back. Everyone, including me, screamed. Still looking at me, Reza twisted as the ball brushed his back and slid under his arm into his hands.

"Hurrah!" his teammates yelled and ran to him.

"That catch saved us," said one.

The tall boy who made the last shot squeezed Reza's hand and said, "Good game. Let's play again soon."

"Uh, sure." Reza blushed.

"Did you see me?" he said, running toward me and his mother. His grin was brighter than the full moon.

"Yes. You were brilliant." I sighed, kicking a stone.

"Mashallah, praise God! I'll die for you, my gol pesar," said Azita Khanom as she pulled a flushed Reza to her and showered him with kisses.

Reza broke away from her embrace, panting. "Don't embarrass me, Mom!" he said under his breath.

But she just laughed her melodious laugh, not caring that she drew stares from two male teachers. "I'm going to get some sabzi for dinner. Do you two want to stand in the breadline?"

We both said yes at the same time. She giggled again and gave Reza some change. "Here! Before I forget."

The sidewalk was bustling with people going home or shopping for dinner. We passed vendors, their merchandise bursting with color, each inviting us to linger. Azita Khanom told a Mullah Nasruddin joke and I laughed, but as we passed sycamores whose branches teemed with unconcerned bright green leaves, my mind wandered back to the trouble I had caused at school.

"I'll be back in a minute," Azita Khanom said when we arrived at the noonvai. She ruffled Reza's hair and left.

"You won't believe what happened," Reza said, not noticing my sullen expression. "Jafar and Mahmood, the dodgeball team captains, argued over me! Over me, Kimia!" he said, pointing at his own chest.

He went on to tell me that after his victorious performance during the oral quiz, his classmates had started treating him like royalty. At lunch he had found a quiet corner as usual. But this time, as he was finishing his cotlet, one by one, boys gathered around him, asking his opinion about different footballers, chewing small quiet bites of their noon-goosht wraps. When the last bell rang, as he was pulling the straps of his backpack over his shoulders, Jafar and Mahmood had magically shown up. The two tallest and most athletic boys in the class had asked him if he wanted to walk with them. That was before they started fighting over him.

"'No, no. I wanted Pirooz,' Jafar said. 'Hey, I got to pick first. I won the coin toss fair and honest,' Mahmood answered. Oh, and Mahmood wants to play again soon. Isn't that amazing?"

"Yup. It's great," I said.

"Wait, you look like your ship has sunk. Who died?"

"Nobody. I got in trouble at school."

"Vay, what happened? Did you take off your scarf again?"

"Worse."

"DOUBLE HOMEWORK," I YELLED when we stepped into Reza's courtyard. "And I have to help Masht Aziz and Fatimeh Khanom for one week after school."

I stopped and grabbed Reza's sleeve. He spun around to face me. The smell of fresh bread he held against his chest wafted over me, but my hunger was huddled in a corner of my stomach, hugging anxiety and despair.

"She's gonna call my mom, if she hasn't already," I said, my voice swelling with a wave of dread.

"I'm sorry, Kimia."

"I don't know which is worse, getting whipped or not being able to go to Baba Morshed's for a whole week."

"Hey, maybe your mom will go easy on you for once. Besides, you'll blink and a whole week will go by. Just like that." Reza snapped his fingers.

"Why are you Mr. Optimist all of a sudden?"

"Ah, you know. Things have a way of working themselves out."

"You sound just like Baba Morshed," I sighed.

Although I appreciated the thought, life didn't pan out as Reza had predicted. As bad timing would have it, Dayi Payam left for Isfahan that day to tie up loose ends. The same afternoon, my mother was wrapping up a particularly stressful day when she received the phone call from Vice Principal Safavi.

I came home to find her putting new tape on my bedroom windows. She was cursing the old, peeling adhesive under her breath. Her hair was unkempt, and remains of a broken candleholder were piled next to a dustpan in the middle of the room. My instinct was to run, but sensing my presence, my mother turned and screamed. "Do you want to be a dancing whore?"

My fingers loosened from my backpack strap, and it fell to the ground with a thump. I looked around the room for a response, but instead I saw the horsewhip on my dresser. She had been waiting for me. Her face darkened, and I turned to shield my own. She struck the whip against my back.

Felfel, who had been taking a nap on my bed, ran and let out a disturbed meow. My mother threw a brush at her. It hit her nose. Felfel yelped and leaped over the mountain of broken glass out to the hallway, meowing even louder.

"I'll kill you!" she screamed, before coming at me again. "Do you know what your little performance will do to my reputation?" she said, lifting the whip once again.

Even though I had transgressed, part of me had hoped she would be on my side—that she would see how the joyless, Draconian laws at school were crushing my spirit; how unjust and ridiculous life had become; how I needed an ally in this madhouse. But all she cared about was herself.

"I hope it ruins your reputation. I hope you die. I want my baba back," I spat through tears.

And then the beating took on a life of its own. If Arman hadn't walked in to interfere . . .

He grabbed Roya and gently took the whip away. Her tight grip on its handle had injured her hand.

Arman was never more like my baba than that day. He knew if he wanted to help me, he needed to first soothe the beast. He wrapped ice in a handkerchief and placed it tenderly on our mother's palm. She eyed him with gratitude as he put his arm around her as if he were a medic helping a victim walk away from a natural disaster. He looked back at me. I was in a ball whimpering on the floor. I watched him take our mother to her bedroom.

"I'll get you some water," I heard him say.

"I'm gonna kill her!" my mother screamed. I pictured her back arching.

"Shhhhh!" he said. "I'll get you some water."

MOVING SLOWLY THE NEXT morning, my body still aching, I surveyed the damage. I ran my hand gingerly over the bruises I could reach. I made a mental note to ask Arman to put a tea compress over the worst parts on my back. Until then, I had been so afraid of being horsewhipped. Somehow the whipping had appeared much more daunting than Baba's belt. Perhaps because the only other time, Arman and I were horsewhipped together. Was it the pain that terrified me or the fact that I was going to be punished alone? Regardless, now that it was behind me, I was relieved. It was horrible, but I could handle it.

To be truly fair, not all was misery and pain. The school janitorial husband and wife team turned out to be kind and lenient. Masht Aziz, who I learned adored Hafez, invited me to a playful game of Moshaereh while we mopped the floor together. With the last letter of the verse he recited, I delivered a new line. He recited mostly Hafez poems. I responded with Rumi, my new namesake.

"'Oh, this old world is becoming new again. Heavenly aromas are gifts brought by the spring breeze,'" he recited.

"'Even if from the sky, poison rains on all, I'm still sweetness wrapped in sweetness wrapped in sweetness.'" I laughed, dipping my mop into the bucket.

Rather than cleaning the toilets, Fatimeh Khanom had me dust tables with a small rag made out of an old chador, a task that was neither difficult nor, in all honesty, required. They dismissed me before their first break, but instead of going home, I sat with them cross-legged under the oak tree and had tea. I dunked my sugar cube that had been procured with newly issued coupons and popped it into my mouth. I poured the tea into the clear glass nalbeki[49] as they did. They sipped their tea slowly, watching the liquid disappear from the saucer.

Every day, when it was time to leave, I held Fatimeh Khanom's hand in mine. "'I am the madman, Majnun, in servitude to you, my Leili. I have become free of both worlds, so I can be your captive,'" I would say, looking them both in the eyes.

"Mashallah, bravo, my daughter!" Masht Aziz always responded, his laughter showing his missing front teeth.

Before exiting the gate, I looked back at the old couple, who sat motionless under the oak tree. They looked elegant and serene, as if they were posing for a painting.

On very lucky days, Reza would be waiting for me on the other side. Even with his increasing social currency, he still found time here and there to walk with me. We had to be careful, of course, so in the more crowded streets he walked ahead or behind me.

---

49   saucer

22. KIMIA — LONDON, HEATHROW AIRPORT, 2009

"WE PUT THE WATERMELON right in the cold stream between two big rocks, while you and the kids played," says Roya. "My naneh even brought her hookah. She smoked after every meal, and camping was no exception. When Amu Doctor put the knife in the watermelon, it was so ripe, it burst with a thud. The coldest and sweetest dessert ever." She blows the steam off her tea and sips noisily, the surge of fond memories animating her face.

I bite into my scone and try to remember that camping trip before I turned eight. It's useless, as I can only recall one or two memories of my life before the Revolution.

We have finally arrived at the London airport. I cannot decide whether I want to reach my destination so I can stretch on a bed, or stay here forever so I won't have to go to Iran. Several remorseful voice mails from Arman tell me he has missed our flight and will be arriving three days later. Roya, who hasn't mentioned him the whole trip, is describing our campsite in great detail.

"You don't remember those frogs at night? There were so many of them, you had to be careful not to step on one," she says.

I suddenly resent her for having a past worth remembering. I resent her for forcing me into a future I don't want.

"We should take some time and research elder care facilities in Shiraz when we get there," I say, not quite sure what I'm hoping to achieve.

"I don't know what you're talking."

A gate attendant has begun a boarding call for a departing flight. Several passengers rise from their tables and wheel their drab luggage toward the gate. My heart beats a bit faster in anticipation of our own upcoming flight.

"Well, Arman and I will only be there for a bit," I say over the boarding call. "You and Amu Doctor might require extra support when we're gone. It's good to plan ahead. That's all."

A sober look crosses my mother's face. She arranges her napkin into neat folds. "I won't need extra support," she says. "You, on the other hand, I'm not so sure." Before I can argue, she bursts into a poem in Farsi: "'This life is our playground and death our nighttime. We must play, returning at night empty-handed and tired.'"

Bernice had offered an apt translation of these verses the day Ruth died. My mother's loud recitation draws the attention of several people who turn to watch us. I'm sipping my coffee, wondering what to do if her behavior escalates, when an athletic blond man approaches our table. "Pardon me, are you Persian?" he asks in an Irish accent.

I watch the residual effects from our conversation dissipate from my mother's face. "Yes, we are," she says, her voice tinged with pride.

"Which do you prefer, Persian or Iranian?"

"Persian," my mother says. "Iranian," I say at the same time. We look at each other and laugh, despite ourselves.

"Join us, please." My mother taps the empty chair near her.

"Persian is better, because *they're* trying to erase our ancient past," Roya says as the man takes his seat.

"I don't know," I say. "I feel like I'm trying to hide my nationality when I tell people I'm Persian. As if I'm ashamed of being from Iran."

"Well, that is quite a dilemma, isn't it? Oh, where are my manners? Hi! I'm Jimmy Delaney," he says, extending his hand to me.

I introduce myself and my mother.

"Kheili Khoshbakhtam,"[50] he says.

"Bah bah . . . Mashallah, bravo! Where did you learn how to speak Farsi?" asks my mother.

"I studied Farsi and Arabic in school," Jimmy says in decent Farsi. "And I brought this in case I stumble." He puts an English-Persian dictionary on the table. "Thank you for giving me the chance to practice."

"I'm glad to help. Are you traveling to Iran?" Roya asks.

"Oh, yes. I'm taking the next flight to Tehran. I'm a foreign correspondent for a new online global news agency and I'm covering the election."

"I'm so happy things might change. I don't trust Mousavi or any candidate approved by the mullahs in the Guardian Council, but a little freedom is better than nothing. These young people don't know what freedom is like at all. They deserve better. You know, we'll be on the same flight," Roya says, her eyes dancing like fireflies.

"Brilliant! Are you visiting family?" Jimmy asks.

I look at my mother.

"Yes," she says.

"Do you feel safe returning to Iran?"

"Yes. Our family has not been back since we left in 1983, but I know many Persians who visit every year and have very good things to say about their trip," Roya says.

I have a hard time imagining having a good time in Iran myself. My mind goes to Shiraz, the city of my birth, and for the first time, I understand the meaning of the Portuguese word

---

50   A pleasure to meet you.

saudade—I miss Shiraz with every fiber of my being, yet it is no longer home.

"Will this be your first time in Iran?" I ask Jimmy after he orders a drink.

"First time. Although, I've been fascinated by the Middle East for quite some time and have covered Yemen, Egypt, and Jordan. But have yet to experience the enigmatic Persian culture first-hand," he says, looking at my mother. "So, when the opportunity arose to cover the elections, I was thrilled. I was supposed get to Tehran last week but better late than never. It wasn't easy jumping through the hoops, the visa, the press accreditation . . . sorry . . ." Jimmy flips through his dictionary. "Permissions," he enunciates. "If only I could speak Farsi the way you two speak English."

"You're doing great," Roya says. "My English is still short, but Kimia learned to speak in three months because she was so young."

As Roya and Jimmy chat about challenges of learning a second language as an adult, my thoughts wander to a day a few months after I arrived in California.

I was sitting between a Brazilian boy and a Vietnamese elderly woman in a crowded ESL classroom. By then, my eyes had stopped flittering about, watching for who might be watching me. My ears had stopped turning, like an animal's, toward whispers. I had stopped listening for sirens or the commotion of someone being taken away by authorities.

It was during a heat wave in San Diego. I read aloud from Mark Twain's book. *Everybody said it was a real beautiful oath.* The teacher asked me to raise my voice above the noise of the window-mounted AC unit. I read the line louder, and the room began spinning slowly around me. I pinched my wrist until I drew blood and the room stopped moving.

That night after dinner, I stayed in the kitchen of our small apartment. I pretended to work on my English writing assignment until Arman and Roya left for their respective bedrooms. I grabbed a steak knife. Hearing Arman's footsteps, I slipped it between my arm and rib cage, beneath my shirt. I squeezed the knife under my arm, walking lopsided, passing him in the hallway. I threw the knife on my bed, and began searching my closet, digging out my father's black Isfahani box. As I placed the knife in the box, I vowed to kill myself after Roya and Arman were asleep.

Sitting at my dresser that night, I looked at my arm. Despite the warm air, I had goose bumps. I made a fist and held my wrist taut on the dresser. Fingernail marks from earlier, three red moon slivers glimmered in the night light. Like diving into a cold pool, the sooner I got up the nerve, the better. The sting, as I pressed the sharp edge of the knife to my wrist, stole my breath and jerked my cutting hand away from the wound. I poised the knife above my wrist again, determined to cut deeper. Crimson beads swelled from the first cut. Time slowed. A thin rivulet of blood rounded my wrist and dripped on the dresser like an ink splash. My breath came back in a smooth long exhale. I wasn't sad or overwhelmed—just aware of every sensation. A new metallic scent blended with the faint yet omnipresent odor of mold in my bedroom. The AC unit purred as I tucked the knife back in its box, its edge still bloody.

My desire to kill myself had vanished, but a new ritual had been born.

"Would you like another drink, Kimia?" Jimmy asks.

I have been looking at the embossed logo on my empty coffee cup without actually seeing it. Roya and Jimmy have been deep in conversation for a while. A waiter is standing near us with a pen and pad in his hand.

"No, thank you," I say, and turn my attention to my companions.

Jimmy orders another tea for Roya and a second gin and tonic for himself before facing us. "I have a theory," he says.

Roya nods with interest.

"The Shiite are like the Irish—all about poetry, passion, and rebellion. The Sunni are more like the Germans: you know, structure, discipline, and purity." He counts the qualities with his fingers, emphasizing each word. "My boyfriend, Andreas, is German. We couldn't be more different, but people don't know that! Similarly, to the Western eye, the Shiite and the Sunni, and in your case, Arabs and Persians, have a lot of parallels, but the cultural differences are vast."

The waiter sets the drinks in front of Jimmy and Roya. Jimmy takes a sip and signals the waiter to bring him another.

"Sorry . . . I don't normally go on the piss like this. Or lecture people I just met. I reckon I do this when I'm nervous," he says, blush rising up his neck.

"You don't worry. You'll be fine. I like the gays very much," my mother says. "My doctor is a gay and he is a very good man."

"Well, I love Iranians. I mean Persians." Jimmy chuckles and leans closer to us. "And you know, I have the biggest crush on President Ahmadinejad."

"*Vay!*" Roya says, horrified.

"Look, all he needs is quite a lot of therapy, a good spa holiday, and he'd come around," Jimmy says.

"If only transformation was that simple," I say.

"Always the optimist!" Jimmy lifts his empty glass with a slight bow. "Enough of that. What about you, Kimia? What do you do?"

In the gate across from us, a new set of passengers is lining up to board the plane. A little girl, clinging to her dad's leg, moves along the line, her eyes glued to the TV monitor.

"She's a life coach," Roya answers for me.

"See?" says Jimmy. "That's what Ahmadinejad needs. That's what I need, really . . . How did you come to be a life coach?"

ON OUR SECOND AND last visit to the marriage counselor's office, Lance announced he had quit the law firm. He said he wanted to take a break.

Anxiety gripping my body, I wiggled upright inside the plush office chair. "Okay. I support you in your decision."

"I need some time to myself. You don't know how it is to feel so, so . . . suffocated," said Lance, yanking on his shirt collar to assert his point.

"There is someone else," I said, looking directly at him.

"I'm in love," he said to the Persian rug stretched under the therapist's feet.

Lance and I drove home in silence. I didn't fight him when he reached for his suitcase. I didn't cry or plead. I locked myself in the guest room and waited until he was gone. Then I went to fetch my black box.

I showed up at work without mentioning my breakup to anyone. Those days, Howard, my boss, was convinced that breaking into the catastrophe-modeling market would help the firm make it to the big leagues. And he kept reminding me it was a lot sexier than the lusterless homeowners and personal-auto-loss projections he had built the actuarial business on. I didn't see the attraction of that. But I loved the eloquent aggregation of data smoothing out the jagged spikes of individual calamity, the predictable comfort of probability distributions, and the generally accepted actuarial methods, my profession's own coded language for loss and death.

Howard had invested heavily in the modeling software, which I had spent weeks learning. That morning, he wanted all hands on deck to close a deal. But I was in no mood for pressure. In the conference room, I sat, unsmiling, explaining the algorithms within the modeling software and answering tough technical questions while Howard pitched to a couple of well-groomed insurance executives. Beads of perspiration appeared on his upper lip as he scrambled to compensate for my terse demeanor. He began making inappropriate jokes.

We closed the deal anyway, and Howard treated us to dinner. He confessed to me, after too many glasses of chardonnay, that his whole motivation for this bold new move into catastrophe modeling was simply to avoid death by boredom.

"For the life of me," he said, sliding uncomfortably close on the round booth seat of the dark steakhouse, "I can't understand how you can stare at those spreadsheets all day."

I excused myself and went to the restroom. I didn't go back to the table. I just left.

After that night, I found myself more and more at my neighborhood meditation sangha. There was something simple and practical, yet utterly luxurious, about having your attention on your breath alone.

I began attending week-long meditation retreats where I learned to chew each bite of my lunch forty times and look into another person's eyes without averting my gaze. The sangha group introduced me to Mahayana Buddhism books, and we attended seminars together. I pored over research articles on the most effective methods of mindfulness.

Other sangha attendees began noticing me. They asked if I had always been this peaceful. My answer? "Does it matter? *This* is the only moment."

Sasha, my first client, was first my meditation partner at a Dharma weekend workshop. Afterward, we went out to coffee, where she confided in me about her messy divorce. Their post-marriage transactions included vicious fights, clothes burning on the front lawn, and even a restraining order. By contrast, at that point, Lance and I had a civil, maybe even amicable relationship. When I told Sasha about the demise of my own marriage, she was shocked.

"You didn't try to cut off his dick?"

I shook my head. I took a bite of my chocolate croissant and closed my eyes to savor the taste.

"And you're on good terms now?" she asked.

"He no longer concerns me," I said, and dabbed my lips with a napkin. "He is like an old acquaintance. He called me last week, as he does once in a while. His new wife is pregnant."

"Oh, for fuck's sake! Are you serious? How did you feel after hearing that?"

"I'm happy for them, I guess," I said, shrugging.

Sasha took a sip of her latte and sighed. "I wish I could be where you are."

"I can give you a few pointers," I offered.

She followed me home, and I spent the next hour coaching her through her anger and resentment. This wasn't that different from finding aberrations in actuarial data. We set outlier emotions aside and kept bringing the focus back to the present moment.

"Can we do this again?" she asked as she was leaving.

"I don't see why not," I said.

Long after I had quit the actuarial firm, I began leading my own workshops and retreats. I even co-wrote a *Present Mind* manual with a famous meditation teacher. Lance's new firm helped me trademark my particular approach. A year later, Lance's third wife, Elaine, became my client.

I spent years practicing and building a career on being at peace. I lapsed only a handful of times in the beginning, when more success led to more work and more clients than I could handle. But I learned how to balance it all. I didn't go looking for my black Isfahani box again until the aftermath of that strange afternoon in Roya's garage.

23. KIMIA — THE VALLEY OF UNDERSTANDING

"Do you have water?"

"No. Do you have electricity?"

"No."

We were now ready for anything. Our shoes kicking up dust, we ran all the way from Reza's house to the Simorgh. Our contagious giggles glided over the honking cars and the hurtling buses. We crossed Afif Abad Street together without a hitch. Neither did I have to drag Reza to the middle, nor Reza had to hold me back until the street was clear. We were two superheroes weaving seamlessly through passersby, invisible to the morality police.

Reza acted as if he were ten feet tall and brave like Rostam. Of course, he didn't look anything like Ferdowsi's mythical warrior, who had a fearsome beard and huge muscles, but I imagined Rostam might have had a similar nonchalant swagger. I couldn't blame Reza. He had received a perfect twenty on each of his pop quizzes, putting him at the top of his class. I watched him singing and tracing the bumpy stones on the hallway Simorgh with his fingers.

"I couldn't sleep a wink last night! I want to know what happens in the next valley," I whispered into the darkness surrounding us.

"Yeah. I couldn't sleep either. I think I ate too many dates dipped in yogurt," he said, aloud.

Frowning, I put my finger to my lips. This is what he was supposed to do to me. I was the loud, careless one. But now, he was different. While I had spent most of the past several weeks buried in a mountain of homework, he had become more popular and confident. Friends came from near and far to play with him, and his parents showered him with gifts and encouragement.

I wrinkled my nose and made a fist to knock, but Reza was too fast. Annoyed, I turned to him and pursed my lips, watching the flash of his eyes daring me to protest. The echo of the knock traveled through me. I took a deep breath and stayed quiet.

"Befarma!" I heard Baba Morshed's booming voice. "Salaam, children! I thought we would take a walk today! What do you think?" Baba Morshed stood near the door, anchoring his worn cane gently in his hand. His old dusty shoes that always sat dutifully by the door were on his feet, and a dark green shawl wrapped around him.

"But the story . . ." I looked over at his clean, empty desk.

"Oh, don't worry," said the storyteller, pointing at his head. "It's all up here!"

While I was beginning to warm up to this unexpected change, Reza looked at his hands, examining his palms like he did when he was nervous.

"Why can't we just stay here?" he asked, no longer self-assured.

"Reza Jon, you should not worry either," Baba Morshed said, holding up a paper bag. "I'm bringing the rosewater noghl candy that you like!" Reza stared at the bag, wiping his hands on his trousers distractedly.

"Well?" Baba Morshed asked with a childlike eagerness.

I looked at the old man's face, his rosy cheeks, the crinkled edges of his laughing eyes, and I didn't have to think for a second longer. "Let's go!" I said, and began climbing.

"I suppose it's settled, then." Baba Morshed's voice followed me to the top of the stairs.

At first, Reza schlepped along reluctantly. Any other time, I would have barked at him to hurry up, but I left him alone, relieved he was back to his old self. He eventually matched our buoyant steps and soon we moved as if we were floating in the air. I marveled that the limp in Baba Morshed's leg didn't at all hamper our smooth pace.

"You've got nalbeki eyes," Reza whispered to me when we arrived at Charrah Moshir Street. Whenever we went to a puppet show or watched our favorite TV programs, Reza said my eyes were wide like two nalbeki tea saucers. I joked that I had to open the doors of my eyes wide enough to invite in all that I loved. Except this wasn't our favorite show. I seemed to be entranced by the hustle and bustle of an ordinary day. My senses, five luminous fires, ablaze inside my body, demanded that I pay attention. The sky was a ridiculous turquoise color, and I could hear a symphony of distinct sounds that normally would have blurred together in the background.

We stopped near a young boy in a torn shirt selling gum and candy. The merchandise was spread out on a beat-up vinyl tablecloth. The scent of bubble gum wafted up from the ground and mixed with traffic fumes. Baba Morshed gave the boy a brand-new hundred-tooman bill and took a small candy. Before the boy could argue that he didn't have that kind of change, Baba Morshed held out his hand.

"Keep the change, son."

"Khoda omret bedeh, agha," said the smiling boy.

The wave of the boy's happiness reached me, tickling my lips. I laughed aloud, before covering my mouth and looking left and right self-consciously, aware of my surroundings. Reza's relieved expression made me feel like I had just swallowed a sliver of light. I wanted to kiss him on the cheek and thank him for being my best friend. But, alas, we were in public. I turned to the old man. "Baba Morshed, I can't wait any longer. Where did the birds go next?"

"Those who survived the fire of Love continued their difficult journey to the third valley: the Valley of Understanding," the storyteller began, pointing to the sky where a loud flock of birds had gathered on the telephone wire. "They followed Hoopoe through dangerous rainstorms, howling winds, and the burning sun. Many birds perished, and many more wished they had never taken the journey." The old man reached into his satchel and with one smooth motion scattered a handful of rice on the ground. The birds swooped in to feast.

"Look at them!" I yelped. "I've never seen them fly together like that. Finches and ducks and parakeets? Look at that! Is that a shahin bird? Like my baba?" I tugged on Reza's sleeve.

"Are you crazy? They're just pigeons!" Reza said, pulling his sleeve away.

I heard him, but I didn't want to argue. Each squawk and tweet made a clear-cut sound, resonating inside my bones. I couldn't understand their conversation, but I could swear it was about something important. "Look at the parakeet . . . have you ever seen such colors? Hey, Duckie, you're kind of far from the water, aren't you?" I thought aloud, ignoring Reza. "How is it that the shahin falcon doesn't eat the others?" I asked Baba Morshed, but he and Reza had moved near the street, watching the approach of a group of young soldiers who marched in military fatigues and shouted slogans. In the distance, several men carried a coffin covered with the flag, flowers, and a framed picture of the young man inside. The sound of their pounding steps reverberated inside my chest.

"War! War! To victory!" the soldiers shouted with their fists in the air.

I shifted my attention to the birds, but the lot of them flew away, probably spooked by the shouting that was getting nearer. They glided across the sky, their colors painting a rainbow above.

A crowd of black-clad mourners followed the young men carrying more coffins. When the man with the megaphone approached, Reza covered his ears and hid behind Baba Morshed.

"Baba Morshed, what happened next?" I shouted over the megaphone.

The old man waved his hand at the crowd. I watched with disbelief as people froze in place, their fists in the air. A young girl who had bent over to tie her shoe was motionless, with shoelaces in hand. The men balancing the coffin on their shoulders were in midstride. A fat droplet of a tear was suspended on a baby's cheek while his mother's hand was cupped centimeters away behind his back. The air around us was charged, and I could smell the impending rain. *It's like life is holding its breath.* I wanted to share that thought with Reza, but I didn't want to miss any details of the frozen sea of people. I weaved in and out of the crowd, examining people's faces up close. I touched the petals of a flower that moments ago had slipped off a coffin and was now suspended in midair. The delicate softness kissed my fingers.

"Kaveh!" I called Reza by his code name, but he didn't come. I turned, wondering. He was still behind Baba Morshed. I ran to the storyteller to see Reza's hands still covering his ears, his eyes squeezed shut. I shouted in his face, "Come on, look!" but he only turned away from me, covering himself from the assault of my voice. The storyteller watched the crowd.

"Hoopoe said: 'In the Valley of Understanding, time stops. All knowledge loses importance. In this valley, you see clearly that light and shadow are entranced in the dance of love.'" The storyteller pointed to the gigantic shadow of a bird flying over the frozen mourners. Oh, the shadow's wingspan was so enormous, there was no mistaking who it belonged to. I looked at the sky, trying to spot the Simorgh. The sky looked back at me, clear, vast, and empty, flaunting its vibrant turquoise-ness.

Baba Morshed waved his hand again. With an imperial sweep of his arm, life exhaled a sharp breath and the commotion returned. The mother rhythmically tapped her child on the back while more teardrops fell. The young girl tied her shoe and resumed walking. The mourners marched away, shouting.

I tore my eyes away from the street and searched for Reza, who was now peeking cautiously from behind Baba Morshed.

"Did you see that?" I asked, but before Reza could reply, I turned to the old man. "How did you do that, Baba Morshed?"

"Do what?" asked Reza, clearly frustrated.

His confused face and the tone of his voice rattled me. I began to question myself. Why did he look like he was miserable? Had I just imagined everything? The world was beginning to lose its vibrancy. I wanted to confer with Baba Morshed, but he was already ahead of us.

"Nothing," I said, and we fell in step behind Baba Morshed. We rounded a corner to watch floating coffins as mourners carried the dead.

"Death to Saddam!" they shouted.

Whatever was left of the magical halo surrounding me burst as a wave of pain and sadness arising from the soldiers' stomping feet reached my chest. Reza didn't look well. I wanted to hold his hand, but Baba Morshed was already kneeling next to him. The storyteller reached into his pocket and brought out a medicinal nabaat[51] and offered it to Reza. Reza put it in his mouth.

"We'd better head back," Baba Morshed said.

We followed him, my eyes focused on Reza. After a minute or two, the color came back to his cheeks and he returned my gaze. I squeezed his hand. Behind us moved the wave of coffins draped with Iranian flags. Beyond the coffins, birds chirped on the telephone wires. In the midst of mourners, a baby smiled at me.

"This is so sad and yet so beautiful. How is this possible?" I said to no one.

"Life, Rumi, life! A well-lived life isn't absent of pain. No, life is much larger than that. It includes pain, it includes sorrow, heartbreak and shekast,"[52] Baba Morshed said. "All states are sacred, and we must treat them each with the dignity they deserve." As I listened, my eyes met a weeping woman, her face twisted in grief.

---

51   rock candy
52   breaking defeat

The anguished look in her eyes pained me from my heart to the tips of my fingers.

"Like Molana says, 'Did you know your suffering is your treasure? Alas, you are the veil covering your treasure.' When you look beyond reason and belief, you begin to find your treasure. You begin to understand." I heard the storyteller's voice. My eyes glided back and forth between the woman and the turquoise sky. The same strange silence of the night at the square shrouded me with a gentle embrace.

I BANGED ON THE Hand of Fatemeh door knocker.

Sara and Dara
Looking at a map
Lightning thunder
clap, clap, clap
Two fell down
One didn't rise
Which one? Which one?
Tell me no lies.

I sang to the door, waiting. I knocked again. "Reza! Reza!"

He cracked the door open.

"Are you coming? Let's go!"

"I can't. I have a lot of, um, stuff to do."

"What kind of stuff?"

"I'm helping my maman and baba with chores."

"Let me in, then. I'll hang out for a little before I go. We can make a quick stone tower," I said, grabbing the edge of the door to let myself in. But Reza firmly held the door in place.

"I can't. Um, I have to go," he said, looking down, his face flushing. And before I could say anything, he shut the door. "Bye, Kimia," I heard him say behind the closed door.

I opened my mouth to shout something, but I was at a loss.

Before that fateful night of the missile attack at the square, we had built countless borj e sangi rock towers in his courtyard. Reza really liked the game. Plus, there was little chance we would get into trouble at the sanctuary of Pirooz courtyard. We had spent our after-school playdates and summer evenings searching for that perfect stone—the one that topped the tower without collapsing it. Of course, since we'd found the underground world of Baba Morshed, we hadn't spent any time on our old hobby. Reza had a lot of friends now, but I thought he would be happy to play at least one game.

I pulled a splinter off the closed door and began walking. Could it be that, unlike the old Reza, the new one was offendable? He hadn't given me any indications. Was he still unwell? He didn't look it. On our walk home the day before, he'd said it was his gorging on yogurt and dates that had got him. He said, "I'm already good, but tomorrow, I'll be aali, brilliant."

He didn't ask, and I was too embarrassed to tell him about my possible hazyun hallucinations. Now that he was popular and could have any friend he wanted, I didn't want him to dismiss me as a little girl with an overactive imagination.

BABA MORSHED DIPPED HIS feathered quill into a heavy brass Qajar inkwell. He scribbled in the big book, the quill dancing as he wrote. I sipped my fragrant tea and perused the bookshelf. There were many fascinating books, but I wasn't interested in any of them—I was just biding my time until Baba Morshed finished.

Without looking up, the storyteller said, "Reza's busy with other things today, I imagine?"

"Oh, yes, he's got chores," I said, pushing a book back into place on the shelf. "I don't think he saw any of the stuff I saw." I headed over to the storyteller. "Baba Morshed, raast begoo. Tell me the truth. Was it my imagination or did you stop time?"

The storyteller paused his writing and looked up. "Ah, Rumi! The magic of the story all depends on you, the listener." I was about to press him, but I considered the possibility that I had some magical power Reza didn't possess. Before I could say anything, the storyteller asked, "Are you ready to continue?"

I set down my tea and jumped in the chair next to him.

"Baleh!"

Baba Morshed set the quill aside and turned the pages of the great book. He adjusted his wire-rimmed glasses. "The birds were nearly halfway through their journey," he said. "Out of the thousands who had started, only a few hundred were left. And now it was time to enter the Valley of Understanding."

Baba Morshed covered my eyes with his callused hands. I gasped as I found myself looking into what I guessed was the Valley of Understanding. The vast space looked like it had been scorched. Besides Parrot hopping and fretting nearby, the place seemed empty. The sky was the same faint gray color of ash and I couldn't tell where the ground stopped and the sky began. Unlike the first two valleys, there was no cacophony of birds, and other than the faint sound of the breeze over smoking ashes, the valley was as quiet as an untold story.

Baba Morshed broke the silence. "The Valley of Understanding has neither a beginning nor an end, and the span to tread it is beyond measure."

I was no longer looking into the valley but standing in it, the old man next to me, his eyes scanning the far distance. Over the horizon, a speck grew and grew. It became bigger, eventually shaping into a bird flying toward us. It was Hoopoe, with his majestic orange-and-black crown. He perched on a naked burnt branch near Parrot. With eyes as black as the ink on the storyteller's quill, he looked at Parrot and then at me. His voice echoed inside my head.

"The body, like the soul, is either growing or declining. But in no way is growth better than decline. When the sun of under-standing shines on a subject, its true worth becomes clear. The furnace of the world becomes a flower garden, and in every moment, a hidden treasure is found." Hoopoe gestured with one outstretched wing to the scorched empty space around us.

Thousands of tiny sprouts began poking out of the ashes, growing rapidly into different flowers and plants. The wind moved the lustrous flowers back and forth, bringing me the scent of Mohammadi roses.

"She who strives to understand will see the walnut in its hard shell. She will no longer be preoccupied with herself, but in each atom she will discover the whole world. Understanding, for each traveler, comes in a rare parcel. You must recognize that parcel and forgo all temporary knowledge. Some will attempt to possess it, but understanding is too clever to be captured," Hoopoe continued.

Shiny gold bubbles emanated from all around Hoopoe. Inside each bubble a tiny treasure glowed. Birds from above the lush new valley swooped down, chirping, squawking, flapping their wings. Magpie, Crow, and Starling chased after the bubbles, but every time they caught one, it burst into nothingness.

I looked to Baba Morshed for an explanation, but he gestured toward Parrot, who was nervously picking at his chest feathers.

"Some will see understanding as a threat to safety. This will only trap one inside the prison of ignorance," said Hoopoe.

Suddenly, a sword made of bright light launched toward Parrot's chest. I closed my eyes and sank my head into the old man's arm.

"Look. Don't be afraid," whispered the old man.

I cracked my eyes to see the panicked parrot shriek and fly to the edge of the valley. The sword had disappeared. Parrot perched at the edge and when Hoopoe beckoned him to come forth, he flapped his wings tentatively toward me and the old man. The sword materialized, meeting him halfway.

"Look, daughter, dear, as soon as the Sword of Understanding approaches Tooti,[53] he goes to pieces. He can't see the difference between reality and illusion. He can't go on to the next valley, and yet, he can't go back to his old life either."

Tooti flew again to the edge, but stopped short from leaving the valley. Magpie, exhausted from chasing bubbles, sat with Tooti and watched as her friends continued their pursuit. A giant bubble containing a perfect gold pyramid came near. The magpie sat still.

"Hurry! This one is so easy to catch! Get it, Magpie!" I shouted.

Magpie didn't move. And when the bubble nearly touched her feather, she closed her eyes. Right then, a quiet flash exploded all around her. I gasped and ran closer to Magpie, the old man following me. I heaved a sigh of relief when I saw Magpie was unharmed. Not only that, she appeared to have been bathed in gold dust, and I could swear she was smiling. I had an irresistible urge to touch her, but as I extended my hand, she looked at her sparkling feathers once more and flew off. With my hand still extended, I watched other birds, moving like dozens of winged golden suns, follow Magpie into the horizon. They too must have passed the test of Understanding. Tooti sat on the edge, his eyes also tracking the departing birds. A single tear fell near his feet.

"Oh no. So what is Hoopoe going to do? Just leave him behind?" I asked. Parrot looked so forlorn, I wanted to cry.

"Watch!" said Baba Morshed.

Hoopoe was pulling a feather out of his crown. He flew to the edge to Parrot. "Light this on fire if life becomes unbearable," Hoopoe said. Tooti thanked Hoopoe and bade the other bird farewell.

"Akhey, poor Tooti!" I cried.

---

53   parrot

WE WERE BACK AT the storyteller's desk when the great clock's bell rang in the stillness of the room. I knew better than to ask about the fate of the parrot. Baba Morshed would just tell me to be patient. I quietly put on my Islamic uniform and scarf and headed toward the door. "I'll see you next time."

The old man waved. "Khoda negahdar. Goodbye."

$\mathcal{P}$ART III

Listen to the story of the reed
As it laments the pain of separation

Since they have cut me from my reed bed
My wails bring tears to both woman and man

—Rumi

24. KIMIA — SHIRAZ, 2009

I AM A STRANGER in my own land. This not-belonging winks at me wherever I turn, as it did when I first moved to America.

Collapsed like a rag doll in the back seat of the taxi, jet-lagged and exhausted with my clothes reeking of traffic fumes, I watch familiar buildings and cypresses zoom by. I lean my head against the window and close my eyes, recalling the game I played as a girl—I would close my eyes, wishing to disappear. Opening my eyes, it was always deflating to find my "un-disappeared" self. No matter, the thrill of a few moments of dark uncertainty was worth the disappointment.

"Where is she from?" The question snaps my eyes open. It is the mustached cab driver addressing Roya through the rearview mirror.

"Where is she from?" he inquires again a bit louder. I lift my head to listen. He is talking about me.

"My daughter is from here, agha. She is a Shirazi, born and raised," answers Roya as if I am a child and she is speaking on my behalf. Her accent has taken on the contagious Shirazi drawl of the cab driver.

"I thought she was a foreigner. She doesn't act like an Iranian," says the driver, still not convinced of my origin.

"Things change, agha. Things change," says Roya.

I don't belong. The cabbie knows it too. I lean my head against the window again.

Upon arriving at Tehran International Airport, we had come across Jimmy in the foreigner line at the airport. He leaned against his suitcase, thumbing through his English-Persian dictionary. Roya was about to say hello when two bearded men in civilian clothing and greasy hair motioned me to step aside. They wanted my passport. The dreadful chill knot in my belly expanded, seizing my breath. I fetched my passport with trembling hands. Flipping through the pages with little attention, the men exchanged glances before asking me to follow them to their office. Before I could react, Roya stepped in front of me.

I recalled my mother slapping me without hesitation when two paasdar guards had come over to complain about a strand of hair poking from under my scarf. I must have been around nine. I had covered my exposed hair immediately when I had sensed the guards' presence, but the damage was already done. My mother hadn't taken the time to even look at me. She had smacked me as she would smack an annoying mosquito, so she could go back to what she was doing.

I was suddenly nine again, bracing myself instinctively. But this time, Roya barked at the guards. "What do you want with my girl?"

The older man coughed. My mother's interference had surprised us all.

"Khahar,[54] we have a few questions—" the younger man began to say before he was cut off.

"Don't sister me, mister. She has nothing to say to you. We came here legally. After years, we are back in our home country. The place we love and cherish. And this is how you treat us?" She hurled her words like stones at them, her volume rising with each sentence. I watched her small, hunched body become tall and

---

54   sister

commanding. The authority of her words stopped the men, their faces frozen in shock.

"You have any problems, you tell us right here, right now." She paused after each word as if it were a lashing on the offenders. Her fury stirred inside, gathering more strength from their incredulous expressions. "Nobody's going to your office," she declared. She spat the words *your office* the way old Shirazi men spat on the sidewalk. She snatched my passport out of the stunned man's hand before grabbing my wrist. She pulled me along, reciting,

> "'They smell your breath,
> lest you might have said I love you
> They smell your heart
> These are strange times, my love
> The butchers are stationed at each crossroad
> with blood-stained clubs and cleavers'"[55]

THE CHAMRAN HOTEL BUILDING towers over us. The modern architecture, sleek and phallic, reminds me more of a current American city than the Shiraz I grew up in. But the familiar soulful eyes of strangers, their hand gestures, the smell of barbecued corn, and the street noises plunge me, against my will, into my childhood. It must be true that early memories imprint differently, for the sights and sounds seem more immediate and less filtered. In my belly screams the same ulcer I thought I had left behind with my childhood. I put my hand on my stomach and breathe. *Nothing matters but this moment.*

Two young boys on bicycles zip past me. Before the Revolution, my father had bought me a beautiful orange bicycle with training wheels. I practiced riding every day after kindergarten as my father ran alongside me, laughing and encouraging me. As soon as I

---

55   From Ahmad Shamlou's poetry collection (1925–2000)

learned to balance on two wheels, I was on my own, racing all the boys. I was the fastest one in the neighborhood until one day, Reza asked me to switch bikes. That day, Reza won the race and we both learned it was my orange bike that was the real champion. Not long after, the Islamic Republic decreed that a girl on a bicycle was too provocative to be legal. In all my years in America, I never got back on a bicycle. It's not until the bikes brush past me that I begin craving to pick up where I left off—somewhere not far from Chamran Hotel, nestled near the Poshteh Moleh, on a dirt road, lifetimes ago.

I see Reza's face as we ride together—he is hunched over his bike handles, his hair swept by the wind when he turns to me and smiles. The sharp tip of the old pain pierces my heart. *I am here, now.* I breathe deeply again. Roya, stooped and travel-worn, needs my help. I take her arm and walk her through the lobby of the hotel I booked against her fervent insistence.

"Ali has invited us to his house," she argued. "He has such a lovely place. And all those empty rooms . . . It would brighten his heart to have us as guests." But I wouldn't hear of it.

"You used to love being with Ali. You're the one who gave him the nickname Amu Doctor. What is this Americanized, 'I need my space' goh o gand?"[56] she added.

We are both notoriously stubborn and hate to lose, but in the end, I won this battle.

As soon as we get settled in the room, Roya says, "The concierge told me they're serving tea in the lobby now. Let's go."

The hotel tea tastes far different from the black tea I drink in San Diego. But really, even the air is different here. Roya, who looks more refreshed, is happy she has a Persian crossword puzzle to entertain her. We're both wearing raincoats and scarves, covering our curves and hair. My scalp itches beneath the hijab I haven't worn in decades. I lean back on the European-style sofa and close my eyes, playing the disappearing game once again.

A fuzzy image of a skinny old man with kind eyes appears

---

56 crap

before me. I blink, realizing my eyes are open. He smiles and his eyes fill with tears. Before I can gasp, my mother, having abandoned her puzzle, surges forth and kisses the man on both cheeks.

"Amu Doctor," I hear myself say in disbelief. The one person I wanted to avoid is right in front of me. I had hoped I could somehow prepare myself before meeting him. I don't want to see him. Not like this.

His face bares no trace of knowledge about what his presence means to me. I shoot a disdainful glance at Roya.

Amu Doctor steps forward and opens his arms. I offer my hand to shake.

"Golam . . ." Amu Doctor weeps, hugging me tightly. The concierge and the hotel guests he is helping pause to watch us, but Amu Doctor doesn't notice or care.

My downright offensive rejection—choosing a hotel over his hospitality—means nothing to him. He chalks my rudeness up to living in America for too long. He has parked his classic Paykan automobile right outside the lobby and won't take no for an answer.

As I pack my belongings in the room I chose and paid for, a cold tide of anger, the kind I haven't felt in years, rises within me. I want to scream at my mother for going behind my back and calling Amu Doctor. But I settle on not making eye contact. She holds the handle of the suitcase she didn't bother to unpack, humming a song about crows coming home from school at dusk. I used to love that song, but right now I don't want to see or hear my mother.

She takes the front seat as we get in the car. As a child I treasured everything about being inside this old Paykan—sitting in the back, delighted that the reliable moon chased us all the way home. I loved watching the shop signs and apartment windows glow against the darkness and inventing stories about the occupants, their lives, and what they might be doing at that moment. Like the old times, Roya and Amu Doctor are already absorbed in conversation.

"They just called in the results and they say Ahmadinejad won," Amu Doctor says. "There is a great silence in Shiraz. Everyone is stunned."

Roya clucks her tongue. "Of course they'd rig the results. They deny even a morsel of freedom to the people. Dirt of the world on their heads. People are not going to just stand by and watch . . ."

I press against the window, my warm forehead on the cool glass. I'm that small girl again, half-listening to Amu Doctor talk to the grown-up in the front passenger seat. But for the first time, I don't want to be here.

As with most Iranians, hospitality is embedded in Amu Doctor's DNA, but as he put our bags in the trunk, he told me he needed to be around me. "Seeing your face enlivened my heart. It's so good to be with my daughter."

Does he have to be so goddamn candid and vulnerable? This is exactly what I was hoping to avoid until after my jet lag subsided and I could be more in control. I squeeze my eyes shut and try metta, the Buddhist loving-kindness meditation, to relax and increase my empathy and compassion. But being here in Shiraz is too disorienting.

In my first years in America, I missed Amu Doctor and Azita Khanom and Reza and my father and . . . and . . . and . . . to the point that out of nowhere, the world would spin around me. Clinging to the hallway wall of my new school, I would will myself to the bathroom, where I tried to wrestle my breath from the clutches of longing. For months, I desperately sought their voices and manners in the people walking in and out of my new life. But there was nothing to remind me of them. Now, sitting in Amu Doctor's car, I wish to fast-forward somehow. I wish I could forget this moment.

LIKE A GHOST, I circle the fountain where many splendid borj e sangi towers were cobbled together ages ago. My body impulsively bends to inspect the stones, but I right myself before anyone notices. The courtyard hasn't changed, yet it appears smaller, and like myself, somehow vacant.

Amu Doctor wants me to take Reza's room, but without looking inside, I switch with Roya. I can hear the echoes of our laughter sprint down the hallway and disappear inside that sea-green room. A numbness reaches in and grabs my tongue. "You'll be more comfortable there," I say mechanically, forcing out the words. "And you can look out over the garden."

Roya begins to protest, but despite my detached tone, she can see how serious I am. And she probably feels guilty about undermining my wishes to stay at the hotel.

"'Did you know your suffering is your treasure? Did you know YOU are the veil covering your treasure?'" Roya softly sings Rumi as she turns toward Reza's room. I shake my head. Subtlety has never been her thing. The wheels on her suitcase sing along, rolling down the empty hallway.

I retreat to the bathroom, trying to regroup, but the sky-blue sink contains more memories.

Lunch is ready, I would hear Azita Khanom announce. Scrubbing my small hands, I would watch a tornado of dirt swirl down the drain.

My turn, Reza would yell from the other side of the door. I would smile watching myself in the mirror. I would make him wait.

I sit at the edge of the bathtub, taking shallow, ragged breaths. I pry my eyes off the sink and watch my hands: they tremble as they clutch a knife I have snuck away from the kitchen. *What am I doing?* My grip slackens, and the knife drops on the floor. The sound of metal hitting the tiles is unbearable. I crawl to the toilet. The hand-painted Persian tiles spin around me as I retch a bitter brew.

"Don't," I whisper, peeling myself off the toilet. Cutting only works if I allow sufficient time to pass between sessions. I angle my wrist toward the light. The three thin lines are still pink. I have to get through this on my own. Slumped over the sink, I splash my face with cool water. I avoid the mirror on my way back to the edge of the bathtub. I pick up the knife, hide it in my bag, and turn the bathroom knob.

25. KIMIA — SHIRAZ, 1981

I CARESSED THE STONE in my hand. My body heat had warmed it to a cozy temperature and the round edges felt soothing against the muscles of my palm. Putting the stone against my cheek, I knew it was the right one. Whether my cheek could calculate the physics of how the stone fared in preserving the integrity of the stack wasn't my concern. The cheek method worked. Most of the time.

I eyed the tall tower that stood before me, holding my breath. I placed the stone on top of the structure as if I was simultaneously letting go of my cherished gem and avoiding detonating a bomb. The high-rise stood still before us.

"Aha!" I exhaled and held my still hand out for Reza to inspect.

"Steady as a surgeon, Reza Khan," I said with a smirk, and collapsed back on the ground, resting on my forearms. "Let's see what you can do. La, la, la . . ." Flicking my chin at the borj e sangi, I egged him on.

Reza, frowning as if solving a complex equation, searched for the perfect stone. Out of our made-up games, this was one challenge he had a decent shot of winning. But he seemed distracted.

It had been a full week since he'd refused to go with me to Baba Morshed's. With my double homework, it wasn't easy for me to slip away, so I had to bide my time until I had the chance to go to the storyteller again. But I wasn't about to give up on Reza. After that morning, I had knocked on his door every day after school. He made excuses each time: Sunday, he had to cram for a test. Monday, Mahmood was coming over. Tuesday, he had a headache. A headache—for God's sake!

My mother and Arman were away that Friday morning, and I had time. I banged on Reza's door, threatening to sing, the way that got me in trouble at school. "Either you let me in or the paasdar guards are going to arrest me and it'll be all your fault. I'm going to start in three, two, one . . ." I yelled at his door.

He let me in. It was awkward at first. We both concentrated on the game and avoided talking about that day with Baba Morshed. But within a few minutes, I felt comfortable enough to tease him. "Hey! This isn't chess. Are you going to pick a stone or not?"

Reza furrowed his eyebrows and picked a round, light cream-colored stone.

"Are you sure you want to use that one? It doesn't look like the most stable rock to me . . . ," I said in a singsong voice.

Gripping the stone, he sat on the edge of the courtyard fountain and gently placed it on top of the tower. For a split second, the structure looked solid and then—bam! Before he could let out the breath he was holding, the whole thing collapsed. We both screamed. A couple of doves flew out of the oak tree.

"Are you kids all right?" Azita Khanom shouted, running into the courtyard.

"Oh, yeah. We're fine." I forced out the words between bouts of laughter. "Sorry for the noise, Azita Khanom."

"I'm just glad no one got hurt," she said, caressing my cheek with the back of her hand.

This is one of the many reasons I adored Azita Khanom. While Roya would have slapped me for scaring her, Azita

Khanom went back inside without giving any impression she was at all upset.

Reza helped me gather the stones, already beginning to withdraw. We placed them neatly along the edge of the garden, the bigger stones before the smaller ones. Our silence was magnified by the courtyard fountain bubbling behind us. I wanted to ask what was wrong, but I was too late.

"Oh, well. You better go before you get into trouble. I know you have loads of homework to do," Reza said without meeting my eyes. He stood and brushed the dirt off his hands.

"I stayed up late last night and finished my homework," I said. "I'm going to see Baba Morshed."

"Baba Morshed's again?"

"Why don't you come with me? The story is getting really scary!"

"That story is for kids. Besides, Morshed is so antirevolution—I could . . . we could get into big trouble hanging out there." He dipped his hands in the fountain and dried them on his pants and continued quietly, "I'm on top of my class now. Me and Mahmood . . ."

"Listen to you! You sound like the falcon in the story, all worried about losing his important position at the palace!" I was burning with jealousy at the mention of the dodgeball team captain. Reza and I had been friends as long as we could remember, and now it was "me and Mahmood"?

I waited for him to defend himself, to call me a name, and to argue, but Reza didn't reply. His unprecedented silence and the way he folded his arms and turned his face away stung more than any insult he might've flung back at me. The recognition that, for the first time, I wasn't welcome in Reza's world sank to the bottom of my belly. I had no choice but to grab my backpack.

"Have fun not getting into trouble," I said before storming out the door.

I regretted lashing out the way I had as soon as I stepped into the street. I had gone there with the intention of not mentioning the storyteller. We were just going to play our game. Instead, I had insulted Reza. At the same time, I was so mad at him. He liked Mahmood better.

I HAD ASSUMED THE storyteller never left his house. When I arrived, the door was ajar and I let myself in.

"Salaam!" I yelled.

"Salaam," Myna replied from the top of her favorite tree.

"What's going on, Myna?"

"Baba Morshed isn't here," she said, her voice sounding like a woman with a Tehrani accent. In the beginning, after we'd grown more comfortable with the storyteller, Reza and I had been curious to talk to Myna. Once, we spent nearly an hour asking her to imitate different people. *That dumb Reza!* I thought, frowning, wishing he was there with me.

"Where is Baba Morshed?" I asked Myna.

"I don't ask, and he doesn't tell me." She flew down and perched on the edge of the desk.

I glanced at the empty place where the giant book sat. I had never felt so far away from Reza, all because of the storyteller, and he wasn't even home.

"Rumi koochikeh,[57] why do you look so perturbed?" Myna tilted her head sideways, looking at me with the dark pupil of her golden eye.

"Kaveh and I had a fight," I said, feeling a bit strange about confiding in a bird.

"Then aashti kon. Make up!" she said without hesitation.

"It's not that simple—" I began to protest, but she cut me off.

"It is that simple."

---

57   little

I was about to argue, but I remembered the way Baba Morshed had taught me to pause before responding.

"I left my best friend in Hindustan. I still miss her," Myna said. "Most of the time when friends fight, they forget what the fight was about. They just remember the feeling of being cut off from someone they love."

26. ROYA — SHIRAZ, 2009

I'M ON REZA'S BED, flipping through old pictures. His sweet presence still lingers in the air, like he is going to burst into the room at any moment, his guileless face lighting up with a wide smile.

Most photos are of Reza and Kimia, looking back at me through the years. *How did my sulky, lanky tomboy in shorts and a Bruce Lee T-shirt become a striking woman with long lustrous hair and feminine curves?*

I close my eyes and imagine Reza as a young man, with a strong jawline and broad shoulders, his eyes still shiny and kind, like his father's. I imagine him sitting across from me on the bed, running a translucent hand to smooth away his hair from his forehead. He isn't here to talk—just to keep me company and look at old pictures.

I find a photo of me, Shahin, Jalal Jon, Azita Khanom, and Amu Doctor sitting in our living room of our old house. The picture has captured us smiling, but I remember how perturbed we all were that night. Arman, being the photographer, isn't in the photo, and Reza and Kimia were already in bed.

We were in the middle of the post-dinner tea, noon khamei,

and discussion, but unlike the evenings before the Revolution, we didn't talk philosophy or poetry. The topic of conversation was a morbid one—the latest wave of executions. The state-sponsored newspapers printed photos of the bullet-ridden bodies of the most prominent victims on the front page. The regime had even hanged people in the street, a barbaric act that caused a miscarriage for Manijeh Khanom. She was heading to work when she came across a body hanging from a scaffold. She went back home to vomit and to lose her baby.

"We did this together," I say aloud to Reza's room. We decided to put an outsider in charge of our country. The man in charge promised more freedom than we would know what to do with. He promised more jobs. He promised to end corruption. What we didn't know was that our revolt against the establishment was going to set us back 1,400 years.

Like a dream that has lost its way to become a kaboos,[58] it started with a murmur of worry, a tiny fracture in our boundless optimism. Whispers surfaced that opposing views wouldn't be tolerated by our new government. Surely that was paranoid nonsense, we thought. But before we could remember our former civil rights, newspapers were shut down, and people of Baha'i faith were targeted as enemies of the state. How could so much calamity befall a people so fast? It must have been some sort of jadoo janbal—the darkest of dark magic.

Those who rose to positions of power were tragically similar in their rampant sexism, bigotry, and lack of qualifications. Women's rights were cut in half. When we took to the streets to protest, we were tear-gassed, hit over the head with batons, and jailed. The men who stood for us were also hit, maybe even more severely, and jailed. Margaret Atwood watched silently from a corner and took notes for her *Handmaid's Tale*.

"Nothing good can ever come out of mixing religion with government—I've always maintained that," Jalal Jon whispered

---

58   nightmare

the night the photo was taken. He was the only one in the group who hadn't gone out to protest. He didn't agree with much of the Shah's tactics, but he never saw some akhund[59] as a savior. "There are a lot of decent clerics out there . . . educated, very reasonable . . . but I bet those men would never want to rule a country," he said.

"I agree, but I don't think we can go back to having a traditional monarchy either," Azita responded. "What we really need is a viable democracy."

"Can we handle it? I mean as a people?" Amu Doctor asked.

"You know, we did just fine under Mossadegh. I was a barely a teenager and bought stocks in our new nationalized oil. Everyone was so energized and involved," Azita said.

"But it didn't last," said Shahin. "The problem is Western interference. The British and the CIA overthrew Mossadegh and we just took it. This whole mess would not have happened if they hadn't staged a coup." He swept his hand over the newspaper.

Arman walked in the room, his hair newly buzz-cut. Everyone drank their tea.

"Arman Jon, take a picture?" Amu Doctor said, handing Arman his fancy camera.

Arman's eyes lit up, "Sure, Amu Jon!"

Everyone posed, smiling.

---

59   mullah

27. KIMIA — SHIRAZ, 2009

JIMMY, THE MAN WE met at Heathrow Airport, is here. In the last two days, the post-election strife has spiraled into massive protests and the authorities have expelled most foreign journalists. Even though internet sites and cellular service have been disabled on and off, footage of thousands of Mousavi supporters who are convinced the election was rigged has been all over social media. Government forces have met them with pepper spray, tear gas, and batons. Rumor has it hundreds have been arrested and several have even been killed.

No matter how much one prepares, or how often one is exposed to it, violence is a shock to the system. I wonder again why I came back to Iran.

Jimmy's boss had arranged for his return, but rather than waiting in Tehran until his flight to London, he hopped on the bus to Shiraz, using Amu Doctor's address that Roya had given him. We are all concerned for his safety, but he has assured us he is working within the bounds of the Islamic law. "As long as I don't cover the protests, I'm fine," he said. "So, rather than being cooped up in my hotel, I decided to come visit you lovely people."

"And we're so happy you did," Amu Doctor said.

"I'll still return the day after tomorrow as scheduled, but this time I'm hoping to take the plane to Tehran. My bum couldn't handle another fourteen-hour bus ride," Jimmy said.

Amu Doctor has taken a liking to Jimmy. He calls him Jimmy the journalist or JJ for short. My mother and I have followed suit. Now, Amu Doctor and Roya are teaching him to make bite-size tacos with the fresh naan sangak they bought earlier from the noonvai. Inside the naan they pack a lump of sheep feta, one soaked walnut, and sprigs of tarragon and basil from the garden. They show him how to wash the bite down with straight black tea. They reminisce about the good old days, the days before the war, before the Revolution.

I take slow sips of my tea, focusing on the taste and the soothing warmth penetrating through the glass of the estekan. I'm hopeful, as after my rough transition to Amu Doctor's house, I fell into a dreamless slumber. My body is beginning to adjust to the time change, but I still can't completely relax around my mother.

"What do you think of my country?" she asks JJ.

"Where shall I begin? Everyone said, 'Be prepared, there are always complications in Iran,' but other than having to go home without a report, I can't complain about anything. So many people have gone out of their way to help me and welcome me. The food, the architecture, and the sheer beauty have surpassed my expectations. And I love, *love* the passion! I didn't see the clashes between the Basiji militia and the protesters, but I talked to plenty of angry men and women. I'm terribly sad for how these intelligent and creative people are risking their lives just to have their vote count."

"Good," Roya says, her voice full of hope. "Maybe the world will take notice. Maybe this time, things will change."

"You think there will be a challenge to the results?" JJ asks.

"Roya Jon, even in America you have had problems with your presidential elections," Amu Doctor says. "This is Iran—do you really think things will change?"

I SWEAR, THE OLD men of my childhood have never left the chai khooneh. They are still reclined against the handmade cushions, sipping tea from nalbeki and smoking hookahs. Maybe it is the way sunbeams cut through the smoke or seeing Reza's smile in Amu Doctor as he tells stories. Whatever it is, I'm brought back to the last time I was here. My hijab tightens against my throat, and I excuse myself and head to the restroom.

I return more poised, making my way through centuries of rosewater and tobacco smell running in the veins of the place. Back at our table, JJ and my mother are speaking in Farsi.

"They gave you a hard time?" Jimmy says. "That delightful customs agent was quite gentle putting my travel bag on the counter. I was ready for the TIA legendary red tape everyone warned me about, but he only gave it a glance before giving it back to me."

"Well, they treated us, their own countrymen, worse than foreigners," Roya says, as I take my seat. "I had heard of these rishoo[60] agents who home in on pretty girls, just so they can inter-rogate them and maybe even send them to jail, where who knows what could happen. I was ready for them. But they searched our bags for two hours."

"It was not two hours," I interject, pulling down my sleeve.

"It was a very long time," Roya says. Like many people in our family, she exaggerates. She doesn't give it much thought, as to stop it is unnatural, like trying to suppress a sneeze.

The server brings our orders. JJ is soon devouring his frozen dessert doused in rosewater. He has learned to pronounce its name with a Shirazi accent: paloodeh Shirazi.

"This takes me back to my summers at Lough Erne Lake, where

---

60   beardie

I sat with my mates on the boardwalk with a cup of ice cream in hand," he says. "We talked *Star Wars* and sports. I wasn't interested in either, but the cold sweet taste made any subject delightful. Good thing I shed a few pounds before this trip, because I know I'll gain them back."

"Well, I have brought Kimia here since she was small. So many good memories . . ." Roya says before her words drift off.

When it is clear Roya isn't going to finish her thought, as she proceeds to eat her dessert, JJ points to the wall with his spoon. "Wow, that's harsh!"

We all look at the mural of the beheaded woman. "Damn! What did she do to deserve that?" he asks.

"That's exactly what I asked when I was four years old." The words rush out of my mouth. I can't pack them back in.

"And?" JJ waits.

"I told her she was beheaded because she had an untidy room," Roya says. "Not my proudest moment." She puts her hand on my knee.

Across from us, two little girls draw pictures with their crayons while their parents chat. The younger girl waves at JJ. He and Amu Doctor wave back with enthusiasm, but Roya continues to stare at the mural, and I, ever so subtly, reclaim my knee.

"I want to make an excuse and say that I was under much stress. But it was wrong," Roya says to no one.

I have never witnessed my mother admit to a wrongdoing. Ever.

I take a bite of my paloodeh and try to ignore the beginning of the hairline fissure in my concrete image of my mother. Everyone looks to me for a response, but I don't have any words. I smile a broad smile and focus on the pleasant coolness of the dessert. But rather than enjoying the moment, I taste my childhood. I taste friendship. I taste heartbreak. I push my cup aside.

"We all have made mistakes, Roya Jon," says Amu Doctor. "It's no use delving in the past. *Gozasht!*" He turns to JJ. "You know this already, but that's a word that means, 'it's in the past.' It also means forgiveness. If you think about it, getting past something is giving it to the past, forgiving it."

"I've never thought about it that way! But it's true," JJ says, bracing his cup with both hands. "I have a lot of gozashting to do."

THE LINGERING BUZZ OF the chai khooneh follows us onto the street. We walk slowly in the cool afternoon air, taking in the scene. Roya appears especially enlivened as she saunters through the familiar streets, more upright and with the same resolve of her youth. Remnants of green banners cling to the bushes. A couple of workers paint over a billboard of Mousavi while a political poster lifts in a gust of wind to the trees. Shops along the way have the same arched doorways I often dream of. Inside those doorways, proprietors add pleasure to their transactions through bargain and taarof. Customers respond in kind with a mixture of pleasantries and deal-making acumen.

"Is that safe?" asks JJ, pointing at a boy hanging halfway out of a speeding bus.

"Yes, of course. He's very good at his job," Amu Doctor says, laughing. "He works for the bus driver. He shouts out stops along the bus route."

Three young girls, green painted on their cheeks, nearly crash into us. With sullen looks on their pretty faces, they don't even notice the near collision.

"Green was Mousavi's color," Amu Doctor says. "We thought he was going to win hands down."

He pauses and we all hear the sounds of chanting in the distance.

"Listen!" Amu Doctor says.

We head toward the raised voices. *"No Gaza, no Lebanon. I die only for Iran."* My steps are reluctant at first, but the faraway chants slip inside my own veins, compelling me to find the protesters and join them.

Amu Doctor turns to my mother. "Are you all right, Roya Jon?"

"Never been better!" she says, keeping her eyes straight ahead. "Remember when we marched together during the Revolution?"

I think of the days before the Shah fell—women wearing colorful shirts and dresses, their hair uncovered, marching along with men sporting neckties and mustaches, fists in the air, smiling. Our neighbors and families spilled into the streets to protest, everyone, even the kids, convinced that a revolution was the best thing for them, the best thing for their country. With one fist in the air and my other hand holding Reza's, I had joined the crowds demanding a regime change.

"Independence, freedom, Islamic Republic," we chanted.

One time when gunshots erupted, my mother and I took shelter in a jewelry store in the Jewish neighborhood. We held on to each other as we peeked outside, watching people run for cover. When it was all over and we stepped out onto the eerily silent street, I stared at the dried blood on the sidewalk.

I remember sitting motionless outside the living room, my ear glued to the door, the night Arman caught me eavesdropping. I begged him not to tell on me, and to my surprise, he relented. The content of the adults' conversation was beyond my grasp, but the gravity of their words seeped through the living room door and into my ear.

"If you think about it, this is not unlike the French Revolution," Dayi Jalal was telling others. "In both cases, people became increasingly frustrated by the ineptitude of the monarchy and the continued decadence of the aristocracy. This resentment, coupled with burgeoning enlightenment ideas in the case of the French and an Islamic democracy for Iranians, fueled the revolts."

The next day, I relayed what I could remember to Masht Aziz, the janitor. "You cannot have a religious democracy that serves everyone justly," I argued, mimicking Dayi Jalal's passion.

We were so fortunate Masht Aziz was a decent man and didn't get my parents in trouble for hosting such discussions.

The protest chants are getting louder. *"Death to the dictator,"* the crowd now shouts. As we walk toward the marchers, I wonder what percentage of the first-generation protesters were later persecuted and killed by the regime they helped bring into power. I wonder if there are any secret records of the fallen children of the Revolution—the refugees, the tortured, the missing, the jailed, and the dead. What if a long scroll of that data written with immaculate calligraphy is locked somewhere, say, a black box in the belly of the Sleeping Man Mountain?

Following my mother's long, purposeful strides, I realize she is not the same person who, shortly after the Revolution, cursed herself and my dad for ever setting foot in the street. She is not the same jaded woman who years later had agreed with Dayi Jalal's conclusion—in France, illiterate masses had risen only to allow the elite intellectuals to rule, whereas in Iran, the elite intellectuals had revolted only to bring the illiterate commoners into power. Now, thirty years later, she is completely convinced that this new revolt is the answer. I have had enough of her capricious and misguided enthusiasm. Plus, she seems fine. She doesn't need me. I can go back to Amu Doctor's, pack my bags, and head straight to the airport.

But my next step brings me into the thronging crowd, a moving forest of green hijabs and neck scarves. Some are holding *Where Is My Vote?* signs above their heads. Others wave green bandanas. A woman chants near my face as others raise their fists. Their faces flushed with passion, everyone is on fire.

We weave through the marchers toward the sidewalk. Someone bumps into me, and the sunglasses I had propped on my head fall to the ground near a wall.

"Bebakhshid," he apologizes.

I nod, and as I bend to pick up my sunglasses, I spot tiny black letters on the corner of the wall. I move closer. Half the *R* and the rest of the letters have faded, but I can see the residues of the $K+R=BB$ equation.

I had teased Reza that day. "The letters look like ants. No one can even see them."

A smile had spread across his face. "That means no one will paint over them."

This wasn't the wall in our neighborhood but one near the chai khooneh. Reza had written our formula other places.

A rosary of sweat forms on my forehead. I feel the cracks on the sidewalk creeping up my legs, splitting me into pieces. I lean against the wall to steady myself.

"What happened, golam?" Amu Doctor yells above the marchers' heads.

I don't answer. My throat is clenched, just like the shoom—cursed days, as my mother puts it. JJ, Roya, and Amu Doctor huddle around me.

Roya's thundering cry slams into me. "But Ali Jon, she has returned!"

"Dear Roya, who has returned?" Amu Doctor holds her frail hand in his.

"The Simorgh! She's seen her too!" Roya says, pointing at me.

"'The Simorgh of my heart is longing to fly again
Until now, this bird was content with ordinary desires
Now, the flame of her passion has burned those seeds
and she is soaring to the seven skies.'"[61]

I straighten enough to see that my mother has the eyes of a madwoman, glassy and hard, seeing things that don't belong to this world. Amu Doctor is about to say something, but a young man approaches us, his eyes flashing with a palpable urgency.

"Excuse me! You need to leave. Right now," the young man says to JJ in English. "You're jeopardizing our movement. You can't be here."

---

61   from Rumi's *Divan e Shams*

Before JJ can respond, the sound of a gunshot in the distance turns chants into screams.

Amu Doctor grabs Roya's hand. "Are you well enough to walk?" he asks me. I nod weakly.

"Follow me," he says, helping Roya to a side street. JJ and I follow without a word. As we rush away, I catch the eyes of a bearded man in civilian clothing hurrying the opposite direction. I turn around to see he is taking photos with his cell phone.

28. ARMAN — FLIGHT 5276, BRITISH AIRWAYS, 2009

I HAVE TO BLEND in once I arrive in Iran. With my scruffy beard, no gold chain, and the boring Target dress shirt, I think I'm pulling off the Hezbollahi look. I dread long plane rides, especially since the destination isn't exactly the Bahamas. These seats are not made for comfort and I keep repositioning the puny airplane pillow behind my back. I still can't believe I missed my original flight.

The morning I was supposed to leave, the doves were cooing outside my window when I rolled over and opened my eyes just a crack. It wasn't noon yet, so I began to close my eyes again, when I realized I had missed the plane by seven minutes. I sat up and grabbed the clock, half double-checking, fully panicked. I rummaged around my crowded nightstand for my cell phone and scrolled through Kimia's missed calls. I dialed her number but it went straight to voice mail. *Fuuuuuck!* I threw myself back onto my bed. The last thing I remembered was taking a final toke, my thoughts drifting to the childhood story of the shepherd of the Sleeping Man Mountain. I closed my eyes, seeing the young man collapse in despair near a bush, his sheep wandering the belly of the mountain. I could hear the melancholy song of the shepherd's ney.[62]

I must've slept through the alarm clock like I used to sleep through air-raid sirens. I squeezed the phone in my hand. Every instance in which I had wronged or disappointed my loved ones managed to culminate in that second. My face heated with shame. I wanted to scream. But I dialed Jason instead. He is probably the only one who doesn't hate me.

A few weeks after I met Jason, I had shown up at his door unannounced, my eyes full of tears. As soon as I was inside, I fell apart right there in the entryway. Jason helped me up, holding my arm, taking me to the living room.

"Brit dumped me," I said through heaving sobs.

"I'm so sorry," Jason said, and offered me a Kleenex box.

"We had just finished, you know, doing it," I said, taking a tissue. "Our man and woman juices hadn't even dried yet."

"TMI, dude, please," Jason pleaded.

"Right. We're lying in bed, smoking a joint, when she gets a phone call. It was her ex, telling her he had left his wife. I could see it in her eyes—I was just a placeholder. She started dressing. So, I asked, 'What about me?' and you know what she said? She said, 'I guess you leave.'" I took a toothbrush out of my pocket. "I mean, I had a toothbrush there!"

Jason was so chill about the whole thing. He wasn't even upset that I had ruined his quiet evening. He ordered us Chinese takeout and played Miles Davis records. He himself has sworn off women since his divorce, which is probably why he acts so sane, but I keep telling him, "Just you wait. The right woman is going to come along, and then bam . . ."

When Jason found out I had missed my flight, he showed up with two coffees. He was so together and capable, I wanted to kiss him. He called his travel agent and booked me on the next avail-

---

62   Persian flute

able flight. Then he did something I hadn't anticipated at all. He invited himself to Shiraz.

"My travel agent thinks it's doable," he said. "I've got dual Canadian-American citizenship and can travel with my Canadian passport. My cousin in Vancouver does some business in Iran and always has good things to say about his visits. He's got connections and I'm sure he can hook me up with a visa fairly quickly. I've always wanted to see Persepolis. Isn't that near Shiraz?" Jason's caffeine must have kicked in. "I'll come a few days after you. Unless you don't want me there. I didn't even think . . ."

I cut him off. "It'll be great." But I can't imagine how it's going to turn out.

The Iranian man in the aisle seat next to me is reading about the post-election mess. He tells me he's a civil engineer. He's about the same age as my father would have been by now.

The sting of tears threatens, knowing my dad won't be there to greet me at the airport. Just like my dad, our Shiraz house is gone too—someone said they leveled it to make room for a high-rise. Such a shame! That sweet living room with arched stained-glass windows opening to the Sleeping Man Mountain—that kind of view would cost a fortune in California.

I can't help but smile, remembering how one time I caught Kimia with her ear to the living room door. I had just finished my homework at the kitchen table and was listening to our parents talk with their guests.

"We all love and celebrate Molavi, but didn't he marry his teenage daughter to that old geezer, Shams-e Tabrizi?" I heard Maman say. "And what did Shams do? Did he beat her to death as some claim? Or did she die because she was so unhappy in her marriage?"

"Wait," my dad said. "What do Rumi and Shams have to do with what's going on right now? Leave it to my beautiful wife to turn the conversation to her favorite subject."

Everyone laughed. Amu Doctor clapped, saying, "Good, good!

What better subject? 'Don't talk of nothing, but beauty, a burning candle, and sweetness.'"[63]

"Thank you, Ali Jon. But I *am* talking about what is happening now," said Maman, her voice full of passion. "The point is, nobody cares what happened to Rumi's daughter, because women aren't seen as people. Society mistreats us and history erases us. So, I don't care who's in charge, they're going to try to sarkoob[64] women. During Reza Shah, they pulled my mother's hijab from her head. No respect at all . . . She didn't leave the house for months. Now they're forcing us to wear rags on our heads."

"You're absolutely right," Dayi Jalal said after a pause. "If you think about it, freedom of thought is a feminine way of governance. In that approach, there is no fear of ideas, political or otherwise. A patriarchal society like this can't handle freedom of thought. Just like women, thoughts will have to be controlled for this kind of government to survive."

"We weren't always like this," my dad said. "Go look at the Persepolis statues—women commanders alongside men . . . Even before then, women were known to be rulers, as qualification determined their position, not their gender."

I didn't know about all that. I mean, could you imagine my mother as a leader? She would burn down the whole country and start World War III with her temper. Besides, I liked the simplicity of the new rules. I knew my place in the world. Upstanding boys like Morteza respected me and were going to introduce me to the commander.

I got up from the kitchen table and headed to the living room. I was about to tell the grown-ups what I thought when I saw Kimia, balled up in the corner like a mouse. I felt the regular urge to slap my sister on the back of the head. She was always breaking rules.

"Please don't tell," Kimia begged, looking at me with sad eyes. Her left cheek bore a pink groove, a pillow mark she must've

63   from Rumi's *Divan e Shams*
64   suppress

gotten from sleeping on her side. She was still wearing her Bruce
Lee shirt. A yellow stain brightened one of Bruce Lee's nunchucks.

I sighed. "All right, go to bed now before I change my mind."

She slammed herself into me, squeezing me tight with her little
body before hurrying to her bedroom. She almost knocked the air
out of me, that little moosh.[65]

By the time I walked into the living room, I had forgotten
what I was going to say and was distracted by Amu Doctor's new
camera.

It dawns on me that only half of us are left from that night.
What was the war all about? All the killings? And what about my
part in it all?

I wish I had my box. Smoking a little would help take the
edge off. I reach for my flight attendant button to order a drink,
but I remember they don't serve alcohol on flights to Iran. For the
second time in a minute, a dreadful realization washes over me: I
have to face everything in Iran stone-cold sober.

---

65   mouse

29. ROYA — SHIRAZ, 2009

THEY TELL ME I have been talking of the Simorgh. Why not? They are somehow surprised that I cannot recall my own words. But they are the ones forgetting life is full of mysteries.

One moment, you're awestruck,
one moment I'm awestruck
You have been drinking barrels of wine,
I'm still waiting for one cup[66]

I sit on Reza's bed again, rummaging through old memories. My rituals have become more elaborate. I wait until everyone is asleep before scattering my letters and photos, like gems out of a treasure chest, all around me on the bed. By the time I begin my one-way conversation with the spirits, I feel rich as a queen.

"Tahereh Khanom," I address my dead mother-in-law. "It must have been your spirit, guiding me to put my valuables in your khatam box." I kiss my index and middle finger and direct the kiss and my eyes to the ceiling. "You're my esteemed mentor and friend. Your death, as sorrowful as it was, gifted Shahin and me with our union and our children. I thank you for making my

---

66   from Rumi's *Divan e Shams*

life so abundant. I thank you for preserving my beloved's letters. Unlike my own mother and stepfather, you and Kamal Jon were the best parents to Shahin. Roohetan shad."[67]

I close my eyes as if I'm using a Ouija board and let my fingers glide over the old letters from Shahin. My hand stops on a letter. The paper feels smooth and comforting between my fingers. I open my eyes. It's the one he wrote a week before he was scheduled to come home—the one I received five, six weeks later. My beloved Shahin wrote to us every week, although we often didn't receive his letters until long after he had mailed them. A rusty paper clip holds together the letters, one to each of us. The edges of the papers are yellowed, and the ink is fading. I separate the first of the three letters and read.

> My beloved Roya,
>
> I miss you and the children from here to the seventh sky. I'm also thrilled to be coming home, hopefully before you receive this letter. Can you believe it? This was supposed to be a two-week assignment, but once again a short trip has been extended beyond my control. Remember the Isfahan project?
>
> I cannot lie, my darling Roya. I'm so afraid. The bastards are targeting schools. I cry every time I listen to the news, yet I have to know. I read and ask all the time to see if Shiraz has been attacked. Do you even know how this war began? It is getting dark, and as the light changes in my office, a muddled notion of a border dispute escalating out of hand is all that comes to mind.
>
> This is going to be a long letter. You know much of this already, but I'm compelled to start from the beginning, and maybe it will all make sense at the end.
>
> Remember when Mr. Noori came to our office that morning? Teymoor had just returned from spending a

---

67   May your spirit always be joyous.

month overseeing the repair of the Pol e Siah bridge right
here in Ahvaz. When Mr. Noori came in to ask us to take
on this project, I understood it was my duty to serve our
country and our Islamic Republic. Dot. Dot. Dot.

I pause and wipe away my tears. The three dots mean he had much more to say but couldn't say it. We hadn't planned this, but I always suspected this must be a code, that he wrote that last line, so if the letter was opened by the authorities, neither of us would get in trouble.

I imagine the dots mean he had mixed feelings when Mr. Noori approached him. It was our own government that crushed Dayi Jalal, executed our neighbor's daughter, and fired me from my teaching job. They were the worst enemy to their own people, and now they were asking him to help them. At the same time, our country was under attack. Kids as young as Arman were being sent to the front line. So many had died already. We had to do something, no?

I continue reading.

"Love appeared simple, but difficulties arose."[68] I
arrived in Ahvaz one autumn day and now it is late
spring. Aside from a few minor details, my work is done.
I will be home in a week, in the blink of an eye. May the
completion of this project help end this war.

I rest the letter on my lap and gaze out the window into the darkness of the night. They didn't reveal the details of his mission, as it was top secret, but my Shahin actually helped design and oversee the installation of a pontoon bridge in the Karun River! The army used it to transport tanks and ammunition underwater to the other side near the Iraqi border without the danger of being targeted.

---

68   from *Divan e Hafez*

"Shahin Jon, you were so gifted," I say aloud. I hold the letter, noticing the way one of my teardrops has smudged the word *autumn*. Grabbing a fresh tissue, I keep reading.

> *I look at the framed photo of us in front of the cypresses of the Bagh e Eram gardens, you with your angelic smile, one arm around my back, one around Arman's shoulder; Kimia in her shorts and the Bruce Lee shirt, remember the one she wouldn't take off until one of us chased her and wrestled her to the ground? I see my whole life in this picture.*
>
>> *"The lover asked her beloved:*
>> *Do you love yourself more than you love me?*
>> *Her love replied, devoid of myself, I have vanished into you*
>> *Nothing has remained of me except for my name*
>> *In my being nothing but you is present"[69]*
>
> *I see your eyes looking back at me through Kimia. Did you know Arman's nose wrinkles the way my mother's did when she laughed? May God rest her soul. The children's hair is a duplicate of yours, lush and black, shining in the sunlight. I've studied your faces so much, I could write a dissertation about this photo!*
>
> *I wonder what Kimia's interests are right now? These days, when I talk to her on the phone, she is so quiet and reserved. But she must be growing like a cedar tree. That kid is so precocious and more full of life than anybody I know. I have enclosed in this envelope a letter for her, a* Shahnameh *story, and something for Arman, a new math riddle. I have a feeling he still doesn't care much for stories. Before I left, he listened politely to some of my*

---

69   from Rumi's *Masnavi*

tales, but he wasn't mesmerized like Kimia. Is he as moody
as when I left him in Shiraz nearly six months ago?

My dear Roya, what attracted me to you was your
fiery passion. I love that fire! But please take care as your
fire can scorch if left uncontained. Please be gentle with
our children until I return. Then you can do with them
as you wish. I'm joking. I miss us laughing.

I wish for your health and happiness.

Your husband, Shahin

The letter to Arman is very short with a very long unsolved math riddle. "Did I even give this to Arman?" I ask the spirits. By the time I received this envelope in the mail, my condition was kharab,[70] in and out of hospitals and one foot out of this world.

I fetch the third letter. His handwriting is simple, not the beautiful nast a aleegh cursive he reserved for me only.

Kimia koochooloo, Ooji Jon,

How are you, my daughter? I am well here and there
is no ache or illness other than missing you. You know
this story already, but here are some more details, so you
can use them in your epic recreations with Reza. Ready?

Once there was. Once there wasn't. Before Eblis,
the devil, became the new royal cook, the palace was
vegetarian and rarely partook of meat. Eblis fed King
Zahhak the blood and flesh of many animals. He fed him
deer, partridge, and white pheasant meat. Soon Zahhak
became dependent on the taste of blood and couldn't be
happy without it. Eblis meditated all night about the
next recipe that would satiate the king's craving and
made each dish bloodier in accordance to the king's wild
appetite.

---

70   destroyed

*One morning, when the yellow ruby of the sun
rose in the lapis dome of the sky, Eblis yet again, with
the taste of slaughtered flesh, bound Zahhak to himself.
Zahhak devoured the meal spiced with saffron, rosewater, and musk. When his belly was full and his mind
at ease, he said, "Oh, devout servant! You have fed us
well again. Ask me for a favor and I shall grant it."*

*Eblis replied, "Your majesty, all I ask is that you
give me permission to show my devotion. All I ask is
for you to grant me the honor to kiss both of your shoulders." Zahhak was prepared to give Eblis land, treasures, strong servants, or beautiful maidens. This was
such a small favor, he didn't hesitate in granting Eblis
this wish.*

*Eblis kissed Zahhak on each shoulder, and then poof,
he disappeared. Soon, from the spots where the cook
had kissed, two snakes sprouted. They began growing
in front of Zahhak's eyes, ferocious, black, and hungry.
The terrified king pulled out his sword and severed the
beasts' heads. He went to bed relieved, but when he woke
in the morning, he heard hissing in his ears — the snakes
had grown back!*

*Zahhak consulted the best healers from far and near,
but no remedy or herb helped. Every time he cut the
snakes down, they grew back like dark branches of a tree.
Eblis, who had planned this all along, appeared to him
as an expert healer and said, "My lord, you must not
kill the snakes. You must feed them. You must appease
them."*

"What shall I feed the snakes, revered healer?"

"Fresh, young human brains," said Eblis simply.

*So, Zahhak ordered his soldiers to slay two young
men and bring him their freshly harvested brains to feed
his snakes. His soldiers obeyed. Eblis had guaranteed this*

offering would succeed — the snakes would wither away and die. But rather than dying, the snakes grew stronger and hungrier.

People didn't understand what was happening to their ruler. At first they went along with the sacrifices, but soon they became angry. But by that time, it was too late, as Zahhak had become even more powerful and demented. He killed anyone who defied his orders and set fire to their home. He ruled for a thousand years, and from beginning to end, the world was under his thumb. A thousand years!

The world had become as black as a raven's feathers, and each day Zahhak grew more vengeful. War and oppression became the norm. If a farmer hid his lovely daughter, Zahhak accused him of treason and killed him, taking the slain man's daughter as a slave.

But darkness, no matter how pervasive and inescapable, doesn't last. Zahhak knew this when he had a kaboos that made him shiver like a newborn chick. He dreamed of a rebellion that reached the palace. The rebel leaders put a rope around his neck and dragged him to Mount Damavand as a cheering crowd followed. He woke up screaming so loud that the hundred columns in the palace trembled. When dream interpreters revealed the meaning of his nightmare, that his downfall and death were imminent, he fainted. But upon waking, he began a new reign of terror . . .

It's getting dark, Ooji, and I still have to write to your maman. I will tell you the rest of the story when we're taking our next walk in the garden.

You take care of your mother and brother and be a good listener. You know I love you from here to the seventh sky. I'm looking at your picture now and can't wait till I squeeze you.

Your father, Ooji the First

It's hard to believe that our thousand years of darkness isn't yet over. How many more young minds need to be sacrificed? Just like the nights of the Revolution, people are taking to their rooftops, shouting Allah o Akbar. Will God ever hear their shouts? "Oh Shahin, would you be surprised by the persistence of the blackness in Iran? Or is this exactly what you predicted? I can't recall."

I place the letter gently on the bed and walk to the window.

"I can see you very clearly now. You're shoving your papers in your briefcase, ready to leave, when your hand touches our framed family photo and turns it sideways. You're about to right it, but your eyes become cemented to the photograph. I see you study the picture until the sun shoots its last rays through the window, right before it sinks behind the Karun River. In the silence of the nearly empty office building, you cradle the picture and you continue to stare at it long after it is too dark to make out our faces. You could have left an hour before, as all your colleagues had."

30. KIMIA — SHIRAZ, 1981

I RAN INTO THE house, yanked off my hijab, and threw my backpack in the corner. I had to finish my dumb double homework before heading to Reza's. He and I were going to vaghean[71] make up this time. Then we would build the most glorious stone tower.

The night before, I had dreamed of the grounds above Baba Morshed's place. Dust danced amid the ruins, the way it had the morning after the missile struck, but the stage was gone. Although I never saw his face, Reza stood next to me, singing.

> *Sara and Dara*
> *Looking at a map*
> *Lightning thunder*
> *clap, clap, clap*

I joined in, spinning in place.

> *Two fell down*
> *One didn't rise*
> *Which one? Which one?*
> *Tell me no lies*

---

71   for real

Sara and Dara
Looking at a map . . .

As my feet came to a stop, there it was: a mound, hiding the trapdoor. I fell to my knees and clawed at the pile of dirt with the urgency of a dog searching for a hidden bone.

"There it is! Help me open it," I shouted.

When there was no reply, I looked to my side and saw a stone tower the size of a skyscraper where Reza would have been.

"Reza!" I yelled.

A woman cried in the distance. Turning, I saw I was surrounded by stone towers.

"Reza!" I screamed, but only muted air fled my mouth. I dragged my unreliable legs through the foreboding stone high-rises. The crying woman was hidden, trapped in a prison made of stacked stones.

I woke up sweating, my heart beating like a chicken's ass. Felfel, who was sleeping on me, opened her eyes and meowed.

"Oh, that was terrible!" I said to Felfel, petting her fluffy head. Felfel let out a consoling meow and circled around to have her tail massaged too.

I was already miserable, but that dream was the last straw. Myna was right. I had to apologize to Reza. School lasted centuries that day. During religion class, I kept mispronouncing words of the Koran, and I forgot to turn in my social studies quiz.

Chewing on my fingernails, I stared at my book bag. Felfel, sensing the direction of my focus, began rubbing her head and brushing her whiskers against it. I knew as soon as I unclasped the book-bag latch to retrieve my homework, my state would sink into the realm of the badbakht.[72] The contents inside were chains, meant to bind me to the netherworld of meaningless tasks. And in that moment, that was far eviler than getting into trouble.

I knew that once I arrived inside the wooden door, looking at

---

72   unfortunate

Reza's smiling face, all would be right. The residue of the dream would vanish as soon as I touched the first stone. He would beat me handily and I would secretly rejoice in his victory. But first, I had to convince Roya to let me go without doing my homework.

With a scheme stowed safely in my head, I took light, Felfel-like steps into the dining room. Arman, hunched over, frozen with his pen suspended above the lines of his notebook, watched the news on TV.

"How can you do your homework and watch TV at the same time?" I yelled.

"*Vay*," gasped Arman, his pen flying out of his hand. "You donkey!"

I giggled and turned my attention to the TV. People were digging through the rubble of a destroyed building. Some wore masks and others had bandanas covering their mouths. The voice-over said: "*This morning, Iraqi warplanes bombed a primary and a secondary school in Borujerd. Sixty school children were killed during this attack. This is following yesterday's attack when the Iraqi jet planes targeted a primary school in the city of Miyaneh, killing thirty-three students . . .*" Images of children's lifeless bodies, like sardines in neat rows, filled the screen.

"Where's Maman?" I said, unable to watch the rest.

"Shhh . . . ," Arman snarled, pointing to her office.

I grabbed a dolmeh from a platter on the table and stuffed it into my mouth as I headed to Roya's office. The sharp shaft of light of the late afternoon sun poured onto Roya's cheeks, giving her an ethereal air. My beautiful mother was absorbed in her writing, a faint smile on her face, as if she were both daydreaming and part of a dream. She looked up to see me, her smile widening. We were finally on good terms.

"Salaam, maman khanom."

"Salaam, Kimia khanom."

We laughed. Encouraged by the good start, I took a step closer.

"How goes the writing?" I said.

"'Attar explored the Seven Valleys of Love. We are still trying to get around one corner.'"

"'I'm drunk and you are mad. Who will take us home?'" I quoted Rumi right back at her.

"Bah bah! Where did you learn that, my daughter?" said Roya, delighted and intrigued.

I almost burst out, "Baba Morshed," but bit my lower lip and composed myself. "Em, I learned it at school."

"Wow! They're teaching you that at school?" Roya frowned.

I held my breath.

"I'm impressed," my mother said with a hearty laugh.

I joined in and laughed again. I was about to begin implementing my getaway plan when the doorbell rang.

"Azizam,[73] will you go see who that is?"

I caught myself before I could utter the words *Why can't Arman do it?* I nodded and ran to the front door, cursing the intruder. I had no idea who would be standing behind the door, but the smiling faces of Mr. and Mrs. Sholeh surprised me nonetheless.

"Salaam, Kimia Joon. Is your mother home, jaanam?" said Mrs. Sholeh, bending down to kiss my head. As Mrs. Sholeh held my head in her hands, I caught a glimpse of Mr. Sholeh, who was no longer smiling. His eyes were swollen and red, the way they had been at Dayi Jalal's funeral. In fact, hollow-cheeked and haggard, he had aged ten years since I saw him at a gathering just a few weeks before. I had played with their daughter Dana while Mr. Sholeh strummed the tonbak and Mrs. Sholeh sang with her angelic voice. The grown-ups were enchanted with the couple's performance, indulging in a much-needed escape into a world of music and poetry.

"Baz havaye vatanam, vatanam aarezoost." I had listened with Dana while the adults, with tears in their eyes, joined in the refrain of the centuries-old poem. The verses, filled with the longing to return home, were the most apt, yet bittersweet expression of what

---

73   darling

we all were going through. We, as a people, had become separated and divided. It hurt. And somehow this ancient song, by anchoring us in an immediate sense of belonging to our history and to each other, helped us feel safer.

Dana and I, piggybacking on the contentment and security of the adults, had watched the show from the dining room, stealing big pieces of kookoo sabzi. Before they left, Mr. Sholeh told me I had grown into a strong young lady. "Your dad will be so proud when he returns from his assignment," he had said.

I had known Mr. and Mrs. Sholeh all my life. My baba and Teymoor Sholeh were high school acquaintances who rediscovered one another at a civil engineering conference in Isfahan years before I was born. Together they formed the Tavan Consulting Firm, traveling all over Iran, overseeing construction of over fifty bridges and dams.

When I was smaller, I was afraid of Dana. She was four years older and physically bigger, but her Down syndrome made her more childlike than me. Unfazed by my fear, Dana had been drawn to me from the first moment, eager to shower me with her toys and her exuberant hugs. As I became older, I felt like a big sister with protective feelings toward my friend. It suddenly concerned me that Dana wasn't with the Sholehs. Had something happened to her?

"Where is Dana?" I asked, searching their eyes for a clue.

"She is at home with her aunt, azizam," Mrs. Sholeh said with a hoarse voice.

"Ah, my mom is writing. Come in," I said, realizing I hadn't welcomed them in.

I was still puzzled about why they had come over unannounced without Dana, but didn't know if it was my place to ask. My stomach tightened as I called for my mother.

"Will you get us some tea, Kimia Joon?" my mother said, sending me out to the kitchen before I could sit with them.

The bird in the cuckoo clock announced it was already five o'clock, and I hadn't left yet. I let out a puff of frustration like I did when I got a math problem wrong and ran to the kitchen to prepare the tea. In my haste, I overfilled the estekan cups, the dark gold tea brimming over saucers.

"Damn it!" I huffed.

I thought about emptying the saucers out in the sink, but decided to get to the living room fast, even if it meant being scorned by my mother. The hot tea splashed and made waves, adding to my agitation, but it didn't slow me down.

"Ey vay! Ey vay! Oh lord, please give me death."

It was my mother's wail I heard, but it felt like it was coming from inside of my own chest. Standing at the doorway, tray in hand, I watched Maman claw the floor as Mr. and Mrs. Sholeh appeared to have piled on top of her. Arman rushed in and nearly bumped into me as I stood frozen.

"What happened?" he screamed, running to them.

Mrs. Sholeh watched Arman while still holding my mother tight. Mr. Sholeh untangled himself and pushed off the ground. "May God rest his soul. You're the man of the house now," he said with a catch in his voice. He stepped to hug my brother.

I stared at my tray and its contents as it fell toward the floor in slow motion. Startled by the sound of shattering glass, everyone turned their eyes to me. In the silence I heard my heart beating in my ears. I ran before the silence ended and didn't respond when they called my name. I ran out of the house. I dared the morality police to spot me and give chase. I ran as fast as my legs could carry me, the cypresses lining Ghasrodasht Avenue zooming past me. I was a ghost who glowed with incandescent rage, flashing past bewildered shopkeepers.

31. $\mathcal{R}$OYA — SHIRAZ, 2009

I CARESS THE PHOTO of my family, the one my Shahin wrote about in his last letter.

"In my dreams, I sometimes fly above the island of blood flowing from your open wound, your frozen eyes looking somewhere past the shattered window toward the horizon," I say to Shahin. "I follow your gaze and find myself in the Karun River, drowning."

I have set up a small altar of my favorite objects on Reza's desk. Other photos and letters are strewn around my khatam box on the bed. I set the photo in the middle of the altar and light the candle I have brought to the room with me.

When they found Shahin's body, his fingers tightly gripped this photo. He lay in a fetal position near his desk. Perhaps if he had assumed that fetal position a split second before he died, he would have survived.

"Why, Shahin? Why? Was it our family's destiny that forced you to sit up right at that inauspicious moment? Oh, so many nights I cried myself to sleep thinking about our ghesmat," I complain to my late husband.

That day thirty-six civilians died in Ahvaz, including Shahin.

But he was the only one who died in that building. The missile had exploded three hundred meters away in an apartment building housing 112 occupants. Altogether nineteen men, sixteen women, and one four-year-old girl died. Thirty-three of the dead were in the upper floors. They had lost the race against time, running down to the basement. The other two were crushed by the rubble at the bottom of the staircase.

I asked Teymoor, Shahin's partner, to gather this information. He wrote it all down, and I memorized every word before burning the paper. The paper felt najes[74] to me, like the war that had killed so many innocent people.

Had Shahin been listening to the radio like everyone else, he would have heard the red siren, warning of the attack. Had he gone home like the rest of the employees, he would have noticed the blackouts and headed for the basement. The only explanation is that he was sitting in his office chair in front of the window until it became dark. The missile attack must have caught him by surprise. Before he had a chance to dive for the floor, a shard of glass had pierced his carotid artery. The window was of course taped, but either the Ahvaz heat had loosened the tape or the junky adhesive hadn't held the glass pieces together. It had been a mercifully quick death.

When they found him, he was clutching the photo to his chest. The frame must have been damaged, as the picture came home without it.

"I like to think that your last instinct was to protect us. But I must confess that sometimes I curse you for that. If you weren't such a great father and husband, you'd still be alive." I let out a bitter laugh.

"Our girl's heart is closed to me." I look left and right and lean closer to his picture, whispering conspiratorially. "Did you know Kimia became an actuary, so she could study mortality data and aberrations, like the one that killed you?"

---

74   unclean

I like to think I made the right decision to tell my children about the circumstances surrounding their father's death. Most Iranian mothers would have taken this to their grave rather than upset their sons and daughters. It is not our way to share these things. One of my own childhood friends grew up thinking her father was on a long trip, when he was in fact, dead. When she finally learned, she was nearly a grown woman. She never recovered from the damage of the lie.

So I didn't hold the truth from my children. In those days, I believed that in our effort to prevent upset for each other, we add buckets of sorrow to the ocean of suffering. I was self-righteous and proud of never keeping anything inside.

But everything changed on the cursed night no one knows about. Sometimes I thought it was God's sense of humor to make me, of all people, the secret keeper of Shiraz.

I turn to Azita Jon's picture—my dear friend. "I meant to make everything as clear and bright as day. I did. But the first time I tried, seeing your face, the words broke like glass inside my mouth. I became do del.[75] I put myself in your shoes and couldn't bear the anguish of knowing. I'm so sorry, Azita Jon. Please forgive me."

---

75   of two hearts

32. KIMIA — SHIRAZ, 1981

"SALAAM, GOLAM!" AMU DOCTOR said, flashing his trademark warm smile.

"Salaam, Amu Doctor," I heard myself say in a faint voice.

"Reza is in his calligraphy lesson right now. Would you like to come in and wait?"

My heart sinking, I shook my head. When did he start taking calligraphy lessons?

"No, thank you."

"What's going on?" Amu Doctor studied my face. I looked away.

"Are you well, golam? Is everything okay?" he pressed.

Instead of answering, I ran.

"HEY! GIRL! WALK!" A woman in a black chador yelled at me. I frowned and ran even faster.

"AH, ASGHAR! HOW HUNGRY are you? Eat, my friend. Maryam, you too. Enjoy. May it feed your soul!" said the storyteller to the hoze pool as he scattered the crumbs. The fish gulped the food, splashing through ripples of their own making. Baba Morshed sang to his fish:

> *"When have you ever seen fish hold a grudge against water?*
> *When have you heard wet clothes curse the sun?*
> *Consider who is hurt by your anger*
> *Whose star is eclipsed at the end?"*[76]

I watched him stooped over, talking to his fish, oblivious to my presence. I thought about putting on a brave face and exchanging pleasantries with him like nothing had changed. But what I really wanted to do was to scream for my baba and start smashing things. I settled for standing at the threshold, whimpering like an injured animal.

"What has happened, dokhtaram?"[77]

My eyes smarted with tears as he walked to me. He knelt and held my shoulders, looking into my face. A flash of understanding changed his expression to sadness.

"Akhey! I'm so sorry, dokhtar," he said without taking his eyes off me.

"Baba Morshed, I know you know magic. Please bring my baba back or help me die, so I can be with him. Tora Khoda!"[78]

He said nothing.

"Tora Khoda! Bring him back!" I shrieked.

He said nothing.

"Do something!" I demanded, and pounded on his chest with my fists. He just knelt there, motionless.

---

76   from Rumi's *Masnavi*
77   my girl
78   for God's sake

Exhausted and bereft of words, I fell into his arms, sobbing. Myna sat on a large blue vase near us, the shiny black of her feathers shivering with concern.

"Let your tears come," whispered Baba Morshed.

No one had ever told me to cry. Everyone was always trying to stop each other from crying. It wasn't like I needed permission. Or did I?

I cried as if I had inside me an infinite well of tears. Perhaps because I had infinite memories of my father: traipsing hand in hand in the garden, eating pomegranates on the balcony while juice dripped down our hands, his eyes, the feel of his hand on my forehead . . . I wailed for him, my baba, every cell of my body mourning the empty place he had left in my world.

With each falling tear, a tiny space opened within my throat. It was as if these tears had been trapped inside me for an eternity and they were grateful to be free. I wanted to cry more than I wanted to breathe. I cherished it more than the best news, the most expensive present, or the best cone of ice cream. I cried for my mother and Arman. I cried for the birds who had died in their journey, for Roxana, for Neda, for Mrs. Hemmati . . . I cried for myself. Baba Morshed held me and stroked my feverish head. His callused hands were balm on my burn.

Much later, when the well of my tears had run dry, I looked at him with inflamed eyes. He chanted *"Huuu"* as he held my gaze. The ripples of the sound penetrated my heart. My mind became calm and empty. As the echo of the sound dissipated, we sat in silence for what felt like hours. I wanted to stay there forever.

"I don't wanna go," I said to the ground.

He held up my chin. "Come back tomorrow. We will see what happened to our friend Tooti, Inshallah."

I shook my head, but I was already standing up. "They won't let me leave the house after this. I'll get the horse whip again."

"Know that when you return, all will be well."

"Do you promise?"

"Albateh!"[79]

I STEPPED INTO THE courtyard to see Arman, followed by my mother and Mr. and Mrs. Sholeh, heading toward me. I stopped in my tracks near the blooming rose bushes.

"Oh, thank God!" said my mother, speeding past the others. "Kimia Joon, I was afraid you were going to run away. Alhamdolellah.[80] I was so worried." She bent to kiss my head. She put her arm around me and escorted me back toward the house. We passed Mr. and Mrs. Sholeh, their heads bowed, and Arman, who seemed more annoyed than grief-stricken.

I entered the house to the sound of the cuckoo. My life was forever altered, but my book bag sat untouched in the same spot beneath the clock, with Felfel curled against it. I tried to read the time, but my mother pulled me into the living room before I could. The broken glass was cleaned up, but the floor was still wet. How long had I been away?

My mother collapsed on the sofa and beckoned me to her lap. I obeyed and folded inside her fierce embrace. Arman appeared at the door and stared at us, his face blank. My mother motioned for him to join us, but he turned and stepped into the hallway. I felt my mother's body shake as her tears returned.

I HID IN THE bushes as the funeral guests trickled in. The smell of roses made me think of my walks with my baba. But then again, everything made me think of him: A man holding his child's hand,

---

79   Of course!
80   Thank God.

football scores, ants . . . Yesterday, when Amu Doctor talked about his shift at the hospital and the shortage of blood, I had blurted, "My baba is O negative, a universal donor," and made everyone cry. Reza was still at school and had missed the whole thing.

Now, craning my neck and peeking between the leaves, I watched Mr. Farrokhi talk in a hushed voice. "A wife and two young kids. And he was supposed to come home this week." He shook his head and glanced toward the door.

The line of mourners coming over to pay respects was getting longer and longer, and the conversation was shifting from talking about the deceased to the shortage of water and electricity.

"We didn't have electricity at all yesterday."

"Brace yourself. It's only going to get worse."

"Do you think *these guys* are going to leave?" Mr. Farrokhi said, nodding his head in the direction of the mosque, hinting at the ruling regime.

"Not so loud, Agha Jon!" whispered Jalil Jon, who leaned closer to Mr. Farrokhi. "They're even arresting people for saying 'Will the weather change?'"

I had heard that rumor. People had begun to use the question about the change in weather as a code for the possibility of a regime change. It was a harmless way to express their anxiety about the current state of affairs and their hope for a better future, but even that had them targeted by the jaasoos agents.

A loud wail came from the doorway. My feet had fallen asleep, and I was getting impatient as the sound was making it impossible for me to listen to people's conversation. The source of the commotion and the bottleneck was a portly woman in a black chador, sobbing lugubriously and blocking the doorway. Mrs. Zadsham and Manijeh Khanom tried to console her and get her to move on, but her feet were firmly planted. Her shoulders shook and her cries reached the whole neighborhood. I crept out of my hiding spot to investigate. I caught a glimpse of the woman's face and realized I didn't know her. Just as the woman left the doorway, my mother spotted me and handed me a tray full of tea.

Serving the black-clad guests, I looked in the plump woman's direction, shooting her an evil eye for hijacking my dad's funeral. A man who had just taken a tea from me now began bawling, his hairy knuckles covering his flushed face, his large belly vibrating. I didn't know him either. Why did these people, who most likely didn't know my father, exhibit such passionate displays of bereavement? I frowned and moved on to the next person. Luckily, I knew Ms. Sasani. She was my dad's secretary.

"May this be your last sorrow," she said, taking the tea.

"Thank you," I said.

This khatm[81] part of the funeral soothed my nerves. As sad as I was, it was nice to see the living room lined with friends, acquaintances, and even these interlopers sitting in an orderly manner. Soon, the rhythm of standing up and bending down took over. I balanced my tea tray and studied how each person reacted to my presence. Most people choked up. All were exceedingly kind. There were relatives, classmates, and Mrs. Sarhang Zangi, who burst into tears when I got close to her. She was the old neighborhood matriarch who had held the Koran up high and insisted my dad kiss it and pass under it three times before he left. "This will protect you, so you will come home safe and sound to us, Inshallah," she told him.

It hadn't worked.

The other ritual that hadn't worked was her wishful nazr of sacrificing a lamb upon his return. Instead, they butchered the lamb for more practical reasons of feeding the mourners. Poor innocent sheep!

Near the akhund, Dayi Payam spun his tasbi rosary beads nervously. He looked at me above his glasses and forced a broken smile. When he was last in Shiraz, we had only played canasta a couple of times. He had on the same black shirt and slacks he wore during Moharram, the month of mourning. But he had lost weight, and the fabric around his shoulders sagged and the big

---

81   the funeral gathering following the burial on the third day

collar made his neck look unnaturally thin. Had I known this was the last time I would see him, I might have abandoned the tea service and sat with him.

Dana, flanked by her mom and dad, who cried intermittently, looked refreshingly cheerful. Seeing Mr. and Mrs. Sholeh made me think of the moment they'd delivered the worst news of my life. Mr. Sholeh looked back at me apologetically and Mrs. Sholeh wiped her eyes with her handkerchief.

"I know the first part of Ayat ol Korsi," Dana blurted.

"Not now, Dana Jon . . . ," said Mrs. Sholeh.

"You want to hear it?" said Dana, too excited to heed her mother's request.

"Yes. Of course!" I said. Ayat ol Korsi was an important surah[82] of the Koran that had taken me a while to memorize, even with my sharp memory. My mother had made sure Arman and I knew it by heart, as she believed it had protective properties. With all the news of recent bombings, she made us chant it each morning before leaving for school.

Dana recited the first few verses of the prayer. "That's all I know!" she said with a nervous giggle.

I put my tray down and kissed Dana on the cheeks. "That was lovely!"

I had held it together this whole time, but now disobedient tears were rolling down my cheeks. I reached for my tea tray, but Mrs. Tavallali tried to wrestle it out of my hands, saying I needed to go rest. I kept my hands on the tray and politely rejected her offer. I squeezed my eyes shut, wringing them of tears, and went to the kitchen to get more tea.

My mother sat in the middle of the living room with her puffy eyes, a kerchief covering her red nose, occasionally letting out a loud cry followed by unintelligible rants. Azita Khanom and other women swooped in to comfort her. The wave eventually passed, and she became silent for a while. And then it started all over.

---

82   a chapter in the sacred scripture of Islam, the Qur'ān

Arman sat with his eyebrows in knots, his eyes dry and his shoulders tense. His bacheh paasdar[83] comrades were similarly stoic; their leader, Morteza, scanned the room as the other two looked at the floor.

Reza sat with Amu Doctor, his head bowed and his hands neatly folded in his lap. He didn't notice me. We hadn't talked since our fight. He had come by a few times, but I had sent him away using homework or my mother's condition as an excuse. Each time, his ears turned red and his eyelashes fluttered, but he hadn't pressed me. Through my binoculars on the balcony, I had watched his crestfallen form amble away.

Out of the corner of my eye, I saw that Neda with her grandmother, who lived next door, had arrived. It was time.

I walked right past Arman and his gang and offered the tea to the person sitting next to them. Arman opened his mouth to say something, but he changed his mind and went back to his robotic state. Morteza twitched in place, looking at Arman and then at me. I could feel his gaze following me out of the living room. I wasn't wearing my hijab.

I ditched the empty tray and ran into my bedroom, locking the door. I put on my headscarf and tied one around my face, so only my eyes were visible. I swung myself out of my bedroom window and climbed down the wall, holding my breath. Once on the ground, I clambered up on top of the garbage can without making any noise. I mounted the wall of Neda's house. Like the ninjas Reza and I used to watch in the movies, I jumped into the courtyard, sending the neighbors' chickens flapping and squawking. A rooster looked at me quizzically as I made my way to the front gate. I opened the gate and ran like the wind to the storyteller.

---

83   kid revolutionary guard

"THAT'S THE CEMENT FACTORY," I said, pointing toward the smokestack in the distance.

We perched on top of Poshteh Moleh Mountain, watching the city. But unlike the times with my baba and Arman, the sun was setting, rather than rising. I looked at the storyteller. The sun illuminated his face and his skin glowed with health, yet the grooves of his wrinkles made him look like he was a thousand years old.

"I can't believe my baba is gone. My mom is devastated, and Arman is acting really weird. I cry all the time now. I don't think I can ever be happy again."

"You will be happy in due time. Night follows day and day follows night."

"Well, this night is lasting forever." I picked up a stone and threw it at the sun. I was about to grab another pebble when my hand touched something soft.

"What's this?" I said, picking up a delicate, long, orange feather with black spots.

"Look, Baba Morshed! A hoopoe feather!"

"Yes, this is what Hoopoe gave to the tooti bird. This could have been a great help to Parrot, but in his confusion and despair, he forgot about it."

Peering into the blackness of a spot on the irised orange feather, I found myself again in the Valley of Understanding. At dusk and in its eerie silence, the valley looked desolate and drought-stricken. A lone bird flew erratically from one end to the other. When the bird came closer, I saw it was the tooti bird, his feathers dusty, patches missing. Hopelessness clouded his eyes.

"Ay vay! He looks awful! What's he doing?"

"He has been roaming the Valley of Understanding in fear and confusion for years."

"Hey, Tooti! Come over here! Remember this?" I yelled at Parrot, waving the hoopoe feather.

The tooti bird squawked and flew right at me and gently took the feather in his beak. The words of Hoopoe rang through the valley: "If life becomes intolerable, light my feather on fire."

The storyteller took a matchbook out of his pocket and lit a match. He offered it to me with ceremonial reverence. I took it, and when Parrot leaned forward, I lit the feather in his beak.

Upon lighting the feather, the flame in my hand became dancing sparkles, forming themselves into a shimmering sword. I snatched my hand away, marveling at the curve of the blade. It made me think of the one Aladdin used to fight the sorcerer from Maghreb. *Oh no!* I thought, realizing what was about to happen. Before I could scream, the sharp point of the blade plunged into the parrot's heart and exited from his back. I wanted to close my eyes but looked to Baba Morshed instead. He was busy guiding the sparkles into my own chest. My body jolted. I looked down at my chest.

"What do you see in your heart?" the old man asked.

"Baba Joon . . . ," I said, tears pouring down my face.

My heart was as vast as the valley. I felt myself in the most loving embrace with my baba. I savored the moment, and my baba, not willing to let go. But to my surprise, after a long time, I became satiated, my whole body relaxing in gratitude. Just then, the image of my dad dissolved, and I looked up.

The tooti bird circled overhead in joyous flight. "Thank you!" he squawked, flying away from the valley.

"Look at him go!" Baba Morshed pointed. "Even though he was tormented by his fear, he trusted his friend. He allowed understanding into his heart. And when he did, our Tooti saw the faces of his lost friends. All he had to do was to understand he hadn't lost anyone. Aren't the simplest things the hardest to understand?"

"MY MOM MADE KHAGINEH halva, your favorite," said Reza shyly, holding a serving dish covered with tinfoil. In the days following the funeral, we had become cordial toward each other, affecting a formal stiffness that was not at all natural.

"May her hand never hurt. Thank you," I said, taking the dish from him. We paused at the front door in awkward silence. I didn't invite him in, and he wouldn't leave.

"I found some good stones for tower building," he said hesitantly.

Every part of me was screaming to put the halva down and hug him tightly and whisper in his ear how much I missed him. I wanted to shout I would go with him right now and build the borj e sangi that would put to shame the biggest high-rise in Shiraz. I wanted to tell him about the Valley of Understanding, the fate of the poor tooti bird . . . But the words choked in my throat. I remembered he wasn't there the day my father died. I remembered he had abandoned our secret adventures. I remembered he had chosen his new friends over me.

"I have lots of homework. And I have to help my maman with cooking." Two back-to-back lies. My homework had been forgiven upon my father's shahadat,[84] and even with the shortage of certain foods, friends and neighbors brought enough dishes that we could have opened a restaurant. My mother seldom left her room to eat, let alone do any cooking that depended on my help.

"Then I'll see you later," Reza said, brushing his hair away from his eye.

"Bye," I said, closing the door.

My heart cold and heavy, I took the khagineh halva to the kitchen and uncovered it. Azita Khanom had made a fancy design out of cinnamon and cardamom powder to decorate the halva. I loved her attention to detail, especially because she had done all this for me alone. Maybe I was doing fine without Reza. I stuck my finger in the middle of one of the powder flowers in the design, closed my eyes, and tasted the sweet halva.

"Go put your scarf on," Arman said, barging into the kitchen. "Morteza and the other brothers are here."

---

84   martyrdom; anyone killed during the war was considered a martyr

33. Morteza — SHIRAZ, 2009

I can sense the morshed's presence. I fix my gaze to the mosque floor as I cannot break the prayer prematurely, but his flowery perfume tickles my nose. After the Imam recites the last verse, I face him. He nods slowly without taking his eyes off me. I leap to my feet, but men all around stand at the same time to greet each other. "May your prayers be accepted," says the man next to me. "You too," I reply hurriedly, and rush to the spot where the old man sat a moment ago. He is not there.

Mr. Dashti has called in sick again. Reports and accounting papers pile next to unwashed estekan cups on my desk. A dehydrated plant droops in the corner, and the birdcage needs to be emptied of waste.

Mr. Dashti hasn't called in sick in all the years he has worked for me. I've thought of visiting him at his home, but there is much to do. I have been working around the clock, as it is my duty to neutralize the biggest fetneh[85] in three decades. But for now, I do my best to focus on entering the numbers in my ledger, as I do every week.

My forearm tingles like an army of ghost spiders is marching up and down. I unbutton my sleeve and scratch my scar. "Look, Lalu—it still bothers me," I say to the black bird, showing her my arm. It does more than bother me: it wakes me from sleep; it makes me think of the morshed and that nightmare of a night nearly thirty years ago.

I have been sleeping in the guest bedroom so as not to disturb Sakineh and the boys. It began days ago when I awakened in the middle of the night to find myself yowling in Sakineh's bosom.

"You kept yelling, 'The blind Afghan was there, I swear it!'" she said, cradling my head. Then she faced the ceiling with both hands, gesturing toward the heavens. "May Saddam burn in hell for an eternity for what he has done to you."

"I'm fine," I said and wiped my brow. "It was just a bad dream. Go back to sleep."

But the next day, I snarled at my youngest, Hossain, when he asked me to help him practice his multiplication table. This surprised us both, as I enjoy helping my boys with their homework. They are both good listeners, and it is rare I have to punish them. But just then, Hossain's squeaky voice was like nails on a chalkboard. He went crying to his maman, and that made me angrier. "Be ashamed of yourself! You need to start acting like a man!" I barked, making both Sakineh and Hadi pout.

I lift my glasses and press my fingers to my closed eyelids. I cannot go on as such.

"Sir, we've found a foreign journalist." I hear Brother Ahmadi's voice and look up. Ahmadi, too, looks tired, his outstretched hand holding a beige file. I open the folder and adjust my glasses to see several photos of a tall foreigner talking with an old couple and a

85   Supreme Leader of Iran Ayatollah Khamenei called the 2009 uprising a fetneh—a calamity.

young woman. The file says *James R. Delaney*, a foreign correspondent with a news agency I have never heard of. His papers seem to be in order, and the report indicates he hasn't been caught using recording devices.

Ahmadi covers his mouth to yawn. "Should we bring him in for questioning?"

"Yes," I say, flipping through the photos once again. Ahmadi is about to leave when a whisper of an idea occurs to me. "Wait."

Ahmadi stops. There is something very familiar about this old woman. She is pointing at something beyond the photo. The men and the young woman look that direction. The young woman has a sour look on her face, but her eyes are full of fire. I flip to the next photo again, but this time I search for something more. This one shows only the back of the foreigner and the young woman who glances back toward the camera. I hadn't seen this the first time, but a lone fuzzy figure is crouched over in the distance. He is dressed in Bakhtiari clothing and cap, bent down to tie his shoe. I flip back to the first photo and remember the contemptuous look on the woman's face.

"Is there something else, sir?" Ahmadi asks.

I have been so engrossed in the photos, I have forgotten my lieutenant is still standing there. "On the second thought . . . Just keep an eye on the foreigner," I say. "What I'd like you to do is find out all you can on Kimia, Arman, and Roya Shams."

"Yes, sir," Ahmadi says as he walks out.

"Sometimes I feel like I wasn't born until that day," I say to the bird when I'm alone. "I have this family to thank for that."

My brother, Arman Shams, was an excellent comrade—always on time, never complaining, and usually anticipating my needs. The two of us, disciplined and strong, reprimanding girls for their lack of modesty, storming into houses to find wretched anti-Islamic items, and sending morally corrupt addicts to prison. We were good together.

But that wasn't all. Arman seemed to possess an ever-present zeal for the Revolution. I believed he would have turned in his own uncle, had Arman stayed in Iran. But he didn't stay. His uncle, a sniveling old mama's boy, ended his days in prison. Or did he kill himself? It is of no consequence, of course. Why waste a thought on a pitiful louse?

I thought so many times of our promising future as leaders of the Revolution. I remember doing push-ups with Arman until our arms trembled, neither of us giving up. But when the fire from that cursed mouth burned me, I screamed his name only to discover that Arman was already gone.

A murmur outside jostles me back to the present. I stick my fingers in between the blinds, already collecting dust in the absence of Mr. Dashti, and peek out the window. The protesters walk in silence, but my tea shakes in my glass anyway. I think of Saadi's poem: "When a limb is pained, the other limbs cannot remain at rest. If thou feel not others' misery, don't call yourself human." But what if a limb is gangrened? Isn't amputation the most merciful act?

34. Kimia — VALLEY OF DETACHMENT

In the days following my baba's funeral, I was free to come and go as I pleased. My mother hardly asked where I was headed, and Arman was spending more time with Morteza, training and most likely pestering people.

I spent nearly all my free time at Baba Morshed's. I saw the storyteller as a kimiagar, my very own alchemist, transforming the banality and the horror of my world into an enchanted garden of story. He dug treasures from beneath the fragrant mulch of ancient words. He made flower arrangements out of disaster. But lately, I found myself to be the lone human among the birds and the fish, as he was rarely home.

In anticipation of his absence, I often arrived prepared with breadcrumbs to feed the fish and the birds. I poured myself some tea and perused the bookshelves. To the sound of the birds chirping and eating, I lay next to the dragon's mouth and read, the reflection of the fire quivering on the pages.

Myna kept me company. She sometimes even shared some of her favorite *Masnavi* tales with me:

"Once there was a merchant who loved his parrot. But who in God's wide world imprisons someone they love? The merchant was about to embark on a journey to Hindustan, and since he was a generous man, he asked the bird what she wanted from her birth home. Tooti asked him to go to the jungle in Hindustan, the same place she was captured, and give her regards to other parrots. 'Please ask them for guidance. That is all I want,' she said to the merchant.

"When the merchant returned from his journey, he told Tooti he had delivered her message, but upon hearing it, all the parrots fell from the trees onto the ground and died. 'It was a terrible sight,' the merchant told her. Right then, Tooti dropped dead inside her cage. The merchant was heartbroken. He cried and cursed and took Tooti out from the cage and threw her limp body out the window. But Tooti had been playing dead. In midair she opened her eyes and took flight, alighting on top of a tree outside the merchant's window. She said, 'The message was: If you want to be free, you must first die.'"

Myna told her stories but always skillfully turned the conversation to Reza. Blood rushed to my cheeks every time she mentioned his code name, Kaveh, but I said I was content being with her and Baba Morshed. I said Arman was happy I had found "more appropriate" activities than spending time with a boy. Then I would remember how being at the storyteller's was a far worse offense. I would stammer that I needed more time before I could talk to Reza.

Once, Baba Morshed arrived at the door, holding his great book under his arm. "Salaam," he said.

"Salaam, Baba Morshed," I replied. "Oh good!" I pointed to his book. "Are you going to continue the story?" He walked leisurely to his desk, humming an old tune to himself. Sitting in his chair, he opened the book, turned to the correct page, and picked up where he had left off.

"By this time, there were only five dozen birds left. They were travel-weary and missed their home. Some had injured wings and could barely fly. But they continued on through lightning and thunder, unfriendly terrains and dangerous obstructions, making their way to the Valley of Detachment," he said, and turned the page.

"This valley was not what they expected." The storyteller paused and looked at me.

I examined the page in the book—it was pitch black. "There is nothing here," I said to the storyteller.

"You are right. But look closer," he replied.

I leaned over, bringing my face right to the page. My body tingled, and I felt a sense of being tugged toward the book. I backed away, scared.

"It's all right, dokhtaram. There are infinite ways to kiss the beloved's hand, and there are infinite ways to hear a story," Baba Morshed said.

I leaned forward, hesitant, and was greeted by the strange sensation again. The pull became stronger, and I took a deep breath, trying to relax myself. I resisted the urge to pull back— Baba Morshed wouldn't do anything to hurt me! My feet began to lift off the floor, and I instinctively grabbed for the edge of the old desk, but it was too late. I was diving headfirst into the book! I sped through a dark tunnel, tossing through several rapid turns, and landed rather gently on the ground. I looked above and below, left and right, but there was only darkness. I held my hand in front of my eyes. Nothing. Fear prickled up my spine and my stomach tensed, but I breathed again and felt a deep stillness emanating from the depth of this strange place. This silence hushed the pangs of fear inside me. An empty wind blew through my hair, making its way to my thoughts.

Baba Morshed's voice danced inside the wind: "Hoopoe broke the silence: 'Friends, in this valley, the storm of detachment destroys all; the seven oceans become no more than a puddle, the seven bright stars a mere twinkle, the seven heavens a carcass, the seven hells a shivering pile of ice.

"'Here, there is neither the want to acquire nor the wish to explore, as nothing old or new is valuable. If all were to be annihilated, from dirt to the moon, and there remained no trace of either human or deev,[86] it would make no difference.'"

A bright light began shining far away but became bigger and brighter as though it was heading toward me. In an instant it was very near, in the shape of a huge bird, flying fast. It came right at me. I covered my eyes and ducked. When I opened them, I was back in the storyteller's place.

---

86   a demonic creature found in Persian folklore

35. KIMIA — SHIRAZ, 2009

AMU DOCTOR AND MY mother play backgammon near the fountain. I step into the courtyard with my own estekan of tea. JJ sits on the bench, under the shade of the oak tree. His suitcase by his side, he is too absorbed in the book on his lap to notice me. My companions' faces don't bear any remnants of the protest mayhem. But the birds who are busy with their regularly scheduled afternoon conference in the oak tree might have spotted us earlier as we stumbled into the courtyard. We had shown up from the street, relieved and shaken by the chaos and violence. Most of all JJ, who regretted his decision to come to Shiraz. Before we went inside, we briefly discussed his options and agreed to have a car take him to the airport immediately. It was the safest path, as if he stayed, he could easily be accused of being a foreign agitator.

"This wasn't smart after all," JJ said, shaking his head. "I thought if I avoided the protests and holidayed outside the capital, I would stay out of trouble. I hadn't counted on the protests finding me! But of course the unrest would spread nationwide. Why wouldn't it? It was daft to think I'd stay under the radar. I mean, look at me." He gestured to himself with open hands. He is tall and blond, not the best physique for going incognito. "I hope I didn't harm the movement as the lad said . . . I hope to God I wasn't spotted by the authorities. The last thing I need is to have the government point to me as the 'foreign influence' with an agenda to take over the country. I mean, I know my history, I just didn't think . . ." JJ rubbed his forehead.

"It's fine," said Amu Doctor. He put a reassuring hand on JJ's shoulder. "I myself have hosted several foreigners in the past twenty years with no problem. These are just sensitive times."

I went inside, thankful to be occupied with a task. I made tea while JJ packed, Roya rested, and Amu Doctor arranged for a car.

I stand at the edge of the courtyard, watching a couple of butterflies circle each other above the fountain while the birds chirp. The familiar sound of dice crashing onto the backgammon board is oddly calming to my senses. My mother mumbles a wish for a double six, rolling the dice with a fast, practiced motion. The courtyard is so tranquil and lovely, it is hard to believe any disturbance at all has occurred in Shiraz. But violence has a way of carving its invisible marks. It shows up in hypervigilance. It shows up in trembling hands. It shows up in nightmares.

I grip my estekan tighter as Amu Doctor cheers for his great dice roll. A bee falls into the fountain and I set down my tea, searching for a stick for her to climb on. A car horn pierces the warm late spring air and I freeze. We all do. Like alert prey animals expecting a predator, we turn toward the old arched door.

"Well, that's me," says JJ, slamming his book shut.

Roya and Amu Doctor leap up, I prop the stick at the edge of the fountain near the drowning bee, and we escort JJ to the door. He kisses us on both cheeks, Persian style.

"Oh, I almost forgot. Here's your book. It was such a pleasure reading—or should I say, attempting to read *The Adventures of Huckleberry Finn* in Farsi," JJ says, handing the book to Amu Doctor.

When I see the cover of the book, the ground begins to lose its firmness beneath me. I only hear snippets of the rest of the conversation. *You keep it . . . no, no, I couldn't . . . you have taarof down so well . . . pleasant journey . . . Khoda hafez . . .*

As soon as JJ leaves, I feign a headache and rush to my room. The rest of the evening is a blur. I can't sleep, yet I can't will myself out of the bed. Roya comes in a few times, insisting I have dinner, but I tell her I'm too nauseated to eat.

"Let me make you some khaksheer then," she says.

"I already had some," I lie. "I'll eat something as soon as it kicks in, I promise."

Before she goes to bed, Roya brings a small plate of food to my bed. "Have three bites," she says like she did when I was little. She watches me eat the bites of naan wrapped around dopiaze aloo before she leaves me in peace.

At four a.m., I throw my covers off, wondering what time it is in San Diego. Does San Diego exist at all? My breathing and visualization exercises have proved useless again.

I dig my stolen knife out of the bottom of my suitcase and head to the bathroom. As I step in, the obituary section peeks out of the newspaper bin in the corner. I study the photo of a young woman who was hit by a car. I imagine her crossing the street, preoccupied with a boy she fancies. She doesn't see the turning car. The driver is looking the other way. Her lips are pursed, keeping all her secrets safe inside. I drop the paper back in the bin.

"It's a real beautiful oath," I whisper.

36. ROYA — SHIRAZ, 2009

LONG AFTER I HAVE completed my nightly ceremony, I feel a warm hand caress my hair. Through all the conversations I've had with the dead, I haven't heard a reply, nor have I expected one. I open my eyes to the darkness and whisper, "Shahin?"

Eager to finally have a proper conversation, I jump out of bed. I have been secretly hoping this moment would arrive, as I have so many questions to ask. I'm about to turn on the light when I hear, "Go to your daughter." It isn't exactly accurate that I hear this. The words pulse inside my body with such urgency that I abandon my attempt to communicate with my dead husband and run out.

I find Kimia's bed empty. Light bleeds from under the bathroom door and I rush to it. I turn the knob and fling the door open to see her standing above the sink. Her white dress glows in the bathroom light. Frozen, she is an ice statue with blazing eyes. Blood drips from her wrist into the basin.

My heart twists with pain. I want to scream, *Why?* But I just look at her without moving, my eyes blinking away tears.

"Get out!" Her whisper is a shout, her eyes flickering with rage. Or is it flashes of shame I see in my daughter? I have a thousand questions, but my mouth is dry as cinder and my words a jumble.

I grab a handful of toilet paper.

"Get out, I said," she repeats in English, pointing the knife at me.

I take a step toward her and seize the blade of the knife. Loose toilet paper twirls around us. Blood is dripping from inside the fist I have made around the knife. She lets go of the handle and stares at me with horror. I caress her cheek with my free hand.

> *"My sweet bitterness*
> *Like the nightingale*
> *I'm in love with the rose*
> *I worship her petals*
> *And I kiss her thorns"*

37. Kimia — SHIRAZ, 2009

WE SIT ON THE edge of the bathtub with the first aid kit between us. My breathing is calm, and the Persian tiles of the bathroom seem shiny, as if they are brand new. When I saw Roya squeeze the knife in her grip, all I could say was, "Oh, jeez." I loosened her fist and retrieved the knife, thinking, *You really have lost it*. But as I brought her to the sink to wash the blood, I had never felt closer to my mother.

I finish bandaging her hand. "Why?" I ask.

"I told you a hundred times . . . How else was I to get through the barbed wire around your heart?" She laughs.

I envy her. My mother is besotted with the splendor of her own madness, while I do all I can to maintain a cordial relationship with my own.

She removes the bloody tissue from my wrist and, with shaky hands, places a bandage on the wound. Having lost so much weight throughout the years, she looks particularly small. The air is charged with the same unreality of my childhood fantasies, but this time, I'm not about to allow myself to trust my altered perception, or this strange dreamlike state.

Roya places a strand of my hair behind my ear. A thought flares in her eyes, and her forehead wrinkles in worry. "It is all my fault. You don't hurt yourself," my mother says in a childlike voice.

This, undoubtedly, is a dream, as I have never heard Roya blame herself for anything. She always blames everyone—my dad for dying, me for not giving her grandchildren, Arman for not amounting to anything, Saddam for bombing her, and the world for being so damned literal. When she isn't composing or reciting poetry, she is screaming at the universe for making her unhappy, imploring and accusing the world at the same time.

"I know in my gut I have wronged you. But my damaged mind doesn't remember how," she says, holding my hands in hers. I feel the bandages covering her injured hand press softly against my wrist wound.

"So, you don't remember taking me to the Museum of Torture?" I ask. Not in a thousand years had I imagined asking my mother about her abusive and neglectful parenting, lest the spark ignite her latent rage. But I continue to proceed as if this is a roya: a dream, like her name.

The bathroom tiles dissolve into the street scene seared in my memory. I see myself as a seven-year-old walking hand in hand with my mother into the town hall that had been converted to the Museum of Torture. I still have nightmares about the horror inside—walls filled with vivid photos of terrified men being scalped next to pictures of dead disfigured bodies, each neatly framed. I had turned the corner to see people's skin hung on the walls and bowls of extracted fingernails next to different pliers designed for that purpose. This was to show what a monster the deposed Shah was to his own people. When we returned home, I spat on the trunk of the willow tree, hit myself on the chest, and fell, punching the ground with my small fists. My baba, who had just come home from work, found me by the tree. He squeezed my dirt-covered body in his arms.

"What's wrong, Ooji?" he asked.

"Marg bar Shah,"[87] I responded, the images too terrifying for me to recount.

"I didn't take you there!" Roya exclaims now, bringing me back to the edge of the bathtub. I look at her. "Ey Khoda! Oh God! I took you there!" she says.

I catch her eyes right before she begins to softly caress my injured wrist, and I see for the first time the architecture of her madness—something imperative is missing in her foundation.

"Do you remember hitting us?" I say.

"A little. I would slap you here and there. This was Iran in those days. That's what parents did." She says, looking at me earnestly, not sure if she has answered correctly.

"You don't remember Baba's belt?" I ask, observing her the way a researcher would inspect a notably interesting specimen. She stares back at me blankly.

"Do you remember how you horsewhipped me for singing in the classroom?" I say. She shakes her head no, her face flushed, not with the guilt of abusing me, but with remorse for what she can't recall.

I'm suddenly bone weary. I sigh and drop my head into my hands. How could anyone be angry with this frail old lady sitting next to me? But even with all my years of training and meditating, I haven't forgotten about any of this. These memories and the pain they contain are as fresh as the day they happened. *I am angry.* And ashamed that I can't let go. Yet my tormentor sits here, with her wide eyes and guileless innocence—a fucking blank slate. It isn't fair.

On the other hand, in all my years of practicing "living in the moment," I have never let her off the hook. I am the judge, each moment condemning her to the prison of her past, over and over again. Who is the real monster? I bury my face deeper in my hands.

She now strokes my head with her good hand. "Bebakhshid. Forgive me. Please don't hurt yourself. Hurt me if you have to," she whispers.

---

87   Death to the Shah

I look up to see tears flowing down her cheeks. She stops abruptly and grabs my shoulders. "I must tell you and Amu Doctor about the day Reza died."

THE GENTLE MORNING LIGHT bathes the hallway as we exit the bathroom. So many questions and emotions bounce around inside me that I might as well have emerged from a different universe. A rooster croons in the distance and I'm reminded I'm most definitely in Shiraz and not San Diego.

We take our seats at the dining room table. Amu Doctor arrives, carrying a tray of tea and breakfast. He slides the tray on the table and kisses me on my head. He is about to say something when he notices our bandages.

"What happened? Did you start a war while I was asleep?" he asks, pointing to our hands.

"I will tell you all about it," my mother says with a rueful smile. She places our tea and plates in front us before calmly buttering her naan.

Amu Doctor makes small bites with his bread and cheese and tells us about Khalil, their gardener's son who is as bright as he is handsome, finishing his PhD. As he eats and speaks, I can sense a natural peacefulness in him, something I have been practicing for years to achieve. I, on the other hand, can hardly eat, dreading whatever Roya has to say about Reza, yet wanting to, as Arman would say, "get it over with."

"Ali Jon, bebakhshid," Roya finally says. "I want to share something that I've kept from you all these long years."

"What is it, Roya Jon?" Amu Doctor asks, setting down his tea.

"It's about Reza," she says, and reaches to hold his hands.

38. ROYA — SHIRAZ, 2009

I CLOSE MY EYES as I hold Ali's hands. The thread of time first slackens and then unravels. When I open my eyes again, I'm back in the kitchen of our house on that fateful night, nearly thirty years ago. I begin speaking and so with each word, the fragments of the old secret dislodge from my heart and become specks of light dancing into the open.

39. ROYA — SHIRAZ, 1981

I HAD NO IDEA where Arman and Kimia were, but my kitchen table overflowed with plates of food: five different kinds of aash, baghali polo, kookoo, and Shahin's favorite, fesenjoon, not the way it's traditionally made, with chicken, but with lamb. I knew this dish had taken Azita twenty-four hours to prepare. I imagined her the night before, teary-eyed, soaking the walnuts while Ali helped Reza with his math homework. I could see her that morning, busy in her yellow kitchen, caramelizing onions in a giant deeg.[88] Singing to herself, she added freshly cut lamb cubes, spices, and the stock. She went on, crushing the walnuts, sprinkling them evenly on top of the lamb and onions before adding the sauce. Did she feel a surge of gratitude while watching the pomegranate syrup simmer in the pot—that her husband and son were alive and well? I wondered if she made lunch for herself and Ali and saved leftovers for Reza before starting on her famous saffron rice.

Ali had brought the dishes while I was still asleep next to a pillow covered with one of Shahin's dress shirts. Salty tear stains covered the shirt, and I sometimes screamed, hitting the pillow it

---

88   cooking pot

covered, cursing Shahin's absence, and sometimes Shahin himself. Those days, Azita and Ali were often over, helping with the dishes, paying bills, and coaxing me to eat.

That afternoon, sometime before the honey drop of the sun melted behind the Sleeping Man, I felt a veil lift from my heart. I opened the kitchen window and took a deep breath, inhaling the late spring air.

"How are you, Maman?" I heard Arman's voice. I turned to see him eating a slice of kookoo havij, watching me intently. My son didn't look like the same boy who had one foot in the world of comics he hid under his mattress. Gaunt, with dark circles under his eyes, his face had the same raw hypervigilance of those who had returned from the front line. I put my hands on the back of the chair to steady myself, a far echo of shame ringing in my ears. My son was falling apart right before my eyes, and I had no inkling what Kimia was up to this late in the day.

"I'm better," I said, sober. "Where is Kimia?"

"I haven't seen her. I went to training after school. Oh, and Morteza is picking me up. We have some work to do later."

I frowned, remembering the tall young man with the menacing eyes at Shahin's funeral. "What kind of work?"

"You know, drills and exercises. Nothing special," he said in a casual tone that made me suspect he was hiding something.

"When are you coming home?"

"In a couple of hours."

"How do I know you'll be safe?" I folded my arms.

"Maman!" he whined like he had when he was small. "We never do anything dangerous, anything we can't handle . . . besides, we'll be near the best bomb shelter in town."

I wanted to argue, but I didn't have a plan. I could keep him at home, but he would only resent me and defy me later—something I didn't have the strength for at the moment.

"Very well. Just meet that rishoo at the door. I'm not going to put a rag on my head in my own house," I said.

"Chashm," he said, but I could see that he wasn't pleased with *my contemptuous tone toward his friend. Why can't he go back to his comics? Maybe I can find some new issues and put them under his mattress. Does he even look there anymore?*

The doorbell rang, and I watched Arman run toward the gate. His limbs had grown even longer in the past weeks, belying the child-self still squirming inside. I went back to my dishes, my ears listening for my daughter. I tidied the kitchen and the living room. I swept the yard and sat on the porch waiting for Kimia, eager to shower her with the attention I had kept from her all these weeks. But the sun was threatening to set, and she hadn't come home yet. I picked up the phone and called Azita and Ali.

"Wait, aren't they at your house?" Ali said.

Reza had told them he was coming over to our house. The hair stood on the back of my neck. *Where are they?* I felt my fists clench, Kimia's unrelenting insolence gnawing at my nerves again. Oh, how she would pay for this! But first we had to find them.

"Roya Joon, why don't you stay put?" Ali insisted. "You can call friends and relatives while Azita and I search the streets. We'll go to their favorite places: the corn vendor, Poshteh Moleh Creek, and the chai khooneh . . . "

"No, no!" I was adamant. "I can't just sit here. I have to go search for them!"

We agreed on a plan. Azita would stay behind, and Ali and I would phone her to check in: I would call her at half past the hour and Ali would call on the hour. I asked Neda, our neighbor's girl, to come over to our house in case the kids showed up. She was to call Azita if they did. I donned my hijab, worry rippling from my center, gripping my entire body. I rushed out the front gate.

A few proprietors were beginning to lock up as I roamed the streets like the madman Majnun in search of his beloved Leili.[89] I had just lost Shahin, and I thought my life was over. But imagining losing my girl brought a renewed sense of purpose and determi-

---

89   Leili and Majnun are famous lovers featured in many Persian tales. Lord Byron called the lovers "the Romeo and Juliet of the East."

nation. While I could live with the death of my husband, I could not bear the loss of my daughter. Oh, Kimia! I liked to think we had raised her to be independent and fierce, but she was sarkesh—too disobedient, too defiant. As much as I despised this Eslam e zooraki, the forced Islam the government was hitting us over the head with, like my beloved Shahin, I was religious in my own way. While looking into the empty shops and searching through the deserted alleys, I made a nazr to send a hundred salavat invocations to compliment the Prophet upon finding Kimia. I would do that every day for a month. After all, wasn't the Prophet partially responsible for this mess?

I was in the midst of ridding my mind of the blasphemous thought when I saw Reza's small body running toward me in an alley. Seeing him, a thin ray of hope began to shine inside my chest. I became certain I was going to fulfill my nazr. But something wasn't quite right about him. He was in such a rush, he almost crashed into me. I held him by his shoulders as I knelt to face him. The faint smell of urine reached my nose. Someone must have relieved themselves in the alley. "Thank God you're all right! Reza Joon, where is Kimia?"

"I—I . . ."

I knew he stuttered when he was nervous. "I don't know," he finally said.

The claw of despair dug into my stomach. Where was she? Reza's eyes were darting around. "What's wrong, pesaram?"

He shrugged.

"You haven't seen Kimia at all today?"

He shook his head no. I searched his innocent face. He wasn't lying.

I wanted to ask him more questions, but first I needed to make a phone call to Azita, who must have been as worried for Reza as I was for Kimia.

"Let's phone your parents, so they can come get you. You should stay with me," I said.

"But . . ." he said, looking behind him anxiously. Was he running from someone?

Just then, we heard the lanati, the cursed red siren warning us an attack was coming.

"Come with me!" I grabbed his thin wrist and pulled him down the alley. I thought about going to the main street and knocking on someone's door, but I didn't know if we had time. The purple and blue twilight of the hour, the pervading silence punctuated by the slip-slap of our hurried footsteps, the peeling paint on a wall, was all a dream scene—one that would haunt me for the rest of my life. I glanced at Reza. He was breathing hard, his boy legs matching my long, fast steps and his little wrist hot in my sweaty hand.

Shahin had taught me that the next best thing to a proper shelter was a concrete building that looked beefy and structurally sound—one without windows.

"Let's go!" I yanked Reza's wrist, probably too harshly. I was thinking of Kimia. That is the truth. I liked to think I loved Reza the way I loved Arman, but for a flash, tentacles of resentment seized my heart. My feet wanted to run for Kimia, not find a shelter for Reza.

I found a thick building at the end of the alley. "You wait here!" I shouted at Reza. "Make yourself like a turtle—you remember how? And don't move until I get back." Reza obeyed, hunching down on the ground and clasping his hands behind his head.

I ran one way, knocking on several doors, and when there was no answer, I ran the other way. *Oh God! Where is she? I hope Arman is safe. How do I know I'm going the right way? Should I find a pay phone and call Azita first?* These spinning thoughts snatched my breath, making me gasp. I turned again, running in the first direction. Reza stayed silent in his turtle position. Then it happened: a violent wave swept my feet from under me with a deafening thud and knocked me sideways. My head collided with the hard cement of the adjacent wall. From my temple, a lightning bolt of pain shot all the way to my fingertips as my body hit the ground. I tried to focus on a shuttered window on the opposite wall, but my vision flickered and blurred. And then, darkness.

Falling into the void, I felt mighty talons catch my limp body, pulling me up, up into the sky. I saw the flash of a savage beak, painted with the blood of the dead. To the whooshing cadence of vast flapping wings, Reza's voice sang, echoing in the black night. "Roya Khanom! Roya Khanom! I'm coming!"

"No, Reza, no . . ."

40. ROYA — SHIRAZ, 2009

A QUIVER OF REGRET lingers on my downturned mouth. Fatigue is clinging to my skin. I take a sip of my tea and continue. "As soon as I was released from the hospital, I went to the bomb site. Two back-to-back bombs fell on that day. One knocked me back to the wall, where I hit my head. That one wrecked three houses and damaged several others. The second one's cursed sound waves burst my eardrums and caused more unseen damage to my body.

"By the time I went to see the aftermath, the cleanup was mostly finished. The bulldozers had already taken away the hunks of concrete and charred debris. It was a warm summer afternoon. Besides the salt seller heading toward me, the alley was as deserted as it had been the evening the bombs fell. The namaki was walking slowly next to his donkey, the beast carrying his owner's salt for sale. 'Namak! Ay Namak!' His shouts bounced around the empty alley. I waited for him to pass before going to the place where Reza had waited for me. The paint still peeled in places, but as I stood, studying the building, sturdy and undamaged except for minor scratches, it came to me. It came to me as clear as the shriek of the red siren piercing the air. My knees buckled under me, and I found myself on all fours, staring at the ground. A strange animal sound emerged from the depths of my marrow. The namaki abandoned his donkey and rushed to my side, kneeling.

"'Did you fall? Are you hurt?' he asked.

"I grabbed his arm. 'He ran to help me,' I cried. A razor-sharp blade slashed at my heart. Darkness.

"Reza's voice called inside the abyss. 'Roya Khanom! I'm coming!'"

41. KIMIA — SHIRAZ, 2009

REZA'S LAST WORDS—*ROYA KHANOM! I'm coming!*—ring in my ears. I lower my chin to hide my agony, but Amu Doctor looks right back at Roya, not angry as I had expected, but with tears pooling in his eyes.

"I'm so sorry, Ali Jon. I'm so sorry," Roya cries.

I tuck away a sob gathering in my own throat. They had found Roya wandering the streets near our house that night—dazed, her head bloodied. She couldn't tell anyone what had happened to her.

My tea sits untouched and the naan has grown cold, its edges curled upward. Roya's paisley dress hanging on her sharp bones appears far too large for her. She began sloughing off weight after that night, shrinking, disappearing bit by bit.

"I dream a thousand dreams of that shoom night," she says. "Sometimes I run hand in hand with him toward safety. Sometimes I don't go into the alley at all. Sometimes I repeat reality and wake up crying." She puts her hand on her heart, her breathing labored. "I knew I had to tell you before I died."

"May God never will it," Amu Doctor says out of pure habit. He has a faraway look in his eyes, peering beyond Roya and through the window into the garden. Both Roya and I turn. A lone hoopoe bathes in the courtyard fountain, drops of water like a shower of tiny pearls around his golden feathers.

"That hoopoe has been visiting me for years," Amu Doctor says. "No matter what mood I'm in, I always feel better after I see him." He lets out a sigh and faces Roya. "Roya Jon, all I knew from that night was that Reza was going to your house to play with Kimia. And now I know you were the last person who saw him alive." Amu Doctor fetches a handkerchief out of his jacket pocket and dabs his eyes. "It turns out my little boy was braver than I could have imagined."

"I'm so honored to have known Reza." Roya squeezes Amu Doctor's hand. "I realize underneath the wretched weight of shame and guilt, I've been so proud of him all these years. Yet I've kept you and Azita from the same treasure."

My mother cries into her hands as Amu Doctor weeps silently. I want to wrap myself around both of them and sob, but my tears are frozen, a lake of ice, unyielding to the amber glow of my elders' Persian-ness.

Right after we arrived in Shiraz, Roya and Amu Doctor had gone to visit the graveyard where my grandparents along with Dayi Jalal, my baba, Azita Khanom, and Reza are buried. I told them I didn't believe in visiting cemeteries, that the dead don't inhabit their graves, waiting for visitors, and I stayed home, staring at the courtyard fountain. But now I wonder whether it is the gravestones I avoid or the part of me I have left behind in the cemetery. The part that rots alongside Reza in that graveyard.

"I have to go now," Roya says, standing abruptly, not a trace of sadness in her voice.

As Amu Doctor and I consider how to respond, she heads into the hallway in the brisk pace of her youth. By now, Amu Doctor has also become accustomed to Roya's erratic manner. He wipes his eyes, folds the handkerchief, and slips it in his pocket. I begin gathering the breakfast dishes. When the sound of Roya's foot-steps grows faint, Amu Doctor reaches for my shoulder. "How are you doing, golam?" he asks.

"I . . ." What can I say? Across from me sits a man who has lost all that was precious to him, yet he is concerned for my well-being. "Amu Jon." I cover his hand with my own. The warmth of his hand is my dad's warmth—it's Reza's warmth, traveling from my shoulders to the cold knot in my belly, piercing it, a pinpoint of light, a promise, a nascent hope. I want to savor this heat, feel the light expand and watch the knot unravel. But the icy hand of fear covers the opening just as fast. A dizzying tightness grips my chest, and the earth becomes undone under my feet as it did last night. I jerk my hand away. "I'm good. Thank you, Amu Jon." I resume piling dishes. The hoopoe circles the fountain and takes off, disappearing above the oak tree.

A low thud comes from the hallway. My hands freeze on a plate as Amu Doctor pushes back from the table and rushes toward the sound. I follow him, dread filling my chest. In Reza's room, my mother lies on the floor, completely still, old photos and letters scattered around her.

42. ARMAN — SHIRAZ, 2009

WELL, I'M HERE. THIS place is out of control, like a different planet, where the atmosphere reeks of rosewater and traffic fumes. As soon as I stepped out of the airport, I was assaulted by people talking loudly, kissing each other on the cheeks, and vowing to die for one another. I know it's all taarof, but it's too much! In the middle of it all, I can't help but notice the women, their high cheekbones, full lips, and eyes that can set fire to the world. Their headscarves are more like fashion accessories than hijab. I mean, some of these girls could audition to be top models somewhere far away from this land that's so bent on hiding the beautiful.

Standing on the airport curb, I wonder how my life would be had I stayed in Iran. Me, a family man, with one of these women as my wife. Tears swim in my eyes. Not only because I'm sad and jet-lagged, but also because my eyes burn from the pollution. I wish I could get a few bong rips to help orient myself.

I sigh, dialing Kimia's number again, but the phone gives me the same message: *The cellular customer is not available.* I overheard someone saying the networks are down because of the protests. I guess I should feel lucky. I missed the major post-election clash at the airport in Tehran. Apparently, the whole place is now barricaded with armed guards in riot gear. I try Amu Doctor's number and the same annoying voice tells me my call won't go through. Fuck it. I'll just show up. Do I even remember how to catch a taxi here?

I HESITATE BEFORE GRABBING the Hand of Fatemeh knocker. When I was a child, I demanded to be the one who knocked on this door. I would stand on my tiptoes, barely reaching the knocker with my small fingers, and throw my body against the thick cherry wood of the door. For the hundredth time, I think about how I'm going to act in Amu Doctor's presence. Everybody knows *it* was a tragedy. No one knows where I was that night. I jump and shake my body like I'm about to begin a race. I knock.

A handsome man with broad shoulders and a movie-star smile opens the door. He has dirt on his hands and shirt and an old-fashioned Walkman clasped on his jeans' waist. The headphones are around his neck, the way Reza . . .

My throat goes dry. I open and close my mouth like a fish.

"Salaam aleykom," the man says expectantly.

"Salaam. I'm Arman," I say and wait for a sickle or whatever weapon the dead use to slash me in half.

"Oh, Arman Khan! Salaam. Good to see you again. Welcome," the man says with warmth. "I would shake your hand, but . . ." He shows me his dirt-covered palms. He must have seen me jump, because he says, "Are you all right?"

"Yes," I say.

"You probably don't remember me."

I shake my head and swallow.

"I'm Kahlil. My father and I used to tend the garden together. Remember my dad? Masht Fatollah? Now that he is retired, I come here when I can. Look, why don't you come in and get settled? I'll get you a glass of water."

I'm still unnerved, but now that I think about it, I have a

vague memory of Masht Fatollah and his son. *Where is everybody?* I peek inside.

"I don't want you to worry," Khalil says, reading my mind, "but your mother fell. She is fine. But as a precaution, your sister and Dr. Pirooz took her to the hospital. Let me wash my hands. I will drive you there as soon as you're ready."

ON THE WAY TO the hospital in his pickup, Khalil tells me he is teaching agricultural engineering at Shiraz University, but he still looks after Amu Doctor's garden. "I owe them everything. Dr. Pirooz and Azita Khanom, may God bless her soul . . . they were my mentors. They helped me with all aspects of my education."

I bounce in the passenger seat, taking in the badly paved alleys I haven't seen in years. Khalil says this is best to avoid the main streets clogged with protesters.

"What do you think of these protests?" I venture.

"To be honest, I voted for Ahmadinejad. I like some of the farming programs he has implemented. Like, the saffron pickers have doubled their salary since he's been in office. I want him to be the president, but I also know yek aalam, a world of Mousavi supporters. All in all, I think it's good for them to voice their discontent. I just wish it wouldn't turn violent the way it has. They say a young girl was shot yesterday," Khalil says, shaking his head.

"Politics is so complex, you know," I say. "We have such a history . . ." My voice trails off as I spot three men in fatigues with rifles on the sidewalk. An unexpected cold fear runs down my spine. I try to finish my thought, but now I'm distracted. "Look, Khalil Jon," I say, remembering the Persian custom that dictates keeping bad news to oneself. "Honestly, how is my mother?"

"I don't know . . . I hope she is doing good," Khalil says, but his voice sounds a little tense.

43. Roya — SHIRAZ, 2009

My head throbs, and my breathing is shallow and pained. Several pairs of eyes peer at me, willing me to look back at them. I blink but can't clear my hazy vision. The shapes look like Ali and my children. They stand over me, by what appears to be my bed. I gaze above them to see the telltale hospital ceiling with the square tiles and rectangular fluorescent lights. My eyes find Arman. *Am I dreaming?* I've had my share of hospital dreams.

"Salaam, Maman Jon," Arman whispers.

I open my mouth to answer, but I become distracted by the IV bag. My bleary eyes follow the tube emerging from it to a needle in my arm. Whatever is in the bag isn't soothing my pain. My strength is evaporating with each strained breath.

"Salaam, pesaram." My voice is raspy and faint, every word a dull ache.

44. KIMIA — SHIRAZ, 2009

WHEN WE BROUGHT ROYA in, Namazi Hospital was overflowing with those injured in the recent protests. Scores of visitors waited their turn to be with their loved ones, but Amu Doctor, a respected otolaryngologist himself, knows most of the staff, so we were granted the rare privilege of staying with our patient.

I vacillate between wakefulness and a dream state—a place I stumble upon when I'm sleep-deprived. The effects of this state vary. Sometimes I become jumpy and skittish, while other times, like now, a pleasant buzz tickles me giddy. Above everything, I'm happy Arman has finally arrived. But he has fared worse than the rest of us. When we mentioned Roya's secret, he broke into tears and left the room. I went outside to find him squatting on the floor against the half-green, half-white wall in the hallway, sobbing into the crook of his arm. It was strange, seeing him so distraught. I hadn't even seen him cry at our father's funeral. Besides, he barely knew Reza. Not like I did.

I touched his shoulder; his body felt foreign to me, a man's body, not the scrawny boy I used to wrestle with. He looked up with red eyes before burying his face in his forearm again.

"She's asleep now. Do you need anything?"

He shook his head.

It's SIX A.M. VISITING hours have long been over. I sit on a patch of grass near the soaring cypresses outside the building. Last night, I begged Amu Doctor to take Arman, who was still a wreck, and get some rest while I stayed close to Roya. "It'll do me good to meditate in the stillness of the night," I convinced them.

While the hospital itself is bursting at the seams with patients, the grounds outside are deserted. Early-morning light seeps into the mist, spreading, covering the building in a soft glow. My eyes drift to the sign above the main entrance, cursive Persian calligraphy swirling inside stylized ocean waves.

The CT scan showed my mother has an intracerebral hemorrhage. They administered diuretics to reduce her brain swelling and wake her up every two hours to make sure her condition doesn't deteriorate.

"She is going to recover, right?" I asked Dr. Moin, a short middle-aged woman with a serious mouth and a blinding white uniform. Amu Doctor says she is one of the best in the country.

"I hope so," Dr. Moin said with an impassive face.

"What are her chances of recovering? Seventy percent? Ninety-five percent?"

"We don't know. I can't give you an estimate right now. The next twenty-four hours will be important. We have a very good team, focusing on her. The rest? Dasteh khodast." She gestured toward the fluorescent light in the ceiling. *It's in God's hands.*

If you can't give me a reasonable probability, what good are you? I thought while thanking her. Before I left, I glanced at my mother and her roommates, a young protester, her head bandaged and her leg in a cast, and a waif of a young woman, sick from chemotherapy. They were all sleeping to the beeping sounds of hospital equipment. As I said my goodbyes, I searched Amu Doctor's face for clues about how he was really sitting with the new revelation. But I only found the same unwavering serenity from before the news, shining through his loving eyes.

45. KIMIA — THE VALLEY OF UNITY

"BABA MORSHED, I HAVE to tell you, last night I had a dream about the Simorgh," I said.

I spread out my arms, brushing Baba Morshed's beard. "Her wingspan was as big as this whole room! She was so colorful, you know, with these huge feathers, like a peacock." I paused. "It was the first good dream I've had since . . . I was a little scared, though. She had this fierce look in her eyes."

"Looking into the eye of the Simorgh again, huh?" said Baba Morshed, leafing through the book.

"What happens next?" I asked, watching the old man's hands with eagerness.

He took his glasses off and looked at me. "Remember sometimes I talk about how life needs to cook things inside your fire?"

I nodded.

"Well, the other Rumi talks of the three stages of life: being uncooked, getting cooked, and burning. Being untouched by life's hardship leaves one uncooked and untransformed. Do you know what that means?"

I shook my head.

"Once there was. Once there wasn't," he began, and I relaxed into my seat, like every other time the storyteller uttered those words. He continued, "A lover knocked on his beloved's door. A voice came from the other side: 'Who is it?' The lover replied, 'It is I, the one who loves you.' The beloved sent him away. 'This house is not the place for the uncooked. Come back when you have been burnt in the fire of love,' said the voice behind the door.

"The lover left his beloved. Sad and with the ache of longing in his heart, he went to work. He endured the torment of separation as he embarked on his solitary journey. He often thought about going back to his beloved, but he knew he wouldn't be welcomed. He was still uncooked. So he brought love to anyone and anything he encountered in his travels. Even so, he suffered many difficulties and faced judgment, rejection, and loneliness. He didn't give up. With each hardship, he felt the jagged edges of his being become rounded in the fire of love, and his heart became fuller and more alive. After a year, he knew he was ready to meet his beloved. He knocked on his beloved's door. A voice came from the other side: 'Who is it?'

"'It is you, Beloved. Only you,' the lover replied. The beloved opened her door. In the house of love, there is room for only one."

Baba Morshed walked over to the fireplace and put a pinch of powder in the dragon's mouth. The flame danced a furious dance.

"You might be wise beyond your age, but you're still young, Rumi! It might be years before my words will be truly experienced by you. There is no need to rush the journey. It will do you no good, as life has its own hesab.[90] The fire of life is an unruly mystery."

I stared at the fire. When I first met the storyteller, I had so many questions. But after the span of a few days, those questions fell away. Somehow our lives beyond the story had become less relevant. It didn't really matter what his real name was or how he came to live under the stage. My questions were now all about the stories. I trusted him. These days, when he asked for my patience, I listened.

---

90   math

As I focused on the dancing flames, they parted, and I was looking into the fifth valley. I inched closer to the fire.

"When Parrot reached the Valley of Unity, Hoopoe was waiting for him," said Baba Morshed.

At Hoopoe's command, all the birds began flying in a curious pattern, dozens of birds, joyful splashes of color in the vast turquoise sky. Near the ground, Parrot flapped his green wings with excitement. The birds began flying in unison, their wings swishing in synchronized motion.

"The Simorgh!" I exclaimed, watching the giant bird move gracefully in the sky, her body made of many smaller birds. Parrot flew into the empty place the birds had left for him—the eye of the Simorgh.

46. ᴚEZA

ON THE DAY I died, I had but one goal: to find Kimia. I had knocked on her door earlier that afternoon, but no one answered. She must have been at the storyteller's.

She was wrong about me. I didn't like my new friends better. I just didn't want to go back to being a chosoo tarsoo, a scaredy-cat. I had climbed to the very top of my class. My friends and teachers admired me. Most of all, I sensed that Kimia looked at me differently. It felt good. The last time with the morshed was really hard. My palms were sweaty and my mouth was dry as a desert. It was the worst. It was so embarrassingly easy to go back to being a failure.

But on that day, I didn't care. I woke up determined that I would rather give it all up than lose my best friend. I had tried a few other times to talk to her, but I didn't have Kimia's talent for persuasion. I was never convincing enough.

I ran through the streets, feeling the breeze in my hair. It was good to be a boy, to move without worrying about breaking the law.

In the open-air market around the perimeter of the square, vendors sat on wobbly stools and chatted with customers while their assistants sorted and weighed fruit and vegetables. They handed paper bags full of produce to shoppers, saying, "Ghabel nadareh." Since the last time Kimia and I were at Baba Morshed's place, I had visited the square often. Every time I went to buy sabzi for dinner, I glanced over at the stage area, wondering if she was there with Baba Morshed. Each time, a different lowly street vendor had set up shop there. Their blanket spread on the stage, they peddled small bowls and plates or plastic dolls and trucks.

I approached with measured steps, noticing they had cleaned up the debris around the stage and discarded the backdrops. This time, it was a blind man selling fortunes and spells on top of the stage. "Jinn giry,[91] fortunes, raml, astrolabe, spells," he yelled. In an inviting gesture, he beckoned people with his hands in the air. On his blanket lay an ancient-looking bronze implement. It was a disk with small delicate etchings on it. I had never seen one before, but I guessed it was an astrolabe, for measuring celestial bodies and such. A bowl of sand sat next to small potion bottles and scrolls tied with flimsy strings. The bowl of sand was raml, with which he predicted the future. My dad had told me it was all khorafat, superstition, but entertaining to watch.

I busied myself nearby, pretending I was about to buy potatoes from a vendor. I watched from the corner of my eye as the blind man talked to a woman and her daughter. He was an old Afghan, wearing a dark green vest over a long shirt covering his crossed legs. His face had the sun-soaked hue of the Afghan construction workers.

"This spell will make a rich and handsome man fall in love with you. He will be good to you, too!" He rocked back and forth as if chanting something sacred, his closed eyelids fluttering. He handed the younger woman a piece of transparent fabric with Arabic scribbles on it. "Put this in a glass of water and drink from it three times a day for three weeks." His accent was the thick Dari we had become used to since the refugees continued to spill into Shiraz from Afghanistan. I couldn't tell whether the young woman

---

91   the service of capturing jinn

really needed the spell or the pair just felt sorry for the blind guy and wanted an excuse to give him money. When they left, I casually walked behind the stage. If I didn't draw any attention to myself, I could quickly slip under.

I heard the blind man's voice. "I would give you a spell, but you really don't need one, pesaram." I looked to see that his head was turned to the side as if he was talking to someone next to him. "I'm talking to you!" he said. I reflexively pointed to my chest.

"Baleh, shoma.[92] You don't need a fortune today. Now go about your business," he said, waving his hand.

I paused for a moment and glanced around before slipping under. I brushed off the dirt concealing the trapdoor. I pulled on the handle, the traffic noise masking the thud.

"KIMIA? BABA MORSHED?" I said as I felt my way down the dark staircase. But my voice just echoed in the silence. I imagined walking into Baba Morshed's place to see Kimia staring into the giant book as the storyteller's voice boomed. They would see me at the door.

"Rez . . . Kaveh! You're here." Kimia's big sparkling eyes would widen with surprise. Her freckles would darken as they did when she blushed. She would smile. The morshed would invite me in and they would tell me what I had missed in the story.

Or Kimia would say, "Kaveh, you're here." Her scornful eyes would look at me as an intruder, walking in on a private moment. I would then rush over and tell her how much I missed her. How I had failed her as a blood brother. How I would go to the seventh sky and back for her. That I wasn't really brave. That I was just pretending to be. I would beg her to forgive me and I wouldn't relent until she accepted me as her best friend.

---

92   Yes, you.

When I got to the bottom, I pushed open the door. It was dark. "Anyone home?" I said to the darkness. Not even the dragon fireplace was lit. The sinking feeling made the corners of my mouth drift downward. I was too late. She had gone back home.

I closed the door and doubled back to the top. Peeking through the crack of the trapdoor, I saw it was about to get dark. The vendors had already packed up for the day, and the square was now empty. I came up quick and began running.

"I'll see you in a minute," yelled the blind man after me. Puzzled, I turned to look at him. He was waving at me, his mouth curling into a familiar lopsided smile. "Be careful you don't fall!" he said. I brushed my hair away from my eyes and watched the street for stones that could trip me. The Afghan's impatient voice followed me. "Boro digeh." *Go then!*

I HAD TURNED THE corner and was running toward Kimia's house when I saw Arman and his gang strutting along and staring people down. *No, no, no . . .* A couple crossed to the other side of the street to avoid them. I averted my eyes and turned around slowly.

I heard their tall, bearded leader's voice. "Isn't that your cousin?"

"Reza!" Arman yelled. I pretended I hadn't heard him and continued to walk, a little faster, toward the felekeh.[93] The gallop of running feet behind me made me freeze. A hand grasped my shoulder.

"Akh!" I cried, as the leader spun me toward him. I couldn't wiggle out.

"Well there, little troublemaker, what sort of plots are you hatching tonight?" He breathed the words in my face.

"I . . ."

---

93   public square

I looked at Arman, pleading with my eyes for help, but he just hardened his expression and chimed in. "Yeah, and where's Kimia, Reza?"

"Uh . . . uh . . . I don't know!" I screwed up my face so I wouldn't start crying right in front of all of them. I just wanted to find Kimia, not be interrogated by these goons.

"So, she's out alone tonight?" Arman asked.

"Uh, yes—I mean, no!" I should have maintained that I didn't know. But my stomach had dropped, and its empty place was soon filling with dread and confusion—the kind that made me stutter during oral exams.

The leader tightened his grip, his nails digging into my biceps. "So, which is it?"

"Uh, she's, uh . . ." A fat tear rolled down my cheek.

"You heard the brother's question!" Arman yelled in my face.

A loud motorcycle whizzed by us, and I yelled without thinking, "She's with the storyteller."

The leader loosened his grip slightly. I looked at the ground, a warm puddle forming beneath my feet.

"Ah man, he pissed himself," the boy with crooked teeth said. Everyone moved back. The leader held my collar with one hand as he stepped to the side. My ears burned.

"You mean the lame morshed, the old man who is rumored to perform at the square?" he said, ignoring the chuckles of the others. I nodded. He turned to the gang. "The commander said those stories are infidel teachings. If we could nab him"—he nudged Arman with his free hand—"we'd be heroes!"

But Arman just nodded curtly, fixing his stare somewhere above me.

The leader grabbed me with both hands again. "Where are they?" he demanded.

"I don't know! I don't know!" I said. "When I got to Baba Morshed's . . ."

"You know where the storyteller lives?" the leader interrupted. He had the smile of a cat that had trapped a mouse.

This was bad. I wasn't good at lying, and I usually offered too much information, especially when I was nervous. It drove Kimia mad. "Um . . ." I looked down.

The chubby boy with pimples and a unibrow shoved me. "Take us there!"

I reluctantly began to walk back the way I had come. They followed as the leader kept me in his grasp. I watched him give Arman a playful punch in the shoulder.

"I should just take him home, so he can change," Arman said, leaning close to the leader's ear.

"Not until he shows us the place," the leader said without taking his eyes off the street. I led the gang through the darkening lanes back to the felekeh. When we arrived, I cut diagonally across the square, toward the stage.

"Hello again." The blind Afghan smiled as we approached. I didn't answer, and the gang mumbled a quiet hello. But he motioned to us eagerly. "Come over here!"

"Forgive me, I don't have any money," Arman said, pulling out the inside of one empty pocket. The other boys snickered, and Arman blushed, feeling silly that the Afghan couldn't see what he was doing.

"This is for free," the blind man said. And he grabbed a handful of sand from his bowl and scattered it onto his blanket. Just then a strong wind blew the sand above my head, hitting the boys in the face. I watched the gang covering their eyes and coughing.

"Forgive me, I can't control the wind," he said, slapping his thigh and laughing as if he wasn't going to stop until we got the joke. Even though my wet pants were uncomfortable, and I wanted to leave more than anything, I could feel the beginning of a smile forming on my lips.

"I told you, you don't need your fortune told," he said, running his hand over the sand. "Today is a good day. You will find what you're looking for."

"Who is he talking to?" the skinny boy asked the leader in a hushed voice.

He's crazy, the leader mouthed, making a swirling motion near his temple with his index finger.

"'Man mast o to divaneh. Ma ra keh barad khaneh,'"[94] the blind man sang, snapping his fingers, his shoulders dancing.

"Listen old man!" the leader leaned close to the Afghan's face. "I'm going to be nice this time, but what you're doing is illegal! Spreading lies and superstition like this!" He swept his hand, gesturing toward the blind man's blanket. He then self-consciously withdrew his hand. "So, let us be on our way."

"Befarma. Help yourselves!" The blind man gestured with his open hands. "But unlike our friend here, you won't find what you're looking for." His voice sounded powerful and kingly, like the hoopoe's voice.

I felt the leader's hand shove me forward. I pointed under the stage.

He grinned. "You're joking!" He ducked under the stage while Arman gave me an apologetic look. After some shuffling around under the stage, the leader popped his head back out. "You guys aren't going to believe this—a trapdoor!" He brushed his hands off. "Who's got a light?"

The fat boy shoved me out of the way while the other gang members began piling under the stage. I was about to bolt when I heard the leader's voice. "Bring the boy!"

ARMAN GENTLY LED ME down the stairs. Someone had lit a match. "There's a lantern!" the leader shouted from below. A moment later, the narrow staircase was abundantly illuminated.

"Get down here!" the leader ordered. I looked at Arman. He gulped and scrambled down the stairs, holding my hand tighter.

---

94   I'm drunk and you are mad / Who will take us home? (from Rumi's *Divan e Shams*)

He had fear in his eyes.

The big wooden door creaked open, and the gang peered in, shoving each other to get a view. The leader soaked in the scene. "The storyteller's storybook world. This is too good to be true!"

There was no sign of the birds. I wondered if they were hiding or they had left. While the boys were busy admiring the place, I was the only one to notice a small table was set with five estekan cups filled with steaming tea.

"Wine!" shouted the unibrow, holding up a dusty bottle. Running his hand along the bookshelf, the lanky boy yelled, "All these books are illegal!" But he lingered by the bookcase. I had stood in the same spot the first time I'd set foot in the storyteller's place. Looking up at the daunting shelves filled with books, I was overwhelmed, but I walked away, feigning disinterest. Maybe the lanky boy was calling the books illegal to cover his own embarrassment for not being able to pronounce the titles. His eyebrows knitted and he was mouthing the exotic words when the quiet one picked up a chess piece and threw it to the leader. The leader's grin widened as he examined the queen. He tossed the piece in his pocket and strolled over to Baba Morshed's collection of walking canes by the door. He picked one out and offered it to Arman.

"Brother, will you do the honors?" he asked. Arman took the cane and stood over a large ceramic vase. He looked at me beseechingly. But then he sucked his teeth and smashed the vase. The others cheered and began their own destruction. I looked on, frozen in horror as books fell on the floor and glass shattered against the wall. The lanky boy began ripping pages out of *The Magician's Nephew*. I remembered the storyteller telling us a quote by its author, C.S. Lewis: "Courage is not simply one of the virtues, but the form of every virtue at the testing point."

Out of nowhere, a guttural rage from the bottom of my feet reached my lips. I cried out, "How dare you?" The others didn't hear me above the noise, but Arman, in the corner of his eye, saw me rush over to the fireplace. He ran after me. I snatched the powder pouch from the floor and threw it into the dragon's mouth. Angry flames roared between the beast's teeth, thundering and spilling beyond the fireplace. I backed away. Arman's grip on the cane had loosened. This time, I didn't hesitate. I ran like I was running away from a wicked deev toward my beloved. I ran and I ran. Into Roya Khanom.

WHEN ROYA KHANOM TOLD me to make like a turtle and wait for her, I listened. But while I was crouching, I remembered how Kimia and I had delighted in the story of Zahhak. Kaveh was just a blacksmith, but he marched into the Serpent King's palace and protested the arrest of his son. His boy was sentenced to be killed to placate the snakes on Zahhak's shoulders. Kaveh stood on the palace steps and shouted for the release of his son. Stunned by this act of bravery, Zahhak granted the demand, but asked Kaveh to sign a letter, appreciating his royal magnanimity and benevolence. Kaveh just laughed and ripped the testament in half as he scolded the bewildered onlookers for serving the evil tyrant. He stormed out of the court, his son by his side. He raised his leather apron on a spear like a flag and beckoned the crowd to join him to defeat Zahhak.

I realized when I threw the magic powder in the dragon's mouth that I was ready to fight like Kaveh. I was afraid, but it didn't matter. My fists clenched. I watched Roya Khanom run. I stood, but my first step landed with a bang, a sound so loud, it made the whole alley shimmer. I braced myself against the wall so as not to fall, watching Roya Khanom hit the ground. I found myself running to her. "Roya Khanom! I'm coming!" I yelled.

I WAS FLYING ABOVE. All I could see was a familiar kid's hand sticking out from under the rubble. I flew on to see Roya Khanom sprawled on the ground. I could hear people screaming and crying inside their bunkers. In fact, if I focused, I could listen to anyone's conversation. Someone was telling a dirty joke.

Still hovering over Roya Khanom, I heard the music of a setar and I wanted to find it. I followed the sound, soaring above streets covered in fire, smoke, and rising dust. I flew across the stream and onto the Poshteh Moleh Mountain, the music pulling me closer. Baba Morshed and Kimia were sitting on top of the mountain, overlooking Shiraz. Baba Morshed looked my direction and smiled, strumming his setar even more passionately. I swooped faster toward them. Kimia looked so exquisite in the diminishing light, it hurt. Her short hair brushed to the side, her eyes were gleaming black pearls and as I got closer, her lips parted in the shape of an O.

I had found her.

47. KIMIA — SHIRAZ, 2009

"IF I'M DYING, LET me die. Don't let them revive me," Roya whispers in my ear.

"Nobody's dying," I say. "They're just going to take you to have another MRI."

In the next bed, Sanam, the young chemo patient, appears less drowsy than yesterday. She is drinking doogh through a straw and listening to her MP3 player. Bahar, my mother's other roommate, has finished drawing Snoopy on her cast and is beginning to fill in words in a bubble above the cartoon dog's head. *Where Is My Vote?*

Roya grabs my wrist. "Don't bullshit me," she says in English. "I can see it in your eyes. I came here to die in a dignified way. Don't deny me that." She takes in a quivering breath. "I want the same DNR thing I had in San Diego. Go tell them now."

I step outside her room to confer with Arman and Amu Doctor.

"She is not in her right mind," Arman says, his voice an entangled murmur. "She had a concussion, for God's sake."

"I know," I say. "But it's consistent with her wishes in America."

"She was crazy there too," he whines, rubbing his forehead.

"Do-not-resuscitate protocol isn't culturally acceptable here," says Amu Doctor. "I don't think they even have forms for such procedures. But if you ask me, I say it is up to her. I'm happy to go talk to her doctors. Although," he continues with a helpless shrug of his shoulders, "I can't promise they will abide by her wishes."

I step closer to Arman. His beard is getting fuller, giving his face an unfamiliar air, yet for the first time in ages, he feels like the boy I grew up with. "This is what she wants," I say, rubbing his arm.

Arman is about to protest again when I hear something. "Shhhhh!" I crane my neck toward my mother's room.

"*Baz havaye vatanam, vatanam aarezoost . . .*" Roya sings, her voice faint, but clear. *I long to go home.*

We all rush into the room. With her eyes closed, and her hair matted to one side, my mother continues singing. She smells like a washed garment, freshly dried in the sun.

"*Baz havaye vatanam, vatanam aarezoost . . .*" The timbre of Amu Doctor's voice rises to meet her. My mother, her eyes still closed, reaches a hand toward Amu Doctor. He wraps his fingers around hers. They sing.

"*I long for the wine maiden who destroys the wine cup.*"

I stroke my mother's face, the gentle mist of warm tears kissing my fingers. She squeezes Amu Doctor's hand encouragingly.

"*I long for the wine maiden who destroys the wine cup.*" Sanam, who has pulled out her earbuds, begins clapping her hands, joining them.

My eyes meet Arman's. He claps along, singing through sobs.

"*It is the hand of dawn that tears the rose's hem. I long to have her bestow the same honor upon me.*"

My mother's face is smooth, except for the wrinkles around her mouth as she forms the words, her voice barely audible. A warm breath slips through my own parted lips and I join the room, singing softly.

"*When I die, instead of a shroud, I long to have the sunlight cover my body.*"

Bahar taps her Sharpie on the upper part of the cast that covers her leg all the way to her hip. She smiles, yet tears begin to well in her eyes.

"When I die, instead of a shroud, I long to have the sunlight cover my body."

We sing the refrain over and over again.

Perhaps it is the lack of sleep, but I have a strange urge to commit every detail of this moment to memory: the humming and the beeping of the hospital equipment; the air, magnetized, like it is about to rain; the merging of our humid breaths as we sing. I swear, there is a whiff of freshly brewed orange blossom tea in the air. My mother takes a long breath through her nose, the corners of her lips curling into a slight smile.

One of the machines begins beeping like a car alarm. My first instinct is to kick and silence it, but the singing stops. My mother is motionless. I shake her shoulders. "Maman?"

48. Arman — SHIRAZ, 2009

I STEP INTO AMU Doctor's courtyard to find Kimia, her eyes closed, meditating in the morning sun. Her hair is still wet from her shower. She hasn't noticed me yet, and I don't want to disturb her. I mean, just because I'm a total mess doesn't mean she can't have a little peace.

My friends always told me my sister was a knockout, and I used that to my advantage—without actually ever really realizing what they were appreciating. But here, this morning, her beauty strikes me and reminds me of our father—her prominent cheekbones, her arching eyebrows. We're orphans now. I start crying again.

She opens her eyes. "How are you doing, Arman?" She pats my arm.

"I'm okay. I'm okay," I say. I'm so not okay. "How are you doing?" I ask, trying to sound more together. Maybe shifting attention from my own miserable self will help.

"I . . ." She shakes her head. "I feel really weird telling you this . . . I wanna grieve Maman, but my thoughts keep going back to Reza." Then she looks me square in the eyes. "I always thought it was my fault that he died."

I freeze. *Please, I beg you.* But she keeps going, completely unaware of what this is doing to me.

"And I still do in a way," she says with a pout. "The thing is, Reza was looking for me. I know it. Even with what Roya said, I still feel guilty. It's irrational, I know. I just wish I had her courage to tell Amu Doctor." Her eyes, big and innocent, remind me of when she was a kid, and I want to punch the wall.

"Fuck!" I say and stand, my hands on my head. "I can't do this anymore."

I storm into the house and find Amu Doctor. He is talking on the phone, making funeral arrangements for our mom. With so many deaths in his . . . our family, this must be somewhat routine for him.

"Amu Doctor, do you mind coming out to the courtyard? I have to tell you something."

49. ARMAN — SHIRAZ, 1981

THE WHOLE MOBAREZIN TRAINING was starting to freak me out. But I didn't know what else to do. I couldn't mope around, helpless because my dad wasn't coming back. And I couldn't stay at home and watch our mother fall apart.

I had a bad feeling when I left the house that day, but then again, my stomach was always in knots when I hung out with Morteza and the gang. Morteza's father had died not long before, and he was so stoic about it. I wanted to be like him so badly, I didn't cry at my own baba's funeral. I thought if I was around Morteza enough, even if it was uncomfortable, I would learn to become a man.

But I was starting to feel we were going about things the wrong way. I hated wrecking people's stuff. I hated seeing fear in their faces as we asked them bullshit questions. The other guys gave me a hard time for not taking charge enough. When I saw Reza in the street, I thought I could pretend to be rough with him. And since I knew him, I could apologize later. I never thought it would end the way it did.

WHEN I SMASHED THAT antique vase at the storyteller's place, I thought I was going to throw up. It was a deep blue jar with delicate fish painted all over it—the kind my dad saw as a piece of our heritage. As soon as the thousand broken pieces hit the floor, something broke inside me.

I stood frozen, watching the destruction, while time slowed: Morteza, intense and focused, his lips upturned in a smile, brought a cane down on a low glass table, sending a turquoise hookah and glass shards flying; Javad flipped a dark bottle of wine out of the rack and whipped it against the wall, the deep crimson splattering like blood; Mohammad emptied the bookshelf and tore out pages of antique-looking books.

I wanted to shout, to stop them, but Reza beat me to it. I watched his little face light with the ferocity of a lion. "How dare you?" he roared, and ran to the fireplace, throwing some explosive inside. The flames were out of control, shooting sparks from the dragon's mouth. Reza watched for an instant and then, with the same determined look on his face, turned around and ran. I let the cane fall from my hand and followed him. I might have heard Morteza shouting my name, but I didn't stop.

I shot up the stairs to see Reza was already gone. Coming up from under the stage in the cooling evening air, I took inventory of the square. There was no sign of the crazy blind Afghan or Reza.

I ran away from the stage while considering where Reza might have run to. Was he trying to find Kimia and the storyteller, or was he heading home?

I had no idea where to start looking for my sister and the morshed. So, I took off toward the known quantity—Reza's house.

I ARRIVED AT REZA'S door and paused. What if he told his parents about what I had done? Azita Khanom would kill me. I swallowed hard and banged on the door. Azita Khanom answered. Her face, wound up in worry, relaxed slightly when she saw me. She obviously hadn't talked to Reza. "Arman, oh God, have you seen Reza?"

"Uh, no, no," I stuttered.

"You must help us find him! And Kimia . . . Your mom is worried sick too," she begged.

"Of course," I said and put on my most reassuring voice. "They're probably together somewhere." I turned to run, hoping this lie would manifest into reality by the time I found Reza. But Azita Khanom shouted, "Wait!"

I stopped. *Oh, God, she's figured me out,* I thought.

"Oh, I'm sorry, you came for something else, yes?" she asked.

I squirmed. "Oh, uh, I wanted, um, Amu Doctor was going to lend me this book on the Sasanian Empire . . ."

"Oh, I'll let him know you came by. He is looking for them too," she said.

"Thanks," I whispered, trying to keep self-loathing out of my voice.

"Call me as soon as you see either of them. Don't forget!" she said, distress wobbling in her eyes.

I ran fast. But then the bombs fell.

50. KIMIA — SHIRAZ, 2009

"I DON'T EXPECT YOU to forgive me," Arman says to Amu Doctor. "I just think you should know." He cries into his open hands. "Reza wouldn't have died and my mom wouldn't have become a mouji if it wasn't for me. You know. I should pay for what I've done." He faces Amu Doctor. "Do you want to press charges or whatever it is you do in this kind of situation?"

Amu Doctor looks at him for a moment. "I have my own secret," he whispers so quietly that I wonder if I have imagined his words. But Arman stops crying and, he, too, searches Amu Doctor's face. The same faraway look casts a glaze over Amu Doctor's features, and for a long while only the bubbling fountain and an occasional birdsong disturbs the silence. A puffy cloud moves over us and covers the stones Reza and I had arranged on the edge of the garden. "Up to now," Amu Doctor says, "I didn't think it was anything I should have shared with you, but here it is."

Arman grimaces, as if bracing himself for a blow. I look away, disgusted. How could Arman have treated Reza like that? But Amu Doctor doesn't seem upset. In fact, the kindness in his face has never been more apparent.

"Shortly after Reza died, he came to me in a dream," Amu Doctor says, his eyes glistening with tears.

Arman and I lean in to hear him.

"He held my face with his little hands and looked in my eyes. He said, 'I love you more than anything, Baba Joon. Know that everything in life is roo hesab—perfectly calculated and precise. No event escapes this. My death happened in accordance to hesab. As will yours and Maman's.' 'But it hurts so much, pesaram,' I cried. 'That's part of it too,' he said with a smile. 'Don't try to make sense of it. Just promise me you will trust life.' I promised him. Then I cried, holding him tight to my chest for what felt like years. When I woke up, I was calm. Like my heart knew something I didn't. I tried to talk to Azita, but she was in a thousand pieces already. Her grief overwhelmed her. That's what killed her. The heart attack was in a way an act of mercy." Amu Doctor wipes his eyes. "You were just a boy." He puts his hand on Arman's shoulder. "Have some gozasht! Be compassionate to yourself!"

And I realize Amu Doctor makes a far better Buddhist than I ever could.

On Reza's bed, I hold the broken drum we found in the wrecked stage area. I can smell him. It hurts. I drop the drum on my lap and pull down my sleeve over my bandaged wrist. I hear a knock.

It's Arman, rapping his knuckles on the doorframe the way he did on the hallway glass after an air raid. "You hate me. It's all right. I hate myself."

I shrug like I'm nine.

He laughs. "You know . . ." His laughter clanks with the hardened lump of remorse. "It feels good to finally feel the hate. I was so afraid of people looking at me with repulsion, the way you're looking at me now. But it's surprisingly . . . liberating."

"What do you want, Arman?" I say, digging my nails into the bedspread.

"Right," he blushes. "Up until that night, I didn't know you had been going to the storyteller's in secret. I found out when Reza told . . ."

I cut him off. "Get to the point."

"I saw Baba Morshed that night."

51. ARMAN — SHIRAZ, 1981

AFTER I LEFT AZITA Khanom, I took off at a run. I knew I would have to retrace my path back through the square. I didn't want to see any of the guys again, so I took the longer way around. The second bomb exploded. I was jolted for a minute, but then I kept running, glancing at the sidewalks and peering into the alleys. But the streets were deserted. People were still hiding, worried more bombs were on the way.

I reached the next alley, exhausted. Panting with my hands on my knees, I peeked around the corner. In the empty alley stood an old man. I could've sworn I had seen him before. With his kolah cap, long old-fashioned shirt, shawl, and white beard, he was perfectly still, like a popup from a children's book. I didn't have time for another mental case like the blind Afghan, so as soon as I caught my breath, I started to run.

As I passed him, he whispered, "Once there was. Once there wasn't," and I stopped cold.

"You! You're the morshed, aren't you?" I pointed in his face.

"At your service," he said in a gracious tone.

"You're the one who's been filling my little sister's head with all the nonsense?" My outrage was justified. He was the reason for this mess I was in. But he just looked back at me with tenderness. I was about to accuse him of more wrongdoing when I remembered how we had destroyed his place. Shame made my skin prickle.

"I had to do it . . . ," I found myself saying aloud.

"Of course," he said, looking at me like I was a book he was leafing through.

"What?" I felt dizzy. "You . . . You're crazy."

"'Love said, you're not mad enough . . . You're not welcome in this house. So, I became mad. So mad, they had to chain me.'"[95]

I was so sick of people around me answering simple questions with cryptic poetry. I wanted to arrest him right there and take him to the commander. Morteza would be so impressed. I let out a harsh laugh. "Old man! You're an infidel. Your house was filled with sinful material. You'll be on the gallows before long. At your age, you haven't learned to follow the Koran's teachings. You haven't learned anything."

"I have learned the only thing that matters in life." He smiled contentedly.

"Yeah? What's that?"

"I have learned how to die."

"How do you die, old man?" I asked with a rush of irritation.

The storyteller lay down right in the middle of the alley and pulled his shawl over him. "Like this!" he said before closing his eyes.

I knelt next to him, staring at his still body. He wasn't breathing. I was shaking when I finally peeled myself away from the ground and braced myself against a wall, throwing up. Then I ran without looking back.

---

95   from Rumi's *Divan e Shams*

52. KIMIA — SHIRAZ, 2009

WE STARE AT EACH other over a bridge made of the ruins of our past. Even though the dark circles beneath his eyes seem like two wells of unshed tears, Arman looks peaceful. The jittery discontent he normally wears like a skin suit has fallen away. He has the resolute composure of a man who is about to walk willingly into the gallows.

"I used to always find you," he says, standing at the doorway. "The one time it really mattered, I failed." He pounds lightly on the doorframe. "Anyway, I'm going to get some noon e sangak for breakfast tomorrow."

I stare at the trampled drum sitting on my lap. When I look up, Arman is gone.

53. Morteza — SHIRAZ, 2009

THE EYES OF THE unholy creature pin me to the wall. I'm paralyzed, less the pouring sweat and my pounding heart.

"Brother Hashemi? Come in, brother, over . . ." An urgent noise comes from a distance over the chatter of two people arguing.

"Brother Hashemi? Over . . ."

Somehow, I'm back in my office, clutching the arms of my chair.

"Brother . . ."

I leap out and turn off the radio that is now playing a talk show. "Hashemi here. Over," I say, pushing the button of the walkie-talkie.

"Brother, we have him. Over."

"Excellent work. Over."

In her cage, Lalu stabs agitated pecks at her chest feathers. I lift my face toward the slow-moving ceiling fan and pull my damp uniform away from my torso. The cooling breeze brings with it a renewed sense of inspiration.

"Bring him to me," I say. "And then position the first squad four blocks to the north of Charrah Moshir. Over."

It is going to be a good evening after all. I throw the walkie-talkie on my desk and take out my black queen. I'm hopeful about my reunion with my comrade, my brother. Plus, God willing, the boot of the Revolution is going to crush these foreign agitators, these dirty cockroaches who keep disturbing the city's peace, once and for all.

54. KIMIA — THE VALLEY OF AWE

FROM THE TOP OF Poshteh Moleh, we watched the dusk soak the sky and drench Shiraz in indigo light. Baba Morshed pulled out his setar and strummed the strings, tuning the instrument. He plucked a single note, letting it ring. The sound reverberated through the mountains. I stared out over the city with wide eyes as the birds approached from the darkening skies.

"*Huuu . . .*" Baba Morshed chanted. My entire body became a cord, trembling to match the sound. I breathed in the cool mountain air and marveled at the flying specks on the horizon. After a long while the sound's echo faded into silence. I looked at the storyteller, my heart filling with a love that only grows in the fertile soil of trust. Baba Morshed was my best friend now. No one had been there for me the way he had. A frown knotted my brow as I thought of Reza.

Baba Morshed began playing his setar, the same bittersweet melody of the night at the square. The birds formed themselves into the shape of the Simorgh and flapped their wings to the music. To the quickening tempo, they soared as one, the graceful bird of my dreams, ascending toward the heavens. The prodigious bird settled into flying a steady rhythm to the music, when a small jet approached behind it. The harsh sound of its engine clashed against the magical notes. The birds broke their formation and scattered in the sky. A dark cylinder fell from the plane onto the city. Effulgent clouds emerged from the spot, and like thunder after lightning, a loud boom clapped all around. But Baba Morshed kept playing his setar.

"In the Valley of Awe, it was neither day nor night. Fire was cold like ice, and the snow scorching hot. It was unbearable for many. The frightened falcon flew as high as he could into the sky. He could no longer breathe. As he plummeted back toward the earth, he said to himself, 'I know nothing. I don't know whether I am or I am not. I am in love, but with whom? My heart is both full and empty.'

"Hoopoe said, 'Yes, this is awe.'"

A second bomb dropped. A bright fire began churning inside the slow-rising puff of dust and smoke. Before I could react, Baba Morshed's fingers strummed faster, coaxing an impassioned tune from the setar. An inexplicable joy burst inside me without warning. I felt the way I did when Reza and I clasped each other's hands, spinning round until we were dizzy and collapsed onto the floor. Listening to each other's laughter, we would crack up even more.

The sound of my own laughter startled me. But then it echoed, making me laugh harder. When I eventually stopped, I noticed Baba Morshed was done playing, his setar by his side, the fire from below bathing his face in a faint light. I looked at Shiraz. The city was both burning and weeping silently.

A question was beginning to root in my mind, but the old man's voice halted my thoughts. "Rumi Jon, I have to tell you this is our last time together." The storyteller locked eyes with me, his face serene, while an inferno burned beneath us. There was silence, save for the sound of my own heartbeat. I wanted to protest. *Why, Baba Morshed? The story isn't finished yet. We haven't even gotten to the Seventh Valley. What happens to the birds?* But breaking that pure silence with my words seemed as bad as breaking my own heart.

"Oh, dokhtaram," he said finally. "I want nothing more than to tell you stories until my last breath. But I have just learned that my time as your morshed has come to an end. You will have adventures and stories of your own."

I flung myself at him.

"I will always be with you. Now, you must go. Your mother needs you. Hurry!" he said, prying me from him. I searched his serious face. He had never commanded me to do anything. Soon I was on my feet, running down the mountain. I wasn't sure what had just happened, but an urgency propelled me to keep descending. In spite of the rush, when I was at the bottom, I turned around. "What's the Seventh Valley?" I screamed at the mountain. The mountain echoed my question.

55. ARMAN — SHIRAZ, 2009

IF THIS WAS ANY other time, I would have been scared out of my mind. But I was already expecting to be struck down by lightning now that my secret was out in the open. I was roaming the streets, trying to find some way to show my repentance, when they nabbed me—like you see in the movies.

I was in the middle of leaving a message for Jason when they threw a bag over my head and hurled me in the back of a van. I didn't resist at all, and when one of the kidnappers jabbed the barrel of a gun into my ribs, I was relieved in a way, thinking he would put me out of my misery.

Inside the bag, I close my eyes. Two men, reeking of sweat and stale smoke, flank me in the back seat, and from the sound of the door slamming, I figure there is another person in the front besides the driver. I haven't felt this calm in a long time.

After a brief drive, the van stops. I'm guided out and into a building. They lead me up a few flights of stairs. I can't see, so I stumble a few times. One of my captors holds my arm in the vise grip of his beefy hand and digs the tip of the gun into my side with the other. They don't say anything, and I don't ask any questions. I wonder if they're surprised.

From the sound of our footsteps, it feels like we're walking through a hallway and into a room. One of the men forces me to sit and ties my hands behind my back.

"Don't move," says a voice in my ear. The man's breath smells like the soggy cigarette butts I've pulled from the Pink Poodle urinals. My thoughts turn to Jason, who is scheduled to arrive soon. I hear the door banging shut and someone locking it, even though I'm tied to a chair.

As I test the zip-tie handcuffs and shift forward and back in place, I wonder if Jason got my phone message. What would he do if he saw me right now? Why was I kidnapped anyway? I still carry thirty years' worth of guilt and shame for what I've done, but this doesn't make any sense. Could this be a ransom kidnapping? But I'm not rich. Maybe they're targeting Kimia, who's better off. Or maybe I'm in a government building. But why? They didn't look at me twice at the airport. I've never been political. I've only been in Shiraz for a couple of days.

I wait for two hours, maybe three. I have a lot of time to think. I think about our mother, how she looked so light and free, her last words, a favorite song. I begin crying. Is the willow tree sapling we planted above my dad's gravestone still alive?

I think about Amu Doctor. If he forgave me, that means Reza forgives me too, right? I think of Kimia, who hates me. Does she even know where I am? I think about how much I love them all. More tears.

The tiny holes of the fabric covering my head are beginning to resemble cells of a beehive. In one AP class, I had to prove mathematically why it's more efficient for bees to construct hexagonal versus circular cells. An urgent need for a pen and paper itches my bound hands. I'm light-headed.

Inside the humid sack, sweat pours down my forehead, stinging my eyes—like when I would arrive home all sweaty from Mobarezin training. I'd go straight to the secret stash of Marvel comics under my mattress. I'd lock the door and kneel by the bed, carefully removing the top comic. I'd put it on top of the bed and open it to the first page. All the dialogue bubbles above the characters were written in English, so I had to invent my own storyline. At first it was frustrating, but then I took a liking to the freedom it offered. I could forge a new story each time. That way, Spider-Man always had something new to say to the Green Goblin. But I never messed with the *KABOOM!* and *POW!* sound effects written in larger letters.

Those days, I loved my Marvels and Imam Hossain—well, mostly Imam Hossain's beard . . . All I knew about him was that he had been martyred in a great battle, and he must've had a great beard. I had to imagine this, too, as Muslims aren't keen on keeping pictures of their saints—something about portraits or statues promoting idol worshipping. What would my kidnappers think of *American Idol*?

The door is flung open. The sound of footsteps enters and stops next to my chair. I want to wipe the drool running down my chin, but that's impossible. I pull myself up and wait. Finally, the sack is ripped off my head in a swift motion. I squint.

It takes me a minute to recognize him, but standing in front of me is a much older version of Morteza Hashemi, my buddy from Mobarezin. The room looks like an office with a cluttered desk featuring a very dead plant, and a bird in a cage. Dressed in wrinkled fatigues, Morteza scowls through an even more massive beard than the one I so envied. He has a thick head of graying hair, which, despite the circumstances, I now find myself envying too.

"Ah, hello brother," Morteza says in a raspy smoker's voice. "At last we meet again." He bends, his face inches away from me, his red eyes peering into mine, searching. "It's been a long, long time."

"Hello, Brother Hashemi," I say, embarrassed of my drool. My eyes scan the room. Does he work here?

"Now, what brings you here, brother?" he says casually as he sits at his desk.

I wiggle my fingers, the plastic zip tie digging into my wrists. My arms have fallen asleep and my hands tingle. This surely is a prank, right? I never imagined my childhood buddies would actually stick with the Revolutionary Guard stuff. We were just teenagers. I think about answering Morteza with a joke. But his baleful smile makes me think twice. "Well, I was brought here by some men I couldn't see . . ."

"Why does your accent sound like a foreigner?" Morteza interrupts, a puzzled frown lining his forehead.

"I guess I'm a little out of practice," I say, self-consciously.

Morteza leans back in his chair. "You always lacked grit, didn't you? Yet . . . I must confess, brother, I saw something in you. Me and the other boys, we wanted recognition. But you, that didn't seem to interest you. There was an intensity about you." Morteza now smiles appraisingly, like I'm a rug he is intent on purchasing at Vakil Bazaar. "Now tell me why you're here!"

"Ahem, as I was saying, someone threw a bag over my head—"

"No!" Morteza slams his fist on the desk, the edge of his smile disappearing into his beard. The dead plant rattles. The black bird flaps her wings in the cage. "Why are you back in Shiraz?"

"Right. My mother . . . She wanted to come back and she was sick . . . She—she just passed away," I offer. *What in shit's name is happening here?*

"May God rest her soul. Tell me, where did you bring her from?"

"From America," I say.

"America!" he laughs for a long time. When he finishes, Morteza addresses the bird. "Did you hear that, Lalu? He was in America this whole time." He lights a cigarette and takes a long drag. "Anyway, tell me what it is you do in America."

"I'm a, uh, a manager."

"Oh?" replies Morteza. With the cigarette hanging from his lips, he picks up the tea kettle on his desk and pours tea into one of the cups on his desk. He puffs on the cigarette, watching me. I lower my eyes from the red glow of the cigarette tip to the steam rising from the tea. Morteza blows smoke in the bird's cage, and the bird turns away from him. He laughs again. "So, what is it that you manage, Brother Shams?"

"A, uh, restaurant." I wiggle my hands behind my back again. No one has called me Brother Shams in decades.

Morteza lifts his estekan to his lips. "Ey, I'm so practical these days that I've become rude." He puts the tea back on the desk. "Let me pour you some tea."

"Oh, no, that's okay, thanks," I say, wondering if I should ask why I've been arrested.

Morteza pours tea in one of the several dirty cups on his desk. "I insist," he says.

I direct my gaze to the floor, unsure whether he is mocking me or just absentminded.

"I suppose I'm also a manager," he says, making a great show of grinding the butt into the ashtray. "I manage the Basiji volunteers for our state. Three thousand men answer to me. But this is a stepping-stone. Soon I will be promoted again."

I'm too weak and defeated to muster anything other than a long inaudible sigh. I haven't eaten in so long, my stomach grumbles loudly. "Congratulations, brother," I finally say.

"That night in the storyteller's place—do you remember it?"

"Yes." My face heats up, and I'm not sure why Morteza has brought up the morshed. In the cage, the bird pecks her feathers.

"You left when the fire started. I've never seen anything like that—not even during the war." Morteza finishes his tea. "I never saw much of you after that night, and then . . . You were gone, just like that." He snaps his fingers. "Tell me, have you been in contact with the morshed?"

I must have misheard him. "I'm sorry . . . what?"

"Oh, nothing . . . Is America everything you thought it would be?"

"America? It's all right," I say, relieved to move on from that subject. But then I remember Jason is en route, and fear churns in my stomach.

"I'm sure you're some sort of big shot over there," Morteza continues. "As for me, things didn't go so well after that night. It's funny, you know, if I was superstitious, I would say that storyteller put some sort of a curse on me! But that's ridiculous, right?"

"Right," I agree.

Morteza downs the tea that was meant for me, and he pulls back his sleeve, revealing an ugly burn scar. My eyes widen.

"You left me," Morteza hisses, his jaw tightening.

I feel my blood turn to ice. Morteza's face is close to mine again. A vein bulges against his forehead. I brace myself for a punch, but he reaches out his hand and strokes my face with surprising gentleness. "It's good to have you back, brother," he says, his eyes lit with genuine affection.

56. Morteza — SHIRAZ, 1981

I HAD JUST SHATTERED a hookah with the morshed's cane when the hellfire from the fiend's mouth leaped across the room. I turned to find it whirling toward me as if I was the target it sought. I tried to duck, but I was too late. The last thing I saw before I shielded my face with my arm was the green of two beastly eyes.

The pain penetrated into my arm bone, blinding me. It grabbed the breath out of my chest and melted my thoughts. My exhalation came out as a scream, a sound so powerful, it brought silence to the entire room. I staggered, collapsing onto the floor by the desk, holding my injured arm stiff at an angle, unable to look it. I could smell the charred flesh and it sickened me. The boys had stopped in shock, staring at me. All at once, I remembered where I was and who I was with. I searched for Arman. "Brother Shams!" I screamed. But he was gone. He had taken the boy with him too. I think Javad was saying something as he walked over to me, but I wasn't paying attention.

Since I had become an orphan months before, relatives had been kind and neighbors had brought me dinner. But it had been the commander's guidance and Arman's friendship that had sustained me. *Where is Arman now when I need him most?*

I stood and picked up the storyteller's fat book with my good hand and hurled it in the fire. "Ahhhh!" The book exploded, sending sparks to the pile of ripped pages on the rugs.

Soon the demonic fire spread, and the black bird started pecking at my head. I snatched her, crushing her wings in my fist, thinking I was going to rip her head off. She looked at me with her yellow eyes, her heart stammering against my fingers. I searched around the desk. I emptied out a cloth sack full of pistachios and put her inside. The fire was getting closer, its hot flames making me sweat, smoke burning my eyes. We had to leave.

We all stumbled out from under the stage, coughing. I choked down the pain that was now spreading all the way to my eyeballs and said, "We must find the commander, immediately."

But they just looked at me, terror naked in their faces. "Cowards!" The scream ripped through my throat before I could catch myself. Predictably, the insult didn't inspire them. They turned and ran to their mothers, and I felt more alone in that moment than I ever had.

Grunting, I allowed myself a quick glance at the wound. The swollen, red-and-white melted flesh made me queasy. The burn extended from the middle of my forearm to my elbow. I sank to the ground, leaning against the stage. I wanted to cry, but my tears had also withered in the fire. My mind had become filled with smoke. Hope was hiding somewhere in the shadows beyond my reach. I was about to leave and return dejected to my empty house when the bird fluttered in the sack I was holding. My thoughts meandered through all my losses, splintering into solutions and stopping on the commander. He was the one I could always depend on even when everything seemed so awful. He had children of his own, but he called me son. The commander was grooming me to be a leader like himself.

I tied a quick knot, closing the sack that contained the bird. I knew exactly where he would be. It was just as well that the boys ran. I would show the commander the morshed's hiding place, and he would put me in charge of a squad of men—not boys—to hunt the storyteller down. But it still bothered me that Shams had deserted the mission. Perhaps even more than the searing burn of the hell I'd just gone through. I was thinking about a proper punishment for Arman and the boys when a bomb exploded, shaking the felekeh. I held on to the stage to steady myself.

Then I saw him, right at the edge of the square. It was the storyteller, limping around the corner into a dark street.

A jolt of fear and excitement sprinted through me. "I've got you now, old man," I hissed, picking up the sack.

I ran and rounded a corner, shouting, "Hey, morshed!" My voice resounded through the empty street. "You can't hide from me!"

Another bomb. With my ears still ringing, it was hard to say whether it had hit close or far. The earth shook just the same.

When I caught my breath, I scanned the streets to see a dark figure disappear into another alley to my right. I took off in that direction, and that's when I saw Shams yelling at the old man. I wanted to go to them, but it all happened so fast. The morshed laid himself on the ground and Shams bolted.

I walked over to the old man. His eyes closed, he was motionless. I knelt by his side and touched his neck. He was still warm but had no pulse.

57. Morteza — SHIRAZ, 2009

"A restaurant." I laugh when I'm alone. While I fought on the front line with a hundred thousand young Basiji volunteers, Arman Shams was in America, serving the Great Satan. I try to imagine this restaurant. My mind goes to bartenders pouring American beer in tall glasses and Shams, wandering among customers, his soft hands on their shoulders and laughing at their jokes.

Shams is either a superb actor or he is innocent. Well, "innocent" might be a strong word. There are consequences for betrayal. But I will soon find out whether Shams is hiding anything.

Ahmadi put a tail on the Shams family for a while. They had been either at home or the hospital the entire time. I told Ahmadi it was best to detain Arman Shams in a discreet manner. In the midst of containing the protests and being shorthanded at the office, I'm grateful to have loyal deputies like Ahmadi.

I take out the queen, holding it in the palm of my hand. It feels uncomfortably warm, making my hand clammy. I glance over at the photos spread on my desk and examine the one in the middle. The identity of the lone figure isn't easy to decipher, but I have a hunch it's no coincidence *they* arrive in Shiraz, and at the same time the storyteller, after all these years, has crawled from the depths of hell to stalk me.

"Five minutes," I say to the guards, who are laughing in the hallway. My voice knocks them to attention and they respond with, "Yes, sir!"

I gather the photos and place them neatly in the folder and lock up the queen. The guards remain silent as I head for the street, where the idling Jeep grunts.

My lieutenant, who sits in the back with an AK-47 on his lap, and the driver both salute me. I climb in, and the driver eases onto the nearly empty nighttime street. *Good*, I think, glancing at the surrounding apartment buildings. *No shouting tonight.* I light a cigarette, regretting the silence a little too. As we drive, I listen for any sound that would give me an excuse to take action. On good days, I pray for the agitators to find the right path, but right now, I just want to rid the city of the filth once and for all. I'm about to take another drag when I see them in the headlights—Shams's sister standing next to a hunched old man with a cane. The old man's gaze rakes over me.

"Stop!" I shout.

"Sir?" says the driver as he slams on the brakes. I shush him without taking my eyes off them. I jump out, running at full speed, but in a flash, the woman and the old man each melt into the shadows, heading in opposite directions.

58. ARMAN — SHIRAZ, 2009

I'M IN SOLITARY CONFINEMENT—WHICH is a good thing. The blend of my sweat, fear, and hunger has produced an ungodly odor I can barely tolerate myself.

I've heard about Tehran's infamous Evin Prison—all the human rights violations, the torture, the brutal interrogations . . . I wonder if Evin is some sort of a chain like KFC or McDonald's. Do they try to be consistent in all their procedures? Is there an employee manual that this Shirazi prison follows? I realize I don't even know the name of this place.

Hours ago—by now I've lost track of time—they took my belt, wallet, phone, shoes, and socks. I was handed a pair of stained and cracked dampaee flip-flops and was escorted to this six-by-seven cell. I slump on the opposite side of a filthy toilet, on a rug that must have been thin even before it was worn out. Why do they call it a cell?

The jiggling of keys in the door snaps me up straight. When the door opens, I shield my eyes. The hallway light shines brightly while the flickering, dim single bulb in my cell threatens to go out at any time. A pudgy bearded man walks in. He reminds me of Haji, the kababi guy, before his shop was bombed. He greets me warmly, shaking my hand. He hands me a photo out of a folder he is holding. "Who is this man?"

I tilt the picture toward the hallway light. Haji points at a blond man. He is talking to my sister, mother, and Amu Doctor, whose back is to the camera.

"I have no idea." I hand the photo back to Haji. I'm curious myself.

Haji smiles and slips the photo back into the folder. "I see . . . I'll be back."

The door clanks shut, and I try to piece together what's happening. Who is that blond man? Why hasn't anyone mentioned him to me? I know Morteza is upset, but did he actually arrest me for going after Reza that night? Or does it have something to do with the blond guy? "Seriously, why am I here?" I say aloud. I know, I know . . . I've been asking this question all my life.

I'm about to settle back into my corner when I hear the sound of someone screaming.

WELL, I'M NOT CURIOUS anymore. I don't care whether the prison guards consult some sort of employee handbook or not. Wincing, I roll to my side away from the toilet. If my feet didn't throb so badly, I'd be certain I have a terrific headache.

After Haji left, I listened to a poor man in the throes of a whipping. I could hear each strike and his shouts so clearly, it felt like they came from inside my own cell. A few hours after the screaming stopped, I fell asleep. Ironically, it was the first peaceful sleep I've had in years. I awoke when the door opened and Haji and a constipated-looking middle-aged man stepped in. Like with Morteza, I had the impulse to make a joke to lighten the mood, but they didn't look like they would laugh either. They took me to a small office. The constipated guy asked my name and address, maybe fourteen thousand times. At one point, I asked why I was there, and the man said they were the ones asking the questions. Haji asked me about the blond man in that photo. I thought about telling them to talk to Kimia and Amu Doctor but didn't want to get them into trouble.

"Are you a spy? A foreign agent?" the constipated man asked.

I laughed at first, but the man just glared. "No . . . I swear to God I'm not," I said, pleadingly.

"Do you still pray?" Haji asked.

"Yes," I answered guiltily.

"Recite the first part of the prayer," the clogged-up man demanded.

Luckily, I remembered all the verses from my teenage religious era. At the end, I was exhausted and both men appeared frustrated, but neither raised their voices.

When they finally stopped with the questions, I thought they were going to escort me back to my cell. But they took a turn down a narrow hallway and into a small room. There was a bare wooden bed in the center, and they asked me to lie there, facedown. My mind raced, realizing what was about to happen. I wanted to attempt a last-ditch effort to make them stop, but I had nothing. I couldn't ask for Morteza. He was the one who had ordered them to do this. It was no use to claim this was a mistake. I didn't have any information to offer about the blond man in the photo and couldn't think of a lie. So I lay down.

They tied me to the bed.

The first lash striking my feet was a lightning bolt. The pain was so jarring that no sound escaped my mouth. Instead my whole body hardened like a knife hand ready to strike back. I squeezed my eyes shut and waited for the second lash.

With each strike, my body felt like a thousand pieces of a jigsaw puzzle, all scattering around the room. In between lashes, the puzzle was put back together minus a piece or two. My screams made my throat raw and I tasted blood.

When they stopped, I thought it was over. But no, they wanted me to walk around the room on my injured feet. I saw Haji, breathing hard and holding a thick cable. That's what he'd used.

Haji's cell phone rang. He answered, "Alo," as I hobbled around.

"Salaam, khanom . . . go ahead and cut the cake," he said, panting. "I'm sorry, you know how it is. We're short-staffed and I have to work late. Khoda hafez." He hung up the phone and signaled me to lie down again.

As they tied me back to the bed, I found myself oddly grateful to Maman, thinking that by horsewhipping me, she might have tried to prepare me for something like this. The lash that followed reminded me she couldn't have possibly prepared me for this— that, khoda biamorz,[96] she was mostly a lousy parent.

They did the whole song and dance twice more before I was led back to my cell. By that time, my swollen feet didn't fit the flimsy prison dampaee. With each step, I was reminded of the number of screaming nerve endings on the bottom of my feet.

As I fell onto the floor of my cell, my mind wandered to Morteza, and everything made sense. He was yet another person whose life I had destroyed. If only I had stopped hanging with him when things began to go sideways, Morteza wouldn't have dropped by my house that day. His timing would have missed Reza. The boys wouldn't have found Baba Morshed's place. Maybe now Morteza would be a gym teacher or a happy bureaucrat somewhere. I breathed in the damp, rank air of the tiny cell. *This is exactly what I deserve.* I let out a sorry moan and crawled to a corner.

Before they left, Haji said, "Treason is a serious crime, punishable by death. You need to start talking if you want to live."

There are three tic-tac-toe games scribbled on the wall inches from my face. One of them is unfinished. Where is a damned pen when you need one?

---

96   may God rest her soul

59. KIMIA — SHIRAZ, 2009

"MAY THIS BE YOUR last sorrow," says Neda, my childhood neighbor and friend. She looks just the same as when I left her years ago. Her husband, a male version of herself, handsome and stylish, kneels to tie their daughter's shoe while other guests weave around them to reach the door.

Neda kisses me on both cheeks. "Where is Agha Arman?" she asks, the corners of her tear-stained eyes wrinkling with concern.

"He's out running errands," I say with practiced calm, but she is already distracted, wrangling her family out the door.

My mother's funeral service is much less crowded and drama-filled than my dad's. There are a few loud mourners, but most are somber and introspective. I only recognize a handful of people, but many guests tell me they remember me as a child. As I say my goodbyes to them, I walk Mr. and Mrs. Sholeh to the courtyard. They both appear smaller, each holding one of Dana's hands in their own. And suddenly, I'm back at my father's funeral, watching them take tea from my tray.

"I miss Roya Joon," says Dana, her black scarf sliding from her head.

"Me too, Azizam," I say.

WHEN THE RELATIVES WHO stayed behind to help us clean are gone, Amu Doctor and I take out the garbage. Thinking about Arman, I wrinkle my nose in frustration. "He tells us he is going to buy bread and then he gets distracted by something else? Typical Arman! But this time he's gone too far. To miss our own mother's funeral is unconscionable."

"I'm concerned for his safety," says Amu Doctor, wheeling out the garbage can.

"I know my brother. He's going to show up in the middle of the night with some excuse."

"Perhaps you're right. Hopefully he will tell us all about it in the morning," Amu Doctor says, his gaze fixed to the door.

Back in my room, I realize that with my mother's death, there are no reasons left for me to stay in Shiraz for a moment longer. I begin pulling clothes out of the closet to pack my suitcase. I call my travel agent, booking my flight for the following evening.

A LIGHT, RAPID KNOCK awakens me. Opening my eyes, I'm surprised to see it's already morning and, for the first time in weeks, I've slept through the night. I rush to the door, expecting to see Arman, but Amu Doctor's worried eyes greet me instead.

"Salaam, golam. Arman still hasn't come home. His suitcase and passports are untouched in his room."

My hand goes to my mouth.

As I search through Arman's belongings to find Jason's contact information, Amu Doctor makes phone calls to the few people he knows in the government. He calmly takes notes and hangs up and dials again. His graying hair and mustache are neatly combed, and his ironed shirt peeks out of his suit jacket. I have resumed a discarded habit from my youth, as I studiously bite my nails to the quick. Arman and I have hardly spoken since he arrived at the hospital on the day Roya was admitted. I haven't told him about hosting JJ or being caught in the protest, and he only mentioned that Jason planned to join us, but he hadn't been able to reach him in time to cancel his trip.

"On what charges?" Amu Doctor says into the phone. He scribbles something on a pad and faces me. "We have to go down there in person. Arman has been arrested, and they won't tell me what the charges are."

Minutes later, Amu Doctor and I exit our car and run toward the entrance of Seppah Prison. I'm sweating inside my black raincoat and scarf, remembering why I especially hated hijab during the summer heat. My mouth parched and my childhood ulcer burning in the pit of my stomach, we approach a booth occupied by a skinny young man. He chews gum with the ardor of a baseball player. A handgun rests in a holster strapped to his waist, and a rifle stands in the corner of the booth.

"Salaam aleykom. We're here to see about Arman Shams. Mr. Noroozi sent us," says Amu Doctor.

"Alaykomussalaam. Let me take a look." To the beat of his rapidly snapping jaw, the young man begins punching keys on his laptop. "Oh, there he is," he says, looking at the monitor. "Wait, no. Bebakhshid." A mystified frown wrinkles his forehead as he clicks on the mouse a few times. "Ah, you have to go to the Basiji headquarters."

"Why?" I say.

"Not sure . . . that's all it says here," the young man says with a shrug, and adjusts his small table fan toward his face.

"You think they got him for using drugs?" I ask Amu Doctor

as we hustle back to the car. "He was using pot in San Diego . . . I can't imagine he'd be that stupid here."

"Baba Jon, he went to buy naan," Amu Doctor says, opening the car door for me. "He was upset, but taking a detour to buy drugs in a city he hasn't visited in thirty years is not likely. I'm more worried that he may have come across a protest and gotten swept up on some mass arrest."

I wait in the steamy car for Amu Doctor to begin driving. The gracious cypresses lining the street salute me, telling me again that I'm home, while a hot pain claws behind my eyes. Arman is difficult, to be sure, but the thought of something bad happening to him makes me ache in a fresh way. As Amu Doctor turns the ignition key, I watch a brother and sister skipping into the shade on the sidewalk, their parents behind them. Arman is the only one I have left. The thought knocks the wind out of me. He has to be all right. He has to.

A small leaf trapped in the windshield wiper shivers against the glass as Amu Doctor navigates the insane traffic expertly. I cringe, remembering how rude I have been to him. He is more like family to me now than ever before. I'm suddenly overcome with such boundless love and respect for him, it's hard for me to contain myself. "Thank you," I whisper.

"'Even though I am me and you are you. You are me and I am you,'"[97] he recites without taking his eyes off the road.

WHEN WE ARRIVE AT the address the young man has given us, they take my phone and imprints of my fingers. They wouldn't let Amu Doctor in the building, claiming he isn't immediate family. I imagine him outside, pacing under the tree shade, waiting for news.

I, too, wait.

There are no clocks in the unadorned hallway, but I must have

97   from Rumi's *Divan e Shams*

been sitting on this foldout chair for two hours, my eyes on the chipped linoleum tile near my foot. For a while, the sound of a collective chant, *"Death to the Dictator,"* kept crashing like a wave into a distant shore. All is silent now.

I eventually stand to stretch my legs. Glancing at the closed door next to my chair, I wonder if this is the place where decades ago, Arman rushed every day before school. I think about what he said about the storyteller. For the longest time, I was convinced Baba Morshed was part of some childhood fantasy, a conjuring of my overactive imagination to deal with, well, to deal with those days. But now, I'm beginning to question everything. Then again, how can I explain shadow puppets having such color and detail to them? How about the strangeness of the Valleys?

The door opens, and a bearded man in fatigues and army boots says, "Befarma. Your time has arrived." His eyes averted, he steps aside to let me in the door. I pass an empty reception area and walk into a messy office smelling of old cigarettes. A middle-aged man sits behind the desk, writing in a notebook. I stand, waiting for him to finish.

"Salaam, Sister Shams. It's good to see you again," the man says, closing his notebook.

"Salaam," I say, searching my memory for all the faces I have come across since arriving in Shiraz several days ago. But I would have remembered this man's thick eyebrows, beard, and hair. There is something familiar about his manner, but I can't place it.

"Do you wear this hijab in America too?" he says, gesturing casually toward my raincoat and scarf.

"Ahem," I begin, half-positive I have missed the first part of this conversation. "Yes," I say with an upward inflection of a Cali girl being quizzed.

"Every day?"

"I wear this one on odd days and I have a brown one I wear on even days," I lie spontaneously. *Does my dress code have an impact on Arman's fate?*

"You don't remember me?"

"Sorry. It's been a long few days."

He laughs in a menacing way and walks over to a cage containing a black bird. "Lalu, she doesn't remember," he says to the bird. *Myna!* But it can't be. Myna's eyes were golden and piercing. From the bird's profile, it appears her eye is just black.

"Look! She remembers you, Lalu!" he says. I watch him, still addled. He appears both amused and angry. I find myself in no-man's land, somewhere between a dream and a childhood memory, the same unsettling whirlwind I have stumbled upon many times since arriving in Shiraz.

"I call her Lalu, because she is a mute myna. At least I can't get her to talk to me! I must confess, it gets on my nerves sometimes. She probably looks a little different than when you knew her. She had an . . . accident." The man grimaces and lights a cigarette. "It's fine, though. I like that she turns a blind eye on me." He exhales the smoke, watching me. The bird turns around in her cage. Myna's shiny, expressive eye looks at me with anguish. Pain clutches my chest.

"It was very cute, if you must know," the man says with laughter in his voice, but anger keeps finding a way back to his eyes. "A couple of times she pretended she was dead, so I would take her out of the cage, but I, too, have read Rumi poems." He taps his head with his index finger and smiles a mouth full of stained teeth.

I grab the edge of the desk so as not to lose my balance. The already stuffy air, freshly polluted with smoke, makes it hard to breathe. I focus on an unwashed estekan on the desk.

He reaches into a drawer and takes out a black chess piece. "Remember this?" he says in a singsong tone, turning the piece between two fingers. Puffing on his cigarette, he waits behind his desk, eagerly, like he is about to watch his favorite TV show.

I suppress a gasp. Of course I've seen this black queen. My mind races to Arman's account of that night. I stare at the man, who looks back at me with bristling contempt. This man is Morteza, and he has Arman. My skin crawls with revulsion. I try to keep my voice steady. "Where is my brother?"

He loosens his grip, letting the chess piece fall on the desk. "Let me answer with another question. Where is Baba Morshed?"

"What? He . . . he died that night . . . when the bombs fell . . . the night you and Arman went to his house."

Morteza shakes his head, disappointed. The silence between us becomes tense like a setar string, the whole room ringing with it. The forgotten cigarette burns to a stub between Morteza's fingers. There has to be something I can say or do to help Arman. "I swear, I didn't see Baba Morshed after that night."

"You're lying!" he shouts. He crushes the butt in the ashtray. "Stop looking at me!"

I drop my gaze to the floor.

"I saw you with him last night." He points at me with a renewed bitterness in his voice.

"That can't be. I was at my mother's funeral last night," I say without meeting his eyes.

He walks over and hands me a photo. "Who is that in the corner?" He gestures to an out-of-focus figure in the background of a photo of myself and JJ. A man in a green shawl is bent, as if to pick something from the ground or to tie his shoe.

"I can't tell who that is. Whoever that is . . . I can't see his face."

"Did the old man show you how to put curses on people?"

"Baba Morshed? He only told stories. I was only nine!"

"Some of the most dangerous people I know are like nine-year-olds." He laughs. He goes to the bird's cage, and without looking at me, he whispers, "It's simple. Bring me the old man or your brother dies."

60. Morteza — SHIRAZ, 2009

I'VE BEEN WATCHING HIM for some time. My brother sleeps on his rug peacefully, completely unaware of another presence in his cell. I could watch him all night. But there is a pressing matter I must attend to. I kneel and touch Shams on the shoulder.

"Dadash, khabi?" I whisper. *Are you asleep, brother?*

Shams jerks awake, his eyes searching the cell. He draws a sharp breath, as if he remembers where he is.

"Brother Hashemi!" He scuttles to sit upright, bristling in pain as he moves himself about his swollen feet. "Listen, I don't know who this foreigner is. I swear it."

"Who? Oh," I say, remembering the foreign correspondent. I sit on the chair I have brought and light my cigarette. "He doesn't concern me right now." I take my habitual first long drag and exhale. "What I want is the morshed." I watch as surprise flashes across his face. "Do you know where he is?"

"He died, brother," Shams answers, his voice resigned. I'm certain my brother wishes he was safely back at his restaurant.

"See, here's the thing. I saw him talking to you that night," I say. I lean back and take another long puff. He opens his mouth, but I show him my palm. "I saw how you left him. Dead. You.

You made a fool of me, brother." I flick the unfinished cigarette on the floor and crush it under my boot. "That's right. I fetched the commander in the chaos after the bombing, because I wanted him to see what we had done to the blasphemous morshed. But guess what?" Shams shakes his head. "He wasn't there!"

I laugh a long laugh, knuckling a tear from the corner of my eye before continuing. "I took the commander to the stage. I actually had him crawl under with me! There was no trapdoor! My hands got torn up and bloody from digging in the dirt. You know what the commander did?" I say through clenched teeth. "He backhanded me for pulling him away from his family right after two bombs fell."

I study Shams's face. My scar burns and I reach for it.

"I'm so sorry, brother. I had no idea," he says. "I had so much to think about those days. But now I understand I wasn't a good friend. I let you down. Please forgive me."

But I smell fear, and where there is fear, there is deceit. For weeks after that night, I watched Shams exit the schoolyard, talking with his friends, but I never approached him. In my naivete, I hoped that Shams himself would reach out. What a fool I was.

"I would've done something if I'd known. I should've talked to you," Shams says, twenty-eight years too late. "What about the others? Couldn't they verify your account?"

"They were too spooked to talk. It didn't help that the commander stripped my rank. I think he encouraged them to not talk to me. They're all gone anyway . . . Be rahmate khoda raftan. They've joined our maker."

"What? I'm so sorry!" He puts his face in his hands.

"That's right. Javad and Mohammad became martyrs when we were all on the front line fighting that devil Saddam. And Abbas had an unfortunate motorcycle accident when he returned home. The commander was the victim of a hit-and-run. They never found the guy."

I run my hand over my beard. "I saw your reluctance at the storyteller's place. You didn't want to harm his things. And then you just left. What I want to know—did you just abandon me, or was it your plan to set me up?" He drops his hands and stares at me with a mixture of horror and pity, like I'm some sort of a ghoul who even frightens himself.

"Here's a funny thing," I plow on. "I go to Bank Melli to deposit a check, and guess who's scurrying away? That morshed, dirt on his head! When the cockroaches spill into the streets, there he is in the middle, marching. But when I go over there, he is gone. Guess who I saw him with last night?"

"I don't know," Shams whispers.

"Your sister! She is still running around with him like she did when she was a child. Did you know that?" I watch bewilderment quiver on his face. Apparently, his sister is still keeping secrets from him. "She came by today. I told her if she doesn't bring the old man to me, I'm going to kill you." I stand. "But really, if she doesn't bring me the storyteller, I'm going to kill her too."

Fear becomes wide in his eyes.

I chuckle and exit. As I lock the door behind me, I feel it jolt as he slams against it, screaming.

61. KIMIA — SHIRAZ, 2009

BEFORE I LEFT MORTEZA'S office, the last thing I heard over the gallop of my own racing heartbeat was his voice, dripping with venom: "If you say one word about this to anyone, he dies."

Jason, Arman's friend, has arrived for his vacation to see us in mourning and Arman in prison. Somehow, this is exactly how I pictured a holiday in Iran.

We gather in the courtyard, drinking tea and brainstorming how to help Arman. Of course, I'm bound by an urgency I can't share with the men. "Think, please think," I beg them.

"The American Embassy is out. I've made phone calls to my contacts, and no one has come through," says Amu Doctor, looking at the oak tree, as if he is trying to coax inspiration from its leaves.

Jason scribbles on his notepad. "Now, this is a long shot," he says, tapping his pencil on the table. "If it's okay, I'd like to talk to my cousin. He knows people in an official capacity in Iran."

"By all means," says Amu Doctor. "Let me show you to the phone."

The two men head inside. Earlier, we had filled Jason in on that terrible night. I told him about my mother and Arman's confession and my own guilt. He admitted he knew Arman had been grappling with an awful secret. "I just didn't know how to help or be there for him," he said, raking a hand through his raven-black hair.

"Well, thank you for being here now," said Amu Doctor as he stood. "The tea should be ready."

"Can you tell me your version of how you escaped Iran?" Jason asked when we were alone.

"Well, my father was an exchange student in Texas. After he moved back to Iran, he maintained a relationship with his American family. They visited Shiraz a few times before the Revolution. My dad, being who he was, had predicted things weren't going to go well in Iran. He asked his American brother, Richard, to help us, should anything happen to him. When my dad was killed, Richard worked with a resettlement organization in the US and sponsored us." My eyes drifted to the stones near the fountain. In this very courtyard, Arman, Reza, and I had flown a paper airplane Uncle Richard had sent us.

We were at our house the day we received the package from DHL. When my father assembled the airplane, we took turns flying it from our rooftop balcony into the yard below. My mother had finally had it with us stomping noisily up and down the stairs and had shooed us out of the house. We ran, laughing, all the way to Reza's and started again until the battered airplane ended in the fountain, limp and soggy without a chance of flying again. Old thoughts of Reza's death mingled with new thoughts of my mother's passing. Jason's hand offered me a tissue and I realized I had stopped talking.

"Oh." I patted my damp eyes with the tissue. I was finally crying. I was a little embarrassed too. I had only known Jason for an hour. "Sorry." I sat tall and composed myself. "I'm just so grateful to Amu Doctor. He arranged for us to leave after my mother was injured. He helped us secure a visa to India, where we could meet with the American Embassy in Mumbai. Richard and his wife had just moved to San Diego from Austin, and that's how we ended up there. Is it close to Arman's version?"

"Pretty close, although his version was more like reading a comic book—a lot of sound effects and heart-stopping action." We both let out a laugh. A dove flew out of the oak tree and landed on the edge of the fountain.

Jason held me in his eyes. "I'm glad you're here. I mean in San Diego." Now, he looked like he was about to tear up.

"And what about you?" I said, not ready to see him cry. "Aren't you glad you came to Iran? I mean isn't this great?"

Jason's lips curved into a sad smile. "This might seem cheesy, but I can't think of any other place I'd rather be. Seriously! Arman isn't just some reliable and ambitious partner I went into business with. He is the most unselfish person I know." Jason blinked, looking at his hands. "I just hope I can help somehow."

I had no idea how close he and Arman were. But was Jason talking about my brother? Reliable? Ambitious? Unselfish? If this was a usual-suspects-lineup equivalent for personality traits, I wouldn't be able to pick Arman in a hundred years. Perhaps I thought I could predict his every move, but there is a side of him I don't know at all. Now, trying to see Arman through Jason's eyes made me miss him from a different place within myself.

"How did you meet Arman?" I said.

"Speed dating." Jason laughed.

It turned out my brother, who was unable to hold down a real job, had run out of money. He was doing double shifts as a pizza-delivery guy when, one lunch hour, as he was delivering a pizza to a downtown office, he spotted an ad for a speed-dating event in the hotel bar next door.

"I was a speed dater, all right," Arman had joked to Jason. "But I had never tried actual speed dating. I mean, I was never good with the ladies, but I hadn't tried this type of humiliation."

At first, Jason hadn't recognized him. Arman's bald head and showy clothes had thrown him off. But around Jason's second drink, an image of the patient Italian boy who had tutored him in linear algebra merged with the face of the guy next to him.

Arman—or Tony, as Jason knew him—was drenched in sweat, slamming back drinks like a man who'd happened upon water after wandering the desert for days.

"Millions of variables had to conspire for us to meet," Arman had said that night. "I mean, what are the chances, right? It was our cumulative choices up to that point and the choices of others we knew and those who knew them and the choices of our collective ancestors, their circumstances, the weather and the stock market, and who knows what else that had us both at that hotel bar at that exact instant. If anything had been altered, we might not be here right now."

Now, at Amu Doctor's courtyard, I begin marveling at the number of unexpected events that have occurred during this trip and my response to it all. Why couldn't I forgive Arman easily, the way Amu Doctor had? I try to picture my life without Arman, and I see blackness surrounding me like a small, stifling box. If my mother were here, she would recite the perfect poem to describe this. My lips tremble and I press the heel of my hands to my eyes, letting the blackness consume me.

When I look up, Jason and Amu Doctor are heading outside. Jason waves his notepad at me. "I talked to my cousin, Simon. He wasn't happy; it's three a.m. in Vancouver. I owe him one." He clears his throat. "Sorry. I told him it was a matter of life and death, and he said he was going to talk to this CEO who knows people in Shiraz."

62. Morteza — SHIRAZ, 2009

I AM STARING INTO the beast's eyes again, fire leaping out toward me. I crouch in a corner of the room, covering my head, as the unbearable heat rises. "Help me! Help me!" I hear myself beg.

A hand touches my shoulder and I turn. It's Kimia Shams, only she is a small girl, with a red scarf covering her hair. "Take my hand. I can help you." She reaches out to me, but in her hand sways a flame.

"Get away from me!" I spit. She shrugs and lopes through the fire like she is playing hopscotch. She pauses for a moment in front of the fireplace and then leaps into the flames, disappearing inside the dragon's mouth. I hear bells toll in the distance.

I'm in my bed. It is my phone, ringing. I consider letting the phone go to the machine, but I reach for the receiver.

"Alo," I say in my most annoyed voice.

"Brother Hashemi. Salaam. How are you?"

"Hazrat Hojatoleslam Jannati! Salaam. How are you, sir? Is everything good?" All the sleepiness leaves me. I sit up in bed.

"Everything is good. I want to talk to you about someone you have detained. Can you tell me why you are holding Arman Shams?"

I hesitate. "Sir, he is under suspicion for treason."

"This is very upsetting to me," Imam Jannati interrupts me, an impatient twang hanging at the edge of his voice.

"Sir, a few more days and I know we can get him to talk," I plead.

"Brother, we didn't have a revolution so we could harass those who have returned to their birth country. Did we?" he asks as a teacher would ask a dimwitted student.

"No, sir," I say, wondering if Imam Jannati knows something. He is a shrewd and fair man. Not much escapes him. But why is he calling at this hour?

"You must let Brother Shams go tonight. Call his family and arrange for them to pick him up. This is not the time to make enemies, brother. Have I made myself clear?"

"Chashm." I can't say no to Imam Jannati.

"Very good. I will check back with you first thing in the morning. Shab bekheir."[98]

"Yes, sir. Good night, sir," I say. My hand drops the receiver to my chest. How did Imam Jannati get involved in this? But it really doesn't matter. What is important is that Shiraz can't find peace until I find the morshed and dispose of him. I throw on my uniform and splash water on my face.

"Who was that?" Sakineh asks from behind the bathroom door.

"Don't worry about it, woman! Go back to sleep before you wake the boys!"

I hear her sluggish steps as she ambles away without arguing. She has listened to me since the first fight in the early weeks of our marriage. In the mirror, I watch a smile form on my lips. That's right! No, none of this is a setback. This only expedites my plan.

---

98   good night

63. Arman — SHIRAZ, 2009

EVERY BONE AND MUSCLE in my body hurts. The skin on the bottom of my foot is torn, and I suspect without some treatment, my wound will soon become infected. But none of this compares to how scared I am for Kimia. A feeling of protectiveness, the kind that only a brother could feel for his sister, fills my chest. Did I ever shield her from harm? No. I know even during my teenage zeal and vigilance, I hurt my sister far more than I ever protected her. Shame creeps inside and heats my face.

I have never wanted superpowers more than I do now. I've tried to pray, but the Arabic words are all jumbled in my head, and I don't even know if there is a God, anyway. It's embarrassing to admit it, but I wish for the strength and bravery of Wolverine. Hell, I'd take Spider-Man's powers. Just don't make me wear a leotard.

I glance at the flickering bulb and wonder why that psycho Morteza is so obsessed with the morshed. The man needs a shrink, not a storyteller. Oh God. What have I done? I put my hands on my forehead.

The dreadful sound of rapid footsteps fills the corridor. I shrink back against the wall as the door flies open. It's Morteza.

He leaps over to me. His hair is disheveled, and a frown knits his thick eyebrows together. "We need to go, brother."

"What time is it?" I ask, and I wonder why I've asked this.

"It's time to go," he says and takes out metal handcuffs. He helps me to my feet. "Now turn around, and bring your hands together."

I obey and Morteza handcuffs me roughly. There is a new urgency in his movements. This worries me.

"Where are we going?" I ask as I hobble barefooted, each step a shooting pain.

"I'm taking you to your Amu's house," he says.

We walk past a few guards, Morteza addressing the one with a question on his face. "Imam Jannati has authorized Brother Shams's release, and I'm taking him home," he says in a hurry and adds, "I know his family."

The name Imam Jannati has a familiar ring to it. Does Amu Doctor know this Imam guy? I begin to feel relieved I'm being released, but why did Morteza handcuff me?

An SUV idles in the front. Morteza helps me get into the shotgun seat. "Brother Hashemi, why am I handcuffed?" I ask.

Morteza jerks the gearshift to D. "It's for your own safety." The car tires screech, and with my hands bound and no seat belt, I lurch dangerously close to the windshield. The car careens through the nighttime streets of Shiraz.

Morteza drives past my old school, and I remember a student rally where my Mobarezin troop occupied the center row. Reza and his classmates were listening to the mullah from the curb. They stood on their toes and craned their necks to get a better look at him before they lost their balance. They repeated this over and over, their small heads bobbing up and down like hungry chicks anticipating a chunky worm. I felt bad for coming down so hard on Reza a few days before. The poor kid was always so nervous, and Kimia, as stubborn and disobedient as she might have been, had helped him relax and be a normal kid. Too bad it was inappropriate for them to socialize. But then again, I didn't make the rules.

My fist and voice rose on cue. *"Death to Saddam! Long live the Islamic Republic!"*

The smaller boys mimicked with fervor, their fists clenched in the air as they shouted. Some of them snickered furtively after their arms were back by their sides. The giggle ripples reached Reza, who covered his mouth as his eyes teared with laughter. I knew it was my duty to do something, but more prepared than I, Morteza shot a wrathful glance at the boys and the laughter was killed point blank.

Now, in the front seat of Morteza's car, I think of the speaker, the Imam who was to marry a little girl from my sister's school. I wondered what the man's name was and whether he had gone through with marrying a ten-year-old girl.

We're getting closer to Amu Doctor's house. "Here's the plan," Morteza says as if I'm his co-conspirator. "We're going to call your sister on your phone. You tell her to take us to the morshed. After that, I'm letting you both go."

I look at Morteza and all I can think is, *Fuck me.*

I weigh my options: If I go along with Morteza and there is no morshed, Morteza will kill me and my sister. If I refuse, he will kill me and then go after Kimia anyway. It reminds me of our dad's favorite riddle, where a guy is caught at a fork in a road, running away from people trying to kill him. Two men are standing at the fork. He has heard about these two men: They're identical twins; one always lies and the other one always tells the truth. One road leads to safety. The other leads to death. The problem is, he doesn't know which road leads where or which twin is the honest one. He is allowed only one question, and the men behind him are approaching fast.

We arrive at Amu Doctor's house. With my hands in handcuffs behind my back, there is no way I can fling myself out of the car. Morteza roots around in the back seat and places something in my lap. It's my confiscated cell phone. He reaches in front of me and takes out his glasses from the glove box. I watch him put on his glasses and search my contacts.

"If I ask your twin which way to safety, where will he point?" I say.

He pauses and looks at me over his glasses. "What?"

"It's the answer to this riddle my dad liked."

"You better be careful. You're starting to go mad," he says admonishingly. He punches a key on my phone. He holds the phone to my ear. "Remember, tell her to come outside quickly . . . without anyone finding out."

"Arman?" I hear my sister's startled voice.

"Hi, Kimia."

"Oh, thank God! Where are you?"

"Run, Kimia!" I yell into the phone. "Wake up Amu Doctor . . . Call the police, anything . . ."

Morteza yanks the phone away from my ear and punches me in the temple. My head slams into the side window. Through the stabbing pain, I hear Morteza shout. "Shut up or I'm going to shoot you right now!" He pulls out his gun from its holster and points it at me while he breathes into the phone. "Listen, you come out here without drawing attention to yourself and your brother lives. We're across the street from your house."

I want to yell again, to tell her to please don't come out, but Morteza hangs up.

"You try anything like that again, and I'm going to shoot her first and then you."

I lean my head against the window toward Amu Doctor's house. The end is coming fast, and I'm helpless.

"I've come prepared anyway," Morteza says. He reaches into the glove box and takes out a roll of duct tape.

64. KIMIA — THE VALLEY OF DEATH

I PUT ON MY raincoat and scarf before tiptoeing into the hallway, holding my shoes in my hands. I'm reminded of all the tiptoeing I used to do as a kid, pretending to be a ninja or a spy. But unlike those days, there is no pretending, and this is not a game.

If I were religious, I would be praying right now. But even the few Tibetan chants I know seem unsuited for this situation. Ironically, I don't have to bring my mind to the present moment, as nothing else in the world could occupy my attention, except for the shallow rhythm of my own breath and the dark textures and shapes in the courtyard.

I close the wooden door behind me, taking care not to make a sound, and survey the street. It's just past four a.m., and the scene has the stillness of a movie set yet to be crowded with the production crew and actors. There is no sound other than an owl hooting somewhere far away. I find the parked SUV on the other side of the street. I put on my shoes, peering more carefully at the vehicle. I see Arman, radiating desperation. Something silvery shines under his nose. As I run across the street, I see his mouth is covered with duct tape.

Morteza steps out from the driver's seat and wags his gun

toward the car. I begin to open the back door when he says, "No. It's better if you drive."

I almost say, *I don't have my driver's license*, but I keep the thought to myself. While Morteza moves to the back, I climb in the driver's seat. I examine my brother. He has a bump on his head and looks more scared than I have ever seen him. Fear, like a contagion, spreads over my own skin. Arman makes urgent noises behind the duct tape and struggles in his seat, but his hands appear to be tied behind his back.

"I'll just sit back here with Lalu," says Morteza, sounding as if he is about to go on a field trip. I turn to the back seat and see he has brought Myna in her cage. Poor Myna! She has been to more exotic places and has more wit and wisdom than most people who come across her cage, yet she is trapped like the pair of us. I recoil at the thought of her being imprisoned, tortured, and rendered mute for nearly thirty years.

I point to Arman. "Can we take off the tape from his mouth?" I ask Morteza in my calmest, meditation teacher voice. "If he promises to keep quiet?"

"You promise?" Morteza asks, to which Arman nods rapidly.

We look at each other. I can see a phrase toss and turn in my brother's eyes—*I'll die for you.* And this is no taarof. *I'll die for you too.*

I slowly bring up my hands, showing them to Morteza. I reach for the duct tape. "This is going to hurt," I say softly and rip the tape from Arman's mouth.

"Ahhhhh!" Arman's censored scream and my "shhhhh" clash.

"Drive, then," Morteza says, pointing the gun to Arman's head. With a quiver of nerves, I turn the key in the ignition and ask, "Where to?"

"To the storyteller! Where else?"

I cast a glance at him through the rearview mirror and begin driving. A fleeting hope, that at any moment I'll wake up in my bed in La Jolla, is a smoke message on the sky of my mind. But the storm of Morteza's words blasts the thought. "It's good that you're both cooperating, because I have no problem with silencing people. I know you, sister—you like stories. So, let me tell you one." He pauses to light a cigarette.

I slow for a turn and feel Arman's eyes boring into me. He must be searching for a plan as desperately as I am.

Morteza grows comfortable in the back seat. "There was this young mother of two, a Mojahedin traitor whom we had been ordered to kill. Four brave men, including myself, stood before her. I was only nineteen. The woman pleaded for her life and her children, but that didn't work. She became cunning. When my friend raised his rifle . . . the woman ripped open her shirt. We, being devout Muslims, had to avert our eyes. We couldn't shoot her. But the answer to these kinds of problems is always simple . . . I approached the woman from behind, pulled out my pistol and put a bullet in the side of her head." From the back seat, Morteza brings his gun next to Arman's head. "Bang!" he shouts.

I slam the brakes, my knuckles white from gripping the steering wheel. Arman falls forward.

Morteza laughs his poisonous laugh. "Shoor nazan, khahar." He waves the gun. "Don't worry, sister. That's part of good story-telling. You should know that. Now keep driving and let me tell you another."

Arman and I exchange glances and I ease my foot off the brake. The streets are deserted in the middle of the night, and I can't decide if this is a blessing or a curse. I drive without a destination in mind, but Morteza doesn't seem to be paying attention.

He continues, "We had received a tip that a family was Baha'i. We knocked and a small boy opened the door. He was six, perhaps seven. I asked him where his parents were. He started telling us, but his grandfather showed up and stopped him. The old man signaled to the boy to leave. We pushed the old man aside and entered the house. I grabbed the boy and put a gun to the old man's head. I gave the boy a chance to do the right thing. But the boy just froze. So I shot his granddad. Of course, the boy told us right after that."

Morteza talks about these killings like he is talking about

the size of the fish he's caught. "Now the boy and all his family are in hell. I know what you're thinking. This can seem cruel to a layman, but when your will is Allah's will, you do what is needed with pleasure. You see, compassion is the true spirit of our Islamic Republic. We eliminate deviants and corruptive influences to keep the fabric of our society intact. So we can be united in caring for the most vulnerable among us. Do you know how many orphan children we've housed, fed, and clothed in the past thirty years? Do you know how many families we've provided for? Of course, not," he huffs, answering his own question. "What do entitled Westerners such as yourselves know about suffering?" He pauses, this time waiting for an answer, but we don't say a word. "Anyway, today is starting on a good note," he goes on, his voice suddenly animated. "In a few hours, if these taghooti infidels continue to spill into the streets, we'll be ready for them. We'll show these foreign agents where their vote is. Fortunately, my men are very loyal."

I detect a jab in the emphasis he has put in the last two words. A shudder slithers through me as I consider what's to come. He goes on describing his new crop of citizen soldiers as I meander aimlessly through the streets.

At the next turn, Morteza's raspy voice fades into the background. An acrid bile gathers in my throat. I slow down. I have taken us to Ghasrodasht Avenue, driving toward the old stage. The stage is now some sort of a shrine with pictures of young men and flowers all around. Every second is an eternity, yet I fear the passage of time.

"They wanted to take apart the stage," Morteza says. "But I convinced the mayor to make this into a war memorial. Look how beautiful it is!"

I stop the car and, with both hands on the steering wheel, I turn my head to face the back seat.

"This is where the morshed is, no?" Morteza says.

"Baleh," I say, nodding with confidence as I open the car door.

My legs are shaking. Morteza jumps out with the birdcage and opens Arman's door. I watch Arman flinch as he stands.

"Are you okay?" I whisper. He nods. He is barefoot and his feet seem swollen. A dormant rage begins to whirl inside me. My fists clench and I want to destroy this man who has hurt my brother. But alas, I'm more afraid than angry.

"Okay, enough! Take us to the storyteller," Morteza says.

I inch slowly with Arman toward the stage. Each step seems to cause him pain and he stares ahead, the whites of his eyes showing.

The felekeh is quiet and empty.

"Okay, hurry up!" Morteza's words claw at the silence. I am running out of time. As we pick up the pace, I think about all the years I have fantasized about killing myself. It's almost humorous that I should be so frightened when the real possibility of death presents itself.

Without thinking, I crawl under the stage, Morteza's urgent whisper following me: "There is no trapdoor anymore!"

But I'm already pulling on the old cast iron handle. I must have been such a strong kid to be able to lift this heavy thing. The door creaks open. Morteza bends to see for himself.

"Is he down there?" he asks.

"Where else?" I begin to climb down into the darkness.

"I'll wait for you to bring him out. If you're not back in ten minutes, I'll put a bullet in your brother's head," he hisses after me.

I continue descending the stairs, using the wall to guide my steps. I breathe in a faint scent of burnt charcoal, clean and ancient. At the bottom, I can't feel the bumpy peaks and valleys of the Simorgh carving, only the same rough texture as the rest of the wall.

A dim light bleeds from beneath the door, and the hair rises on the back of my neck. I curse myself for ever opening this door all those years ago, and like before, I consider running back up the stairs. But just as before, I push the door open.

It's Baba Morshed, holding an old-fashioned lantern, a cap on his head and his green shawl wrapped around his shoulders. He smiles and sets the lantern on the floor. Besides the ash covering the ground, the vast room is empty. We both pause. He looks as he did years ago. His eyes sparkle with the same enduring affection, but I am taken aback. I have never seen him from the vantage point of my adult height. He is not bigger than life, like I remember. As he approaches me, the familiar lines in his face squeeze my heart, and I choke down a whimper. He holds my face between his hands, his eyes brimming with tears. "Ah, dokhtaram! You are the light of my eyes."

I have never seen him cry, and it makes me weep, too. "Baba, why did you abandon me?"

"My child, questions have been simmering in your fire. It's time to open your eyes and see clearly."

The lantern light twinkles, and a forgotten sensation washes over me—the same one that bathed me while I listened to Baba Morshed's stories. "The Seventh Valley . . . ," I whisper.

"Yes, Rumi! But I am not going to be your morshed for the last valley. The Valley of Death is a solitary journey."

"I've tried to kill myself, but I can't," I plead.

"There are a thousand ways to dance at the beloved's feet, and there is more than one way to die." He holds my hands in his.

"I'm so afraid, Baba Morshed."

"What are you so afraid of, Rumi Jon? Of this?" He gestures with both hands, looking around at the emptiness surrounding us.

"No, no, Baba. I'm afraid of something else—"

"There is . . . ," he interrupts, his eyes ablaze with a deep flame. "There is nothing else." His words echo as the light below us flickers one last time and extinguishes. I grope in the dark, but he is gone.

"Baba Morshed?" I say to the darkness, cursing myself for not asking him to come back up with me when I had the chance. "Baba Morshed!" I yell. "Morteza is going to kill Arman!" I take a step forward, but the ground gives beneath me and my foot slips into a hole. Catching my balance, I step back gingerly and fall against the door.

I groan. I put my hand on my pounding heart and take a breath, trying to bring my mind back to now. But the whirlwind of thoughts makes this impossible. In the center of the storm, Baba Morshed's first question, from that first day I stood at his door, keeps repeating: "Some people argue that we have free will . . . do you think we have this choice?"

Competing answers whip around, making my head hurt. On the one hand, Arman is going to die, because instead of buying naan, I chose to go hear stories. His confession made me furious with him, but I'm the one to blame—not just for Reza, but for all of it!—for what happened to my mother, for Amu Doctor and Azita Khanom's pain, and even for Morteza. Had I killed myself long ago, at least Arman would be happy in his club. Had I not convinced him to come . . . None of this is logical, but it doesn't make it any less true. The thorny cloak of shame and regret digs into my skin.

On the other hand, if it is ghesmat that has brought so much suffering to me and those around me, then like my mother, I spit on destiny! *Tof!* Either way, not only have I not had the life I wanted to live, but I'm also punished by the one I have. Either way, unlike in the stories, no one is going to save the day.

I pound on the door. "No! No! No!" I am forced to face Morteza empty-handed. This is it. I stand, my knees threatening to buckle. What will my clients think of this ending? My bad karma? Will my death dissuade Bernice from traveling to Afghanistan? I head to the hallway. My steps have grown clumsy, as if my feet have forgotten their task. I haven't written a will. Who will inherit my house? Are these my last thoughts? What is it like to get shot? Will he shoot me or Arman first? This must be what it's like to go crazy. Suddenly, I laugh: At least Morteza will be in good company.

I step on the first stair, but like a falcon about to soar into the skies, an ascending feeling begins to arise inside me. My mind is illuminated with the image of Reza, only a child, his face burning in fierce determination, his hair covering one eye, standing up to oversize bullies.

"I'm so scared," I whisper. The shards of a bitter cold radiate from my center to each limb, making my fingers numb. I double over and bury my hands in my armpits.

Through the cobweb of forgotten memories, I remember Baba Morshed telling me all states are sacred. I had no idea what to think of it then, and I'm not sure what it means now. How can fear be sacred? My mind keeps rushing back to Reza at his last moments. He was afraid, but he didn't run away. "Roya Khanom! I'm coming."

And for the first time, like Majnun who has finally united with Leili, I embrace my fear, letting its icy kiss caress my lips.

Your life is over. Arman's life is over. You're completely helpless. I lose my breath and my teeth chatter. I don't turn away. I hold my beloved tightly, taking in the darkness.

You're going to die. I don't turn away.

I peer into the deep blackness, quivering. I let my body shake the way I let my tears flow in Baba Morshed's arms. With each tremble, fear unclings itself from me. "Where are you going?" I yell after it. "Your beloved is right here. Come back!"

"Come back!" The hallway repeats my words. As the echo subsides, all becomes still. I listen to the blooming silence, no longer shivering.

"There is nothing else," Love whispers, pouring out of me into the empty space around. The darkness reciprocates, and I'm showered with wave upon wave of gratitude. As I let out my first full breath, the sound of *"huuu"* flows from my lips, my breastbone humming with it. The five dying fires of my senses stir, drawing power from the mysterious vibration, growing even more brilliant and roaring than even in all my time with the storyteller. I let their flames move me.

"Arman! I'm coming!"

65. ARMAN — SHIRAZ, 2009

WHO KNEW HOW SLOWLY ten minutes could pass? Morteza keeps pacing back and forth like the berserk mountain lion I once saw at the San Diego Zoo. I've tried talking to him a few times, but he just goes apeshit. He says he doesn't trust anything that comes out of my mouth.

Sitting on the edge of the stage, I inch closer to the trapdoor, so that when Kimia comes out, I can jump in front of her. Maybe I can take the bullet and she can run to safety.

As I wait, I check out the war memorial Morteza is so proud of. There is a dusty rug covering the center of the stage while framed pictures of shahid martyrs line the perimeter of the rug. Plastic flowers around the pictures look beaten up and sun-bleached. I wonder about the young men in the pictures. *How many people did they kill before they were killed themselves? How does it feel to kill someone? And more pertinent for me right now, how does it feel to be on the receiving end of this equation?*

A thud comes from under the stage. Morteza points his gun nervously. Kimia scrambles out. I try to remain inconspicuous, but I'm holding my breath, ready to pounce.

"Ah, there you are!" Morteza says, excited.

I'm about to make my move, but Kimia holds out a hand to me and steps forward. She seems different. For one thing, she is covered in black soot, and it's difficult to see her expression in the dark. For another, it's hard to describe, but she doesn't seem like my sister—her movements are more pronounced, almost theatrical.

"So, where is he?" Morteza asks, gesturing with his gun.

"Right here," Kimia says, pointing at herself with imperial confidence. "I am the storyteller." Her eyes drill into Morteza, and I momentarily forget the plan I have in mind.

"This is not a game." Morteza shakes his head and raises his gun. "You disappoint me, sister. You haven't learned your lesson."

"I'll tell you what," Kimia interrupts. Her voice is deep and calm. Her words are coming from all around, and I'm strangely reminded of being at the movies. "I'll tell you a good story. If you don't like it, you can kill us." She gestures to herself, to me and the bird in the cage.

I want to react, but like Morteza, I'm too surprised. I throw a glance at the trapdoor. Maybe Kimia is still down there and this is some jinn impersonating my sister.

"You see, a well-told story reveals more precious truths than a thousand lessons." She pauses, but we don't move. Her eyes are definitely Kimia's. Even in the relative darkness I can see them sparkle, the way they did when she was small.

"Once there was. Once there wasn't." My sister says these words, and I don't know what Morteza feels, but suddenly I'm a child again, the child I was before I gave up on stories.

"There was a young boy who had a heart as pure as the shining sun," she says, sweeping her hand slowly over the stage. Morteza and I watch as the rug on the stage shimmers like the waves of a river. If my hands weren't tied behind my back, I'd rub my eyes. I steal a quick glance at Morteza. Even though his gun is still pointing at Kimia, he seems more interested in the waves on the carpet. I let out a breath I've been holding.

An image of a boy of eight or nine appears on the stage. The boy begins walking, and I can't look away. The ripples of the wave reach the edges of the rug and the scene becomes clear. The boy meanders on a dirt road toward a noonvai on a corner. The street looks like Felekeh Ghasrodasht before they paved it in the mid-seventies. The boy stops near the edge of the oven, looking into it, watching the naan cook on the hot pebbles. The baker hands the bread to a man with lamb-chop sideburns and bell-bottom pants.

"Thank you, agha," the hippie says, taking the naan. The baker's eyes follow the man as he leaves and turns to the boy.

"Salaam, pesar! How's your naneh?"

"She's still sick," the boy says.

"Here." The baker looks to his left and right and slips the boy the freshly baked naan. "Take this to her. She will get better, Inshallah!"

Morteza has lowered his gun and watches the stage intently. Good. I bring my attention back to Kimia.

"But it wasn't his mother's ghesmat. She didn't recover," she says softly.

The scene changes to a schoolyard. Kids play, but the boy, in a black dress shirt, sits by himself in a corner. The bell rings and he wipes his eyes with the back of his hand and heads to the classroom.

"That was the first time the boy's life changed," Kimia says.

Morteza and I watch the scene change to a sparse room in a small house. The boy takes off his shoes, puts his book bag on the bare floor, and enters the room. He looks at the bedroll and pillow in the corner before walking into the kitchen. He begins slicing onions into a pot. He tears up.

"Even though his heart was still as big as the world, it ached. It wasn't fair. His naneh was forever gone, and nothing would bring her back," Kimia narrates.

The boy's father enters the kitchen. "What's for dinner?" he demands, and the expression on the boy's face hurts my heart.

The scene blurs and Morteza's free hand reaches for the carpet, waving, mimicking Kimia, as if he can adjust the resolution. Kimia gestures at the rug and the scene becomes clear, but Morteza's satisfied face tells me he believes it's him. The boy now scribbles into a notebook, doing his homework on the floor of the small room. His father lies near him, taking a nap.

"He didn't know it then, but his childhood had ended already. He went to school, he studied, and he worked. This went on for years. The boy got used to the routine, but he knew something was missing in his life. He only had time to ponder this for a few moments before his exhausted body succumbed to sleep. Then the great Revolution came, and he was right there with the rest of the country."

The scene changes to a protest. From people's clothes and the signs on the shops, it looks to be Charrah Moshir Street in the late seventies. In the sea of faces marches a teenage version of the boy, with whiskers and a headband, shouting slogans alongside men and women. I recognize that boy! It's Morteza before I met him. I kick myself for not realizing this earlier. I have so many questions for Kimia. This all feels like the time I took mescaline and tripped my balls off. But the pain in my feet as I wiggle my toes reminds me of the dire reality of my situation.

"By now his heart, like his hands, had callused on the tender parts." Kimia's soothing voice gently carries me back to the story. "He was becoming a man. But more importantly, his life was infused with a resolute passion to serve God."

The screen on the rug shows the parking lot where Morteza and I used to train. I gasp, and with disbelieving eyes, I scan the faces of the boys, trying to find myself. But I'm not among them. Morteza stands at attention in the front row as the commander paces, giving a speech.

"Death changed the boy's life for a second time. But it wasn't the death of his baba, who had departed with God's grace a few months before. This time, it was the death of someone he barely knew at all—a child.

"A number of people and events, including our boy, helped put the child in the wrong place at the wrong time." I hear Kimia's voice, and before the scene changes, I start to cry. This time I know what's coming. I blink away the tears and watch Reza run in a long alley. He pauses and raises his face to the huge wall collapsing. A brick dislodges from the wall and glances off the side of his head. He falls. The earth around us rumbles and the wall comes down on Reza, covering his body in the rubble.

I first wonder if Morteza even remembered Reza, but I'm taken aback when I see him from the corner of my eye. Morteza's face is so twisted in agony, I'm torn between tackling him while he is distracted and giving him a hug. Kimia's glare tells me I should do neither.

She sweeps her hand over the rug again. "The boy was so consumed with his own pain that he hardly gave a second thought to the dead child."

The scene changes, and a teenage Morteza sits, leaning against the makeshift stage, hugging his knees to his chest. His hair full of dust, his arm with the fresh burn rests by his side. He winces as boys leap from under the stage and one by one run away without even giving him a glance.

"But his heart knew better. After all, the dead boy's destiny was linked to his. Each night, vague notions tugged at him right before he fell asleep. He didn't pay heed, as he was too distraught, too weary to notice."

Morteza continues to stare at the screen, but my belly roils in the anticipation of the moment he loses interest in the story or becomes angered by it.

"Our boy decided to become more diligent. He poured himself into doing God's work."

Morteza is now near the trenches of what looks to be a battlefront. His wide eyes are fixed on the pistol he holds in his hand.

"A corner of his heart had darkened, and the darkness was expanding. A howling despair whirled in the desert of his soul."

Morteza steps over a dead woman's body and stumbles behind a military tank. He pukes, holding his stomach.

"He thought the best course of action was to build his tolerance. He reminded himself of the first time he killed a mouse in the kitchen. It was hard, but it had to be done. He needed to crush anything that got in the way of his mission. But the darkness in his heart kept beckoning him, asking him to remember his story. The boy ignored the calls, all the while feeling something was wrong. After years, the calls shrank to small whimpers and eventually stopped. His nightmares, on the other hand, grew more vivid. He saw the storyteller as his enemy. He thought the morshed was coming for him."

Kimia waves her hand, and all I can see is the rug covering the stage again. I've been dreading this moment, as I'm sure Morteza is going to shoot us both.

"This is not the case," Kimia bellows. "The boy is confusing the message from the darkness with darkness itself. The darkness calls: 'Did you know your suffering is your treasure? Alas, you are the veil covering your treasure.'[99] When you look beyond reason and belief, you begin to find your treasure. You begin to understand. But first you must acknowledge the darkness."

The air becomes electric with a strange magnetism. It's as if atoms whirl around us in an ecstatic dance. I sway a little myself as Kimia reaches her hand toward the birdcage. She opens it. Morteza lifts his gun, and even though I'm completely out of my element, I take a step toward him. But he only shrugs and mumbles something unintelligible. He brings the gun back to his side.

"'Love has set fire to my past and freed the bird of truth,'" Kimia recites.

The bird steps out, perching on the stage. She looks back and forth between Kimia and Morteza, then flutters her wings. To the shiver of her wings, the ground begins pulsing with an ominous hum. The bird flies around our heads, and the hum rises into a frenzy.

"Can you stand still?" Kimia's voice carries above the commotion. A dark wave of snapping wings approaches above the buildings behind the stage, joining the black bird. High-pitched battle cries come from above. Thousands of screaming birds churn the air.

---

99   from Rumi's *Divan e Shams*

"You're afraid," Kimia's voice booms. "You think these birds are going to tear you into pieces with their talons and beaks and feed you to the fishes in the Caspian Sea. You want to take cover. But don't."

Morteza and I stand still. Kimia locks eyes with him in such an intense way, I'm positive he is going to burst into flames. Sweat beads above his brow and his grip tightens around the gun, but he doesn't move.

"You want to defend yourself, but don't. Instead, watch them. This is just a story, and these are just birds." She breaks her gaze away from Morteza and opens her arms to the sky. "Remember, the magic of the story all depends on you, the listener."

Except for a few dozen, the birds scatter and fly away. Their cries change to tweets and chirps and a calming feeling washes over me. The sky is beginning to turn from black to violet, revealing some of the remaining birds in different sizes and colors.

"For the third time, death changes the boy's life. What he doesn't know is that his destiny isn't just linked to the people in this realm. His ghesmat, along with that of everyone he knows, is connected to the destiny of the birds in an ancient myth: the myth of the Seven Valleys of Love. Legend has it that thousands of birds set out on an arduous journey to find the mythical Simorgh. Each valley claims hundreds of birds, and at the end only thirty survive. The survivors have suffered disappointments, heartbreak, and loss. But when they reach the Seventh Valley, they realize something so obvious, it makes them laugh." Kimia points to the sky. The birds come together in the air and begin to take the form of a giant bird, like the Simorgh. The sky grows lighter, and with a swoosh of the enormous wings of the Simorgh, a ripple of joyous laughter travels down to us.

"They see themselves: the Simorgh—*si morgh, thirty birds,*" Kimia says in a whisper as the giant bird disappears behind the buildings.

The sound of azaan, the morning call to prayer, emanates from the mosque in the distance. Morteza's mouth is half open, as if he has just finished talking with the strangest of jinns. I follow Kimia's gaze and turn to see people standing behind us. Amu Doctor is with Jason next to a skinny boy in a plaid shirt. Next to him, a woman with sad eyes holds a black chador under her chin, two small boys by her side. The boys, who look a lot like Morteza, stare at Kimia, like they hope to hear more of the story. Behind them, three men in fatigues stand stiffly next to Haji. My pulse quickens and I shudder. I don't know whether I should run or beg. But Haji's focus is on his commander, who has also turned to face the small audience, his arms by his sides and the gun dangling from his limp fingers.

Haji glides over and puts his hand on Morteza's shoulder. "Brother, go home and get some rest. We'll take care of things from here."

Morteza doesn't say a thing. He slides the gun back in its holster and is about to leave when he stops and faces Kimia. He fishes something out of his pocket and offers it to her. She holds the object to the light. It's a black chess piece. She closes her fingers over it and smiles, but Morteza is already turning, taking slow steps toward the woman and the boys. They all pause for a moment and then walk away from the stage without saying a word.

Haji opens his hand and shows me a small key. He gestures with his head for me to turn. I obey and he uncuffs me. My upper body tingles in protest or maybe in gratitude while my feet scream in pain. I move my arms slowly to the front and open and close my fist. Haji nods deferentially to Amu Doctor, and Jason, who seems unnaturally pale, before stepping back. Kimia runs over and slams her body into mine. She holds me tightly in her arms.

"Akh!" I yell.

The moazzen, calling everyone to prayer, continues to sing in his sweet voice. I fall to my knees and lay my face against the cool dust of Shiraz, weeping.

66. Arman — SAN DIEGO, 2010

It took Jason more than a month after we returned to get my permission to ask Kimia out. I mean, not like it was mine to give— but it was a classy, you know, gesture. I sat between them on our flight back from Iran, totally caught in the crossfire of the sparks flying back and forth. I tell you, it was exhausting. And amusing.

Anyway, I said, "Yeah man. That's cool." But it took Jason another month before he got up the nerve. I had always known him to be so confident and smooth; I was surprised he was so nervous. He kept saying, "I gotta do something first." He went to China, saying he needed to meet with his relatives to improve products and working conditions in their factories. But I really think he was trying to score points with my do-gooder sister before he asked her out.

The clock shows six a.m. Sitting on my bed, I open my box and fish out the vial of peppermint oil. I put it under my nose and take a few deep breaths like my sister taught me. Man, I'm awake now! As I put on my gym clothes, I still smell traces of the mint odor going deep into my lungs, making my breaths fuller. That Kimia! First, she convinced me to go to Iran, and now she's having me sniff essential oils. What's next?

Heading over, I text Jason and fill my water bottle.

Before we left Shiraz, workers were pouring the foundation for a new Chinese hotel chain. Haji pointed that out to me as we were leaving the square that morning. He asked to talk to me privately. Haji isn't his real name, of course, but he told me not to tell anyone his identity.

"Don't mention me or anything that happened to you to anyone," he said before giving me a salve to put on my feet. "It helps with pain and swelling," he said, patting me on the shoulder. "We live in dangerous times. We have to be very vigilant."

I like to think that was his apology. He was very polite and courteous the whole time, I'll give him that. I'm not sure what happened to Morteza after that night in the square, but I could see Haji as the commander type.

I grab my gym bag and give the pile of letters on my dining room table one last look. Amu Doctor and I have been writing to each other the old-fashioned way. He writes about Khalil's research and the new modern apartments they're building near our old house. I tell him about how Kimia and her friend Bernice have been running a drum circle for refugees and veterans. I don't see how this hippie-dippie stuff helps victims of war, but Amu Doctor is a lot more open-minded than I am. I tell him about my fall enrollment at UC San Diego. I'm going to finish my degree like my mom wanted me to—like I want to.

I close the door and head to my circuit-training class. *I'm going to be the healthiest man alive.* I can't help it. Like my mother, I'm an exaggerator, and that'll never change.

Є PILOGUE

AT MY VANITY, I trace the edge of my box with my fingers. Oh death, so universal, so banal, and so fickle, comes wrapped in many packages. For years I chose to wrap mine in this box. Then I went back home. In Iran, my loved ones inspired me in how they responded to death. Amu Doctor became a saint. Arman became sober. My mother died with poetry on her tongue. And me?

I open the box. There, nestled in the felt-lined interior, is my mother's leather-bound *Masnavi* book. My dagger is now a conversation piece, hanging on my office wall, above the fountain.

When I open the book, the picture of the Simorgh greets me— the same creature that my five-year-old self found to be the most ridiculous-looking thing. What kind of bird had a fox head and a peacock tail? I had no idea, but it definitely needed a mustache.

Throughout my childhood I reveled in stories about the Simorgh. I dreamed of the Simorgh. I recited poems about the Simorgh. Now, I know her as a witness so ever-present that she has seen civilizations rise and fall. She has seen stoic men weep and small children become as brave as Rostam. But only a few souls have the eyes to see her.

My phone vibrates on the vanity table. Jason's text reads, *I'm on my way.*

The fragrance of my mother's old Rumi book reminds me of her.

If my mother were here, she would recite a poem to show that, like the Simorgh, our story is everlasting. Our story has kept our spirit alive despite invasions, wars, and despotic leaders.

I imagine Baba Morshed smiling and stroking his long beard upon hearing the poem. He would respond, "A well-told story, one that includes pain, sorrow, heartbreak, and shekast will outlive all of us." He would say, "Those who see with the eyes of the Simorgh will tell a new story, and the whole world will become new."

My mother's death has been the only part of my trip I have shared with my clients, but I no longer discourage them from telling me about their past. My own story has just begun.

As I touch a teardrop with my finger, this verse repeats in my head: "Baz havaye vatanam aarezoost." I long to go home.

Once there was. Once there wasn't. Once there was a girl who was supposed to go to the bakery. Instead she went to the square to hear a story.

About the Author

ARI HONARVAR IS THE founder of Rumi with a View, dedicated to building music and poetry bridges across war-torn and conflict-ridden borders. Her writing has appeared in *The Guardian, Teen Vogue,* the *Washington Post, Slate, Newsweek, Vice,* and elsewhere. She is the author of the oracle card set and book *Rumi's Gift.* She lives in San Diego, where she has befriended a hummingbird named Taadon.

Acknowledgments

THIS BOOK WOULDN'T HAVE come to fruition without my global village of loved ones and supporters.

Thank you to my hamnafas, Brian, the one I breathe with. Without you as my love and my muse, I doubt I would have written a single line.

Thank you to my brilliant mentor, Rene Denfeld, whose invaluable insight made the novel what it is now. You also recommended my remarkable publisher, Laura Stanfill! Thank you, Laura, for your ingenious edits, for your unwavering commitment to amplifying own voices, and for celebrating each small step along the way. I'm so fortunate to have you as my fellow literary traveler in the mysterious journey of life. I'm thankful to the production team, especially Maya Myers, Gigi Little, and Olivia Rollins for their painstaking contributions and polishing touches.

A thousand thanks to my marvelous beta readers, Kim Balkan, Nilou Minovi, Satya Bella, Pat Sherwin, Parke Troutman, Krista Bruemmer, and others who took the time to read and provide feedback. Thank you to the kind actuary who helped me with terminology and accuracy. Thank you to the phenomenal seasoned authors Marivi Soliven and Sahar Delijani, who believed in *A Girl Called Rumi* and offered their loving support as I was preparing my manuscript.

To my wonderful big sister, Azi, who helped me remember what I could not and had nothing but encouraging words for me: I love you and thank you. I'm grateful to my mother, Afsar, who immersed me in the enchanted world of poetry before I could read, and to my father, Gholamhosein, whose gentle guidance and love continue to envelop me even twenty years after his passing. Thank you to my brother, Basseer, who took me in under extraordinary circumstances when I was fourteen and made my life in America possible.

A Girl Called
Rumi

Readers' Guide

FOREST AVENUE PRESS
Portland, Oregon

Author Ari Honarvar at age nine,
trying to blend in as a boy in
Iran, 1982

Afterword

WHEN I WAS SIX, women of Iran lost their right to sing or ride a bicycle in public. Just as this war on women was becoming our new normal, Saddam Hussein attacked Iran, starting a bloody war that lasted eight years. Like our ancestors, my family turned to the soul-saving power of poetry and storytelling to survive those dark days. *A Girl Called Rumi* was inspired by my experiences growing up in such times and emigrating to America, where in order to fit in, I abandoned my immigrant story.

My own journey and work with current refugees and asylum seekers who have escaped unspeakable violence lead me to believe that the arts are a powerful means of transforming suffering into treasure. This book is a love letter to all the displaced souls who yearn to become their own alchemists.

All characters and events in this book are fictional. Translations and any mistakes are all mine. A number of scenes are derived from my own experience growing up in the seventies and eighties in Iran. The name Roya, *dream* in Farsi, is to commemorate our neighbor's teenage daughter, my sister's classmate, who was brutally executed during the post-revolution crackdowns. Her murder shook all of us to the core, yet we couldn't protest or mourn her properly for fear of retribution. As I wrote *A Girl Called Rumi*, I saw an ageless Roya bearing witness to the lives of those residing in the Ghasrodasht neighborhood of Shiraz. Unlike Kimia's painstaking and precise actuarial work, what she recalls of her childhood is often wondrous and not exactly logical—feelings and sensations are palpable while actual events and timelines are subject to dreamlike malleability. Not all the math in the opening scene and throughout the book adds up as a result. The Seven Valleys of Love, of course, are timeless, and the chapters they appear in don't include a date.

The bit about the horse purchase and burial is true. My teenage brother purchased and hid a horse in our basement. We rode the horse during the day while our parents were at work. I also remember being four and watching my brother and sister dig a hole behind our house to bury a horse. The birthday party raid is also based on a true story. My essay on that experience, "I Lived through the 'New Normal' & Don't Want to Do It Again," was published by *Elephant Journal* in January 2017.

As for my translation process, there were a few delightful hurdles: The Persian language doesn't have gender-specific pronouns. This makes for intriguing mystery novels and poetry. In my translations of *Attar's Conference of the Birds*, I took the liberty of assigning genders to different birds. And adhering to the Persian way, I have chosen the gender-neutral *their* instead of *her/his*. The Persian language doesn't have articles either. The Simorgh is the only bird distinguished with an article from other bird characters in the story.

Rather than using Perglish (a blend of Persian/English words), I chose to add the English counterpart to pluralize. For example, I chose *paasdar guards* and not *paasdars*. There are a few Perglish words sprinkled throughout, mostly used by Arman.

My translations of *Masnavi*, *Shahnameh*, and *The Conference of the Birds* tales aren't scholarly. The stories are told the way a storyteller would interpret and embellish a tale according to the audience and their own temperament. Adhering to the original verses of Persian poems, the translations don't include punctuation. I enjoy footnotes when reading novels that contain foreign languages, so I opted for providing them for this book.

The Iran-Iraq War cost more than 600,000 lives. Numerous cities on both sides suffered air raids, with the most intense attacks occurring between 1984 and 1988. Six years into the war, Iranians designed a pontoon bridge to transport tanks and ammunition underwater to the other side near the Iraqi border. For more information, see Laura Secor's "The Man Who Refused to Spy," an essay published by the *New Yorker* on September 21, 2020.

The end of the war in 1988 didn't result in border changes. The US was selling weapons to both Iran and Iraq during the war.

Book Club Questions

1. When Kimia is in her mother's house in California, she finds the red scarf she once used as a cape in Iran. What do you think it represents? Why is it important to the author to have that object show up at the beginning of the novel? Which objects endure throughout the novel and which ones quietly disappear?

2. Author Ari Honarvar believes in joy as a revolutionary act. Even in the midst of trauma and the most brutal of circumstances, storytelling, music, and beauty can help people survive. How do you see those themes play out in *A Girl Called Rumi*? What are some of the scenes where you see joy appear in the midst of despair within the novel? How about in your own life?

3. In the Seven Valleys stories, which bird reminds you of yourself and what holds you back? Why or how?

4. Why do you think Roya wants to return to Iran? Does she accomplish what she sets out to do?

5. Kimia and Reza build stone towers in the courtyard and take a blood oath. Did you have a best friend in childhood? What games or memories do you hold dear?

6. Why do Kimia and Reza give false names to Baba Morshed? Do you suspect the old man knows they are lying? What's the significance of each name?

7. Where does the number thirty appear in the novel? What does it mean, if anything?

8. Morteza has been holding a deep grudge and letting the anger gnaw at him for decades, while elevating his own sense of importance. How does he treat his staff and his family? Does the story change him? What do you think about his future?

9. What do you make of Kimia's cutting? What do you think it means to have someone so successful in counseling others not be able to let go of her own past?

10. Kimia and Reza write their initials in tiny print on walls around Shiraz. Kimia spots one set of them during her return trip. What do you think the author is saying about the endurance of the written word?

11. Kimia says, "My mother is besotted with the splendor of her own madness, while I do all I can to maintain a cordial relationship with my own." How does madness manifest in each character? Are there differences between the glorious madness experienced by mystics, neurodivergence, and/or mental health issues in need of care?

12. What objects or scenes stand out to you as you think about the author's use of color? The red cape, the emerald eye of the Simorgh . . . what else?

13. Do you admire Amu Doctor? Why or why not? Each character has experienced significant losses in their lives—but Amu Doctor forgives quickly and with graciousness. Do you think you would have handled learning the truth about a situation, so many decades later, with the same calm he shows?

14. The calligram of the dancer featured between sections of the novel features this Rumi verse:

    Even if from the sky
    poison befalls all
    I'm still sweetness
    wrapped in sweetness
    wrapped in sweetness
    wrapped in sweetness . . .

    Is this a lens through which you can view Kimia's journey? Arman's? Roya's?

15. Who's the hero of *A Girl Called Rumi*?

Please consider sharing your thoughts about *A Girl Called Rumi* on social media and your favorite book reviewing sites.

To tag Ari Honarvar:
Twitter: @rumiwithview
Instagram: @rumiwithaview

To tag Forest Avenue Press:
Twitter: @forestavepress
Instagram: @forestavenuepress
Facebook: Forest Avenue Press

For the latest about the novel, and to learn more about Ari's work with refugees, see rumiwithaview.com.